Born and a variety of office jobs and as a cabaret singer under the name of 'Linda Gaye' in the sixties.

She began writing seriously in 1981, and her first novel, a romance titled *The Sheikh*, was published internationally in 1991. She has continued to write bestsellers, with *Heart of the Outback* and *Whispers Through the Pines* being outstanding successes.

Lynne was the inaugural president of Romance Writers of Australia Inc. in 1991, an association that grew considerably under her commitment and expertise.

When not working, Lynne loves to read, garden and travel. Married to John, Lynne has two adult children, Karen and Brett, and grand-daughters, Liah and Tara.

*Outback Sunset* is Lynne's seventh novel.

# OUTBACK SUNSET

# OUTBACK SUNSET

## LYNNE WILDING

**Harper**Collins*Publishers*

**HarperCollins***Publishers*

First published in Australia in 2004
by HarperCollins*Publishers* Australia Pty Limited
ABN 36 009 913 517
A member of the HarperCollins*Publishers* (Australia) Pty Limited Group
www.harpercollins.com.au

**HarperCollins***Publishers*
25 Ryde Road, Pymble, Sydney NSW 2073, Australia
31 View Road, Glenfield, Auckland 10, New Zealand
77–85 Fulham Palace Road, London W6 8JB, United Kingdom
2 Bloor Street East, 20th floor, Toronto, Ontario M4W 1A8, Canada
10 East 53rd Street, New York NY 10022, USA

National Library of Australia Cataloguing-in-Publication data:

Wilding, Lynne.
   Outback sunset.
   ISBN 0 7322 7184 3.
   1. Family farms – Fiction. 2 Cattle ranches – Northern
   Territory – Fiction. I. Title.
A823.3

Cover photograph by Terry Underwood, photographer and author of
*In the Middle of Nowhere* and *Riveren: My Home, Our Country*.
www.terryunderwood.com
Cover design by Darian Causby, Highway 51 Design Works
Typeset in 10.5/13 Sabon by HarperCollins Design Studio
Printed and bound in Australia by Griffin Press on 50gsm Bulky News

7 6 5          05 06 07 08

*To my daughter, Karen, with love . . .*
*For her strength and resilience*

# CHAPTER ONE

Standing in the wings of the Theatre Royal, Kerri Spanos watched the audience rise to their feet on the fourth curtain call. They clapped, whistled and stamped their feet in an explosive approval of the performance.

A self-satisfied smile lit her Greek-English features as she glanced towards the cast of Noel Coward's *Private Lives*. They stood centre stage, footlights and overhead lights illuminating them. Kerri's smile widened to one of triumph because there had been an element of risk to bringing her star 'down under'. But here, Vanessa Forsythe, English dramatic actress of extraordinary talent, was a success. Mmmm, and what was even better, the nervous breakdown her star client and friend of many years had been on the verge of having thirteen weeks ago, no longer loomed as a threat.

Kerri waited for the curtains to close permanently and the stage lights to dim before she moved backstage towards Vanessa's dressing-room. She sensed, as she walked, a mixture of melancholy and relief from the leads all the way down to the backstage doorman, that the production had ended ... Final performances were like that.

All in all though, she thought as she trundled past stage props and behind-the-scenes workers, the experience for Vanessa had been worthwhile. In England, Vanessa Forsythe was almost a household name due to an impressive list of stage performances and her first foray into films of quality, a Spanish drama that had won critical acclaim at the Cannes Film Festival two years ago. She and Vanessa could return home now knowing Vanessa had left a mark on Sydney audiences and expanded her reputation internationally.

*Home.* Back to the bustle of London, the high cost of living and the notoriously inclement weather — so different from sunny, casual, outgoing Sydney. Thank God she was going, though she wasn't looking forward to the flight. She'd missed London, her family, her office. A wry smile lifted the corners of her thin lips as she admitted that. Sydney was a nice place, the people were friendly enough, but she, one of the best management agents in the entertainment business, lived for the cut and thrust of making deals, placating clients, discovering new talent and so on ... Still, holding Vanessa's hand, figuratively if not literally, and helping her through her 'crisis', had been a necessity. Over the last twelve weeks she had flown to and from London twice to make sure Vanny's emotions stayed on an even keel.

She rapped on Vanessa's dressing-room door, turned the knob and entered the room.

'Vanny, luv,' Kerri's made-over from cockney to pseudo English public school accent echoed around the box-like, windowless room. 'They absolutely loved you. You made the role of Amanda in *Private Lives* yours, a real triumph.'

A pair of sharp, penetrating black eyes ran over her client who was several centimetres taller than herself. Willowy was the apt term to describe Vanessa's figure rather than model slim. With her olive skin and large brown eyes — courtesy of a Spanish grandfather — combined with striking features and honey blond hair — the actress was an agent's dream. Doubly so because Vanessa Forsythe had real talent without the contrary temperament that often accompanied talented artists.

'Yes, it went well,' Vanessa's reply was circumspect. Already she was creaming her face prior to removing the stage make-up.

'Well?' Kerri laughed at the understated reply. 'You had them drooling. Even the critics couldn't fault your performance.'

Vanessa's gaze locked with her agent's. 'Yes, well, we know how lucky that was. When I arrived here I was a mess . . .'

'You were,' Kerri conceded but added quickly, 'You're also a professional. You got on with it 'cause that was your job. Now you can think and talk about David without dissolving into tears like you did back in September, constantly!'

Vanessa's eyebrows flew upwards in acknowledgement of Kerri's statement. 'Thanks for reminding me.' She reached for the box of tissues, pulled several out and began to wipe her make-up off.

'So, luv, what are you going to wear to the after-show party?' Kerri asked. She trotted over to the portable wardrobe from which several outfits wrapped in plastic bags hung. Her fingers flicked one after another along the railing. 'The blue full length? No. The cream suit then?'

'I was planning to give the party a miss.'

'No way.' Kerri's tone was uncompromising as she turned to stare at Vanessa. 'Several top notch journos will be there as well as the cast, crew and the backers. Remember, you're on show till you board the plane and we wing our way back to London tomorrow evening.'

For close to thirty seconds silence greeted her agent's order. Vanessa sighed before she said, 'Okay, I'll go to the party, but,' she breathed in deeply, 'I'm not going home tomorrow.' Though her eyes were fixed on her reflection in the mirror she glanced briefly at Kerri to gauge her reaction to what she'd said.

'What?' In an instant Kerri's hands rose to her abundant hips. Short and loving everything she cooked and ate, the forty-five-year-old woman was no longer slim but blessed with generous proportions. 'What did you say, Vanny? Of course you are. We're both going home tomorrow.'

Vanessa shook her head. 'I rang the airline this morning and changed my booking.'

'Explain?' With difficulty Kerri masked her dismay. What was going on inside Vanny's head? Some kind of delayed reaction to her fiancé, David Benedict's death? She'd thought her protégée and friend had worked her way through the worst of her grief, that she was ready to return home but ... Her confusion expanded, had she?

'Don't be cross, Kerri, I need some time out for myself.' Vanessa began to uncoil the French roll and brush her long hair till it fell around to frame her heart-shaped face. 'I've enjoyed my time in Sydney, but while I'm here I want to use the opportunity to see more of Australia. I have three weeks off before rehearsals start on *The Glass Menagerie*. I want to spend my leisure time here.'

'You can't be serious. By yourself?' Kerri fixed her with a dark, speculative stare. 'I see. You want time out. Fine.' Her tone was clipped and irritated. 'Come home and spend a few weeks at Bourton on the Water, you love that little cottage of yours in the Cotswolds.'

'Not any more.' Vanessa's full lips thinned. 'David and I, we spent a lot of time there. I don't want to go,' a slight quaver in her voice was discernible, 'where I'll be reminded of him, of us. I'm even thinking of selling the Belgrave Square flat and buying elsewhere.'

Kerri let the statement about selling the London flat go by without comment. 'Go somewhere else. Cannes, the Costa del Sol.'

'No, I'm going to Kakadu.'

'Kakadu.' Kerri gave her a funny look. 'Where and what the bloody hell is Kakadu?'

Vanessa's tentative grin displayed perfect teeth. With a tinge of amusement she informed her agent. 'It's up north, south-east of Darwin. Kerri, Australia is a big beautiful country, so everyone tells me. There are Aboriginal cave paintings up there, crocodiles and all kinds of bird life and other sights to see. It's very unique and different to the UK or the Continent. I want to see just a little of it before my next engagement.' She added a touch imperiously, 'What's wrong with that?'

'Nothing, I suppose,' Kerri conceded, almost choking as she said the words. 'Why didn't you tell me before this?'

'Because I knew how you'd react, that you'd try to talk me out of it.'

Kerri clicked her tongue at the thought of being so predictable, even though she knew she was. 'So, what you're telling me is that you intend to be a run-of-the-mill tourist?'

'Yes,' Vanessa smiled at her agent winningly, 'it's a role I'm going to enjoy playing.'

Kerri's grunt was a comment in itself. In silence she took note of the lighthearted answer and as she looked more closely at Vanessa, noted the determined set of her jaw, the duelling sparkle in her eyes, a gleam she hadn't seen there for months. 'And ...' her head of dark hair shook from side to side, 'I can't talk you out of it, can I?'

Kerri was well aware that her question held a tinge of fatalism. They knew each other too well. Vanessa's grandmother, Rhoda Forsythe, a part-time actress who had supplemented her irregular stage performances by working as a supermarket food demonstrator, had introduced her to Vanny as a skinny seventeen year old, straight out of school and desperately wanting to act. Since that day, they'd had a personal and professional relationship for more than eleven years. And over that time she had learnt when she could talk Vanessa around and when she couldn't. This, she believed glumly, was one of the couldn'ts.

'Not this time, Kerri, but don't think I'm not grateful for all you've done,' Vanessa added quickly. 'You saved my life and my sanity by bringing me to Sydney and helping me get over David. I'm truly appreciative, but seeing part of the outback is something I really want to do.'

Kerri's ample shoulders shrugged good-naturedly in defeat, 'I'm not happy about it, but ... okay.'

Vanessa Forsythe yawned, stretched then unzipped the ankle length, shoestring strap cinnamon-coloured satin gown. As she stepped out of it she glanced at the bedside clock: 3.14 a.m. She yawned again, inelegantly, as her gaze skimmed over the serviced apartment with its minimalist kitchen and sitting area that had been home for two months. She sighed slowly and rubbed her eyes as she took in its state of bedlam. How had she managed to accumulate enough odds and ends, clothes, souvenirs and other trinkets to fill an extra suitcase? Packing was going to take forever!

Then she smiled as she reminisced over several shopping forays she and Kerri had indulged in. Her agent was of the firm belief that shopping till one dropped cured ninety-nine per cent of a woman's ills and, maybe she was right! They had done that — shopped to the point of exhaustion — on a day trip to Melbourne. Then, when Kerri had come out again, on a two-day break on the Gold Coast. She slipped on a baggy, over-long T-shirt, her usual night attire. What would she have done without Kerri? Fallen apart. Become quagmired in a trough of emotional depression.

She set the bedside clock alarm for 8.30 a.m. Too much to do tomorrow to indulge in a sleep-in. Stretching under the sheet she tried to drop off ... One eye opened to check the clock: 3.28 a.m. Damn. Sleep should have come easily, she was very tired, but with the final curtain call, the party afterwards, and being excited about her Top End holiday, she was too wired up to sleep. She had weaned herself off the sleeping tablets prescribed before she'd left London and didn't want to start using them again for fear of becoming dependent on them now that the worst of her emotional trauma was behind her.

She thought that sentence three times before it merged with her subconscious. Thirteen weeks ago she had thought the pain and the sense of loss would never end. Unconsciously she sucked her lower lip between her teeth as, unbidden, memories of David flooded her brain. Memories of the trauma that had changed her life and expectations, that had haunted her waking and sleeping hours for weeks ...

The night of 12 July 1988 was — for summer — one of the wettest on record. Vanessa remembered hearing that on the radio before she booked the taxi to take her to the party destination in Soho. She took a black, full length leather coat from the wardrobe and slipped it on as she contemplated why she was leaving her Belgrave Square flat on such a beastly night. She was doing it for Melody Sharp, a childhood friend. They had grown up in the same block of council flats in Brixton, played together, got into the occasional scrape together, attended the same high school too — and while they didn't see much of each other these days, each having different careers — the bond of friendship remained. Melody, now a successful nightclub proprietor in Soho Square, was throwing a lavish party to celebrate her thirtieth birthday in grand style. Only Melody and perhaps two other people, Kerri and David, could make her leave home and hearth on such a miserable night.

Sandy, her Jack Russell terrier, watched her get ready to leave, and gave a plaintive yelp. He didn't like being left alone on stormy nights. She picked him up, cuddled his small body to her and whispered comfortingly, 'Won't be for long, Sandy. I promise.' He licked her hand as she put him on the bed, then she picked up her evening bag and headed for the door.

As the taxi battled the weather and the traffic, Vanessa's thoughts turned to David. Her fiancé had been away for three weeks and she had missed him like crazy. Dear, dynamic David. At thirty-nine, he had clawed a niche for himself in the competitive world of international finance. With almost movie star looks, an engaging personality and an excellent education (Eton, Oxford and a Harvard business degree), David had been seen in certain circles as the well-to-do, perennial London bachelor. Until he and Vanessa had met and fallen in love. Many people, including members of the media, had been surprised when their engagement had been announced — they'd thought him marriage proof, but not anymore.

Vanessa smiled and twisted the engagement ring on her finger as the taxi crawled through the sodden streets. David was happy, she was exceedingly happy and they were going to be a superb married couple: everyone said so. Their marriage was going to be as vibrant and contented as that of her parents, Rosa and Edward Forsythe. Unfortunately, there was a lingering sadness about that ... Orphaned at twelve, she'd been brought up by her grandmother, Rhoda, but now, not even Gran, who'd passed on last year, would be present to share the joy of her wedding day.

The taxi lurched to a stop outside *The Spot*. It was an incongruous name for Melody's nightclub and she'd teased her friend about it, claiming that the name was better suited to a dry-cleaning shop than a quality nightclub. Vanessa paid the driver and waited until the doorman and club's bouncer, Geoffrey, came forward with a large umbrella and escorted her into the lobby.

The nightclub, with its redecorated 1930s art deco interior, was jumping, and the eight-piece band was doing its best to make the guests deaf. A smoke haze hung over the room, half a metre or so below the ceiling, and a crush of people were eating, dancing and drinking the free booze.

As well, she couldn't help but notice several guests indulging in a variety of other illegal and questionable pleasures. Everyone turned a blind eye to the drug taking, but if one couldn't, one left.

Vanessa could have enjoyed the night by being inconspicuous and playing *spot the celebrity*, there were plenty in the crowd, but Melody soon spied her, screeched her name and drew her into the party's crush.

By midnight Vanessa had had enough. This was not the type of party she enjoyed. It was too noisy and brassy, too crowded, too everything. Without saying goodbye, she slipped outside. Breathing in the air, damp but smoke free, she waited for Geoffrey to flag down a taxi to take her home.

She wanted to be home when David came in. She was expecting him to arrive any minute from Dorset where he'd been visiting his friends. Two overseas business trips then a combined business/pleasure trip to Dorset meant that she hadn't seen him for three weeks. Vanessa wanted to show him how much he'd been missed, in the most acceptable manner she could think of. Her chuckle, too soft for Geoffrey to notice, held a note of sexiness as she contemplated how to achieve that. Perhaps a trail of rose petals from the front door to the bed, a bottle of champagne, Dom Perignon of course, in the ice bucket and two glasses on the bedside table. She'd be wearing the black lace, fur-trimmed teddy that David had bought for her twenty-eighth birthday last month. That was guaranteed to impress.

She heard her dog, Sandy, whimpering with fright because of the weather as she opened the bedroom door, and, shivering, he bounded up into her arms from his hiding place under the bed. Sitting on the bed, she hugged him so tight that he yelped. She loosened her grip and began to stroke the back of his head, then his back until he settled.

Lulled into a mild reverie of anticipating David's arrival, the phone on the side table rang, startling her. As she picked up the receiver she noted the time: 12.40 a.m. God, who would be calling her at this time of the morning?

'David?' she said expectantly.

'It's Lloyd. I've been trying to reach you for hours.'

David's older brother had a fondness for whisky and when he had too many he, occasionally, wanted to talk to his brother about old times, but ... Tonight Lloyd didn't sound as if he had been drinking.

'What's up, Lloyd?'

There was a brief silence. 'Ummm, Vanessa. It's ... about David. Th-there's been an ... accident.'

Vanessa went cold all over and all the energy drained from her body. She dropped Sandy and it took all her strength to cling to the receiver. 'An accident,' she repeated dully. Her throat was tightening up, so much so that she couldn't ask the question she wanted to ask. Lloyd's words saved her from having to.

'There was a twilight hunt at the Cooper's and you know how he loves to ride the hunt. Came off his horse over a hedge. Damned silly fool.'

'How,' she took a deep breath, 'badly is he hurt?'

'The medicos aren't sure. He was taken to the local hospital but he's since been taken by ambulance to London. He, we're at Guy's Hospital right now. He's still unconscious and the preliminary examinations have revealed a skull fracture, internal bleeding and a broken leg. He's having more tests, a CT, I think, as we speak.'

'What's a CT?' Vanessa asked.

Lloyd, who had no medical background, explained as best he could. 'As the doctor described it to me, it's like an x-ray only more comprehensive 'cause it shows bones, organs and soft tissue damage.'

Vanessa bit her lip to stop its trembling. Her voice was quavery as she said, 'I'm coming over.' As she spoke she stood and grabbed the black coat and evening bag. 'Be there in twenty minutes.'

God, how could she sound so normal when inside everything was being shattered. She had woven David into the very fabric of her life, her emotions. David — hurt, unconscious! She tried to stop her imagination from going into overdrive and couldn't. What if ... Oh, what if ...? No. Don't think that, you must think positively. And don't cry. You don't want him to wake up and see red rings around your eyes. David will be all right, he has to be ...

Lloyd and Robyn Benedict met Vanessa in the casualty area waiting room at Guy's Hospital. She studied their tense faces as she approached. Robyn had been crying, her eyes were red and puffy. Lloyd, an older, taller version of David, and usually poker-faced, wore a haggard look.

They hugged and then sat in the near empty waiting room.

'How is he?' Vanessa asked breathlessly.

'We're waiting to hear. A team of doctors is with him,' Robyn said in a hushed tone. 'It's so awful.'

'Was he wearing his riding hat?' Vanessa knew David was vain about his thick, wavy blond hair and hated having to wear the mandatory riding hat.

'I believe so. Neville said that his chin strap wasn't done up and when he fell the hat came off. He hit his head on a log near the hedge.' The corners of Lloyd's mouth turned down. 'A bad business, I'm afraid. Nev and Prue Cooper are devastated.'

13

They were devastated? Huh! She was finding it hard to hold on to her self-control. Somewhere inside the double swinging doors to the right of them was the man she loved and he was badly injured. She couldn't imagine life without him. They had such wonderful plans, they loved each other so much. Surely God wouldn't, couldn't take him away from her. He'd taken her parents, Gran. Wasn't that enough? Not David too.

Two white-coated doctors pushed the swinging doors open. They came towards the trio who were holding hands for mutual comfort.

'Mr Benedict?'

Lloyd nodded and introduced the women with him. 'My wife, Robyn, and David's fiancée, Vanessa Forsythe.'

The younger doctor's eyes lit up. 'Of course, Miss Forsythe, I'd recognise you anywhere.'

'I'm Dr Thomas, the neurologist,' the older man with the neatly trimmed beard said. 'I've examined David and we have the results of the scan. There is a build-up of pressure, caused by a collection of blood, against the brain. An operation is necessary to relieve the pressure.' He stared speculatively at Lloyd. 'I assume you're the patient's next of kin. I need you to give consent for the operation.'

Vanessa's throat constricted but from somewhere she found her voice. 'An operation, doctor. There's no alternative?'

'Not if we want to save him, Miss Forsythe,' Dr Thomas said with an almost impersonal frankness. 'Time is an important factor. My surgical team can be ready within the hour, and the longer we delay, the greater the risk to the patient.'

'I see.' Lloyd looked at Vanessa. As she was David's fiancée, he obviously wanted her to approve. 'Well?' His raised eyebrow became a question mark.

Vanessa heard herself say as if she were a long way away, 'All right, if there's no other choice.'

The younger doctor smiled at her, then nodded to Dr Thomas. 'I'll organise the paperwork.'

Vanessa sat in the chair, her brown eyes glued to David's face. His head was swathed in bandages. There were tubes up his nose and in his mouth, IV drips attached to his arms and an abundance of electronic equipment — several different types of monitors — behind the head of the bed. His right leg was encased in a plaster cast and elevated via a pulley system. The monitors, with their digital numbers, their graphs, the sounds some made, fascinated and the more closely she watched them, terrified her. A kindly sister had explained their function but because she wasn't medically inclined and had good health herself, she found them intimidating and confusing.

She, Lloyd and Robyn were taking turns to sit beside David in his intensive care bed. Already, it felt as if she had been there a week when in real time it had been less than twelve hours. In hospital, time seemed to crawl instead of flowing at the normal pace as it did in the outside world. Her back ached, her eyes were sore from staring at the monitors and her brain was as weary as the rest of her from the act of willing David to get better. She needed to see him open his eyes, to move, even fractionally, either of which in her mind would signify the operation's success. The night sister-in-charge, had told her it was too early for any real sign of recovery because he was heavily medicated and wouldn't respond to stimuli for another twelve hours at least. But still she hoped for some sign, anything to ease her anxiety.

Another twelve, then twenty-four and thirty hours ticked by and David's condition did not change. Vanessa heard the word 'coma' whispered by the attending sisters. Dr Thomas kept popping in to check the observation charts. He would stand at the foot of the bed with a serious, considering expression, not saying anything positive or negative, but playing, she assumed, like her, a waiting game.

It was hard to sit still for long periods of time. Eventually one's mind became as numb as one's backside. In the early daylight of the fifth day Vanessa watched rain drops slide down the window to the right of David's bed. The weather was still atrocious. Just for something to do she stood and walked towards the glass, to stare down into the street below. People, early shift workers most likely, hurried by, their umbrellas forming an almost unbroken line along the street. Great-coats, trench coats, scarves and mackintoshes were almost uniformly grey, black and fawn. She couldn't remember any other time when she had felt so weary.

And ... as each hour stretched into another day, and another, the hopelessness of David's situation increased, instinct telling her even before Dr Thomas had, that some sign of recovery should have been evident by now.

Oh, David. She blinked back a rush of tears. What if he suddenly woke and saw them? No, she had to be strong for him. When he woke up she could relax and have a good cry; they would be tears of relief then.

Standing there she continued to slip into deeper emotional misery by remembering happier times. How they'd first met, during, of all things, a literary luncheon for Australian author, Colleen McCullough, in a Savoy function room. He had been standing behind her in line, waiting for the author to sign a copy of her book, *The Ladies of Missalonghi*. He had introduced himself and they'd started to talk. He'd asked her to join him for coffee. She had said yes, and that was how their relationship had begun.

At the beginning of the sixth day, Vanessa gathered enough courage to ask Dr Thomas the questions she had so far been afraid to ask. 'Why isn't David responding? What's wrong?'

Dr Thomas pursed his lips while his mind formulated an answer. 'We're not sure, Vanessa. Sometimes after the surgery David's had, the brain, well it goes to sleep. That's why he's in a coma. That can be a healthy sign, a sign that the brain is healing itself in its own time.'

She stared at him. 'You don't think that's the case with David, do you? I — I've heard the staff saying things like 'diminishing brain activity,' 'less response to stimulus'. You've put him on a respirator.'

Anxiety added a touch of anger to her tone. 'I may not be medically wise but neither am I naive. I know those aren't positive signs.'

He returned her challenging stare for a moment as he deliberated over how much to tell her. 'No, they aren't. The coma's deepened I'm afraid, and ...' he paused, stroked his beard with his hand, 'all we can do is keep up the support systems, the intravenous feeding, the respirator ... and hope! We've done everything that's medically possible ...' He cleared his throat and, uncomfortable with her stricken expression, averted his gaze.

But then, as if to a macabre cue, the cardiac monitor gave a beep, a different kind of beep. Vanessa's gaze flew to the electronic graph. It was making uneven strokes. Up and down, then flat. Up and down again then flatter for longer and another sound, a continuing beeping that went on and on. The sound scared the hell out of her. In a flurry of activity, four or five sisters plus Dr Thomas converged around David's bed. She heard the words over the ward's speaker system, 'Code Red, Code Red, room two three eight.'

'Get her out of here,' Dr Thomas barked to the closest sister, jerking his head to mean Vanessa, as he was given the electric paddles from the defibrillator.

Entirely alone, Vanessa stood in the corridor leaning against the wall. At first she stared at the closed door of room two three eight, praying for it to open, willing the staff to come out wearing expressions of relief. Seconds ran into minutes. Five minutes passed, the door remained closed and no-one entered or left. A frightening emptiness began to invade her body, stripping her energy away and slowly, hands trembling, she covered her face and began to cry.

After David's funeral, Kerri Spanos had been Vanessa's salvation.

Kerri tidied up the flat, talked her through the early, worst days of her grief, comforted her and made Vanessa stay as her guest for almost a week to maintain a constant watch on her friend. She kept the media away, ensuring the message got through that Vanessa wanted privacy and no interviews would be given.

The short-term contract Vanessa had, to play one of the leading female roles in a Sydney production of *Private Lives*, had been a godsend. It allowed Kerri to whisk Vanny away from a morbidly curious media, snuffing out their nosiness, and it gave her friend something other than being miserable to focus on.

That Vanessa came good both on and off stage in Sydney told Kerri something she would keep to herself. Vanessa believed her heart had been broken by David's death and, yes, it had been traumatic and dreadful but she, personally, believed Vanny wasn't as grief-stricken as she might have been.

How she concluded that was . . . complicated. Her dear friend and client had had several relationships over as many years. None had worked out and when David came along, Vanny had pinned her future happiness on their marriage, partly because she had dreamt of having the same kind of successful marriage her parents had enjoyed. She had believed David would provide that for her. Her Vanny would be sad for quite a while but she would get over this loss. However, she silently prophesied that it would take a different, special kind of man to re-awaken her. Yes, someone quite special.

# CHAPTER TWO

Playing tourist was the kind of therapy Vanessa needed. Able to dress down, wear a floppy hat for protection from the sun, and sunglasses, she looked like everyone else on the bus as it drove from one tourist destination to another in and around Kakadu. Single blokes keen to crack on to the English tourist soon found out that she preferred her own company to theirs but she also enjoyed participating in group activities. After almost two weeks of never-ending sunshine, the sun had streaked Vanessa's fair hair with whitish-blonde strips and noticeably darkened her already olive skin. With her day pack strapped to her back, a water bottle slung around her waist, she had become comfortable in shorts and singlet tops, socks and hiking boots which had, at first, been foreign garb.

Resting her head against the bus's seat on the return trip to Darwin at the end of the tour, Vanessa smiled as she wondered what Kerri and some of her London friends would say if they saw her dressed as she was today. There wouldn't be too many compliments, she felt certain of that.

As the bus began to off-load passengers at their hotels, the woman in front of Vanessa, Fay Whitcombe, a retired Darwin businesswoman, turned back to her and asked, 'This is your last day, Vanessa?'

"Fraid so, more's the pity. I'd love to stay another two weeks, longer even. I can't believe this country, it's spectacular. I've enjoyed every minute,' Vanessa replied, her praise genuine.

She had begun the holiday with nothing more than a sense of adventure and an inkling of how pleasant it would be to see outback Australia. What she hadn't expected was for the experience to touch her deeply. It defied logic, because she was English through and through but, curiously, something about the land, perhaps its vastness, its uniqueness had become imbedded in her psyche. So much so that she knew, one day, she had to return to explore more of its ancient landscapes and learn about its original inhabitants and those who'd come more recently to colonise what Territorians called the Top End. Having seen first-hand the ruggedness of the land, the magnificence of the outback sunsets — they were so unique — as well as the isolation, she had considerable admiration for what Aborigines and others had achieved.

'Some of us, ten or fifteen people or so, plan to have farewell drinks and watch the sun set at the sailing club at Fannie Bay. Would you like to come along and say a proper goodbye?'

Vanessa didn't need to think long about Fay's invitation. 'I'd love to.' During the tour she'd got to know at least half the people on the bus and was comfortable in their company. And, wouldn't Kerri get a kick out of knowing they thought she was an out-of-work actress rather than how well known and well paid she was in the United Kingdom and, because she spoke Spanish fluently, the Continent. Contrarily, she liked the anonymity of not being recognised, of not being thought of as special. 'What time?'

Fay rolled her eyes with amusement. '*Before* sunset.'

Embarrassed by her silly question, Vanessa laughed. 'Oh, of course.'

She should spend the night packing because her flight time was mid-morning, but that was too boring and much too sensible for her last night in Australia. She could and would be sensible, she decided, when she got back to London, and Sandy. God, the one thing, apart from Kerri, that she'd missed was her Jack Russell. Bella De Mondi, a fledgling actress, whom Kerri had vouched for, was house-sitting and caring for Sandy in her absence.

After being dropped off at Rydges Hotel, she read the faxes waiting for her in her suite. One was from Kerri double-checking that Vanessa was taking the flight in the morning. Her eyebrows lifted at her agent's lack of faith. The second one was from a London property agent; a buyer was interested in her Belgrave Square flat and had made an offer.

Hmmm. She didn't know about that. Lately she was having second thoughts about selling the flat. Initially the thought of living there with the memories of David had been unthinkable. But then, the nuisance value associated with moving, packing and relocating ... was a headache, especially with her schedule for the next six months. Three months as star of *The Glass Menagerie* on the West End and, later, working as the presenter of a pre-recorded television documentary series on a selection of historical homes in England for *National Geographic* were scheduled. Both would keep her occupied, too much so for the draining business of buying and relocating.

Over several calls, Kerri had almost convinced her that the smart thing was to hire a professional decorator to redo every room to erase the memories of David's presence. The exercise would be costly, but less arduous than moving ... and ... she and Sandy loved the flat because it was close to his favourite park.

After a much appreciated shower, Vanessa changed into casual evening wear, lightweight slacks, a midriff top and sandals. One did not overdress in the Top End at night simply because, with the wet soon to arrive, it was as hot and humid in the evening as it was during the day. On The Esplanade she flagged down a taxi to take her to the club.

Sunset was disappointing because there were no clouds to enhance the pink sky before night fell over a glassy, smooth Arafura Sea. Fay and Barry Whitcombe were natural organisers. The couple had commandeered two tables, well away from the three-piece band, for their group so people could talk without sending themselves hoarse. Over her gin and tonic, Vanessa sat back and let the conversation flow over and around her while, in a melancholy mood because her holiday was at an end, she reflected on her time in Australia.

Several months ago, on the flight into Sydney she had been steeped in misery, certain that the time in Australia would be a drag. It had been anything but. Kerri and the cast of *Private Lives* had seen to that. She had found it impossible to be constantly depressed when everyone around her was upbeat and optimistic. She knew many Australian actors and entertainers in London. Making the best of things and brimming with optimism — sometimes without sufficient reason — was a definitive Aussie trademark. Their welcoming ways and friendliness had helped her shrug off the gloom, and talking to Trish, who'd played Sybil and Tom Reynolds who'd been Elliott in *Private Lives,* had been instrumental in whetting her appetite to see more of the island continent.

She had begun the holiday with no comparable yardstick to judge it by, and though it defied commonsense that she should bond with a country so different to where she had been nurtured, curiously, she had. And when she first heard the guttural sounds of a didgeridoo, its sound had vibrated through her chest in a most peculiar manner, as if it were calling to her.

'Wanna dance, Vanessa?' asked Peter Kosh, a Canadian backpacker who sat across the table from her. An engaging grin punctuated his invitation.

Vanessa glanced at the dance floor. Two other couples were dancing. She and Peter had danced several times at the crocodile-shaped Gagudju

Hotel, in the heart of Kakadu. She smiled at him and got up. 'Sure.'

'Barry,' Fay looked at her husband. 'Ask the band to play *The Nutbush*.' She grinned at Peter and Vanessa. 'You two dance that so well.'

Vanessa considered the energetic steps of *The Nutbush* more of a workout than a proper dance and one for which one had to be reasonably fit to last the distance. Fortunately, the walking, swimming and climbing she'd done over the last two weeks had toned her muscles as efficiently as a daily two-hour workout at a gym would have. Besides, she loved to dance. Her mother, Rosa Constancia del Rios-Forsythe, had been a professional dancer in her youth, before she had met Vanessa's father. Her mum had taught her many of the dances she had learned as a child on the back streets of Madrid, so Vanessa had no trouble picking up more modern dance routines.

Halfway through the four-four beat of *The Nutbush*, Brendan Selby, his glance more curious than interested, looked up from his glass towards the dance floor and saw her. Barefooted, head tilted slightly back, smiling, she was moving to the music's beat with a fluidity he suddenly found riveting. Damn it, she was good, much better than her dancing partner. His gaze slid towards his brother. Curtis was playing pool with a couple of blokes. Waiting his turn for the ball, he also watched the dancers while he leant on his pool stick. A swift glance around the lounge-bar area surprised Brendan. Everyone was watching the free, impromptu entertainment.

He picked up his glass, stood and moved to the edge of the dance floor for a better look. The walk was worth it. What a sensational-looking woman she was! Almost as tall as he, she looked good enough to eat, with her tanned skin, high cheekbones, flashing brown eyes, wide smile and pearly white teeth. The dance ended to a round of applause after which the dancers gave each other a friendly hug and returned to their table. Barely able to tear his eyes away from the woman, Brendan moved to the bar for a refill, positioning himself so he could see her without being obvious. Was she with her dancing partner, or was she ... available?

Hell, even if she was available, why would she be interested in him? He didn't look his best. He and Curtis had spent most of the day at their mother's house, by the shores of Cullen Bay. After doing several maintenance jobs for Hilary Selby, they hadn't bothered to freshen up, deciding to come to the sailing club for a steak and chips dinner washed down with a few beers before turning in for an early night. Tomorrow morning, at sunrise, he and Curtis would head home. Home being a five hundred plus kilometre chopper ride to the Kimberley region in Western Australia. Content at this point to observe, Brendan stayed on the bar stool, sipping his beer, his fascination for the blonde woman growing by the minute.

Inexplicably, he had an overwhelming need to know who she was, what she did for a living, and was she *involved?* Anyone as beautiful as she probably was. The thought depressed him. Still, by the way she responded to the men at the table he sensed that she wasn't overly interested in any of them though she was friendly enough and joined in the conversation. Covertly studying her he sensed her reserve, it was recognisable from where he sat.

He waited an hour or so, watched the numbers at her table thin, checked out what she was drinking, then ordered one for her, after which he sauntered across to where she sat and put the drink down in front of her.

'For the dance you did, Miss ...? Having two left feet myself, I really appreciated your skill.' He held out his hand. 'I'm Brendan Selby from Western Australia. Most people call me Bren.'

Vanessa looked dubiously at the gin and tonic, and at the man who'd bought it for her. In one glance she took in his grubby shorts, the singlet top that showed off his well-developed chest, and his dust-encrusted sandalled feet. 'Thank you, but I don't think ...'

'Please,' Bren entreated. 'I'm strictly a beer man so if you don't have it, it'll be tipped down the drain.'

After giving Bren a mother-hen once over and an ever so slight nod of approval, Fay Whitcombe intervened. 'Go on, Vanessa, it's all right. I'm sure Bren doesn't bite.' She threw him a speculative stare, 'Do you?' When he said that he didn't, she smiled and invited, 'Sit down, Bren.' Fay formally introduced Vanessa. 'This is Vanessa Forsythe. Tonight's her last night in Darwin. She flies home tomorrow.'

'And home is ...?'

'London.'

'Oh!' Brendan disguised his disappointment. Well, that's that. She might just as well live on Mars. Even so, as he couldn't help himself, he took another, closer look. An alien ache twisted in his chest until it hurt and at that moment the fact that she was out of reach, somehow, crazily, didn't matter. He just wanted to talk to her, get to know her a little and to watch those expressive brown eyes and forget that after tonight he'd never see her again. Such thoughts were as un-Brendan like as could be and they surprised him. He mentally shook himself as he sat opposite her, admonishing himself to be sensible.

'Vanessa's an actress,' Fay put in to start the conversation.

'Really!' Bren absorbed that with a nod. 'I thought maybe a model or a dancer.'

'My mother was a dancer who, being Spanish, specialised in Flamenco dancing,' Vanessa said. 'She taught me how to do a lot of different dances when I was younger ... b-before she passed on.' No-one at the table knew, because she'd not talked very much about herself and what she did, but she could dance the bossa nova, the cha cha, the tango, even the provocative lambada, at a professional level, if she wanted to.

'I'm sorry for your loss,' Bren said, his tone sincere.

Vanessa's returning smile was tinged with sadness. 'It was a long time ago. I was twelve when I lost both my parents in a train crash.'

Bren nodded solemnly. 'That must have been tough. My father passed away seven months ago. I inherited his cattle station and run it with help from my younger brother.' He pointed to Curtis who was leaning over the pool table to make a shot. 'That's him over there. Curtis is a crack pool player.'

Vanessa's gaze flicked towards the pool table then back to Bren Selby. Polite interest was in her tone as she asked, 'Where is your station, Bren?'

'In the Kimberley, a hundred or so kilometres south west of Kununurra. It's not as huge as some, roughly one hundred and ninety-five thousand hectares. It's called Amaroo Downs. We run about eight thousand head of cattle there, mostly Brahman.'

Vanessa laughed, 'That sounds huge. Isn't that about the size of Wales?'

'Not quite, but it is pretty big,' Bren advised with a pleased grin.

'Must keep you busy,' Fay interceded. 'You know Linford Downs Station, of course? Barry and I are friends of Simon and Kathy Johns.'

'The Johns are our closest neighbours.'

The band started to play again, and this time the tune had a slow beat to it. Bren gathered his courage and looked at Vanessa. 'Care to dance?'

'What about your two left feet?' Vanessa teased.

He smiled as he got to his feet. 'I'll do my best to control them.'

Holding Vanessa in his arms, not too close, but not too far away, did the most amazing things to him. He hoped she wouldn't notice his sweaty palms, and the hesitancy in his steps as he tried his darnedest not to step on her feet. Miraculously he didn't. She was so tall that they could look into each other's eyes. Hers were a rich, warm brown flecked with gold. Very unusual, he decided. Vanessa Forsythe, such a nice name, was the loveliest woman he had ever met, and he'd met a few in his thirty-four years. He'd loved a few too, and been engaged twice, but *this* woman ...

Christ, he couldn't believe what was happening to him. He was falling under some kind of spell and the spell-maker was — Vanessa. Another interesting thing was that she had no idea of her capabilities. From the responses she made he knew that she was just being pleasantly polite. But an English reserve was there, below the surface politeness and it made him wonder, was she getting over a broken relationship? That could explain the stand-offishness and why a gorgeous-looking woman such as herself was travelling alone. There had to be a reason why she preferred her own company. He longed to ask so many questions other than the standard, 'Are you enjoying yourself?', 'Do you like Australia?', but commonsense and the manners drummed into him by his mother, stopped him. Besides, he'd rather she vouch information about herself instead of him trying to prise it out of her.

They enjoyed another dance — and he only stepped on her foot once, something of a record for him.

'I think I have to call it a night,' Vanessa announced as the dance finished. 'I've heaps of packing to do and ...'

'How about one for the road?' Bren tried to talk her into another drink.

'Thanks, not this time, Bren. Really, I should go.'

Desperate to keep the contact going as long as possible he offered, 'We could share a taxi back to town. I'm staying at the All Seasons Hotel, it's near Rydges. That's where you're staying, isn't it?' He'd heard Fay mention the hotel's name in conversation.

'I don't think so.'

'Okay,' he accepted her decision. She didn't know him from Adam and she was smart enough not to hop into a taxi with a stranger. Fair enough. A woman on her own had to be careful these days. 'When's your flight?'

'10.00 a.m.'

He watched her say goodbye to the people at the table, those she'd been touring with.

'I'll write in a few weeks, after you've had time to settle,' Fay Whitcombe promised.

'Please do, especially if you and Barry plan to come to London in late June, for Wimbledon. We'll catch up then,' Vanessa answered as she gave Fay, then Barry, a hug.

Bren insisted on staying with her while she waited for a taxi. Unfortunately, a vacant one came along too soon as far as he was concerned.

'Nice to have met you, Bren Selby,' Vanessa said with an informal smile. She held out her hand. 'Don't work too hard on that station of yours.'

As he grasped her hand in his large one, Bren was extraordinarily conscious of his reaction to her. It made him feel — bloody fantastic. God, how could he walk away from her, from what he was feeling? It was too damned special. Somehow he controlled the urge to let her see his reactions. Too soon for that.

'Yeah,' he grinned at her. 'I know the axiom: all work and no play ... Have a safe trip home, Vanessa.'

Bren could have asked for her phone number, her address. He didn't, but not because he didn't want to. He did, desperately. He didn't because he believed she wouldn't give it to him and he chose not to risk a second rebuff. Closing the taxi door after she'd got in he watched it until it was out of sight. He had a lot on his plate right now: Amaroo Downs was in need of attention, and his mother was becoming more, not less demanding as she tried to cope with being a widow. Somehow, though, he would track Vanessa down ... And when he did, he'd use every means at his disposal to make her fall in love with him.

His jaw clamped down with determination as he turned on his heel to go and find Curtis. People, family, those who knew him well, knew that when Brendan James Selby put his mind towards a goal, he didn't give up until he'd achieved it.

'You're out of your head. You do know that, don't you?'

Bren threw Curtis a baleful glance before he continued to pack his bag. 'You don't understand, mate, I have to go. I can't think straight, haven't been able to for two months, not since that night at Fannie Bay. Geez, Curtis, you saw her. Saw how beautiful she was. It's like something is eating me up inside, in my gut. If I don't ...'

'Christ, Bren, she's only a woman,' Curtis cut in, ignoring his brother's annoyed intake of breath. It wasn't the first time he'd heard his brother wax lyrical over Vanessa 'what's her name' but flying half way around the world to see her 'cause he had the hots for her made no sense. 'Fair bloody dinkum,

Bren, wise up,' he let his exasperation show. 'She doesn't know you exist.'

'Just because you've turned into a woman hater because of what your wife, Georgia, did, don't judge all women by her actions.'

'My ex-wife, thank you!' Curtis corrected. 'I don't hate women, I just don't trust them and,' he paused to gather his thoughts, 'don't change the subject. What you're doing is madness. You're likely to come a real gutser, you know.'

'Perhaps I will,' Bren conceded matter-of-factly. 'Be that as it may, I've never felt like this before about any woman, not even Donna and Maddy when I was engaged to them. All I know is, I have to try. If she turns me down, well, then I guess I'll have to live with that.'

'But it's the worst time to go. There's work to do here. And, in case it's slipped your mind, the station's not exactly flush financially,' Curtis reminded him. 'Dad, the poor bugger, due to his illness, made several unsound business decisions. The debts are killing us. We'll have to work flat out and live lean for a few years to pay them off.'

'I know.' Grey eyes looked directly into Curtis's. 'It's a risk I'm prepared to take. Besides, you and Reg can organise and run Amaroo Downs as well if not better than I can.'

Curtis had to agree with that. 'We both know that Reg, by himself, could run the place with one hand tied behind his back.' As head stockman, Reg Morrison was exceptional and had been at Amaroo for almost eighteen years. 'That's not the point though. Dad left the place to you, not me.'

There was no rancour in his brother's tone, but Bren felt compelled to say, 'Which wasn't my choice, as you well know. Dad had this outdated nineteenth century idea about the eldest son inheriting the property. It wasn't what I wanted.'

'I'm okay with it, Bren.'

Matthew Selby had seen that his wife and his other children, Curtis and Lauren were well catered for financially. That Matthew had decided to keep up the tradition set by their grandfather, English-born Robert Selby, of the eldest son inheriting the main property, Amaroo Downs, was something Curtis didn't agree with, but would never legally dispute. Their father had continued the tradition because *he* had inherited Amaroo the same way, over his brother, Stuart. At the time Stuart had been mightily disgruntled by Robert's will. His uncle had taken his cash inheritance and forged a successful career in the pearling industry in Broome, and later, in tourism. Today, Stuart and his wife, Diane, were reputedly multi-multi-millionaires with a lifestyle that far outstripped what Curtis and Bren had at Amaroo Downs.

'Mum won't be pleased that you're running off to chase a piece of skirt.'

'It's not Mum's business and,' Bren gave him a dark look, 'I don't care for your tone. Vanessa isn't just "a piece of skirt" to me. Show some respect. If things work out the way I hope, she's the woman I intend to marry.'

Curtis ran a hand through his short, brownish-blond hair. Bren had a short fuse temper and it wasn't clever to rile him when his emotions where tied up in knots. Younger by three years, Curtis was taller and slimmer than Bren and in earlier days had never beaten his older brother in a wrestle or a fair fight.

'Marry? Hell, Bren, if you could hear yourself, you sound like a moonstruck adolescent.'

'I'm a bit old for that, but,' Bren shrugged a shoulder diffidently, 'I don't care. This is something I have to do and nothing you, Mum or anyone might say will make me change my mind.'

'Okay, okay!' Curtis threw up his hands in defeat. 'How long will you be away?'

'I don't know. As long as it takes,' Bren replied, his smile a silent challenge. 'Felicia and Alex Montgomery have offered to put me up at their flat in Mayfair.'

Alex, an old school mate who lived in London had, during the month, faxed him some interesting and enlightening information on Vanessa Forsythe, information that might have put a lesser man off. She was not the out-of-work actress she'd purported to be to her tourist friends. Vanessa was an exceedingly well known English dramatic actress with a string of successes and awards to her name. He hadn't told Curtis that because he knew what his brother would do; try to throw more obstacles in his way. That Curtis didn't want him to get hurt was obvious and brotherly of him, but going to London was something Bren absolutely, positively had to do.

'When will you be off?'

'My flight leaves the day after tomorrow.' He gave Curtis an appealing look. 'I'll need to hitch a chopper ride to Darwin tomorrow morning.'

An unhappy, gravelly sound issued from Curtis's throat. 'Sure, you're the boss,' he grumbled tongue-in-cheek, then he hightailed it out of the room before the boot Bren threw at him could find its mark.

Shaking his head, Bren chuckled at his brother's quick response. Curtis could still move fast. For several minutes, while he packed, he thought over what his younger, eminently sensible brother had said. Was he making the biggest mistake of his life? Was he chasing a dream that had no chance of becoming a reality? Maybe he was a fool ... Curtis hadn't exactly said that he was, but the expression in his eyes to that effect had been child's play to read.

Bren stopped doing what he was doing to move to the window. He pushed the curtain back to look beyond the machinery shed and the stockmen's quarters to the land. Puddles that were left over from the rain dotted the front lawn and the various yards beyond the homestead's fence and were beginning to dry up. A welcome, fine layer of green grass was sprouting from the red earth. Within weeks, as the sun dried the moisture, the grass would turn yellow but still be nutritious for stock. In the distance the foothills of the northern part of the Durack Range were greening too, under a cloudless sky.

The muscles in Bren's chest tightened with pride as he breathed the air coming in through the open window. It was still moist, with a faint earthiness to it. Amaroo Downs, his very own considerable piece of land and sky. Near the fence that separated the house from the other station buildings and stock, stood two Brahman poddy calves. They were waiting for their bottles of milk and getting impatient to be fed.

He fancied that he knew just about every centimetre of Amaroo and he knew the risk he was taking in leaving. Christ! Hadn't he spent more nights than he cared to number weighing up the pros and cons? All to no avail. He sighed and turned back to the bed. He had to go, something deep inside him was pulling him towards Vanessa and the need was too compelling to resist. He couldn't sleep or function properly for thinking about her. It had been going on for two months without abating — that had to mean something. Incredible as it was, in just one night he had developed feelings for her and they ran deep.

It was as if she had infected his blood, his heart and his soul. He knew one thing: he had to take up the challenge of finding her and, if he were lucky — he'd always been a lucky bugger when it came to women — he would win her heart. What came after that, lifestyle, career decisions, well, frankly, he hadn't a clue. He and Vanessa would work that out when the time came . . .

# CHAPTER THREE

Bren was nervous and he didn't mind admitting it, if only to himself. He'd arrived in London two days ago, been met by the Montgomerys and slept off the jet lag, after which he had fielded an angry phone call from his mother, who had suggested in the strongest possible terms that he come home immediately. His equally forceful rejection of that suggestion had been met with several seconds of stony silence, then she'd hung up on him. Grimacing at the memory of it, he shook his head as he fiddled with the angle of his bow-tie. Sometimes his mother was a real trial . . .

Since his father's death, Hilary Selby's life had lacked direction and because it had she took her frustration out on other members of the family. When Dad had fallen ill, his mother had taken over the running of Amaroo Downs, much to his and Curtis's frustration. After his father's death Hilary Selby had wanted to continue running the show, but the specifics of the will, that he had to manage Amaroo Downs to secure his inheritance, had precluded that, and added disgruntlement to the grief she'd felt at losing the man she loved.

In a fit of pique, Hilary, who'd been well provided for in the will, had bought a beautiful home in Cullen Bay, a Darwin seaside suburb where, with the Selby name being well known, a good social life was guaranteed. But that hadn't satisfied her. He shrugged a shoulder defensively as he acknowledged that nothing seemed to satisfy his mother these days. Which was regrettable because, periodically, she made his, Curtis's and Lauren's lives hell with her demands and attempts to impose her will as she had in bygone days.

Bren had settled into his room at the Montgomery's spacious flat in Mayfair. He had come armed with Vanessa's phone number and address, courtesy of an obliging Fay Whitcombe whom he'd contacted through their mutual friends on Linford Downs Station.

Alex and Felicia had bought him, and themselves, tickets to the opening night of *The Glass Menagerie*, in which Vanessa starred. He looked at his reflection in the wardrobe mirror. Opening nights were special events in London with first-nighters wearing their best clobber, according to Alex. Hence the hired dinner suit and other paraphernalia.

Would she remember him? God, his hopes would be dashed if she didn't. In her profession, she undoubtedly met a lot of people, males, from varying backgrounds and, perhaps, the unpalatable thought crossed his mind, she was seeing a new man by now. Damn! He should have come sooner but Curtis would have thrown a fit if he'd taken off before the post-wet muster.

'Ready, Bren?' Alex asked as he knocked on the bedroom door.

'Don't you look super,' Felicia complimented as the two men came down the hallway then added as an afterthought to her husband, 'you too, darling.' Ready herself, she went to stand by the front door to wait for them.

'Mmmm, you can tell we've been married for a while,' Alex grumbled good-naturedly, his grimace directed at his wife. 'The longer one is married, so I've noted, the more rare and sometimes questionable are the compliments.'

'Don't be such a bear, darling. It's Bren's confidence that needs boosting, not yours.'

'No, it doesn't,' Bren said staunchly as they walked down a flight of stairs to street level. He knew he looked good in the dinner suit. He had the height, the breadth of shoulders and the tan to carry it off. It was bitterly cold outside, it had been all day, and a sensible man would have worn his sheepskin coat over the dinner suit. That wouldn't have looked sophisticated so the coat stayed where he'd thrown it on arrival, over a chair next to the bed.

'I wangled tickets through a friend to go backstage afterwards, to meet the cast,' Felicia murmured to Bren as Alex flagged a taxi. 'I didn't tell you before 'cause I thought it might make you nervous.'

'Thanks, I believe they're hard to get.' Bren gave Felicia a grateful smile, letting the fact that he was impressed show. It was obvious that Felicia was trying to make him feel comfortable and help him in his romantic endeavours. It was nice of her to have made the effort. He didn't know the English-born Felicia as well as he knew Alex. He and Alex'd been mates at boarding school and had flatted together in Townsville while they'd done their respective university degrees; farm agriculture for himself and a business degree for Alex. After getting his Masters, Alex, now a stockbroker, was doing very nicely on the London Stock Exchange.

From their dress circle seats, the Montgomerys and Bren had a good view of the stage. Bren's gaze followed Vanessa as she performed her role though he was more interested in watching her every movement and listening to the sound of her voice, than following the play's plot. Before Vanessa made her entrance, he had admitted to, suddenly, having doubts. What if, when he saw her, he felt nothing? What if the fantasy he'd built up in his mind was just that, and seeing her in real life burst the bubble of his dreams? But then she had come on stage and her presence was so powerful that the audience hushed, eager to hear every line she uttered.

She looked very different to the woman he'd met in Darwin. Her hair was formally done. She wore stage make-up too, and her role played a part in that. However, as he listened to his erratic heart pump faster than it should, and became more aware of the blood coursing through his veins, he knew his feelings were true and that nothing mattered more than getting Vanessa to reciprocate them.

The evening passed in a blur. Alex, Felicia and he talked about the play and about other topics but he'd be damned if he could remember a single word.

He was focussing on that backstage party. God, so much hinged on making the right impression.

These feelings, these anxieties were new territory for Bren Selby. In the past, with women, he could either take them or leave them — often the latter — in spite of the outback lacking a surplus of females, a fact that had never worried him. Having seen Curtis go through a ruinous divorce to that bitch, Georgia, and seeing him lose contact with his only child, had been a salient lesson, enough to put him off contemplating settling down. Until now!

Since he had first laid eyes on Vanessa he had thought, many times, that he was embarking on an impossible dream yet, curiously, there was something romantic, even old-fashioned about his quest, considering it was almost the nineties. These days, people shacked up together, changed partners as frequently as they liked, were promiscuous in their love lives and didn't seem overly concerned about contracting AIDS or any of several other nasty, communicable diseases. Social ethics had blurred dramatically as the century was drawing to a close and while he considered himself a modern kind of bloke, there was enough of the traditionalist in him to want to do things the right way.

It was bedlam backstage after the final curtain went down. Vanessa hated it and at the same time, contradictorily, loved it. There were so many people, cast, crew members and the public milling around to congratulate and, occasionally, criticise the performance. Champagne flowed freely, and there was a lot of noise, laughter and compliments, sincere and otherwise. After years of experience she knew that by the time the critics' reviews went to print, she would be pleasantly exhausted and her cheek muscles sore from so much smiling.

From the other side of the stage Kerri Spanos gave her the thumbs up sign. Yes, she too believed the audience had loved the play. *The Glass Menagerie* had been originally made memorable by the late English actress, Gertrude Lawrence, long before Vanessa had been born. She hoped none of the critics would compare her performance to the legendary Gertrude's. She had played the role the way she had felt it, not copying it from any past performances.

Someone touched her on the shoulder. She turned around to see who it was.

'Vanessa Forsythe, I presume?' A deep voice with an Australian accent spoke, corrupting the renowned Stanley meets Livingstone introduction.

'Oh!' She looked into a pair of grey eyes that were studying her intensely. They belonged to a ruggedly attractive man in his early thirties. 'It's you.'

A shiver of delight went through her. She knew him, didn't she, but from where and how? Something about him ... She pondered over the tingle of recognition, her brown eyes sparkling as the memory clicked into place. 'Aahhh! The jackaroo with two left feet, from Darwin.'

'The same. But how unkind of you to remember my two left feet, considering I only trod on your toes once,' Bren threw back at her with an engaging grin.

His answer made her smile, slowly. He'd been nice, she remembered that. Friendly and easygoing, a lot different to the average uptight, straight-backed Englishman. And, she recalled admitting as she had packed her bags that night ... there had been a momentary regret that they'd been like ships passing in the night.

'What are you doing here?'

'Combining business with pleasure,' he fibbed convincingly. 'Inspecting livestock breeds in Middlesex and staying with an old school friend in London.' He waggled an accusing finger at her as he said, 'You could have told me you were *the* Vanessa Forsythe. The actress who has articles written about her regularly in women's magazines, who's been nominated for several acting awards and has already won one.'

Wanting to know all he could, over the last two months he had compiled a dossier on Vanessa, thanks to her fan club. He had press clippings from her Sydney performances. He knew about the death of her fiancé, David Benedict. Knew a little about her parents, her on-the-stage grandmother ...

'Forgive me. I was on holiday, travelling incognito.' She jiggled her eyebrows melodramatically. 'I chose to be an ordinary person. That's not always easy for me in the United Kingdom.'

'You could never be ordinary, Vanessa.' His voice rang with sincerity. 'Though I understand the reason for your secretiveness.'

'Thanks, but I'm afraid you have the advantage. I'm sorry, I can't recall your name.'

He stopped the wince before it started. Of course she couldn't. Why would she? 'Brendan Selby of Amaroo Downs. People call me Bren.'

'Bren. Yes, of course. Come meet my agent, Kerri Spanos. She's standing beside the lighting control panel over there, giving us the "stare". Kerri's very protective and, clearly, wants to know who you are.'

Vanessa took hold of his hand. 'She's a dear friend as well as my business manager and,' she giggled as she admitted her agent's greatest flaw, 'when it comes to her clients, the world's biggest stickybeak.'

'We can't disappoint the world's biggest stickybeak, can we?' he agreed. Following her, they wove their way through the crowd until they'd made it to the other side of the stage.

'Kerri, meet Brendan Selby from Australia.' Vanessa made the simple introduction.

'Australia.' Kerri's dark eyebrows winged upwards. 'So, do I presume that you two have met before ...?'

'Fleetingly,' Vanessa supplied the answer. 'On my last night in Darwin.'

'And now you're in England, Bren.' The question was more in Kerri's eyes than her tone of voice as she submitted him to a thorough inspection.

'Yeah. A combined business trip and holiday. I read the promo about the play in the paper and recognised Vanessa's name. Thought I'd look her up and say hello.'

'Really, on a first night too! How interesting,' Kerri said with a cool smile.

On the surface Kerri Spanos's expression gave nothing away but Bren could tell that Vanessa's agent's mind was ticking overtime. Bullshit, she was probably thinking. He might fool Vanessa with his casual approach but he could tell from the agent's sharp look that she *knew* he was smitten.

'How long will you be in town, Bren?' Kerri wanted to know.

'I'm not sure. A month at least, maybe longer.'

'Your property can do without you for that long?' Vanessa queried.

'My brother runs the place as well as I do, perhaps even better,' Bren admitted with a chuckle. 'I won't be missed, too much, not until the spring muster.' Though he knew Curtis would kill him if he stayed away that long!

'Oh, Vanny,' Kerri was the only person who dared to use that nickname for Vanessa, 'Mike Harley from *The Times* wants an interview. He'd like to do it now so it can make tomorrow afternoon's paper.'

'No problem.' Vanessa gave Bren a regretful smile. 'That's the problem with being *known,* not enough time to oneself.'

'Perhaps I could give you a call? Take you to lunch or something?' Bren offered, striving to keep the eagerness out of his voice.

'Of course, I'd like that,' Vanessa said with a smile. 'Kerri will give you my number.'

'No worries. I got your number from Fay Whitcombe. Fay was kind enough to give it to me before I left Darwin,' he said with a self-satisfied smile.

'Oh,' Vanessa looked impressed. 'How clever of you to do that. The Whitcombes are coming here in June, you know.'

'You'd better go and find Mike, Vanny,' Kerri reminded Vanessa, encouraging her client to move on.

Bren watched Vanessa melt into the crowd, but with her height and fair hair, she still stood out. Pleased that he'd accomplished what he had, he was about to turn away to go and find the Montgomerys when Kerri put a detaining hand on his sleeve.

'Bren Selby,' she said coolly, her coal black eyes probing his. 'I think we both know what you're after, with regard to Vanny. She ...' Kerri paused, pursed her lips for a second or two then decided to go on and say what she wanted to. 'The last six months have been rough for Vanny ... I don't want her to be hurt again.'

Bren nodded that he understood the gist of her words. 'I know about David Benedict.'

'You do?' Kerri didn't disguise her surprise. She gave the man from the Australian outback another longer, appraising look, and there was a glimmer of interest in her black depths.

'Yes. Believe me, Ms Spanos, the last thing I'd want to do is hurt Vanessa. She's become ... quite special to me.'

Kerri took his words in with a nod of her head. Her set features would have been the envy of a poker player for they betrayed nothing of her inner thoughts. 'I accept that. But be warned, Bren, if you hurt her, I'll do my utmost to make your life hell. And ...' she added with steely purpose, 'with my contacts I have a reputation for being able to do that, no matter where you might be in the world.'

Bren took Kerri's threat in his stride. He was astute enough to see that Vanessa's agent could be a formidable enemy or she could be a valuable asset and that it would be smarter to have her on his side than otherwise. 'I promise you won't have to, Ms Spanos.'

'Good, and you can call me Kerri, Bren.'

'Thank you, Kerri.' He didn't want to say anymore, he'd said enough. Intuitively she'd worked out that he was either infatuated or in love with Vanessa, so all he could hope was that she wouldn't use what influence she had with Vanessa to cruel his chance with her. Before he could make a speedy exit someone came up to Kerri and spirited her away without so much as a backwards glance at him.

Theatricals! Watching her totter off in her stiletto heels, his mouth twisted in a cynical smile. Vanessa's world was one he knew nothing about but he had the feeling that over the next month or so he was going to do a crash course on actors, agents and those involved in live theatre ...

Vanessa could not sleep. She should be able to because the performance, the backstage party, then the vigil at a restaurant in Soho until the morning's first edition reviews came out, should have exhausted her. The reviews were good. Better than good; they had been excellent. The newspapers' hard-to-please theatre critics, male and female, had waxed lyrical in their overall praise of the production, and especially the performers. That should have made her relaxed and happy but, confusingly, she was unable to fall asleep and she knew the cause. It wasn't the reviews or her performance. Drifting in and out of her consciousness was a particular face, a very interesting face that belonged to ... Bren Selby.

Why? What was it about Bren that made him so memorable? She scarcely knew the man, and though he was attractive, he wasn't the most handsome man in the world. But something — his ruggedness, the air of well-being, his congeniality, the no fuss attitude when compared to other men of her acquaintance — had an obvious appeal. Ohhh, she reprimanded herself, she was being silly. He probably wouldn't call her, he was probably only being polite. Though, if he did call, how would she react? Right now she had no idea.

*You're an idiot, Vanessa Forsythe. Why are you allowing yourself to lose sleep over something so trivial?* She unscrewed her eyes, opened the lids and glanced at the bedside clock: 4.32 a.m. Aargghhh! Irritated by her foolishness, and dog-tired, she thumped the pillow several times, sighed and repeated over and over, 'Go to sleep, go to sleep . . . go to sleep.'

Bren had been to London twice before so for his first date with Vanessa he hired a compact car and they drove to Lower Slaughter, a pleasant village not far from London, for lunch. He already knew that to see her he'd have to work in with her stage commitments — six nightly performances and a matinee on Saturdays. All the while his heart was telling him to go fast, but his head was saying the opposite; go slow, don't try to rush a woman like Vanessa or he'd end up blowing it.

Over a traditional ploughman's lunch and a pint of beer at the Bald Stag Hotel, they talked, and talked, then, despite the crisp, winter's day — spring was around the corner, so the Montgomerys assured him — they went for a walk. Suitably rugged up in jackets, scarves and hats, they strolled arm in arm around the picturesque village.

'You know, if I wasn't an Australian, I wouldn't mind being English,' Bren said as he peered into the many-paned window of an antique-cum-bookshop. 'I love the old buildings here, the sense of history.'

She laughed. 'And if I wasn't English, I think I'd like to be Australian. I loved Australia, the vastness, the freedom, the sunsets — God they're wonderful. I'm not sure why, but I felt at home there. I'm sure there's no other place on Earth like the outback.'

'You'll have to come back then,' he said quietly, with a sly look in her direction.

'I intend to, when the opportunity arises. As we speak,' she confided, 'Kerri is negotiating with a British and Australian film consortium on a role for me in a movie being made next year in South Australia.'

'I see. So, tell me, do you see yourself as a movie star or a stage actress?'

'The stage will always be my first love, but Kerri says I'd be crazy to knock back any movie making opportunities that come up, providing they're suitable. The pay and the exposure, providing the movie's made well, is too good.'

'Do you see yourself doing something else one day, something away from the stage perhaps?' The second question was asked casually, but Bren held his breath as he waited for her answer.

'Honestly, Bren, I don't know.' His question made her think about David, about the plans they'd had for her to scale down her stage career to be a wife and eventually a mother. She stifled an internal sigh. That was history now and ... remembering ... could still bring about a melancholy mood. 'Who knows what the future might bring? At this point in my life, well, I'm keeping my options open.'

'You are wise, Vanessa Forsythe,' he responded with a chuckle. He appreciated her honesty and her answer implied that she wasn't wholly fanatical about her career. Such knowledge gave him reason to hope.

They gravitated to a park which bordered a small river that wended its way around the village's perimeter, and because a watery sun had deigned to shine on one of the painted benches, they sat to take in the scene. By a bend in the stream — it was really too small to be called a river — stood a two-storey mill with a water wheel. The mill was very old with its rough cut, lichen encrusted greyish stone walls. And beyond was a single arch stone bridge that spanned the stream, its supports laden with dark green ivy. The couple waved to an occasional holiday barge operator as the craft passed, heading west to Cirencester, Oxford and beyond. In this part of the world many streams had, in bygone days, served as waterways to transport goods to larger towns and to London.

'That would be a nice, leisurely holiday.' There was a note of wistfulness in Bren's voice.

'It's supposed to be. Ronnie Ashton, an actor friend of mine, owns a barge moored in a canal off the Thames. He rents it out during the tourist season for an obscene amount of money. He's tried talking me into using it in the low season, such as now.' Vanessa looked at him. 'If you're interested, I could talk to Ronnie.'

The suggestion was tempting but Bren didn't want to go anywhere or do anything that didn't include Vanessa. 'Maybe later on.'

'You haven't told me much about yourself,' he asked, changing the subject. He wanted to know all he could about Vanessa, more than what he'd read about in magazines. 'What was your childhood like?'

Her reply was endearingly honest. 'Poor. My father, like my grandmother, was an actor but roles were few and far between, even though he was very good, according to Gran. When Dad had no stage work he would do anything to bring in money. Labouring on building sites. Once he took a job as a shoe salesman, but he hated dealing with people's smelly feet!' She made the appropriate grimace. 'He worked as a travelling salesman too, and would paint houses or do people's gardens. Dad was prepared to have a go at anything to make enough to keep us together.'

She stopped for a couple of seconds to gather the right words. 'My mother, Rosa, developed a health problem, asthma, when I was little. She was used to the dry, hot climate of Madrid and after a while she couldn't dance anymore. Dad became the sole provider. We could only afford a cramped, cold water flat in Brixton — you may not know but it's a pretty tough suburb. I went to school there too.' Vanessa screwed up her eyes and brought her hands across her chest, hugging herself as if she was suddenly cold.

'The flat was like an ice chest, even with the heat on and, sometimes we couldn't afford coal for the fireplace. Still,' a ghost of a smile lifted the corners of her mouth, 'no matter how miserable the flat was, my parents were happy because they had each other.'

'They met when Dad was doing a stint working on stage as a magician's assistant. My mother, Rosa del Rios, came across from Spain with the Bartoleni Flamenco Dancing Troupe. Both were appearing at the same theatre in Margate during the summer.' She smiled at him. 'They were so in love ... Gran used to tease them about their kissing and cuddling, but I remember that I thought it was terrific.'

Intrigued by her tender tone, he asked, 'Why did she tease them?'

'Gran's husband, my grandfather, walked out on her when my father turned six. She never forgave Hector Forsythe for abandoning them. He came crawling back ten years later and got short shrift.' She shook her fair head. 'Gran was not a forgiving woman. She said Grandfather only came back 'cause he was sick and wanted her and his son to look after him.'

'Sounds like a tough lady.'

'She was when she had to be, but never with me. I was staying with Gran when my parents were killed in a train crash — Dad had got work in a stage production in Glasgow and Mum went with him. Kind of a short holiday for them both. The train crashed head-on into a freight train. Sixteen people died.'

Bren made a sympathetic murmur. 'Losing them both at the same time must have been awful for you.'

'It was. I don't know what I'd have done if it hadn't been for Gran. Welfare wanted to put me in an orphanage but Gran insisted she could care for me. She did.' The smile she gave him turned radiant as the reminiscing continued. 'Through her I learned so much about acting and stagecraft. She was my first and best drama teacher and when she thought I was ready, she introduced me to Kerri.'

'You don't have any other relatives?'

She shook her head. 'No one in England, and in Spain my mother was a rare, only child. I've a few distant cousins on the maternal side, they're scattered about Spain. I've never met them but we still exchange Christmas cards. That's all.' She gave him a quizzical glance and said, 'That's enough about me. What about you, Bren?'

He shrugged at her. 'My life reads like an open, and not very interesting book. Apart from boarding school and time at university, I've spent my life in the outback, on Amaroo.'

'No girlfriends, sweethearts?' she teased.

'A few. I was engaged twice but neither arrangement worked out.' Thank goodness they hadn't otherwise he wouldn't be here talking to her, watching her, falling more in love with her as every minute passed. 'I've a brother, Curtis, you almost met him in Darwin, and a sister. Lauren's the youngest, she's married to Marc, who manages a station, Cadogan's Run. They have three boys. Then there's my mother, Hilary, and my father's brother. Uncle Stuart — he's mega wealthy — lives in Broome with his family ...'

'How I envy you. It must be wonderful to have a big family, people to be with at Christmas, and birthdays to celebrate together.'

Bren thought about his mother and wasn't so sure it was wonderful, then he glanced at his watch. 'Hell, it's 3.30.' He got to his feet and pulled her up in front of him. 'We'd better be getting back. You'll want to rest before tonight's performance, won't you?'

Impressed by his thoughtfulness, she kissed him impulsively on the cheek. 'Guess so. I've enjoyed today. Thank you.'

'Thank you!' He grinned back at her. 'Could I impose and invite you to supper after the show?' He raised an eyebrow at her. 'Or does Kerri frown on that sort of thing?'

'She probably will but,' she wrinkled her nose cutely, 'we'll do it anyhow. And tomorrow night, after the play I'll take you out, to meet my friend, Melody. She manages one of the best disco-nightclubs in Soho.'

As they walked back to the car, Bren issued another invitation. 'My friends, the Montgomerys, would love you to come for Sunday lunch. That is, if you don't have anything special on.'

'Not this weekend. I'd love to.'

From that day on Bren spent as much time as he could with Vanessa, monopolising every spare hour whenever he could get away with it.

Sometimes they did ordinary things, like shopping or just walking along the path that bordered the Thames, or wandering through Hyde Park or Kew Gardens.

Bren's ongoing worry that she'd get tired or bored with his company, didn't eventuate and, as each date led to another, he got the chance to know the real Vanessa, not the stage and public persona she donned for the media and theatre-goers. He wasn't a worldly man but he knew one thing: because of her experience with David — the unhappiness it had caused — he would have to win her trust before he could win her heart.

# CHAPTER FOUR

Despite his broad-rimmed hat, Curtis shaded his eyes from the glare of the sun as the chopper, an expensive McDonald Douglas MD Explorer, circled twice before setting down on the runway next to their own chopper. Damn, and several unkind thoughts sprang to mind straight away as he recognised the craft. His uncle hadn't bothered to learn how to fly so he employed a pilot to swan him around, wherever and whenever he wanted. Well, he thought dourly, the old moneybags could afford it. Their seasoned but well-maintained Cessna they used for checking the herd and travel to and from Kununurra and Darwin was parked in the cavern-like tin shed, affectionately called the hangar.

So ... dear Uncle Stuart was deigning to pay Amaroo a visit. He didn't have time to entertain rellies, there was too much to do and who knew when Bren would be back. His brother should be here doing his share, not leaving it all up to him and Reg, not gallivanting overseas to chase Vanessa what's her name! Boots dragging in accordance with his level of enthusiasm, he walked towards the chopper.

He watched Stuart exit from the chopper and wave. The pilot got out on the other side, as did another person. Curtis gave a low whistle through his teeth. She was back, Nova Morrison, Reg's prodigal daughter. Those swaying hips, her cheeky look-at-me saunter, was Nova's trademark walk, and one he'd recognise anywhere. He rubbed the two-day-old stubble along his jawline as he thought, how long had it been since she'd been at Amaroo? Two years, maybe longer.

'Hello,' he shouted to them over the chopper's diminishing whine and mentally put aside the list of things he'd planned to do today. He would be lucky to get half of them done now. Fixing a welcoming grin to his lips, he continued on towards them.

'Ooohh, Curtis.' Nova ran the last three metres between them and hugged him exuberantly. 'You haven't changed one bit,' she purred. 'You're still the handsomest Selby, you know.'

Curtis gave a deprecating laugh. 'And you're still an outrageous flatterer, Nova. How are you doing?'

'Very well.' She preened herself against him, standing as tall as she could, which brought her up to the middle of his chest. 'I brought my degree in Arts-Science to show Dad, proof it was worth what it cost him. Since uni I've been working my way around, doing casual stuff, waitressing, bar work, hospitality receptionist shit, you know. In Sydney, Perth, and more recently, Broome.' She glanced towards Stuart. 'Bumped into your uncle in Dampier Street and he offered me a lift home.' Nova's smile showed a set of perfect teeth. She smiled a lot when she was talking to a man. 'I said yes 'cause I thought it time for a visit.'

'Hi, Curtis,' Stuart greeted his nephew. They shook hands. 'You know Rolfe Weston, my pilot?'

'Yeah. Hi.' Undiplomatically, Curtis came straight to the point. 'What brings you to Amaroo, Stuart?'

'Just a social call. Haven't been here since . . .,' he cleared his throat, 'since Matthew died.'

'Let's get out of the sun,' Nova suggested, attempting to break the underlying tension between the two men who had, for no obvious reason other than a personality clash, never got along. 'I'm sure everyone's dying for a cup of tea and some of Fran's pineapple scones.' Standing between them, she linked an arm through each of the Selby men as they walked towards the house. 'Where's Dad, Curtis?'

'On the northern boundary. We're mustering the stock there for branding.'

'Matthew used to bring them into the yards to do that,' Stuart remarked conversationally. He was studying the wide, low, single storey timber homestead that had been the station's main dwelling for just on thirty years.

As a young bride, Hilary Selby had insisted that she couldn't live in the five room stone house that Robert Selby, Amaroo's founder, had built with his bare hands more than fifty years ago. Coming from a wealthy Brisbane family, and used to the best of everything, she knew that the Selbys were wealthy enough to afford a house to match their standing in the Kimberley. And because Matthew could deny her nothing a Perth architect had been commissioned to design and build a large, comfortable home that other station owners in the region would envy.

Designed to deflect the heat, with high ceilings, a good airflow and an abundance of overhead fans run by a petrol generator, to cool the rooms at night, it had become almost a stately mansion in this part of the world. Like most cattle stations, the kitchen was the homestead's heart and contained a larder big enough to store food for a small restaurant. Because of Amaroo's remoteness groceries were ordered in bulk and trucked in from Kununurra every few months. A thriving vegetable plot outside the back door and a chicken coop to provide eggs, plus the easy availability of beef for butchering, meant those on the station ate well.

Six bedrooms and two bathrooms, a timber-panelled study for Matthew, a 'reading' room for Hilary, and wide, shady verandahs on three sides of the rectangular shaped house that doubled as sleep-outs when it was unbearably hot, more than adequately housed the family Matthew and Hilary had had.

East of the homestead stood a fenced, much neglected tennis court and beyond the paved patio area covered by a canvas pergola, was a large hole, fenced with barbed wire. A swimming pool had been part of Hilary's original grand plan but over the years the project had been shelved and never completed. The sturdy one-metre high picket fence around the perimeter of the homestead and the outdoor area was in need of a coat of paint. The fence kept unwanted animals — domestic and feral — off the bore-watered lawn and Fran's vegetable garden.

'Usually we do,' Curtis responded to Stuart's remark about the branding. 'But as there's good feed near the boundary to the Linford Downs Station, it makes more sense to do it the old-fashioned way — this time we're taking the branding iron and other paraphernalia to them.'

'Ugh, even now I still hate branding,' Nova shuddered, 'it's cruel.'

'But necessary to keep track of stock.' Curtis grinned at Nova, his hazel eyes giving her a thorough appraisal. She was petitely built. Black straight hair, cut short, olive skin from her Asian and Australian parentage and she had a trace of her Malaysian forebears in her features too. She would be about twenty-three years old now and was pretty to look at. No, more vivacious than pretty, he corrected himself. He groaned silently as he thought about the stockmen's quarters. At present there were four bachelors in the bunkhouse, all capable of competing with each other for her attention.

Curtis, seven years older, had known Nova since she was five years old. That's when Reg and his second wife, Fran, had come to work at Amaroo, and from an early age, Nova had a knack for creating ... disruptions. As a child, her mercurial, demanding temperament had reminded him of a mischievous kitten that constantly craved attention. She had been indulged by Reg and treated with kid gloves by Fran for fear of her making their lives more difficult than they already were and had, as a teenager, used her questionable *skills* — a certain slyness and a desire to manipulate people and situations — to get what she wanted, which was to break up Reg's marriage. That's when Reg had taken a stand and sent her to boarding school. The

Methodist Ladies College at Claremont in Western Australia had, apparently, straightened her out. Her animosity towards Fran — Amaroo's cook and housekeeper who was the gentlest, kindest person he knew — had lessened as Nova had matured. So, if they were lucky, Nova's return to Amaroo might be a peaceful one. He'd keep his fingers crossed over that possibility.

Besides, with Bren away he had enough on his plate without having to referee a family that couldn't get along. Grimacing to himself, Curtis scraped dirt off his boots on the back verandah step and stood back to let everyone else enter the house before him. *Referee,* that was a role he was becoming increasingly familiar with because his mother, as much as he loved her, was a difficult woman. Manipulative, prickly, she wore her widow's discontent like a badge of honour and sometimes nothing the family did made her happy for long. He knew she missed his father. Hell, he missed him too. But, as his father had said when he was alive, 'Life goes on and you'd better get on with it before it passes you by'. He smiled as he remembered his father's words of wisdom. It was a credo he was trying to follow in spite of personal problems — a broken marriage and losing substantial contact with his daughter.

As they sat around the table in the roomy kitchen, cups of tea in front of everyone and a fresh tea cake sliced and half demolished, Stuart got the conversation going. 'How's your mother, Curtis?'

The question broke through Curtis's reminiscing. 'She's well. Lauren and the boys are with her at the moment, taking a break from station life.'

63

'Bren? Where's he?'

'You haven't heard?' Fran Morrison, slender and grey haired, and as tall as the men in the room, put in dryly as she placed a batch of scones — she baked a dozen and a half every day — on the table. 'Bren's in London, been there more than two weeks.'

'Good God! What's he doing there?' Stuart queried.

'He fancies himself in love,' Curtis's reply was sharp. Everyone other than Fran looked at him expectantly which forced him to relate the tale of Bren's infatuation with the English actress, including his plan to win her love.

'How wonderfully romantic,' was Nova's comment. 'I didn't think Bren had it in him.'

'The boy's off his head,' said Stuart Selby, put out by his other nephew's behaviour. 'Should have more sense. There are plenty of Australian girls for him to fall in love with.'

'I saw her act in Sydney,' piped up Rolfe Weston. 'Vanessa Forsythe is an excellent actress. She's very talented.'

'Yeah, that's what worries me,' Curtis's tone was frank. 'I hope her acting finishes at the stage door. I don't want her *pretending* or play-acting that she's in love with Bren.' He shook his head in disgust. 'He's bloody serious about her.'

'Oh, don't be so down in the mouth,' Nova chided. 'Bren's in his thirties, it's time he settled down and this . . . Vanessa could be the right woman for him.'

'Maybe. But he's needed here. Decisions have to be made regarding stock, and the breeding program we want to introduce is behind schedule.'

'And — it's not *your* place so you don't want to make decisions by yourself,' Stuart put in succinctly, a smirk on his face.

Curtis's sideways glance at his uncle told everyone that he didn't appreciate the remark. 'That's right.'

'You have my sympathy. I was in the same position after Matthew inherited Amaroo. That's why I got out.' Stuart grunted as he recalled. 'The best decision I ever made. Now I have more money than I know what to do with.' How typical of Stuart to rub everyone's noses in his inordinate tourist success — it was one of his less admirable traits.

Stuart's gaze locked on to Curtis's. 'Perhaps that's the kind of decision you should be making. You have the funds to, don't you?'

'My money's tied up in a venture with Lauren, besides, I'm not interested in leaving Amaroo. It will always be home to me. I can't imagine living anywhere else.'

'Even though you'll never own the place?' Stuart put in slyly. He leant back in his seat to wait for the answer.

'Being here is enough,' Curtis's answer was direct. 'I don't cast envious eyes over Amaroo. It's Bren's and I've accepted that.'

Nova glanced from Curtis to Stuart. She shook her head at them. 'You two! Amaroo, Amaroo ... Can't we talk about something else?'

Curtis gave her a cheeky grin and with a twinkle in his eye, teased, 'What else of mutual interest is there to talk about?'

Exasperated, she picked up a half-eaten piece of cake and threw it at him. It landed on his chest and he promptly popped the remains into his mouth.

'Pig!' Then in typical Nova style, she changed the subject. 'I saw Georgia in Sydney when I was there.'

'And ...?'

She'd known the mention of Curtis's ex-wife's name would get his attention. 'Georgia looked fantastic. She asked how you were.'

The hazel eyes hardened. 'I'm sure she did. She's making a nice income with the child allowance I pay, on top of what she earns as a freelance journalist-photographer. It's in her best interests for me to be in good health.' His tone changed, softened. 'Was Regan with her?'

'No, it was night time, at a pub in The Rocks. She was with a few people who were farewelling her before she flew to Paris for the spring fashion shows.'

'And dragging Regan with her, no doubt.' Curtis shook his head. 'That's no life for a young kid.'

'Curtis, you have to accept that you've lost Regan. I know it's hard, but it's a fact,' Stuart put in quietly. 'Georgia built up a lot of resentment over the divorce, mostly because you fought tooth and nail to have sole custody of your daughter by implying that she wasn't a fit mother because of her affairs. That made her mean enough to make it difficult, almost impossible for you to see a lot of Regan.'

Curtis gave him a withering look. 'Easy for you to say, Stuart. You have four daughters, two of whom are in your various businesses where you see them regularly and the two youngest still live at home. I have one child and if I'm lucky I see her for two weeks of every year.'

The phone rang and Fran got to it first. She looked at Curtis. 'It's Linford Downs Station. Bit of a problem, I think.'

Glad for the diversion, Curtis scraped back his chair on the vinyl as he rose to answer the call.

'What's up, Simon?'

'Curtis, one of our men has just ridden in from the range bordering our properties. Your stockman, the one named Tony, has had an accident. His horse spooked and he came off. Reg is pretty sure he has a broken leg,' Simon Johns reported. 'He said to relay that Tony's in a lot of pain, too much to be put into splints then on a horse and brought in.'

'Okay, I'll come out in the chopper. Where exactly are they?'

'Approximately ten kilometres north of where Gumbledon Creek runs into the Chamberlain River.'

Curtis knew the place. He checked the time on the kitchen wall clock. He would have to fuel up the chopper before take off. 'I can be there in an hour or so. Thanks, Simon. Bye.'

He glanced at those seated at the table. Now he had a good excuse to be up and away, literally! 'Got to go. One of our men's had an accident. I'll have to fly him to the hospital in Kununurra.'

'What bad luck,' Nova said. 'I'd like to see Dad. If there's room on board, can I come too?'

'Sure,' Curtis shrugged a shoulder at her. 'We've a Robinson 44 now, it'll take the three of us, with

Tony in the front seat. You can even play nurse if you want to. Tony would probably like that.' She pulled a face at his sarcastic tone and he grinned.

Curtis shook hands with his uncle. 'Hang around if you want, but I'll be away for several hours.'

'It's all right. We're on our way to Darwin anyway and just called in to break the journey.' He gave his nephew a casual salute. 'I'll be seeing Hilary while I'm there. Want me to pass on any messages?'

'Give her my love, and tell her that everything's fine here.' Curtis, with a goodbye nod, went out the back door without wasting any more time, with Nova trailing behind and doing a slow jog trot to keep pace with him.

Vanessa chose a CD, popped it into the hi-fi and pressed the play button. Spanish music filled her redecorated living room. She loved the new look Maxine Richards had created for her.

The building had central heating so Maxine had opted to pull up the carpet in the living and dining area, polish the floor boards and spread two subtly patterned Turkish rugs across the floors. The colour of the walls was a soft apricot-orange and the new sofa had apricot tones with several loose cushions in cream and varying shades of apricot. Over the fireplace stood a large gilt bevel-edged mirror and two exquisite chandeliers, plus several strategically placed table lamps to provide adequate lighting. Two one-metre high, hand-painted Greek urns, a glass-topped mahogany coffee table and a nouveau Provincial French bureau completed the look of understated elegance. As she caught the tempo of the music, Vanessa began to dance.

Around the sofa, past the window, pirouetting sensually to the tango beat, her invisible partner was Bren. *Bren* ... They had become almost inseparable apart from career commitments ... but, they hadn't made love! Kerri, busybody that she was, constantly asked, 'Have you done it yet?' Embarrassing, really. If she wasn't such a good friend she'd have told her in no uncertain terms to mind her own business.

She was waiting for Bren to pick her up. They were going to take advantage of Ronnie's offer to use his houseboat. Three carefree days during which her understudy would play her role in the play while she and Bren sailed down the Thames, and along a series of canals to Oxford. There was no telephone on board and no fax machine, and no curious Kerri! Just the two of them.

Vanessa stopped but still swayed to the beat in front of the mirror over the mantelpiece to study her reflection. Was she in love with Bren Selby? She stared critically at her image while she catalogued her features. Her mouth was a little too wide, her eyebrows were too straight — she'd rather they arched a little even though straight did suit her. The high cheekbones, inherited from her mother, gave her face a slightly aristocratic look. She sucked in her cheeks and the bones stood out even more. Good bone structure. Gran had said she would age well. Christ, who cared about that, she thought as she flicked her hair back? She was only twenty-eight, a long way from being *old*. As she stared into her brown depths she tried to analyse her feelings for Bren.

Without a doubt she liked him, a lot. He was easy to be with. No pretensions, no bullshit, no sugar-coated compliments to get into her pants. That, in itself, set him apart from most of the men who came on to her. Her cheeks tinted pink at her frank thoughts. Did *she* want him to? Hmmm! There was a strong, growing physical attraction between them, she couldn't deny it. She dreamt about him, thought about him so much, wondered, yes, what would it be like to run with her feelings.

Her fiancé, David, had been an experienced lover, skilled in the art of getting a woman's total response. Bren, obviously, wasn't a worldly-wise man but that might be a nice change. After losing David she'd thought a good deal about the attributes she wanted in a man: sincerity, loyalty, honesty. Bren had all these things and more. She smiled at her reflection. Yes, it would be easy to fall in love with him. Indeed. Dead easy.

The front doorbell rang. *Bren.* Vanessa turned the hi-fi off and went to let him in. 'Come on, Sandy,' she called, listening to his pit-patter footsteps behind her, 'we're going on a holiday.'

Manoeuvring the brightly painted, six metre barge along the narrow canal was not as simple as Ronnie, Vanessa's friend and their instructor, had made out. Bren had learned that after a few kilometres down the main canal. It was still early in the season, so there wasn't a lot of craft on the water. Vanessa had said that at the peak of summer, barges waited for hours to go through the several locks along the way. Bren glanced at the countryside as he steered. After a wet winter, the countryside looked so green his eyes hurt. He couldn't imagine Amaroo having the lushness of England. If it did, he could run three to four times the number of cattle he 'grew' on his property.

The barge's motor, a simple engine, putt-putted away, trailing a column of greyish-black smoke from the narrow funnel above the cabin. If Curtis could see him now, with his cap on — Vanessa insisted that as the barge's captain he had to wear it — a woollen checked shirt and a sleeveless nylon zip-up vest and black corduroy pants, no doubt he'd get a sneer and a horse laugh from him.

Bren didn't care. He couldn't remember being happier. Vanessa was like nothing he had ever experienced. Most of the time he stood in awe of her beauty, quietly amazed that she enjoyed his company. She was lovely, and unaffected, perhaps even unaware of the massive effect she had on him. He watched her come out of the cabin, bearing mugs of hot tea.

'We should reach the next village by lunch. We can tie up there and have a meal at a cafe on the main street,' she said as she handed him a mug.

'Sounds good.' He looked up at the sky. 'The weather looks as if it's closing in.'

She looked up too. 'Just a shower, that's all.'

He grinned. 'I wish I could bottle some of your weather, the countryside too, and transport them to Amaroo.'

She lifted an eyebrow at him. 'Are you getting homesick?'

'Not at all. I've missed out on a lot of hard work, and the heat. In late summer, going into our autumn, it's pretty warm in the Kimberley. My brother will be down in the mouth at not having me around, but he'll manage.'

'You're lucky to have family to rely on. I envy you that.'

He glanced at her over the rim of his mug. 'You envy me! You, who has everything. The theatrical world's at your feet, adulation from fans, financial security.'

She shook her head at him. 'What I envy is your family. You've a brother, a sister, a mother, nephews and a niece. I . . . have no-one except Kerri — she's the closest thing I have to family. Sometimes, even in a city as crowded as London,' she confided, 'one can feel very much alone.'

He put his free arm around her and drew her closer. 'I'll share my rellies with you,' he offered. 'How about that?'

'That's nice of you.' She kissed him on the cheek.

Very quickly he turned her face-on so he could kiss her lips. The kiss deepened and her arms slid up around his neck. The hand not on the barge's tiller crept around her waist and pulled her hard against his chest.

Vanessa experienced a slow, sizzling sensation. It enervated her spine and a certain breathlessness accompanied the lightheartedness which began to invade her. She tried to think straight and couldn't. Then, she decided she didn't want to and gave herself up to what he was arousing in her — marvellous, wonderful feelings. When they separated each stared deeply into the other's eyes, for several seconds, trying to gauge the other's reactions.

Bren cleared the huskiness from his throat before he said, 'I could take a lot of that.'

Brown eyes sparkled with mischief, and something deeper, more mysterious. 'And I'm pleased to oblige,' she said, and promptly kissed him back.

The barge, not being steered competently, edged towards and bumped against the side of the canal.

'Damn,' Bren muttered half under his breath. He let Vanessa go so he could correct the barge's course. 'Too many distractions on deck.'

Smiling, Vanessa gave him a mock salute. 'Yes, Captain, I'll go below decks, Captain. Keep your eye out for that village. We'll put in there for lunch and supplies.'

Over a light lunch then shopping at a market nearby for basic supplies — bread, milk, cereals, juice — Vanessa's mind wandered. All she could think of since they'd kissed on deck was — that kiss! How it affected her, what her expectations were, what his might be.

Increasingly, she was finding Bren Selby very attractive; she was too honest with herself to deny that. But, she had to ask herself the question, how far did the sexual attraction go? After David, she had become apprehensive about allowing a romantic situation to get out of hand. She didn't think she could bear to be hurt again. But then she found herself tallying Bren's good points, looking for negatives and not finding any. Their budding romance was ... perfect. They enjoyed each other's company and while he'd made no sexual demands, she knew from his hastily masked expressions and the tension in him that such thoughts dominated. It was almost as if he didn't want to spoil the perfection of their courting, if she could use such an old-fashioned term, by taking their relationship to a deeper level.

And the depth of her feelings for him had been tested when he'd left London for two days and nights, to inspect a breeding bull at a farm in Lancashire. She had been miserable *and* conscious that something important was missing in her life. She had been unable to think about anything other than his return and the welcome back dinner she'd planned for him.

Perhaps ... the thought crossed her mind as they made their way back through misty rain to the barge with the groceries, and Sandy jumping at their heels, it was up to her to make the first move for both of them.

After stowing the groceries in the compact, functional gallery, Bren was about to don an oilskin, start the motor and cast off when Vanessa closed the hatch and drew the bolt. She turned towards him. 'No need to rush. The rain will last for an hour or so, and the next lock is less than an hour away.'

'Okay, I'll see what's on the telly.'

'You can,' she agreed, 'but ...' She walked up to him and faced him. Her brown eyes stared into his. 'Telly isn't the only activity one can indulge in below decks.'

His eyebrows shot up in surprise at her not very subtle suggestion, and his Adam's apple wobbled nervously when he swallowed. The smile she radiated contained a mixture of allure and invitation as her fingers found the top button of his shirt and prised it open. And then ... her fingers slid inside to stroke his bare chest.

Bren wasn't slow on the uptake. His arms came around her and drew her close, the fingers of one hand tilting her chin up. Unerringly, his lips found hers and she felt a shuddering sigh go through him as his arms tightened around her. As she surrendered mentally and physically to the magic of the moment, she was aware that the attraction between them was spiralling out of control but she was beyond caring.

His lips were warm and firm, his questing tongue knowledgeable and curious as it delved into her warm, responsive mouth and found a sensual match. Their breathing grew ragged as they pressed together, closer and closer, hands and fingertips exploring each other's body. Both eager for greater intimacy, they began to undress each other and, with stumbling steps, bumped their way down the narrow passageway to the main bedroom in the forward section of the barge. By the time they reached the bed, they were half undressed.

Bren rained a dozen feather-light kisses over her face, but then moved back to regard her seriously. 'You're sure you want to ...?'

Vanessa's fingers explored the contours of his face, noting the hesitation in his eyes, his concern for her. 'Yes,' she whispered. Suddenly, without forethought, without analysing it, she knew she had never been more sure of anything in her life. Amazing as it seemed, considering the brief time they had known each other, she was falling in love with Bren. And it was the most marvellous feeling. She couldn't recall how or when the attraction had deepened to something more serious, and neither had she expected or wanted it to happen, but it had. The symptoms that went with being in love were not unknown to her — blood racing through her veins, feeling dizzy and the next second giggly, and shy. Neither did she want to think about later, about tomorrow or next week, next month, she just wanted *now* ... with him.

Smiling at the reverence of his touch, she let him finish undressing her, her self-consciousness at being naked on the bed betrayed by the rosy flush that coloured her cheeks and warmed her body down to her toes. His caresses were gentle, almost as if he feared she would break, until she showed him she wouldn't and began to boldly stroke his body and show him what she wanted. She quickly learned that Bren was a well-built man. His shoulders were broad and his torso muscled from years of working out of doors and he was deeply tanned to below the waist. Curiously, her fingers began to undo the belt on his trousers, then fiddle with the zipper. At that, his hand rested over hers, stopping her.

'I think I can manage,' he said with a husky laugh, his eyes glinting with desire as they roamed over her.

'I-I'm being too forward,' she said softly, embarrassed.

'No, I love your honesty, darling. It's so refreshing.'

The smile she gave him was a trifle wobbly around the edges. Seducing a man was an experience she lacked. In the past the opposite had occurred. There had been men, not exactly a stampede of them, only five full-on affairs over her adult life, and in the lovemaking her partner had taken the initiative. She didn't know why she was behaving differently with Bren, maybe it was because she wanted him so much. Deep inside an unsatisfied ache resided and feelings — she had been keeping them suppressed for fear of being hurt again — bubbled and boiled, creating a head of steam that craved release.

She shivered, not from the cool air inside the barge, but with anticipation as he lay on his side next to her on the bed. He wasn't going to rush things, though she could tell he wanted her quite badly. His breathing was heavy, his eyelids were drooping, his body, hard and tense, touched her from chest to knees, exposing the evidence of his arousal. Its heat scorched against her lower stomach, tantalising and tormenting her with the promise of fulfilment.

He kissed her again, deeply, passionately, then he rolled her onto her back and began a trail of kisses down her chin, to between her breasts. He paused there to suckle each one until she writhed against him with impatience. His lips moved lower, to her navel, to the dark vee of curls at the junction of her legs and, lower still, exploring, tasting, anointing her with his hot, wet tongue.

Was his intention to drive her insane, she wondered as wave upon wave of desire, each stronger than the last threatened to shred her self-control? In a half-strangled voice she whispered close to his ear, 'Bren, I want you ... Now.'

Knowing she was ready he plunged into her, long and deep and hard. Vanessa's body bucked as the first orgasm shuddered through her. Her fingers dug into his buttocks, urging him on further as their bodies rocked in the frenzy of passion each had unleashed, until, finally, their energies and appetites expended, they lay in each other's arms and drifted into a light, dreamy sleep.

That afternoon the barge didn't make it to the next lock. For the rest of that day and most of the night, Bren and Vanessa remained closeted in the barge's bedroom ... talking quietly to each other, making love, sleeping and making love again until overtaken by exhaustion.

All too soon their idyllic break came to an end. As they tied up at the dock and offloaded Sandy and the bags, Bren's sense of regret that their time together had been so brief, deepened. He knew, without a shadow of a doubt, that he was in love and Vanessa ... He had high hopes that she was learning to care for him too.

Vanessa sat in Kerri Spanos's office, listening to her agent talk to a producer in Hollywood. To occupy herself she studied the interior of the office. It was a testimony to Kerri's success as an agent. Autographed photographs of famous actors, producers and directors covered almost all the available wall space. On her desk was a photo of Kerri's husband, Yannis, and their son Nick. Yannis had decided years ago that the go-getter, the business head of the family, was his wife. She had the acumen and the drive, and he'd been more than happy to become a gentleman farmer in Sussex while Kerri ran her business, the Spanos Artists Management Agency from her London office and lived in their fashionable flat in Knightsbridge. Kerri and thirteen-year-old Nick would motor down to Nutley and their farm most weekends. Most considered it an odd arrangement but it worked for the Spanos — they were a happy family unit.

A similar arrangement wouldn't suit her, Vanessa thought. When she married she would want to be with her husband every possible minute. As she thought that, Vanessa sucked in her underlip. That's why she was here, taking up Kerri's valuable time. She had an important matter to discuss and she had more than an inkling that her agent, and friend, wasn't going to like the topic, not at all.

Finishing the call, Kerri put the phone down. 'So,' her dark eyes regarded Vanessa assessingly, noting her radiant expression, how relaxed she looked, but that she seemed nervous about something. She could always tell when Vanny was nervous. 'What have you come to tell me that's so important? I cancelled lunch at the Ritz with an important client, so it had better be good.'

Vanessa took in a breath and the words all came out in a rush. 'Bren's asked me to marry him.'

'What?' It took several seconds for Kerri to recover her aplomb.

'He proposed last night, at the flat. Insisted that I not give him an answer straight away. Bren said I should think about it because there were quite a few matters to consider.' Vanessa's eyes widened as she went on. 'I didn't get a wink of sleep thinking about everything, but,' she smiled again, 'I phoned him this morning and said . . . yes.'

Kerri shook her head, hoping that she hadn't heard right. 'Yes. You said yes? Are you out of your mind? You've got contracts, commitments for the next two years.' She stared hard at the actress, disbelief glinting in her expressive eyes. 'I suppose he wants you to live in some outback shack and to turn your back on your career. Have you any idea what you might be giving up, Vanny?'

'We didn't get into details but, yes, it's natural that I'd want to spend a lot of time at Amaroo. I'll commute back here and elsewhere for roles.' She added succinctly, 'Other actors and actresses around the world do so successfully.'

'You're kidding yourself if you think that will work. In three years, maybe less, backers, producers, directors will forget who Vanessa Forsythe is, and you know there's a queue of younger actresses panting to step into the shoes you vacate.' The stare she gave Vanessa was hard-eyed and business-like. 'It's quite possible that you and your career will fade into oblivion.'

Vanessa winced at Kerri's frankness but, gathering confidence and determination, her chin jutted forward. 'Well, I can't expect Bren to give up his station and spend his time in London with me. That wouldn't be fair and after a while he'd hate it.'

She had done a lot of soul-searching last night, getting little sleep and, as daylight had pushed through the bedroom window, her decision had firmed. Her career might suffer if she married Bren, but what was she to do? Throw away the chance to be happy and fulfilled? After losing David she thought she might never find that special someone, but now she had. She would be a fool to walk away from him!

'So my career may not reach the dizzy heights we thought it would,' she rationalised. 'Gran was the ambitious one in the Forsythe family. It was her encouragement that drove me to stretch my talents in a variety of roles.' She threw Kerri a sly look. 'Besides, I imagine that no matter where I live, if I have a good agent who knows my capabilities, I should get ample work in the industry.'

'Don't soft-soap me, Vanny.' Kerri waggled a finger at her. 'Experts have tried and failed.'

For twenty seconds or so, silence fell over the agent's office. Vanessa checked her nails, fiddled with her hair, adjusted the folds of her frock, studied the photos adorning the wall again. There was one of herself as well as other famous faces Kerri represented.

Vanessa took a different tack. 'I'm not getting any younger. I'll be twenty-nine next birthday . . .'

'Your biological clock is ticking over, is that it?'

Vanessa shrugged elegantly but didn't give a straight answer. 'I want a home, a family and, eventually children. It's still harder for career women, and in most marriages she, more than he, does the compromising. If the trade-off for those things is that I surrender a chunk of my career, well, so be it.'

Kerri shook her head, her sigh long and expressive. She had never seen Vanny more determined than she was right now. Perhaps the tragedy of David's death was playing a part in what she wanted. Or, maybe she saw the idealistic picture of domestic life passing her by and she remembered too well how happy her parents had been and she dreamed of that kind of happiness for herself. She knew that because Vanny had spoken often of wanting a similar relationship with the man she fell in love with.

Personally, she had her doubts that someone like Vanny could find permanent happiness on a cattle station in the middle of the Australian outback. She would get bored and frustrated with the life in a couple of years but, for the present Vanessa believed Bren Selby could give her what she needed and, thinking fatalistically, who was Kerri to say otherwise?

'You really want to do this?' Kerri asked, her tone unusually gentle.

'With all my heart.'

'Then,' grudging acceptance brightened Kerri's voice. 'I guess all I can do is wish you every happiness, luv.'

Vanessa gave Kerri a beaming smile. 'Oh! I thought you'd try to talk me out of it. I was sure we'd end up having a big fight.'

'I'll be frank,' Kerri's reply was swift, 'I can't see it working, the two of you are just too different but you deserve your shot at happiness even though it might cost you your career.'

'If I was with another agent I'd say it would,' Vanessa agreed, 'but I know that you'll look after my interests, and while I will live in the outback, there are planes, and communication devices. I still want to act and Bren agrees that I should. What it will take is organisation and planning, something,' her brown eyes twinkled cheekily, 'we know you excel at.'

Kerri nodded her dark head, silently accepting Vanessa's compliment. 'Speaking of which, you've got the part of Annie in the Australian movie, *Heart of the Outback*. They'll be filming it next summer, their summer of course. Now, and depending on when you set the wedding date, I'll try to juggle dates, postponements, cancellations etc,' she grimaced. 'No doubt I'll have to pull in a few favours.'

'Bren really has to get back to Amaroo, so I'm thinking two weeks from now. I'm free of commitments then and he's suggested that we have a quiet wedding here then fly to Darwin a week later for an official reception at his mother's home.' Vanessa paused just long enough to let that sink in. 'And because you, Yannis and Nick are the closest I have to family, I'm hoping that Yannis will agree to give me away and that you'll all come to Darwin for the reception, my treat of course.'

'Two weeks! I'm *thrilled* you haven't made it too tough,' Kerri muttered tongue-in-cheek. 'The Spanos family accepts.' She stood and moved around her desk towards the row of filing cabinets. 'Let's go through your file now, work out your commitments. See what we can get you out of without it costing you too much.'

# CHAPTER FIVE

Vanessa came out of the bathroom of the classy presidential suite, which doubled as the bridal suite at Darwin's Novotel Atrium Hotel. She looked towards the bed. Bren was sound asleep. It had been a long day — going over the reception arrangements — and afterwards, cocktails at Bren's mother's home and dinner at a restaurant where she met the rest of the Selby family. The Spanos family, Kerri, Yannis and Nick, her only guests apart from Fay and Barry Whitcombe, were ensconced in the suite next to theirs — all was quiet in that direction so she assumed they had retired for the night.

She should too, but she was too keyed up. Walking onto the balcony she checked out the night view of Darwin. Still damned hot, even at 1.30 a.m. As she sat on the lounger and studied the lights she pondered over her reaction to meeting the Selbys. They were an interesting bunch. Vanessa enjoyed studying people — she believed it helped her acting by trying to figure out what and why people did what they did.

Hilary Selby was ... she tried to conjure up a suitable description and the word *formidable* came to her with ease. Instinctively she sensed a need to be on her guard around Hilary. In her mid-fifties, the chain-smoking widow was still an attractive woman but very possessive, especially of Bren. She had found Hilary's expressions, at times disdainful, at times condescending, and the aura of tension she emanated towards herself and Bren had been palpable, telling Vanessa that Hilary was masking her true opinions. Deep down, her mother-in-law was not for the marriage and was accepting the situation because her son wanted it. But looking at the long term there was a large plus. Hilary lived in Darwin and, according to Bren, rarely visited Amaroo, something Vanessa believed she would be grateful for.

Hilary had organised the official reception details herself. A catered dinner for sixty people was to be held, at sunset in the garden of her home, with the tables scattered around the sides of the pool.

Vanessa's thoughts moved to Bren's sister. Lauren was married to Marc, an ex-patriot of the Ukraine. She came over as a nice person and their three sons were adorable. Marc managed the cattle station Lauren and Curtis had jointly bought with money inherited from their father. It wasn't far from Amaroo Downs. Then there was Bren's uncle, Stuart Selby and his wife, Diane. She had found Stuart a difficult man to talk to. Extremely wealthy, he was smug and arrogant and much too vocal about his wealth as if he enjoyed rubbing the other Selby men's noses in his affluence. Something else too ... During dinner she had detected that Stuart and Curtis, Bren's younger brother, didn't get on mainly because they spent most of the evening swapping sly digs at each other. She wondered, albeit fleetingly, why they didn't get along.

Curtis Selby was a complex, taciturn individual. She found him neither likeable nor dislikeable, though he had one point in his favour, a clear affection for his brother. Vanessa knew about his failed marriage. Bren had told her everything and she'd concluded that his sour attitude was caused by 'life' dealing him a cruel blow. She felt sorry for that, and that he appeared to exist in the shadow of Bren's more friendly, outgoing personality. How she and Curtis would deal with each other when they were both living at Amaroo would be interesting.

Another guest, Nova Morrison, had caught her attentive eye during the evening. The young Australian-Asian woman was beautiful and, because she'd grown up at Amaroo, was comfortable with family members. Nova had accepted her as Bren's bride without reservations which implied that in time, and if Nova remained at Amaroo, they might become friends. Just as well. She had the feeling that, initially, she would need all the friends she could gather to her.

Her thoughts turned back to Bren and she smiled in the semi-darkness of the balcony. Due to Hilary's dictates, chores and wedding preparations they had scarcely had a moment to themselves since their arrival. As she rose from the lounger her smiled widened in dreamy anticipation. They were man and wife now and they would be together . . . always.

*Memories are like snapshots in time.* Vanessa remembered her Gran saying that. As the sun slipped over the horizon and a brief twilight fell across Hilary's garden, she tried to capture and store the moment in her memory forever. Gifted with an abundance of fairness, she gave credit where it was due. Hilary had proven herself a superb organiser. Every detail: flowers, table decorations, scattered rose petals across the patio's tiles and lawn, had all been executed with professional precision.

After Yannis made the official speech that welcomed her and Bren as a married couple, the celebration and congratulations began, starting with a few hundred coloured balloons being released from nets into the darkening sky. Coloured bulbs and fairy lights strung through the trees and shrubs were switched on. Champagne began to flow, hors d'oeuvres circulated and the four-piece band started to play. Vanessa knew that Kerri could find no fault with anything either but her agent wasn't wrapped in their hostess and had been ready to pounce on anything that went wrong. Nothing did.

The weather was perfect, the food delicious and the guests were behaving congenially, until . . .

'Sir,' the head waiter came up to Curtis. 'There's a young woman at the front door. Says she's a professional photographer. She'd like to come in and take photos of the bride and groom for a London newspaper.'

Curtis's eyebrows shot upwards. 'A London newspaper?' He turned to Bren and Vanessa who were close by. 'Vanessa, has UK media coverage of the reception been arranged by Kerri?'

'Not that I know of.' Vanessa searched among the guests for Kerri but couldn't locate her.

'I'll check it out,' Curtis offered and strode off.

He saw her waiting just inside the front door, her photographic paraphernalia in a black bag on the tiles next to her feet. His heart sank as he recognised her titian hair, the shapely figure and striking, well made-up looks. 'Georgia.' *Damn.* 'What are you doing here?'

'Nice to see you too, Curtis. Trying to make a living, what else! I've just flown in from Singapore, en route to Sydney. I saw the notice about Bren's reception in the local rag. I'm freelancing, as you know, and Vanessa being who she is in the United Kingdom, I'm sure I can sell the photos to *The Times* or *The Telegraph*. Good publicity for her and the Selbys.'

'Really! I'd have thought the money you gouge out of me on a regular basis would have lessened your need to chase work.' His gaze raked over his ex-wife with a mixture of dispassion, and, yes, he cursed himself as he admitted it, reluctant interest. In her scandalously brief miniskirt, high heeled sandals and a skimpy midriff top — all intended to show off her sleek, tanned body, she looked bloody fantastic.

'Don't start.' Georgia Selby wasn't fazed by the sarcasm in her ex-husband's voice, the glacial gleam in his eyes. 'It was a court decision we both agreed to abide by, for Regan's sake.'

His expression and tone softened. 'Regan, how is she?' He wouldn't see her for another five months, probably after Christmas. That was the deal they'd struck. He had his daughter for two weeks annually during the wet, but through his solicitor he had Georgia provide him with regular photos of her, and copies of her school reports. Almost seven, Regan was tall for her age and had a mass of curly red hair, like her mother. The time they spent together, with him trying to cram a whole year's love and attention into a fortnight, was not and never would be, enough.

'She's well. Growing like a weed.' Georgia smiled impatiently, she was focussed on getting what she wanted — the photos. 'She's with Mum and Dad while I've been on assignment.'

Grudgingly, he admitted as he looked away, 'Divorce seems to agree with you.'

'Thank you. I'll accept that as a compliment.' Her lips thinned and her next sentence was businesslike. 'Now that we've done with the pleasantries, may I come in and take photos or not?'

'If it were up to me, I'd say no,' Curtis replied, knowing that he sounded mean-spirited. So what! Just looking at her was making his gut tighten, and talking to her made him remember how much she had hurt him, and that deep down she was a cold, mercenary bitch. 'Bren and Vanessa should decide.'

Georgia picked up her equipment. 'I'm sure they'll be more ... receptive. It'll be good publicity for Vanessa too. Lead the way.'

He shrugged as if he couldn't care less. 'Okay, but as soon as you're done, you leave. Agreed?'

Georgia gave him a look that said as clearly as words that he was a bastard. 'All right, Curtis. I get the message — loud and clear. Just let me do what I'm good at.'

He curbed the urge to retort that she was a better photographer than she ever had been a wife because it sounded childish. After Bren, Vanessa and her

89

agent okayed it, he watched his ex-wife take her photos. Georgia was a professional and she didn't rush. An hour ticked by, during which he was painfully conscious of her presence, before she packed everything up and without a goodbye or so much as a thank you, left. Typical Georgia!

Damn her. They'd been divorced almost a year and she could still churn up his insides. Not that he loved her anymore. Those feelings had died long before the divorce. It was the way she had gone about things that, when he thought about it, made him as mad as hell.

The bald-faced lies she'd told in court about their marriage. The affairs — with two stockmen at Amaroo, and others. She and her bloody lawyer had screwed him for every dollar they could, including a portion of his father's inheritance and there were the restrictive visiting rights with Regan. He had only agreed to the terms because commonsense told him it would be detrimental for his daughter to be shuffled backwards and forwards. She needed stability in her young life and she needed Georgia more than she needed him.

'You all right, Curtis?'

He had retreated to a secluded spot on the patio, where a screen of potted palms afforded him anonymity, to lick his emotional wounds. Turning, he saw Nova behind him. He didn't have to pretend or put on a brave face with her; she knew him too well. 'Guess so.'

'Georgia had a nerve turning up like that.'

He grunted before he responded. 'We both know Georgia isn't short on nerve.'

'We talked for a while,' Nova confided. 'She's doing well, getting heaps of work.'

'Perhaps I should take her back to court and she can start paying me maintenance,' he threw back, accompanying his words with a derisive laugh.

'Knowing how Georgia loves money, I don't like your chances,' Nova stated matter-of-factly. Her gaze moved and fastened on the bridal couple. 'They make a handsome couple, don't they?' she said, in an attempt to get his mind off his ex. She watched the Spanos family claim Vanessa's attention. The bride and groom separated and Vanessa disappeared from view.

'Can't deny that,' Curtis admitted with good grace. 'All I hope is that she makes Bren happy.'

'Why shouldn't she? They seem very much in love.'

'Sometimes, in the outback, love isn't enough.' His reply was cryptic. 'Don't get me wrong, I love my brother but, in a way, I think he's being selfish.'

'Selfish?' Nova's unlined forehead creased in a frown. 'How do you figure that?'

'I question how much thought he's given as to how Vanessa's life will change. His won't. He'll still run Amaroo, be where he's always been. For her it's, as the Yanks say, a whole new ball game. Not the same as she's known.'

'I chatted with her for a while last night. Vanessa seems very capable and keen to adapt.'

'Mmmm. Of course. Right now she's seeing everything through the eyes of love.' His mobile mouth twisted cynically. 'Like Georgia, when she first came to Amaroo. As we found out, she couldn't bear the isolation, couldn't become self-sufficient and didn't want to learn about life on the land. She wasn't interested enough.'

'I think you've forgotten that Georgia was happy for a while. She used to ride out and take photos. Remember that wonderful coffee-table book of photographs? It was very good.'

He nodded that he remembered and continued on. 'Then Regan came along and she became tied down with a fussy baby.' He paused to reflect for a moment or two. 'That's when things started to change. It took me a long time, too long, to realise she was bored and desperate to get away from Amaroo, permanently. By the time I realised the problem it was too late ... And all the love between us had gone.'

'I don't think that will happen with Vanessa,' Nova defended Bren's bride. 'I don't think she's like Georgia. I'm sorry, but we both know now that Georgia was, and always will be, self-centred and wilful.'

Curtis thrust his hands into his trouser pockets and rocked backwards and forwards on his heels — something he did when he was thinking seriously. 'Maybe not, but ...'

Vanessa, who'd just left the Spanos family, saw Curtis and Nova talking and walked down the hallway to join them. For a few seconds she stood indecisively by the patio doorway, not to eavesdrop, but she would have had to have impaired hearing not to catch what Curtis and Nova were saying.

'I give the marriage a year, two at the most,' Curtis decreed. 'Have you looked at her hands?

Vanessa hasn't done a hard day's physical work in her life so, if she's going to be the kind of wife Bren expects her to be, she'll have to undergo one hell of a change. Don't get me wrong, Vanessa is lovely to look at and very decorative. And,' he scratched his head as he deliberated how to phrase the words, 'it might be presumptive of me, but I think she lacks substance. In time she'll tire of the unappreciated role of "outback wife", get bored with it. She'll miss London too and her stage buddies as well as the high life.'

'She intends to work. Her agent will see that she gets roles, just not as often as in the past,' Nova, striving to keep Curtis's interest, defended the woman she had recently met. 'I think you're being prejudiced and unnecessarily hard. Wait and see. I think Vanessa will surprise you. Maybe she'll surprise all of us.'

He shook his head in disagreement and his features set into serious lines. 'You and I know it takes heaps of intestinal fortitude to cut it in the Kimberley. Like it or not, she's too soft and while I'd like to be proven wrong, I simply can't see her surviving.'

'Goodness!' Nova suddenly changed the emphasis, teasing him, 'and you've come to that conclusion after knowing her for less than forty-eight hours.'

'I'm not the only one. Mum and Stuart think the same.'

Nova's expression showed what she thought of their collective opinions. 'Well, I believe she's tougher than she looks and that Bren's made the right choice.' Her up-slanting gaze moved towards the pre-fabricated timber dance floor in the middle of the lawn.

'Come on, enough about Vanessa. The band's playing and you owe me a dance.' She pulled him from his hiding place and half dragged him down the patio steps to the platform dance floor.

In the shadows, Vanessa watched them begin to dance. She had to blink furiously to hold back the urge to cry. Eavesdropping, she accepted the home truth, was rarely good for the person being commented on. Her heart had plummeted as she'd heard Curtis say what was on his mind. Curiously, it hurt that he thought so little of her on, as Nova had noted, a relatively short acquaintance. Curtis, Hilary and Stuart seemed to have made snap, first impressions, before they really got to know her. That was so . . . unfair.

She was soft, lacking in substance and intestinal fortitude, was she? How little they knew about her, about what she had already accomplished in life. There had been enough experiences in her life, as a child, as a teenager and as an adult, to question their ill-informed opinion — if they'd bothered to ask. What did any of the relatively wealthy Selbys know about her background?

Living in the back streets of Brixton it had been a challenge not only to survive, but not to be dragged under by the ever present cycle of poverty. She knew all about that, and more. Standing up to crooked shopkeepers who tried to give her, when she'd been very young, the incorrect change. Not knuckling under to street gangs that intermittently roamed the area, making it unsafe to play outside. And by ignoring the jeers and insults from school mates by getting good grades when few of them cared enough to bother because they knew when they left school, they'd go straight onto the dole and eventually have a council flat for life. Vanessa had wanted more than that.

She had to stand up for herself in so many ways. Even early in her career, she'd had to fight to win worthwhile theatre roles. That made her soft? How dare they try and sentence her without knowing who she really was. And that wasn't all . . .

Since saying yes to Bren's proposal, she had immersed herself in and done all she could to learn about outback life. She always thoroughly researched roles but this — the life she and Bren were embarking on together — was more than a role, it was the most important thing in her life. She was a success in the theatre and she intended to be a success as Bren's wife. She knew she had a lot to learn, that she'd make mistakes, but she was one hundred per cent certain that she would be successful.

Vanessa tossed her head angrily and her fingers clenched into fists as she went over again what Curtis had said. Curtis Selby was a jaded and cynical man who had no idea what she was made of. He knew nothing about her resilience, her determination, her ability to focus and to learn. Where would she be today without such attributes? Certainly not at the top of her profession.

She heard Kerri calling her name and straightened her spine as she turned towards her friend, vowing that if she did one thing this year she would prove Curtis Selby and the other Selbys wrong. Her chin lifted with the pride her Spanish-born mother had instilled in her from an early age. And ... she wouldn't be doing it for Bren, she would be doing it for herself.

# CHAPTER SIX

Rays of sunlight peeped through the window as Vanessa felt Bren move, then roll out of bed. She listened to him stumble around, dressing without putting on the light.

'I am awake,' she said sleepily, and fumbled for the lamp switch on the bedside table.

'Sorry, hon, it's early. 5.30.'

'Oohh,' Vanessa screwed up her eyelids and threw her forearm over her eyes to diffuse the brightness. 'Let's go back to Hayman Island ...' she murmured in a wistful tone. The resort island and their one-week honeymoon had been delightful, but too short. She sat up and yawned.

'Love to, but can't. Curtis is close to frothing at the mouth with impatience to get things done. He's lined up so much work we'll be lucky to get half of it done by sunset.'

Curtis! She hadn't forgotten his opinion on their marriage, that it wouldn't last, and as a consequence, when they were in the same room her manner towards him was politely cool. Not that he noticed her frigidity. Yesterday afternoon, when he'd picked them up from the commercial flight to

Kununurra in the station's chopper, all he'd done was talk to Bren about cattle, and other stuff she didn't as yet understand. Quite rude, really.

He kissed her cheek. 'Go back to sleep if you want to. Everyone, the dogs, the cattle, we all have chores to do on the station.'

She wondered what the cattle had to do other than eat and grow fat for market? 'What about me? I want to work too.'

Bren's grey eyes softened with amusement. 'You don't know anything about station work.'

'I know,' she promptly confessed. 'You and everyone here are going to teach me, starting today.'

'Okay,' he grinned, inordinately pleased by what she'd said, 'I'll have Nova show you how our communications work, the hf radio and the uhf units. She'll take you on a grand tour of the place too.' His hand reached across to touch her cheek and then smooth several strands of hair off her forehead. 'See you tonight.'

Leaving the light on, he left. Vanessa, now wide-awake, listened to the silence for a few minutes before throwing the sheet off to get up.

After their arrival last night, she had been too travel-weary to take in the details of their bedroom. She did so now as she padded about the room, taking clothes out of a suitcase. It was a typical man's room. Dark-stained furniture, noticeably untidy with pieces of Bren's clothing draped over a tallboy and over knobs on the wardrobe doors, boots and shoes where he'd dropped them. Clearly Fran, the head stockman's wife, whom she'd met at the reception and briefly again last night had instructions not to service his room because everything looked just as he'd left it more than three months ago. Hmmm! There would be changes, no, *improvements* in that respect, of that she was certain, when she settled in.

She had so much to learn and get used to. Curtis had been right about that even though she believed his opinions were skewed. After dressing in the clothes she had bought from Delaney's in Darwin, the store that stocked RM Williams Clothing — lightweight moleskins, a checked cotton shirt and brown elasticised boots — she made the bed. She was about to leave the room when she heard a bleating, no, more of a lowing sound that disturbed the dawn's silence.

At the window Vanessa pulled the curtain back and looked out. The morning sun, already bright, made her blink and for several seconds she stood there taking everything in. A mist was rising off the ground, breaking up to reveal the front garden of the homestead with its array of plants. Australian natives that could survive the heat, she presumed, and beyond the fence, the flat land flowed into the distance in an undulating plain. Stands of ghost gums, she knew that from her Kakadu holiday, starkly white, stood close to a creek — one of several on the station — and way over on the right was a cluster of reddish-brown boulders — red sandstone, she believed — just beyond what looked like it had once been a tennis court. Perhaps the court could be rejuvenated so they could play at night, she thought.

And everywhere she looked was the red soil, the trademark colour of the outback, in the yards, on the dirt road that twisted and turned snake-like until it disappeared around a corner and between clumps of yellowing grass.

Her gaze wandered back to where the mist had lifted. Glimpses of low, rounded, dull green foothills were visible. They resembled a multiplicity of camel humps. Amaroo — home, her first real home apart from her London flat. A place she could imbue with her character, her tastes, where she and Bren could live and raise a family.

Two Brahman calves came into sight. They were nudging the fence's gate and making frustrated, lowing noises. Was something wrong with them? Had they become separated from their mothers? Vanessa watched Fran walking towards the calves. Fran, hat on her head, carried two huge plastic drink bottles full of milk, with teats, under one arm and she had a plastic bucket in her other hand. The calves, seeing that breakfast was on the way, bounded towards Fran, almost knocking her off her feet in their eagerness to get fed. Vanessa smiled at their antics, amused to see their tails swish to and fro with satisfaction as they gulped the milk down. The scene was natural and peacefully rural, yet set against a vastly different background to the English countryside she was familiar with.

Seeing the calves brought Sandy, her Jack Russell, to mind. Poor little mite was isolated in Darwin's quarantine station — a situation deemed necessary by the authorities to prevent the importation and spread of a variety of animal diseases. Three months would pass before they could be reunited. She missed him, for apart from the clothes and keepsakes she'd brought with her, he was the only piece of England intended for the Kimberley. She knew he would fret dreadfully but when his 'detention' came to an end and he reached Amaroo, with so much space to run around in, he was going to be in heaven. That prompted another thought. She hoped Sandy would make friends with the station's dogs. Bren had told her about them. Bubba and Kimbo were blue heelers and, Ringo, Curtis's dog, was a kelpie-cross. They were real station dogs who earned their keep working cattle, guarding the fenced-off chicken coop and the vegetable garden against the predatory dingoes at night and other feral animals, catching as many as they could chase down.

Finding her way through the long, ranch-style house to the kitchen gave Vanessa an interesting, if brief, tour of Bren's home. As she familiarised herself with the rooms she couldn't help noticing that they were in need of some t.l.c. She was sure Hilary Selby was a woman of impeccable taste, so she assumed that with her husband being ill for almost two years before his death, she hadn't the time nor the inclination to keep the rooms up to scratch. A coat of paint on the walls and ceiling wouldn't go astray, and she would like to replace some pieces of furniture, her taste being different to Hilary's.

Hilary preferred modern, understated elegance which suited her home in Cullen Bay but *she* pictured Amaroo having more of a casual country look. Leather armchairs, rounded sofas in attractive soft patterns, dressers and colonial style bookcases on either side of the rough rock fireplace which was rarely lit because most of the year it was too hot. A few paintings, Australian landscapes, naturally, two or three colourful rugs to complement the polished floors and light, translucent drapes, would give the entrance, dining and living rooms a real spruce-up. She would probably have to order catalogues and have the necessities sent from either Geraldton or Darwin.

She found Fran in the kitchen tidying up after Bren and Reg's breakfast.

'Morning,' Vanessa greeted the middle-aged woman who stood at the kitchen sink.

'G'day, Vanessa. I trust you slept well?'

'Like a log. Must be the fresh air.' Her cheeks coloured delicately. And the comfort of being in Bren's arms all night, she thought, but didn't add.

'What can I get you for breakfast? Muesli, bacon and eggs, an omelette, cereal, toast, fruit?'

'I don't know, I'm just getting used to the breakfast thing.'

Fran clucked at her with her tongue and said in that frank way of hers, 'On Amaroo everyone, even Nova who's obsessive about her weight, has a hearty breakfast. It'll take ten minutes to cook you a nice hot brekkie. Start you off well for the whole day, it will.'

Breakfast. Vanessa smiled because eating it was still a novelty. Until their honeymoon, she'd rarely eaten breakfast because of her different lifestyle but, intending to fit in, she looked at Fran who, in anticipation, had a skillet in one hand and a spatula in the other. She said enthusiastically, 'Bacon and eggs and some fruit would be nice.'

Nova arrived as Vanessa was finishing her coffee. She gave Bren's bride an assessing once-over as she sat opposite. 'Nice clobber.'

Vanessa blinked twice. The word was unfamiliar. 'Clobber?'

'Clothes,' Fran translated the Aussie-ism, grinning conspiratorially at her step-daughter. 'I see that we're going to have to educate Vanessa on the lingo.' She winked at Bren's bride, 'Language to you.'

Entering into the lighthearted conversation, Vanessa countered, 'Should I take notes?'

'Not if you have a half-decent memory,' Nova replied. 'Come on, we'll go into the office and you can talk to your sister-in-law, Lauren, via the high frequency radio.'

Eager to impress Vanessa with the uniqueness of Amaroo, and her knowledge, Nova gave her charge the grand tour of Amaroo, and, not in a hurry, it took the better part of the morning. Vanessa found it fascinating and awesome, unlike anything she had expected. Amaroo Station did not resemble an English farm or the Cooper's manor house in Dorset in any way. Buildings, other than the homestead and the original cottage, were rudimentary and stark. They were built from unpainted timber and corrugated iron to weather according to the elements of rain and sun under which they managed to exist. There were several equipment sheds, a saddle room, and the stockmen's bunkhouse — and she learned that Fran, Nova and Reg had a two-bedroom flat attached to the far end of the bunkhouse. They walked the perimeter of the original stone homestead, built by Bren's grandfather and Nova told her that Curtis lived there, alone.

Away from the homestead stood several fenced stockyards, a breaking-in yard with a two-metre high railing fence around it and further out still stood another high, tin structure — a hangar of sorts, which housed aeroplane equipment and tools, a lot of motor bikes and a chopper. A single engine plane stood outside on the packed earth runway.

'Because of Amaroo's terrain, horses aren't always used to muster stock. Sometimes bikes and the chopper handle the rougher ground better — and the bikes are more practical to run too,' Nova told Vanessa as they browsed through the bike area, looking at the variety of bikes the station had.

'How far away are our closest neighbours?'

'That's Linford Downs. It's about two hundred kilometres due west. Lauren and Marc's station, Cadogan's Run, is a bit more, something over two hundred south-west as the crow flies.'

'Can you fly that?' Vanessa asked, pointing to the chopper, which looked as if it were well-maintained.

Nova thought about that for a few seconds. 'I've never had any lessons, but I've watched Curtis and Dad work on the motor and fly it. Reckon I could, in an emergency.'

'I'd like to learn how to fly one day,' Vanessa said with a decisive nod of her head. 'It must be a super experience being up in the air, looking down at everything.'

'Bren or Curtis could teach you initially, but you'd have to be tested by the authorities to get a pilot's licence. Curtis is the better chopper pilot, and he's more patient than Bren.'

'Really?' Vanessa's left eyebrow lifted on hearing that. Curtis Selby was not high on her totem pole of nice people. 'I would have thought the opposite.'

Nova's grin implied that she understood what Vanessa meant. 'His brusque manner can be off-putting, but Curtis is a good bloke. Honestly.'

Vanessa's smile accepted Nova's vote of confidence on Curtis but the expression in her eyes said something different. 'If you say so.' She gave her guide a quizzical look, then asked, 'What do you do when you're at Amaroo?'

'This and that. A bit of everything except cooking. I'm a regular jillaroo,' she said proudly. 'I help with the musters, repair fencing, branding, do artificial insemination and whatever needs doing at the time. Sometimes I visit the Aboriginal camp in the hills. I've several friends there.'

'You don't get bored?'

'One only gets bored at Amaroo if one wants to. I've always found plenty of things to do.' As she looked at Vanessa her expression became serious. 'That's the trick to the outback, you know, keeping busy and,' she grinned, 'there's always plenty to keep one busy.'

'Why?'

Nova shrugged her shoulders. 'I guess ... because when you're doing stuff you don't think about the isolation or how hot it is, or that it's too dry or too wet. Do you ride, Vanessa?' Nova asked, as by silent, mutual consent they began to walk back to the homestead.

'In a fashion,' Vanessa was too modest to boast and admit that she was an accomplished horsewoman with dressage and gymkhana experience. Something she'd learned as an adult. 'I've enjoyed riding over several weekends at a Dorset manor house, owned by one of David's friends. That's ... where David joined the hunt and ...'

Vanessa's tone and her inability to finish the sentence alerted Nova that something was wrong. She remembered why. 'Sorry! That was a stupid question. I forgot about your late fiancé.' Then by way of explanation she added. 'Bren told the family how he died.' God, why hadn't she thought before she said that. On meeting Vanessa she had seen the future potential in being nice to her, to becoming her 'best buddy'. She didn't know how, yet, but she suspected she could learn a lot from the sophisticated, but easygoing actress — things that could be to her advantage one day.

'That's all right,' Vanessa assured Nova though her smile was tinged with a touch of melancholy. 'It's in the past now.'

And it was. Falling in love with Bren had eased and, over time, eradicated most of the pain associated with David's untimely passing when she had once believed that she'd never be happy again. Her gaze took in her immediate surroundings and then she stared into the distance. It wasn't at all like England but ... she liked it.

The starkness had raw appeal, and she sensed the challenge in the ruggedness and the unforgiving quality of the forever-the-same Kimberley. She intended to make a good life with Bren, and fervently embrace what had to be learned with a willingness that would show Curtis and anyone else who doubted her capacity to adapt, that she could contribute something worthwhile to the station.

'When you've settled in, we'll go exploring,' Nova offered. 'There are some great places on Amaroo. There's a narrow gorge with ancient palms growing everywhere. It has a waterfall and a pool deep enough to swim in.'

Understanding that Nova was trying to make up for her recent faux pas drove Vanessa's melancholia into her subconscious. Smiling, she pulled at her shirt to let the air flow inside and cool her skin down. 'I'd like that . . .'

She looked down at her new boots as she stepped up onto the verandah. They were scuffed and covered in a film of red soil. Her smile widened. They didn't look new anymore, and that was just fine with her.

On her second day at Amaroo, Vanessa began to assume the role Hilary Selby had exulted in for so long, being the station's boss lady, but she did it smoothly and subtly so as not to offend anyone, especially Nova and Fran. Both women were going out of their way to make her feel comfortable, and giving her snippets of information to help run the station and homestead. That day she helped Fran feed the poddy calves and the following day she did it by herself. She organised furniture catalogues to be sent from a Darwin home furniture store and learned that because it was over a thousand kilometres from Amaroo, delivery of the pieces would take several months. Still, as far as she was concerned, it was important that all the Selbys, as well as others connected with the station, knew that she was 'moving in' for keeps and that the homestead was not simply a base from which she took off to complete acting engagements.

On a July morning Curtis watched Bren throw a rope around Runaway, a four-year-old mare singled out from several other horses in the stockyard. Bren brought the mare to the rails and put her bridle on. Morning shadows were shrinking across the earth as the sun came up. Sun-up was Curtis's favourite time of day. It was still quiet, apart from the occasional twitter of a bird. Dew hung on the tips of yellow grass, and on the spider's web attached to the corner doorway of the saddle room, and there was a pleasant coolness to the air. The coolness would soon evaporate and turn into a sizzler as the day heated up. In the Kimberley June, July and August had the most moderate weather. The heat was not too extreme, the humidity was bearable and there was an unwritten guarantee that today would be the same as yesterday, and tomorrow the same as today.

That suited him because Curtis wasn't overly fond of change and there had been several changes around Amaroo over the last few months. Vanessa had successfully put her stamp on the place — 'staked out her territory', more or less. She had redecorated half the house, restored the tennis court and had lighting installed so the court could be used when it was cooler. Bren said she was even talking about doing something with the thirty-year-old hole in the ground near the court. Not putting in a swimming pool but a huge spa or some other kind of watery nonsense — ridiculous and impractical for the Kimberley climate.

It was obvious that she didn't like him. He lifted a shoulder carelessly then let it settle. He wasn't particularly thrilled with her either, but he was a fair man and he could see that she made Bren happy. His brother hadn't had a mood for months nor got stuck into the whisky because he felt down. So, as far as he could tell Vanessa was good for Bren, but only the passage of time would see if that continued to be the case.

His thoughts shifted away from his brother and Vanessa to his daughter. God, he was looking forward to the wet though it was still several months away. Not because the rain revitalised the land and helped the animals in the Kimberley to put on weight but because he could take time off to see Regan. How he missed her. It was as if a part of him was numb, cut off, and like a man desperate for information he would read and re-read her letters, written in her childish handwriting, over and over again, till he knew every word off by heart. He would fly to Sydney and spend a small fortune on accommodation and spoil her over a couple of weeks of quality time together.

Bren brought a saddle out of the saddle room and put it on Runaway. The horse pawed the ground and neighed. She hadn't been ridden for a while. Curtis squinted against the sunlight as he looked at the frisky Runaway. He'd not seen his sister-in-law ride and as she was going to accompany them on a muster being done on the station's southern quadrant, the last thing he wanted was an accident.

'You sure Vanessa can ride okay?' he asked, 'Runaway's not known for her gentle nature.'

'Nova reckons she can handle her. Vanessa rode her up to the Aboriginal camp last week.'

Curtis made a snorting sound. 'That's a short ride, three hours tops. You think she can sit in a saddle all day long?'

'Nova says she'll be fine. Vanessa's tougher than she looks. I thought you'd have realised that by now.' Bren studied his brother over Runaway's rump for several seconds. 'Look at what she's learned. She can refuel the engine that runs the generator and fix the fanbelt when it loosens and the motor cuts out. Nova's shown her how to fix pumps at bore water outlets when they clog up with mud and roots, and she's learning how to keep the station's books up to date as well as the records on the breeding program.' He stared challengingly at Curtis. 'Bro, when are you going to give her some credit for what she's achieved?'

Curtis took note of the muscle twitching along his brother's jawline, a sure sign that Bren's short fuse temper was on the rise. 'Okay.' He lifted his hands in defeat. 'I admit it, she's scrubbed up better than I thought she would.'

Bren's mouth widened in a grin, as if he knew that was a reasonable concession. 'Good. That wasn't too hard, was it?' He tightened the saddle's girth strap, adjusted the bridle and reins. 'Would you go and give Nova and Vanessa a hurry up. Reg's riding and Warren's in the support truck. They have a half hour's start on us.'

Ten minutes later, with a jaundiced gaze, Curtis watched Vanessa mount Runaway, and she did it with the ease that came from years of practice. As soon as she settled into the saddle, she flicked the reins and cantered off after Bren who was flying across the bottom paddock. She knew how to ride, he acknowledged sourly as he and Nova followed. Oddly, it irked him to see that she was accomplished in that regard but then, his lips compressed together with annoyance . . . why should it?

She was making a fair fist of life at Amaroo too, better than his ex-wife had. Everyone seemed to admire her, not only for her looks which were exceptional, but for her nature, her pleasantness and her intellect. She picked up things quickly, and she had a good memory too. He should be happy for Bren. He was, but he couldn't take to her, couldn't drop the barriers, or the feeling that deep down this, her life at Amaroo was just another role to her and for actors, all roles came to an end one day, didn't they?

Nova had warned Vanessa that mustering, cutting out the weaners then branding and castrating them was hot, dirty work, and her tutor hadn't been wrong. They had been riding the mob, several hundred head, towards a small gorge which, because of its shape made a good holding yard, for what seemed hours. Vanessa had red dust in her hair, her eyes, in every pore of her body, she was sure of that. Astride Runaway, she sat atop a small knoll watching Bren, Curtis, Reg and Warren, the part-Aboriginal stockman, separate the cattle into three groups. Mature bulls and cows, weaners and calves, which were destined to be branded and most of the males, castrated.

Vanessa could see that it was hard, back-breaking work but those doing it made it look easy. No one appeared to hurry, but the separating got done with a minimum of effort because everyone knew it was important to conserve as much energy as possible, because the day was going to be long and arduous. She looked up at a cloud-swept sky and then down at a vehicle being driven by Warrem. It carried their food, water and swags and was some distance away from the cattle so they wouldn't get spooked. They'd be eating and sleeping out tonight, her first experience at sleeping under the stars.

She watched Bren and his dog, Kimbo, herd three strays back to the mob and admired the ease with which her husband did the job, whistling and yelling commands to the dog, and occasionally cracking his stockwhip. If Kerri could see Bren now, see his expertise, ran the thought through her head. See her too, all sweaty and dishevelled. Her agent wouldn't believe her eyes. Her client, the darling of London's West End, was far removed from her usual well-coiffed, made-up self.

As Vanessa watched the milling herd, clouds of dust sprang up as Reg raced ahead of the cattle to reach down and open one of the roughly made gates. Because she lacked experience Vanessa had been delegated to the position of observer, allowed to watch the action from a safe distance. Even so, she was gaining some understanding of what Bren, Curtis and the others did on a regular basis —

pitting their skills and will against a mob of undisciplined animals in one of the harshest environments on earth. Their sense of achievement must be extraordinary and, suddenly, she was humbled by what she was seeing. Each person did what they had to do without expecting praise, or reward.

One day, not this year but maybe the next, she would be experienced enough to do what Reg and Bren were doing. That thought excited her more than hearing the applause of two thousand fans in a theatre.

After lunch, which consisted of thick slabs of homemade bread, sliced roast beef and pickles, plus fresh fruit, washed down with billy tea, the work continued. Lunch, she learned, was always light because of the heavy workload that didn't let up until sunset.

There wasn't much of a physical nature that Vanessa could do, other than watch the proceedings, but she helped to control the gate that sent the male weaners single file into a smaller holding area where they were leg-roped and branded. Watching was bad enough and the smell of burnt animal hair soon mingled with the smell of cattle, dust and honest sweat. Grudgingly and silently, she admired their teamwork. All were old hands at the tasks and knew, without having to be told, what had to be done. Nova, by far the smallest physically, worked as hard as the men, impressing Vanessa with her stamina.

When she saw Curtis castrate the first young male Brahman, she was unprepared for the shock of it.

'Oh, that's so cruel,' slipped out, over the protesting calf's bellow, before she could stop herself.

Curtis, who'd deftly applied a rubber band around the calf's testicles and twisted it several times, looked up from the task, his expression puzzled. 'It's not as cruel as cutting them off then cauterising the wound with a hot iron. With this method, after a few weeks the balls just fall off. Castrating males not suitable for the breeding program is a widely accepted practice. It makes them less aggressive and more inclined to fatten up, too.'

As she listened to Curtis's explanation, her gaze turned towards Bren, who was getting the next animal ready. 'Still, it must hurt, mustn't it?'

Curtis answered for his brother. 'Vets say the discomfort is minimal, compared to the other method. They hardly feel a thing.'

Vanessa's expression became sceptical. 'Oh, really! Then why do they bellow? What you've said is hard to believe, Curtis. They feel pain like us, they bleed like us. I'm sure that if the same thing was done to a man he wouldn't say, "I hardly felt a thing".'

Bren burst out laughing. He undid the leg ropes on the weaner and shooed him off. 'Reckon she has you there, Curtis.' He crossed his legs and held his crotch for a moment. 'The mere thought of castration makes me feel bloody crook in the nether regions.'

Annoyed that Vanessa had got the better of him, Curtis's response to her was brusque. 'I'm sorry if it offends your sensitivities, but that's the way it is. If it makes you queasy, why don't you go and help Warren set up camp? We'll need wood for a fire to cook dinner too.'

'That's a good idea, hon, and Warren could do with a hand,' Bren intervened smoothly in an attempt to diffuse the tension between Curtis and his wife.

'Sure.' Though her tone was agreeable she resented being summarily dismissed so she delivered a withering stare at Curtis before he stomped off to rope another unfortunate male calf. She turned on her heel and walked away from Bren, Curtis and the cattle.

The steak and sausages barbecued over an open fire with jacketed potatoes rolled in aluminium foil and cooked in the embers together with damper freshly made by Warren, smelled and tasted so good. Warren produced half a dozen cans of beer, still reasonably cool, from the bottom of the cooler, to eat with the meal.

Twilight soon gave way to nightfall which was relieved around their stock camp by the fire and a single tilly lamp. Six swags had been rolled out around the fire in preparation for an early night but after the billy tea and biscuits were consumed, everyone sat back when Reg produced a battered harmonica from his saddlebag and began to play.

'Give us a song, Nova,' Bren requested. He was sitting beside Vanessa, an arm casually draped around her shoulders. 'Our Nova's got a passable voice, you know.'

'Passable?' Reg stopped playing. 'She's bloody good, mate, and you know it.' He glanced towards his daughter and his rugged, lined features — he was not a handsome man by any stretch of the imagination, having a broken nose, a receding hairline, bushy eyebrows and a thin, crooked mouth — broke into a grin, 'She could win the best new talent award at any country music festival if she put her mind to it.'

'Go on, do that Peter Allen tune, *Tenterfield Saddler*, I like that one,' Warren encouraged. He picked up two sticks close to the fire and as Reg played the opening notes on the harmonica, struck them against each other to the beat of the music.

Leaning against a boulder, her hands tucked into the pockets of her jeans, Nova began to sing.

'That was wonderful.' As everyone clapped after the song ended, Vanessa said, 'You're very good. Why aren't you doing something with that voice of yours?'

'She does. Reg says she sings in the shower all the time,' Bren teased, and chuckled when Nova poked out her tongue at him.

'I mean something professional.'

'I'd have to go east. That's where the top country and western singers live and perform,' Nova said. 'I'd rather stay at Amaroo.'

'But you're so talented,' Vanessa persisted, dismayed by Nova's apparent lack of ambition. 'Some people would kill for a voice like yours.'

Nova shrugged, 'One day I will, maybe.'

Vanessa watched Nova's gaze rest on Curtis for several moments before coming back to her with a smile. The significance of the younger woman's glance sank in and instantly she berated herself for not picking up on it sooner. She, who was supposed to be good at observing people! Nova was romantically interested in Curtis. Of course. Many of the things she had noted — how Nova defended him, that she'd danced with him at the reception, that she sang his praises to her — made sense now. Nova had a huge crush on Vanessa's brother-in-law.

Reg began to play a tune everyone knew and the solo singing turned into a general sing-a-long for an hour or so, until Bren suggested they hit their bed rolls because tomorrow was also going to be a busy day.

'Once the branding's done, we'll herd the mob towards Gumbledon Creek for a drink then lead them to the western plains. There's better feed there at this time of the year.'

Vanessa did her best to stifle a moan. Her muscles were stiff and reacting from a day in the saddle. She crawled into her bedding. A layer of compacted foam was her mattress and underneath, the ground was rock hard. She didn't want to think about how sore she would be by the time they returned to the homestead; she would not give Curtis the pleasure he would derive from seeing her saddle sore. Still, soreness aside, she had enjoyed the day. There had been a lot of hard riding and she had learned a good deal. Even the debate with Curtis about the castrating had been a valuable lesson, with Bren explaining later, when they had a moment alone, that the method used really was the most effective and a relatively pain-free way of accomplishing the deed.

That made her think about the two poddy calves back at the homestead. She had christened them

Fergus and Andy. Poor little things. She would have to make sure she wasn't around when Curtis did the deed on them! Yawning, and with a last look at the black sky above with its millions upon millions of stars, she settled into her swag, certain she wouldn't fall asleep for ages. In less than five minutes she was sound asleep.

Bren woke her with a kiss, her favourite way of waking up.

'I've planned for us to spend the whole day together. No work, no other people, just us,' he whispered as he drew her into his arms.

'Without Curtis's approval?' she said slyly. The last muster before the wet came was about to start, and some of the stock had to be herded to a pick-up point for the road train to take it to Derby for export to the Middle East.

'To hell with Curtis and his workaholic ways,' he said, criticising his brother good-naturedly. 'I'm the boss and today is ours to do with as we please.'

And they did . . .

It took an hour and a half of steady riding, past the old quarry, past an aborted gold-mining attempt by Bren's grandfather, then along a narrow trail that wended across a plain and through a valley of knee-high spiky, yellow spear grass, slowly climbing towards the gorge. A trickle of sweat pooled in the depression at the base of Vanessa's throat, filled then slid down between her breasts. She ignored the discomfort of the heat because she was enthralled by the scenery.

They entered the gorge which, Bren had told her, wasn't a gorge in the strictest sense of the word. It was more like two steep rocky hills with a fifteen to twenty metre wide space in between. Vanessa was astonished by the change in the flora; even the earth beneath their horses hooves was a different colour and texture. Bleached by aeons of flooding during the wet, it wasn't the fine red soil she was used to but a yellowish-white in colour. Spindly gums — she didn't know what they were called — clung for dear life to crevices in the rock and a mixture of shrubs, reminiscent of tea trees, plus tall palms and clusters of what she'd been told were ancient cycads, gave the gorge a spectacular, primordial look.

'It's so beautiful,' she exclaimed.

'My grandfather was the first white man to see the place. He named it Exeter Gorge — because that's where he came from in England. See there,' Bren pointed to a horizontal mark that was a different colour to the upper wall of the gorge, 'that's how high the water can get during and after the wet.'

'Remarkable.' Vanessa gauged the mark to be about one and a half metres up from the gorge's floor.

'Wait till you see the waterfall. It won't be running at full pelt — we'd have to come in after the wet to see that — but it's still quite a sight, 'cause the fall is so high.'

She looked around for a sign of a creek. There wasn't any. The ground was bone dry. 'Where's the water now?'

'Evaporated or gone underground. Geologists aren't sure. It does that in the dry.'

She shook her head in wonderment and Bren gave her a quizzical look, 'What?'

'I was thinking of England, trying to compare. I can't. This place is just so ... special.'

His grin was a wide one. 'You're beginning to sound like a native.'

'That's one of the nicest things you've said to me.'

'Come on. Race you to the waterfall,' Bren challenged. He dug his heels into his horse's flanks and raced off.

She spurred her horse forward and followed but not at the breakneck speed at which her husband rode.

Bren was off his horse and releasing the saddle's girth before removing it by the time she rode up and dismounted. She loosely tethered the reins then stood, staring at the splendour before her.

Water cascaded over and down sheer walls that must have been approximately fifty metres high. Spray from the falling water was, in the sun's light, creating a rainbow halfway down as it fell into a naturally formed, almost circular pool. A variety of flora abounded because of the constant water supply. Vanessa watched the water hit the pool, bounce up in a small wave then in ever-widening ripples, move towards shore. 'This is magnificent.'

Bren came up behind her and put his arms around her waist. '*You* are magnificent. Every day I say a prayer of thanks — not an easy thing for me 'cause I'm not a godly man — that you fell in love with me.'

She leant back onto his chest, smiling as he nibbled her neck. 'Thank you. That's my second compliment for the day and as they say, straight back at you, my darling.' She turned in his arms to face him and offered her lips for his kiss.

After a delightful interlude Bren broke away and fanned his face with his disreputable looking Akubra — he refused to buy a new one because this was his lucky hat. Over time he had pushed and pulled the brim into a unique shape and she'd noticed that most of the station hands had done the same, seeming not to appreciate the work the manufacturer had gone to, to give the hat its individual style.

'I thought I was hot before; I'm steaming now.' His eyes moved away from her to the cascading water and the pool it emptied into. 'Let's cool off.'

'I didn't pack bathers.' She gave him a prim look but, contradictorily, her smile was one of anticipation.

He gave her a wicked smile. 'All the better, we'll skinny-dip.'

'What about crocodiles?' She'd heard and read enough stories about crocodile attacks to be nervous about the idea of swimming in pools where the merciless reptiles might lurk.

'It's safe because the river stops at the top of the falls. Crocs aren't going to bother coming down into the gorge — there's no food here for them.'

She gave him a tentative smile. 'There's us.'

'Believe me, hon, if I thought there was a skerrick of a risk I wouldn't get my big toe wet. I've seen what crocs do to animals and humans.' He began to unbutton his shirt and his belt. 'Besides, the chopper regularly flies over this area. One of us would have spotted croc slides if they were around.'

'Fran's packed us a wonderful lunch, with wine. Let's put the bottle in a cool spot first,' Vanessa suggested.

They stayed in the water, which was refreshingly cool, for an hour before hunger of a different kind pulled them back to the shore and they made love. After that they lay naked on the large towel Bren had packed, letting the sun dry them.

'Now that's what I call an appetiser,' Bren whispered in her ear as he lazily stroked her body. 'Could we put it on the daily menu?'

Playfully, she slapped his hand away. 'I concede it might be nice but also hard to achieve, what with people wandering in and out of the homestead.' Everyone, she had noticed, seemed to have carte blanche and came in and out of the place as they pleased. The station hands didn't, but Reg, Nova and Fran, as well as Curtis could often be seen walking through various rooms — the kitchen, the office to send messages, the living areas too. Privacy wasn't something anyone worried about and over the months she'd finally got used to that.

'Just a thought,' he said, his tone still husky in the afterglow of their lovemaking.

'I'm starving, let's have lunch.' Vanessa threw her singlet top over her nakedness and reached for the lunch box. Bren liberated the bottle of wine from its watery resting place and they drank it in plastic cups.

'Fancy some exploring afterwards?' Bren queried while munching on a corned beef fritter.

'Depends . . .' She quirked an eyebrow at him.

'There are Aboriginal cave paintings up one side of the gorge. It's a bit of a climb to get there.'

Vanessa's eyes sparkled with enthusiasm. 'I'd love to see them, once lunch has settled.'

'Okay, you rest while I clean up.'

Bren tidied the remains of their lunch and put what was left in his saddlebag while Vanessa spread the towel under a patch of shade and lay down, protecting her face from the sun's glare with her hat. As she relaxed she listened to the faint and occasional hum of bush insects, but apart from that there was silence — not the stirring of a breeze to rustle the scrub or overhanging tall palms. There wasn't even the sound of a bird to disturb the absolute quiet.

Too hot, she decided. The animals and insects who called this part of the land home were smart enough to be taking it easy in some shady spot, she thought as she drifted into a pleasant, fatigued sleep.

Bren, grabbing Vanessa's toe and pulling it, roused her from the dream she'd been having. She and Bren had been the only inhabitants on a tropical island, a paradise with plenty to eat and drink, but dark clouds were forming and a wind was stirring the vegetation — a storm was about to hit paradise and ... She opened her eyes, blinked at the semi-darkness of the hat which had half fallen off her face. Her gaze on Bren, she sat up with a jerk and was about to stand when Bren's eyes suddenly focussed on a spot behind her. His 'wake up now' smile froze on his face.

'Don't move,' he hissed at her, a sense of urgency in his tone. *'Don't move a muscle.'*

Still watching something to the right of her shoulder, he got up, very slowly, and edged backwards to the saddles. He removed his Winchester 30/30 rifle with great care from the leather holster attachment strapped to his saddle.

Vanessa was perplexed and, because his behaviour was strange, she was becoming more anxious by the second. She saw beads of sweat — he was close enough for her to see them — form on his upper lip as he brought the rifle up to his shoulder and aimed it. But ... her eyes widened, her heart began a rapid acceleration, he seemed to be aiming at her!

Almost frozen with fright, her throat muscles in spasm, she dredged up the courage to whisper, 'Wh-at ... are ... you doing?'

# CHAPTER SEVEN

His answer came in a heartbeat when he pulled the rifle's trigger. The noise echoed down the gorge, around the waterfall and pool then faded away to nothingness.

Bren dropped the rifle and raced to Vanessa. He pulled her up and into his arms. 'Sorry, hon, there wasn't time to explain.' He pointed to something partly hidden in the grass behind her. 'Look.'

Trembling, she swivelled sideways in his arms to stare down at a two-metre long, dark brown smooth, *something*. God, it was a snake! His shot had blown its head off yet its body still wriggled in a final death throe.

'That's a King Brown, otherwise known as a Mulga snake. Their venom sacs hold more venom in them than any other snake in the country. They can kill a person but not quickly, takes half a day or longer, so I've heard.' She shuddered and he tightened his arms around her. 'They're cold-blooded and like the heat, but they're not usually aggressive. Guess he felt threatened 'cause we were a little too close to him.'

'I ... I ...' Her mouth was dry and she almost choked on the lump of fear lodged in her throat, a bubble of nausea threatening to make her throw up. 'I, oooh, Bren.' Her arms clung to him as if she never intended to let him go. She couldn't tell him that for one or two crazy seconds she had thought he was going to shoot her. That had been her first immediate and, she realised, foolish reaction.

'It's all right. You're safe. Wait.' He disentangled himself and went back to his saddle. From one of the bags he extracted a small flask with an outer, polystyrene skin. 'Drink this.'

Vanessa took a swig. Warm, smooth brandy heated her mouth and slid down her throat into her stomach, the alcohol calming her. She took another mouthful, coughed and gave the flask back. 'Do you always carry alcohol with you?' The trembling was easing, and so was the nauseous feeling.

'Sure do. Strictly for medicinal purposes though. You've got to carry it the right way, in a protective flask, or the stuff evaporates in the heat,' he said with an unrepentant grin. He took a mouthful himself, then returned the flask to the saddlebag.

She shook her head at him, then the full import of what had happened struck her. 'You saved my life.'

'My pleasure,' he said lightheartedly. 'I was slack though. I should have checked the ground before you lay down, made sure there were no nasties in the grass.' He touched her cheek, tracing his fingers down her jawline, down her throat in a sensitive caress. 'You okay now?' He waited till she'd given him an affirmative nod. 'Still want to look at those cave paintings? We can do it another time if you're too shaky.'

She raised an eyebrow at him. 'Are there likely to be snakes up there?'

'No.' He saw anxiety mirrored in her brown eyes, and responded to it. 'But I'll take the rifle just in case. Okay?'

'Okay.' Vanessa smiled a relieved smile. She didn't want Bren to think she was scared, but that had been a harrowing experience — another snippet for the diary she was keeping about acclimatising to the outback. She was trying so hard to get used to the ins and outs of outback life, to its attractions and the dangers but she knew that learning and knowing all she had to know was going to take time. She pointed to the rifle. 'Perhaps, one day, you should teach me how to handle one of those things.'

'A good idea,' he smiled encouragingly at her. 'I'll put it on my list of "Essential things to teach Vanessa".' He held out his hand to her, giving her fingers a squeeze as they entwined with his. 'Let's go, shall we?'

At first, the changes on Amaroo over the next month or two were so subtle it took a while for Vanessa to pick up on the fact that something was wrong.

Then, slowly, small occurrences began to gather weight at the back of her mind, things that didn't make sense. Bren vetoing the proposed spa she had set her heart on till the next year was the first. Then, one day, Fran let it slip that she had been told to keep household and other expenditure very economical. Ten days later the two casual station hands were laid off. Vanessa now knew enough about station life to know that with the land they had, plus herd numbers, two pairs of hands were going to be missed. And, she didn't need a high IQ to know that week by week, Bren was quietly introducing other belt-tightening strategies.

But the most remarkable change was in Bren. His relaxed, easygoing nature gradually underwent a change, beginning with him becoming more of a workaholic, like his brother. Occasionally he lapsed into brooding moods as if his thoughts were a million miles away. He began to drink seriously after dinner — something he hadn't done before, when they were first married — and would continue until he was tipsy or clearly inebriated. As well, he spent hours in the office, poring over the station's accounts and when he emerged his mood was blacker than when he went in.

However, worst of all, after a month or so came the realisation that he was distancing himself from her. It was something quite odd considering they'd only been married a short while. Vanessa tried to initiate discussions about what was worrying him but to no avail. He refused to talk about the problem, to share it with her, which made her deduce that some peculiar Selby credo wouldn't allow him to.

Whether he was doing it consciously or unconsciously, she considered that he was treating her like an outsider. It hurt that he didn't have the confidence to confide in her. She had expected their marriage to be a partnership, in the truest sense of the word — a similar relationship to that which her parents had enjoyed — but Bren was shutting her out and she was at a loss to know how to break through his reserve. Her concerns were compounded because, in less than a week, she was leaving for England to play Katharina, a role she had played several times, in *The Taming of the Shrew* at a Stratford on Avon Shakespeare Festival.

One day the station's accountant, Fabian Costello, visited Amaroo and stayed closeted with Bren and Curtis for most of the day, which told Vanessa something. If she must, she had to force the issue and not allow Bren to fob her off with platitudes that everything was fine, when her heart and her intellect told her it wasn't.

When Fabian left early next morning, with Reg flying him back to Kununurra, Bren still refused to be drawn on what was wrong. By bedtime that night Vanessa had had enough of tiptoeing around and of respecting Bren's 'space'. She had built up sufficient hurt and anger internally and she intended to have her say. After dinner, sitting in a leather chair with Sandy asleep on her lap, she watched Bren refill his whisky glass for the third time and began with a casual remark. 'Considering the remoteness of Amaroo, isn't it unusual for an accountant to pay a client a personal visit?'

'They do sometimes.' He took a sip of whisky. 'We've known Fabian for a long time — he's been Amaroo's accountant for ten years.'

'I see. So you got things sorted out?'

He pulled a face, more of a grimace, as he moved restlessly on the sofa. 'Some things, yes, others, no.'

'Such as?'

Bren's features tightened into a scowl. He threw her a dark look. 'What's with the third degree,

Vanessa? I've said before, it's nothing for you to worry about.'

'So you say, but I am worried.' She stared straight at him, her eyes locking with his. 'I can't help it. I thought our marriage was a partnership — in every way. I don't hold back on matters that concern my career, such as contracts and acting opportunities — they'll always come second to us. You are not reciprocating.' When he didn't dispute what she'd said, she went on, 'I don't like being shut out.'

Bren stared at her for twenty seconds or so then looked away. 'It's complicated.' He stopped, swirled the ice cubes around in his glass and listened to them clink against its sides. 'Vanessa, I don't want you to worry . . . You're right though, something has happened but Curtis and I will get it sorted. It's just that . . .'

He stopped again and when he didn't continue she prompted him. 'What, Bren?'

'Look,' his voice rose half a decibel, 'for God's sake, let it be. Just trust me.' Restless, he stood and began to pace about the room.

Stung by his tone and his attitude, Vanessa's chin lifted, her hot Spanish-inherited blood heating up. 'It isn't a matter of trust, it's . . . you're making me feel like an outsider. As if I'm a guest at Amaroo, that I don't really belong.'

Bren's head shook in denial. 'That's crazy talk, Vanessa. You're my wife, of course you belong here.'

Her expressive features, trained by her craft to show emotion, disputed his comment. 'Look, I don't know if I can help but it's just that you don't appear to have enough confidence in me to talk about the problem. That's what really hurts.'

'I don't want to argue over this ...' He stood, walked towards her, his arms outstretched. 'It isn't that important.'

She didn't agree. Having observed the situation silently, for weeks, seeing him become more morose and less the 'Bren' she knew, she had a different opinion.

'Is that so?' her hands went to her hips aggressively. 'It's important enough for your accountant to visit you. It's important enough for you and Curtis to walk around with grim expressions and shaking your heads as if the weight of the world is on your shoulders. It's important enough to embark on belt-tightening strategies and to put off workers.' Her voice rose in tune with her temper. 'Do you think I'm stupid, that I haven't noticed? Or is it that you think Amaroo's problem is too complicated for someone like me to understand?'

'Geez,' Bren backed away. He sat down again in response to her anger. He remembered something her agent had hinted at, that being half Spanish she had a temper but, apart from the altercation with Curtis, months ago, he hadn't been exposed to it. That she was mad made her look more fiery and beautiful than she normally was, and ... so utterly desirable that what he wanted to do was to take her in his arms and forget the problem he had, to kiss away her anger and to make passionate love with her.

'God, Vanessa,' he back-pedalled, 'I-I didn't think you felt so intensely about it. Curtis and I, well, I guess we misjudged your level of interest.' He tried a boyish smile, its intention to calm her down. 'I haven't been thinking clearly for weeks.'

Unimpressed, and doubly so after he said he and Curtis had talked about her — probably discussed tactics — brought the tart retort, 'I have noticed.'

The gleam of battle was still in her eyes and, fatalistically, he knew that she wasn't going to be fobbed off with excuses. He also saw that she was at the end of her patience towards him being miserable. And that she cared so much was a pleasing revelation! She was astonishing, more than he'd expected, more than he could have hoped for. Hardly a day went by without him acknowledging his good fortune and now she was proving herself even more.

'I care about you, Bren. I care about Amaroo too. I know I haven't been here long and I can't explain it well, but the land, everything here has kind of gotten into my blood.'

'All right.' He patted a space next to him. She joined him on the sofa. His shoulders slumped forward, his head went down and he couldn't look at her. 'I don't think I'm doing a very good job of running Amaroo.' He stopped her before she had the chance to deny that. 'When Dad was alive, I didn't have to worry about things, didn't have to be responsible. That was his job and until about twelve months before his death he ran the property well.' He shifted with discomfort. 'Life here has always been relatively easy. I did what Dad told me to do and everything was fine. Now I have to make decisions that affect the welfare of the station and the people here. I don't know if I've got what it takes.'

'Oh, Bren.' His confession dissolved her anger. Her arms went around him and she disguised the fact that his admission shocked her more than she cared to admit. He was like a small boy in need of reassurance, and far removed from the confident man she thought she had married.

'You're too hard on yourself,' she soothed, 'Amaroo is a big concern. I know that. You're in a competitive business in a harsh, uncompromising climate. Running this property successfully would test the resolve of nine out of ten men.'

He turned his head, his expression one of enlightenment. 'You're right, hon. You've tapped into that already and you're a relative newcomer.'

'Tell me about the problem. Maybe I can help. If I can't at least you'll know that I have some understanding of what's wrong, and I'll stop pestering you about not knowing,' she said gently as she stroked his brown hair.

'Okay. As I said, it's complicated. The provisions in Dad's will — bequests to Mum, Curtis and Lauren — drained Amaroo's capital reserves. I wasn't worried about that because Dad had invested strongly in international shares — a teak plantation in Malaysia — and the share value was going up. I intended to sell when the shares reached a unit price of $2.20 and recoup enough to tide the property over till a percentage of stock is sold for export.' He stared into her eyes. 'About six weeks ago, the bottom fell out of the Asian teak market and the shares, worth $2.91 are now worth 27 cents and the price is still falling! I had Fabian increase our overdraft with the bank — we're going to be in the

133

red until we sell more stock — but the bank manager,' he curled his lip in disgust, 'is playing hard ball. There's a small mortgage on Amaroo and they want a portion paid back, or more surety, before they'll increase the overdraft. I don't have anything else to pledge and we won't have an appreciable injection of funds till the muster after the wet.'

'Can't you get an extension?'

'I've had one extension. That's why Fabian came. The bank's putting the screws on him and there isn't enough in our working accounts to appease them.' He shook his head. 'Bloody, bloodsuckers, that's what our banks are.'

'What about Curtis and Lauren? They received sizeable inheritances. Can't they lend you what you need in the short term?'

He grunted. 'They would if they could. Unfortunately, they put what they had — Curtis got screwed by Georgia for a chunk of his inheritance — into buying Cadogan's Run. They also had to borrow which means they don't have sufficient equity in the place to help me out.'

Vanessa hesitated for a second or two. 'Your mother?'

'No way,' his tone was adamant. 'I'd never live it down. You only met Mum briefly, but I imagine you formed an opinion as to what she's like. It was hard to get her to leave Amaroo, so Curtis and I could run the place the way we think best. If I borrow from her she'll want to come back to continue her rule.' He glanced meaningfully in her direction. 'Would you like to share Amaroo with her?'

Vanessa grinned in spite of the seriousness of things. 'That would be ... difficult.'

'I love her, but you bet it would!' he said with feeling, 'My Uncle Stuart has offered to loan me what I need but Curtis is against that.'

She didn't often agree with Curtis, but she did in this respect. Something about Stuart Selby caused her to have a niggle of discomfort when she thought about him. She hardly knew him, yet she — like Curtis — was loath to trust him when it came to his financial generosity. Some inner sense told her that it would come with provisions more beneficial to Stuart than to Amaroo.

'I agree with Curtis. It isn't a good idea to borrow from your uncle.' Then she had an inspired thought, but first she had to know ... 'How much do you need?'

'Initially, two hundred and fifty thousand dollars and in six months another similar amount. Stock sales should cover the second payment though.'

'I could realise that and more by selling my cottage at Bourton on the Water.' Her tone was contemplative and, smiling at his profile she added gently, 'It's yours, my darling.'

A tense silence pervaded the room for maybe twenty seconds, then Bren moved away from her and stood up. 'No bloody way!' Frustration and pride caused his temper to snap. 'I won't sponge off you. God, your agent would love that. I saw the look in Kerri's eyes when we first met. She thought I was after what money you might have.'

'But it would only be a short-term thing, surely ...'

'No, thanks. I do have some pride. I'll find a way of getting what I need but not from you.' With that comment resonating throughout the room, he strode down the hall and out of sight.

Wide-eyed with shock, Vanessa stared at the sofa and at the whisky glass on the coffee table. Then tears began to prick at her eyes. Had she been wrong to offer what she had? No. A small flame of anger began to burn inside her. What was the matter with Bren? Why couldn't he accept that her offer was sincerely meant, intended to benefit him and Amaroo? Was it pride or was it something else? For the life of her she didn't know and ... didn't understand. But she knew one thing, now was not the time to be faint-hearted or passive. Amaroo meant a good deal to her — she thought of it as her home. This was where she wanted to live and one day to raise a family with Bren. Her lips thinned with growing anger.

So, she'd be damned if she'd sit back meekly and not do her utmost to correct the property's financial bind. Flicking her hair back angrily, she clicked her fingers for Sandy to follow her, but ... where had Bren gone?

She wandered through the house. In their bedroom? He wasn't in the en suite or the bathroom, nor the kitchen. She stepped through the kitchen doorway onto the back verandah and saw that the lights were on in Curtis's cottage. Had he gone to his brother for what ... solace? Understanding?

Steaming at his pigheadedness, for she was certain that's what it came down to, and with Sandy trailing behind, she marched towards the cottage, up to the front door and knocked. Within seconds the door opened wide.

'Vanessa.' Curtis wasn't quick enough to hide his surprise. Both were aware that she'd never knocked on his door before.

She began without a polite preamble. 'Is Bren here? I need to talk to him.'

'He's in the kitchen making coffee.' Curtis stood aside for her to enter the cottage. 'Do you want one? A coffee?' he asked belatedly.

'No, thank you.' Her tone was sharp and for the moment she forgot that her anger was directed at Bren, not Curtis. She took a deep breath to calm herself down. Almost reluctantly, as she moved further into the room, she took a curious look around and found the cottage's interior a pleasant surprise.

The living room was surprisingly cool. Two walls were cement rendered, and on one a variety of Aboriginal artifacts hung on wooden pegs. The second wall housed a timber bookcase almost completely full of books of all sizes and shapes. The two remaining walls were of hand-hewn natural stone. Near an oval dinner table stood a cabinet with an interesting array of Aboriginal artifacts, she discovered that as she moved closer to inspect it. Through an open doorway she caught a glimpse of a modern kitchen, not large like the one in the homestead, but adequate, and the floor of both rooms was made from huge, time-smoothed red sandstone blocks. A colourful scatter rug in reds and browns, in front of a sofa, softened the living-room floor's rugged appearance.

'I didn't know you were a reader,' surprise made her say as she gazed at the bookcase.

Curtis's forehead puckered in a frown. Clearly he was confused as to why she was here. He watched her studying the books, she trailed a hand along one of the rows.

'Sometimes I find it hard to sleep,' he found himself admitting. 'Curling up with a book helps me to relax. My grandfather, Robert, was a learned man, an inveterate reader. Being the second son of a moderately well-off country squire, with few inheritance entitlements, he came to Australia with his wife to seek a better life. The ship they were on foundered just off Darwin. After they were rescued and instead of travelling on to Brisbane, their original destination, he and my grandmother forged west from Darwin with a group of immigrants thirsty for land. That's how he came upon Amaroo.'

'How long ago was that?'

'The late 1920s. Dad was born here in 1935.'

'How did he accumulate so many books?'

'Over the years, most came from England but when Mum had the new house designed, she chose not to waste space on a library. As I got older, went to uni and stuff, I took the books out of the storage shed where they were deteriorating due to the weather — the humidity plays havoc with old paper and the glue, you know.' He paused then went on. 'The temperature in here is fairly constant because the walls are thick and the windows small. They survive better here.' He stopped speaking as Bren came into the living room with two mugs of coffee.

Not good at disguising his feelings, Bren's discomfort at his wife following him to Curtis's was obvious. It made Vanessa remember how angry she was. She watched him hand Curtis a mug of coffee, after which he stared disconsolately at her but didn't say a word.

'That discussion we were having isn't over, Bren,' Vanessa began, 'so unless you intend to saddle a horse and ride off into the night to avoid me, we are going to settle the matter now.'

Curtis shifted his weight from one foot to the other and, clearly uncomfortable said, 'I'll step out onto the verandah.'

'No, I want you to hear what I have to say.' Her stare, aimed at Curtis, vetoed his escape. 'I'm sure Bren told you I offered to sell some property in England and use the proceeds to get the bank off our backs.'

Her use of the word 'our' wasn't lost on Curtis. His eyebrows rose momentarily then settled. 'Bren told me.' Pointing to an easy chair, he invited, 'Please sit down, Vanessa.' He glanced at Bren then went on. 'I believe Bren said he wasn't interested, that he'd find another way to get the funds.'

Vanessa's mouth tightened with impatience. She had expected a united front and that's what she was getting. 'We know that's impossible, unless he accepts your uncle's offer or asks your mother. He says he doesn't want to do either.'

'In the end he might have to do one or the other,' Curtis said matter-of-factly, but his tone was not enthusiastic.

'I think we both believe that would be a mistake.'
Vanessa was trying to keep her cool. If she was
going to convince both Selby men she would need to
keep a clear head and a cap on her temper. She
watched Bren, trying to gauge what he was feeling,
thinking. That he wouldn't look at her told her
something, and in response some of her anger
diffused. He still looked as he had a little while ago,
so ... lost, as if solving the problem of Amaroo was
beyond him.

'My offer still stands and I'm hurt that neither of
you,' she stared first at Bren then at Curtis, 'will
consider it. Amaroo has become my home too. I
don't want it put in jeopardy, especially when there's
no need to.' She spoke with a patience that amazed
her when, deep down she wanted to scream at their
joint male bullheadedness.

'Like you, I have a stake in what happens here. If
you must, look upon it as a business proposition, a
straight out loan,' she said. *To ease your pride*, she
thought. 'It makes sense, and there won't be any
problem selling my Bourton on the Water property
— the Cotswolds is a popular, picturesque part of
England.' She waited for one of them to respond.

'It would only be acceptable if it were regarded as
a loan to be paid back when the property's profits
allow it.' Curtis made the suggestion on Bren's
behalf. His gaze flashed to Bren who had his head
down and appeared to have his thoughts elsewhere.

'If you like,' she agreed. If that proviso created a
balm for their male pride she had no problem with
it. 'Pay me when you can. Afterwards, I'll invest it in
a Darwin property from which I can derive an

income. That would be a win-win situation for all of us.' She didn't like it that Curtis appeared to be doing all the thinking and the talking for Bren and the property. She didn't like that at all. But she had to put that thought behind her — the important thing was that both of them understood that she wouldn't be diverted from doing what had to be done, wounded pride or no wounded pride!

'What do you think, Bren?' she asked quietly, seeking a response from him.

'It could work that way,' Curtis said slowly, having thought it through.

Bren looked, not at Vanessa but at Curtis, and said, 'You think so?'

'Yes.' Curtis and Vanessa said in unison.

'The important thing is to keep Amaroo going. The problem is short-term, but we know that the bank could get nasty.' She had a mental image of the bank trying to foreclose, of Bren losing everything his parents and grandparents had created. 'Curtis,' she stared directly at him, 'it's up to you to convince Bren to accept my idea. I believe you can be persuasive when you want to be.' More than once she had seen him diffuse tension between Nova and her parents, and mediate between arguing station hands.

The corners of Curtis's mouth turned down, implying that he didn't appreciate her frankness. 'It could be a few years before you'd be fully paid back.'

Vanessa shrugged a shoulder, unconsciously mimicking his earlier movement. She continued to observe him chew the side of his mouth for a few seconds, mulling over what she'd said. Normally his features were inscrutable; but for a brief time she had seen distrust be replaced by something else — respect. God, had his ex-wife done such a job on him that he was loath to trust anything a woman said? She hoped not.

'Look, I know you don't like me very much. I can live with that as long as you understand that I sincerely want to help. Not you,' she saw him wince, 'but my husband and Amaroo.'

'Phew!' Curtis's head jerked back with surprise. 'You come right out and say what you think, don't you?'

She noted that he didn't dispute what she'd said about him not liking her. So what! She was sufficiently mature to know that one couldn't be liked by everyone.

'When I have to.' She stood and moved to the door. 'I love Bren and I love Amaroo. If you feel the same you'll help Bren to see that this offer is what he needs at this point in time.'

And then, without waiting for him to answer her, and not looking at Bren either, she made her way out of the cottage. From what she had gleaned about Curtis, he wasn't the type who made snap decisions. He would think about what she'd said, weigh things up before he made up his mind. Grudgingly, she was developing a sense of admiration for Curtis Selby. He seemed more in tune with Amaroo's needs and more businesslike than the man she'd married. And, the bottom line was that she believed he was the only one able to persuade Bren that using what she offered was smart, and that he'd do it in such a way that her husband's pride was not seriously dented.

Back in her bedroom, Vanessa checked the time on the digital alarm clock. It would be early morning in London. She wasn't going to wait until Bren and Curtis debated her suggestion. She would call Kerri now and instruct her to put the property on the market, and she wouldn't allow any argument from her friend should she try to sway her otherwise.

After Vanessa left, Curtis stared at the closed door while he reorganised his thoughts. He didn't like changes or surprises and tonight Vanessa had dumped a change *and* a surprise on him. Maybe he'd have to rethink his opinion of her. Maybe — a growling sound erupted deep in his throat as that thought settled in his mind — she wasn't just a beautiful, artistically talented woman. Maybe there was more to her than he thought.

For reasons he didn't understand such thoughts made him feel uncomfortable because he believed himself a good judge of character and he didn't like to be proven wrong. Her sincerity and flashes of fieriness had caught him off guard. But could she be believed when she said she loved Amaroo? Could she, in such a short space of time? He stroked his chin reflectively as he thought about that. God, this place was so different to where she'd come from. And it was clear that she was made of sterner stuff than he'd thought. Another surprise. Somehow, after tonight, he had to believe that this wouldn't be the only surprise Bren's wife would thrust at him.

Curtis's gaze moved to Bren. His brother's expression was a mixture of confusion, bewilderment and surprise over Vanessa's passion. 'Come on out to the hangar, Bren. We'll talk things over while we clean up Nova's bike.'

'What's wrong with her bike?'

'She was showing off to Warren and Tony, doing wheelies. She came a gutser down by the breaking-in yard. Half buried the bike in the dirt and now the motor needs a good clean.'

'Nova can pull down a motor. You should make her do it.' Bren's tone was dour.

Curtis nodded. 'You know Nova, if she doesn't want to she'll find a way to con one of the blokes into doing it for her. I'd rather do it myself. That way I know it's done properly.'

The brothers walked onto the verandah, the old boards creaking under their combined weight. Curtis lifted his head to stare up at the night sky and, as always it enthralled him. There was sufficient moonlight to illuminate the way to the hangar, and he whistled for Ringo to follow them as they walked towards it. Life, he decided, was becoming interesting at Amaroo in several different ways.

# CHAPTER EIGHT

Vanessa angled her face slightly to see Bren's profile as, intent on getting the single engine Cessna airborne, the dials on the plane's panel and the wheel had his undivided attention. She had spent half of her six weeks in England analysing how they'd parted, friendly on the surface, but with an undercurrent of tension between them, and how that had made her feel. That Curtis had convinced Bren to accept her offer by the following morning was a relief and though they had talked it through, unfortunately, their relationship had remained strained. The Bourton on the Water cottage had sold quickly, the financials being settled while she was in Stratford on Avon.

Before flying out of Kununurra a bank cheque deposited in Bren's bank account had delighted the branch's bank manager, and Bren and Vanessa had celebrated at the Country Club Hotel with a bottle of champagne in the hotel's beer garden.

With the debt off his mind, Vanessa was pleased because Bren became the pleasant, easygoing husband she'd hitherto known him to be. She would never know for sure whether Curtis had been instrumental in returning her husband's nature to normal. Any negative thoughts she had had on the flight home disappeared the moment she and Bren had met at the airport and Bren had given her a beaming smile and a bearish hug. Their love and their marriage were too strong to be permanently strained by financial matters. However, the episode had been a salutary lesson during which she had learned that Bren, lovable as he was, had flaws. But then she rationalised the thought, who didn't, including herself?

She tucked her arm through his as the plane levelled off.

'You must have a good case of jet lag, what with the international flight, then the domestic and a visit by my mother?' he communicated through the mike and headphones, while at the same time, squeezing her hand against his ribs.

'I'm used to flying, and I can usually nod off.' She hadn't this time because she had been concerned as to how things would be when they met. She needn't have worried. Bren had made it clear that he had missed her, even suggesting they stay overnight in Kununurra, but she wanted to get home to Amaroo.

'Get on okay with Mum?' There was a pensive note in his voice as he asked the question.

'There wasn't a lot of time between flights. She met me at the airport and we had coffee.' She smiled as she remembered Hilary Selby's pinched features, trying to appear at ease with someone she didn't care for. 'It was pleasant enough.'

He chuckled as he adjusted the throttle. Over the motor's hum, he commented, 'I bet. Mum can be difficult when she puts her mind to it. Don't worry, in time she'll accept you. It took her ages to accept Lauren's husband 'cause he came from Eastern Europe and had an accent. She and Marc get along famously now.'

'Your mother made it clear that all she wants from me is more grandchildren. Another grand-daughter would be nice, so she intimated.'

His quick glance was followed by a suggestive leer. Briefly, his left hand stroked her inner thigh. 'I think you might need help accomplishing that.'

'I will. We might seriously consider having a baby after I've done the movie in South Australia.'

'I'd forgotten about that.' His tone changed. 'You'll be going away again.'

Vanessa heard his obvious disappointment and her heart skipped a beat. 'It's hard for me too, darling, but Kerri couldn't get me out of every commitment. We had a long talk in Stratford on Avon about future work. She knows I want to space my work out, only two engagements a year. But with regard to the movie, at least the Flinders Rangers are closer than London. The production schedule is for five weeks on location, depending on the weather.'

'Okay. You have to shoot a rifle in the movie, don't you? After you've settled in we'll go down to the creek and I'll teach you how.'

There was a pause before she said, 'I know I should, but I hate guns of any sort.'

Bren shook his head, his tone firm. 'Women who live in the outback should know how to shoot, even if they rarely have to use a firearm.'

'Why?'

'Remember the snake at Exeter Falls? There are feral animals — goats, foxes, cats and dingoes out there. It's general policy for outback folks to kill them if they sight them because they damage and kill stock, or eat the grass. They're all considered vermin.'

Vanessa knew he was right, that over the time she'd been at Amaroo, she had learned many things that few women who lived in suburbia needed to know. And that knowing could make the difference between life or death. 'I suppose you're right,' she murmured. Masking her lack of enthusiasm she settled back into the plane's seat and let the hum of the motor loll her into a semi-trance.

It was late afternoon, an hour before sunset. Astride the bike, she watched the distance from the creek bank drop away as she followed Bren and Nova. Kerri and some of her friends would have a good laugh if they saw her on the trail bike. She was trying to stay in the tracks Bren was making through the dirt because she was more cautious than the other two who had years of experience. She was pleased to have mastered the bike, though she preferred a horse. Even so, she languished five metres behind the others. The station's dogs and Sandy, who'd come for the run, had bounded off and were in front of her too.

The land, the people who lived in the Kimberley, the cattle too, were waiting for the wet. Everything that could droop did — leaves, branches. The grass was flat and sparse because the stock had eaten it down to ground level and the creek, which had been full on her arrival, was now a muddy trickle with the occasional waterhole. The drop in the level of water exposed the creek's banks and the roots of gums and willow barks, which now resembled oddly shaped ribs as they reached thirstily and in vain for what was needed to sustain them.

Directly above, beyond the tree branches, the sky was clear but over the Barnett Range, purplish grey clouds were gathering. They were heavy with the promise of rain but, with the humidity still close to one hundred per cent, rain wasn't likely today ... maybe tomorrow.

Bren and Nova were waiting for her. The Winchester 30/30 lever action rifle was in Bren's right hand. Last night he had spent an hour briefing her on the rifle, showing her how to clean it, as well as how to load bullets into the chamber. Still, familiarity had not bred ease regarding the weapon though she secretly admitted that it made sense to know how to use it.

'Nova's going to set up several targets on the other side of the creek, about fifteen metres away,' Bren said.

Vanessa watched Nova clamber down the bank and head for the other side of the narrow creek. 'Perhaps I should aim at a tree. I might be able to hit something that big.'

'You might, but the tree wouldn't appreciate it.' He passed her a box of bullets. 'Load the chamber, as I showed you to.'

In her nervousness, Vanessa fumbled and two shiny bullets fell onto the ground. Eventually she had all of them in place.

Bren came around behind her and showed her where to place the butt of the rifle, against the inside hollow of her shoulder. He put a folded piece of cloth behind the butt, explaining as he did, 'To protect you from being bruised. The rifle weighs less than eight kilos but it has a strong kickback for a woman.'

'Thanks.' She tried to quell her nerves. Her legs felt shaky and her mouth had gone dry. The feelings were as bad as the first on-stage entry of a new performance.

'Okay, Nova and the dogs are back. Sight one of the targets, close your left eye, like I told you. Now, squeeze the trigger, do it slowly . . .'

Bang! Vanessa didn't know which was worse — the noise the rifle's discharge made or how it kicked against her shoulder.

A previously silent flock of little corellas squawked with fright and outrage then took to the sky. Sandy, sitting next to the bike, began to howl. A lone kangaroo napping in the shade scrambled to its feet and, indignant at having its rest disturbed, bounded into the scrub.

'Did I hit anything?'

'Which target were you aiming at?' Nova teased, holding back the urge to snigger at Vanessa's ineptitude. She was getting very good at pretending to be her best buddy.

'The biggest, of course, the drum.'

'Nope,' Nova's reply was dry, 'it didn't move.'

'Patience, hon, you've got to "get your eye in". Prime the rifle then empty the chamber at the target. It's going to take a while for you to hit what you aim at.'

'I might still be trying when the wet comes.'

Bren grinned at her frustration. 'It takes patience. Nova can supervise you with an hour's practice on a regular basis till you're competent.'

'Gee, thanks, Bren,' Nova muttered softly, her expression saying as clearly as words what she thought of that idea. 'I was planning to "get out of Dodge" so to speak before the wet arrives, to visit friends in Sydney and Melbourne.'

'That's okay. I'll do it,' Bren said. He glanced towards the ranges, his gaze narrowed against the fading light. 'Pack your bags soon. The wet'll be here in days, if not hours.'

'How do you know that?' Vanessa was curious as to how he could predict the wet's arrival so accurately.

'A feeling. After enough years watching and waiting, you, umm, kind of sense when it's on its way.' He took the rifle off Vanessa and blew on the chamber to cool the mechanism. 'Reload it, hon.'

Vanessa was on her third reload when the dogs started to bark at someone coming down the creek bed. It was Curtis riding hell for leather on his horse. He was waving his hat in the air as if he had something important to tell them. Reining in hard made his horse neigh and snort in protest. He and the horse were soaked — his sandy coloured hair was plastered to his head, his T-shirt to his body.

Nova gave a low whistle. 'Hey, what's this, wet T-shirt time? Darn, we didn't bring any grog.'

'The wet!' Curtis grinned at them. 'It's raining in the foothills, bloody lovely. Buckets and buckets of it.'

'Which means you'll be taking off to see Regan,' Bren remarked astutely.

'Too right. My bag's already packed.'

Vanessa's gaze settled on Nova who was giving Curtis a brief, hungry look. She supposed her brother-in-law was attractive in a lean, wiry way, but his features weren't as strongly pronounced as Bren's. Poor woman. Nova had it bad and it was sad that Curtis had no idea how she felt, no idea at all.

'Can I cadge a ride to Darwin with you?' Nova asked.

'Sure, if you can be ready to leave when I am.'

Nova smiled at him, 'Oh, I'll be ready.' She was more than ready for a change. After playing 'little miss nice' to Vanessa, of going out of her way to be friendly and informative, she was somewhat weary of the play-acting. How and why Vanessa did it for a living, she couldn't understand. The Englishwoman was okay, in her own way, and she had gleaned a good deal of interesting information about acting, agents and famous people, but she needed to be somewhere where she could be herself and hang out with her friends, not just Bren's wife.

Bren took the rifle off Vanessa. 'Guess that's it for today.' He glanced towards Curtis and Nova. 'They have other plans.'

Vanessa wasn't sorry the shooting lesson was over and she felt slightly more at ease with the weapon now. She hopped back on the bike, started it, then motioned for Sandy to jump up into her lap. As she rode back to the homestead distant claps of thunder and flashes of forked and sheet lightning in a darkening, northern sky, provided a wonderful sound and light show of what was to come.

Experiencing the wet for the first time gave Vanessa a new perspective on where she lived. Being English, and used to it raining, she marvelled that any piece of land could absorb as much water as Amaroo land did. The tennis court — she, Fran and Nova had scrupulously weeded the court, applied white paint to show the correct lines, and repaired the wire fencing where it had rusted through — lay submerged beneath several centimetres of water and would be unplayable for months.

She shook her head, remembering that two weeks ago they had held a late in the afternoon to evening tennis day. Lauren, Marc and the boys had flown in from Cadogan's Run. The Johns had come from Linford Downs, with Fay and Barry Whitcombe, and it was nice to see them again. It had been a marvellous afternoon and evening culminating in a barbecue and a sing-a-long around a communal camp fire. Nova had been the star performer, accompanying herself on guitar, and even the quiet, laconic Reg had performed a solo on his harmonica.

The depression where the swimming pool was supposed to be had turned into a lake, to the appreciation of local waterfowl and a few wild ducks. Vanessa had read and been told that people in the outback went troppo, slightly mad, during the build-up to and after several weeks of being confined by isolation due to flooding. She soon found out who and how people were affected on Amaroo.

Reg didn't find it hard to relax — he caught up on his reading and listening to his much-prized record collection. Fran coped by working her way through a basket of mending and sewing that built up throughout the year, by reorganising the pantry and doing advance food orders, cooking and freezing. Bren was like a caged animal. Inactivity was anathema to him — he hated it, and with Curtis and Nova away from Amaroo there were too few distractions to occupy him.

Bren's restlessness caused Vanessa to recall what Nova had said on her first day at Amaroo — 'the trick to not getting bored is to keep busy'. She found plenty of tasks to keep herself occupied, including reading and memorising her lines for the forthcoming movie. Having Bren read the other parts helped her to learn her own and to immerse herself in the character of Annie Brompton, the English woman befriended by jillaroo, Sara Jones, and the adventures they had in the movie. 'Annie' wasn't the leading role, but hers was a solid character part and she found herself able to draw from her experiences at Amaroo to give her character depth and individuality. She hoped the director would appreciate her efforts to get into the character's head and indeed to become Annie.

'Don't know how you do it,' Bren complimented after they'd worked the final scene through. 'You've got Annie's part down perfectly, hon.'

'A good grounding at Amaroo has helped that.' She scooped Sandy up into her lap and the dog responded by resting his front paws on her chest and licking her neck. After a while, giggling because his tongue tickled, she said, 'Enough, boy', and ruffled his fur and patted him till he settled.

'You know, if you could get a movie part every year in Australia, you wouldn't have to work in England, Europe or America.'

'True, but actresses have to go where the parts are. Unfortunately, movie roles don't come up often here — the Australian film industry is small. Even so, Kerri — she has many contacts in live theatre, and films — will find work for me in Australia.' She smiled at him. He was getting restless again. 'I'm registered with the Media Entertainment and Arts Alliance — the equivalent of the United Kingdom's Actors Equity and get their quarterly magazine, *Equity*, which details future stage and film projects. Evidently, major cities on the east coast produce quite a few dramatic projects during the course of a year.'

Bren rubbed his thumb and second finger on his left hand together, to imply money, 'Wouldn't pay as well though.'

'No,' she agreed, 'the trade-off would be that I'd be closer to home.'

'I'd like that.'

With the script out of the way, Vanessa watched as he continued to fidget. He got up, walked to the living-room window and looked out. Rain still beat down steadily, if not torrentially, as it had for the last two weeks. Inside the air was musty from the dampness, and the furniture when touched had a sticky feel, and while the air wasn't as steamy as it had been before the wet, a good night's sleep was still hard to come by. No one was working at their usual pace and, therefore, not as tired when they went to bed. Thinking about that — the lack of exercise — gave Vanessa an idea!

She put Sandy on the floor, got up and went to the hi-fi system where she chose a CD and pushed the play button. Classical Spanish guitar music, accompanied by castanets and tambourines, flooded every corner of the room. She pushed the coffee table out of the way, moved one of the leather chairs back to make more space and, barefoot, began to dance a traditional Spanish dance, one her mother had taught her. Hearing the music, Bren turned back to her, grinned with delight and sat on the arm of the sofa to watch. When the music's beat changed to a cha-cha, she sidled over to Bren.

'Time for you to learn how to dance, husband of mine.'

'I'm hopeless,' he tried to get out of it, 'no sense of rhythm.'

'I don't believe that.' Shaking her head made her blond hair sway this way and that as she moved in front of him to the music's beat.

'You know I have two left feet,' he protested.

She ignored him and pulled him upright into the space she had created. 'Practice will change that.'

'You reckon?' His expression was doubtful.

Vanessa smiled confidently. 'I am a very good teacher.' She put his right hand on her shoulder, his other hand on her hip. 'It's easy, just follow me, one two three, stamp, cha cha cha. See, like this.'

After several minutes of stumbling, treading on her feet and becoming increasingly frustrated, Bren growled deep in his throat and muttered, 'I can't do it.'

156

'Bren, you're not hearing the beat. *Listen.*' She grabbed both his hips and began to rock them from side to side with the beat. 'Yes, yes, that's it.'

Her patience paid off. Two minutes later he wasn't stumbling. Another two minutes and he was getting right into it and then ... As his expression relaxed, his gaze ran appreciatively over her gyrating form. He stopped dancing to pull her into his arms, and kissed her long and hard and deep.

'We can find something more interesting to do than dancing ...' he whispered in her ear. Her responsive tinkling laugh sent a ripple of arousal through him. His grip on her tightened.

'And I was beginning to think you'd never cotton on to where this might be leading,' she teased, batting her eyelids coquettishly.

He laughed as he picked her up in his arms and carried her into their bedroom ...

Nova Morrison sat on a bench that afforded her a good view of the Archibald Fountain in Sydney's Hyde Park. She was waiting for someone. More correctly for two someones — Curtis and Regan Selby. At her suggestion they were going to spend the day together. In truth, she would rather have been alone with Curtis but that wasn't possible because of his daughter, so she accepted the alternative knowing she would only receive a percentage of Curtis's attention, not all of it.

She squinted behind her sunglasses as she studied the scene, and waited. Hmmm, just how long had she been waiting for Curtis to notice her as a woman? Her cheeks warmed as she recalled the teenage crush she had had on him. At fourteen, and home on holidays, she had noticed for the first time that he was gorgeous, and masculine, and ... unattainable. By the time she went back to school in Clermond she was in love ... Then he had met Georgia and theirs had been a whirlwind romance. Curtis had married before she'd grown up and she had told herself that was it, that he was out of reach.

But, wonder of wonders, the marriage hadn't lasted. Curtis had fallen out of love with his wife and now he was free again. But ... was he really free, she asked herself? She knew him as well as anyone at Amaroo, enough to be aware of his continuing hostility towards his ex. Rightly so. Georgia was a conniving bitch and she had taken him for a massive emotional and financial ride, after which he had developed — though he kept it hidden under a mantle of diffidence — a chip on his shoulder when it came to women. Look how he felt about Vanessa! She crossed her legs and pulled her short skirt down when an older man in a three piece suit, probably a lawyer or a doctor because he'd come from Macquarie Street, walked by leering at her. Perv!

From the moment Curtis laid eyes on Vanessa, he'd done nothing but find fault with everything she did. She was too beautiful. She was too soft. She'd get bored with Bren and Amaroo. She was role-playing. According to him the list of her shortcomings was endless. Curiously though, his prophecy that the marriage would sour, that Vanessa'd get bored and want to return to England, hadn't come to pass, at least not yet. Who the hell cared? Deep down she didn't. Long ago she had decided to milk Vanessa for all the information the woman was worth and, the funny thing was, Vanessa — who tended to look for the good rather than the bad in people — was being calculatedly cultivated by a woman several years her junior and she didn't know it.

She smiled as she remembered seeing Vanessa work her guts out to fit in, to learn all she could — much to Curtis's ire. The man *she* wanted, had wanted, it seemed forever, didn't like to be proven wrong about anything. Then a thought found its way into her head — if he could be wrong about Vanessa, then wasn't it possible that he'd come round and see her, Nova, as a woman, not just the kid he'd watched grow up.

Nova was not abnormally vain but she knew she could just about take her pick when it came to men. She had a good body, looked fantastic and she was smart, but the only thing she wanted, Curtis — more than recognition and fame as a country and western singer — remained an elusive dream. She sniffed back a tear of frustration. What was the matter with Curtis anyway? Emotionally, he was over Georgia and he wasn't interested in anyone else so what did she have to do to make him see her as the future Mrs Curtis Selby?

Because of her background and living with Fran, the most down-to-earth person she knew, she was practical enough to realise that it was smart to have a long-term backup plan. That was why, as a result of Nova's questions and sly suggesting, Vanessa's agent had asked around and got the name of a contact. While in Sydney she was going to see an agent who specialised in bands and artists who worked the country and western show circuit. As early as tomorrow evening she had an appointment with Anthea Dennison, with the possibility — her heart thumped heavily in her chest — of doing a live audition at a Sydney club.

Thinking about the audition made her restless and she shifted along the bench, seeking some dappled shade. It was her hope that seeing Curtis away from the station's environment, and with her looking spectacular, would create a spark of attraction. Her lips pursed with irritation because she recalled what her stepmother had said before she'd left. Fran had twigged a good while ago that she was in love with Curtis and had remarked in that frank way she had that she didn't think Curtis would reciprocate. What did the old fart know? Bugger all! Her jaw clenched with annoyance and she quickly dismissed Fran's opinion as un-important. She had waited too long to give up when, now, she had her best chance. Somehow she would win his love, no matter what it took!

Through her sunglasses she saw Curtis and his daughter coming towards her and waved a welcome.

Curtis, in jeans, a striped casual shirt, a peaked cap on his head and sporting joggers, looked pretty cool, like a real city bloke. He was holding Regan's hand and she noted that the girl was tall for her age with red hair like Georgia. She hoped the girl's temperament was different to her mother's — that would make the kid easier to like. Still, she would do the right thing and compliment Regan on her height and hair. Girls liked you to notice that they were growing up.

Mentally she reviewed the plan she had devised. First: win over the kid. That was easy if you sounded sincere and gave them plenty of attention. Second: work on the father, let him see that you'd make an ideal stepmother, and be so damned attractive, alluring and pleasant that he wouldn't be able to resist. She knew what not to do because of Fran! She and her stepmother had never hit it off because Fran, in the beginning, had tried too hard. From an early age, Nova had resented Fran taking her birth mother's place, though Lucy Lee, her real mum, had had no difficulty in giving her up because she was 'tainted' with white blood. What had resulted was an overall distrust of Fran's sometimes clumsy attempts to mother her.

'Hello.' Nova bounced up from the bench as they got close. 'Regan, how you've grown.' She winked conspiratorially at the youngster. 'I guess everyone tells you that?'

Regan nodded. She was shy because she didn't remember who Nova was.

'Nova works at Amaroo,' Curtis reminded his daughter. 'She's known you since you were a baby.'

Nova winked again at the girl. 'But I didn't do nappy-changing duty so you don't have to feel embarrassed. I used to play with you and take you for rides on the little grey pony, Peter Pan. Do you remember him?'

Regan smiled politely, 'I do.'

Curtis grinned at his daughter, and the warmth of his smile included Nova as well. 'Any idea as to what we might do today?' he asked Nova.

'Have you been on the Manly ferry?' Nova asked, focussing her attention on Regan.

'No, I've been on the Taronga Zoo ferry on a school excursion but that's all.'

'Why don't we take the ferry to Manly, visit Oceanworld and have lunch on the wharf?' Nova suggested. Having worked in Sydney she was familiar with several tourist-type places.

'Sounds great.' Curtis glanced towards Nova, and his expression said a silent thank you. 'We can walk to the ferries at the Quay, it's downhill all the way.'

'Walk! *You?*' Nova queried, punctuating it with a chuckle. Bren and Curtis weren't keen on walking. At Amaroo they rode horses, bikes or flew wherever they had to go.

'You're right,' he admitted his weakness. 'We'll grab a cab.' He threaded his arm through Nova's and still holding Regan's hand, they headed towards Circular Quay.

Nova allowed a smile to curve her well-shaped mouth. The day was starting well and if she had any influence over things, with Curtis being in Sydney for another week, there would be several more days like today.

The night Nova auditioned for Anthea Dennison's Management Agency, Curtis came to the club to watch her perform, and it was his presence more than Anthea's and the gathering of members that made her nervous. Perched on a bar stool, she strummed her borrowed guitar in an elongated arpeggio as she stared into the bright spotlight and sang the opening lyrics of 'I've Never Been To Me'.

Then the desire to and thrill of performing took over. She forgot about Curtis, forgot about the audience and lost herself in the lyrics and melody of the plaintive ballad with flair and an unmistakable, unique style.

Sophisticated week night club crowds weren't always appreciative of artists plying their trade but this audience took to Nova straight away and applauded long and loud enough for her to do an encore. Nova was pleased, as was Curtis and the agent. Afterwards, they sat at a table together.

'You're a natural, Nova. You need to work up a good repertoire, get charts done and have moby backing discs so you can work without live bands. Do that and I'll have you working your tail off in no time at all,' Anthea declared with an accompanying sleek, professional smile.

Overwhelmed by the agent's enthusiasm, Nova began to prevaricate. 'The charts and CD, they cost a lot of money, I suppose?'

'Yes, but they're necessary investments for your future as an entertainer. There's a lot of competition around and you need to be professional, if you want to get regular work,' Anthea responded without hesitation. 'I can help in that respect, give you a few contact names. You should also get a professional to help you organise your repertoire — work out numbers that suit your voice and style, as well as what's popular on the club scene.'

'Do it, Nova,' Curtis encouraged, 'you've too much talent to waste on camp fire sing-a-longs at Amaroo.'

'It's a big step, Curtis. I-I want to think about it.'

'Sure, it is a new world, a new life.' Anthea agreed. The reed slender woman with shoulder length chestnut hair finished her Campari and soda and stood up. 'Don't wait too long. The window of opportunity can close as quickly as it opens.'

Later that night, as she lay in her modestly priced hotel bed, wanting to fall asleep but unable to, Nova did some serious thinking. Anthea had given her a glimpse into a very different life, the world of entertaining, of possible adulation and appreciation but, was it what she really wanted? She thought about Curtis and the years she had waited for and wanted him. If she followed her other dream it was unlikely that he would be a part of it. Damn it, she sighed into the darkness and thumped the pillow for good measure. She wanted both but instinct and commonsense told her that might not be possible. She had to choose one or the other ... Curtis or the music.

In the morning the state of the bed — sheets and covers twisted, pillows askew — was evidence of the restless night she'd had, mentally debating the problem. Just before dawn she made her decision. She cared too much for Curtis and he was more important than a singing career.

# CHAPTER NINE

As soon as the worst of the wet subsided, and the rain eased to a steady downpour which was safe to fly in, by way of giving Vanessa a break, Bren whisked her off in the Cessna to Broome to visit his uncle and family. This year the wet had virtually bypassed Broome but with a supply of water from up north guaranteed, the town wasn't suffering from a water shortage.

The Selby's home was all and more than Vanessa expected it to be. Two storeys high and of palatial dimensions, it had an internal spa room and all rooms were climate controlled. The sculptured outdoor pool and the sub-tropical gardens reflected an Asian influence which wasn't surprising because much of Broome had originally been settled by Malay and Japanese divers and their families late in the nineteenth and the early part of the twentieth century. Vanessa was particularly envious of Diane's garden with its lushness and tall palms, and compared it to the difficulty of keeping a half-decent garden alive at Amaroo.

A few hours after their arrival, Stuart came home. Dressed in shorts, sandals and a singlet top, he looked more like a run-of-the-mill tourist than one of Broome's most prosperous residents. The only give-away that he was a businessman was his expensive crocodile skin attaché case. He gave the case to Ling, the house boy, to deposit in the study as he came in.

As she sat in the spacious living room with its view of sandhills and sea, something in Vanessa's expression must have shown her surprise at the way he was dressed. Stuart prefaced his words with a laugh and said, 'We dress for comfort, rather than to impress. I've been at the pearl farm. It's located in an estuary and it's always bloody warm there.'

After all round greetings, the four gravitated to the pool with its covered cabana and wet bar and were soon joined by the two youngest Selby daughters, Gillian and Anna, who were in their late teens.

As Bren and Stuart organised drinks at the bar, Vanessa, watching them, found herself noting a strong family resemblance. They were about the same height and build, though Bren's hair was brown with a curl to it while Stuart's was sandy coloured, like Curtis's, with distinguishing flecks of silver at the temples. There were other similarities too — their eyes were the same colour and when they smiled, their mouths quirked in a similar manner. Quite remarkable, really, because when she mentally pictured Curtis's features and from photos she had seen of Matthew Selby, Bren bore no close resemblance to his brother or father, but then she shrugged off the observation. Perhaps he was more like Hilary's side of the family.

Bikini clad Gillian and Anna came out of the cabana and dived into the deep end of the pool where they began to horse around, trying to dunk and out-splash each other.

A wave of water sloshed up over the pool and onto Stuart's feet as he carried drinks back to the table. 'Keep the splashing down the other end, girls,' he ordered, his forehead knitting in a disapproving frown.

'Oh, relax, Stuart, they're just having fun,' Diane defended the girls.

His deepening frown was the only outward sign that Stuart had heard her comment. He directed his conversation to Bren as soon as he'd settled. 'So, you got over your financial hiccup at Amaroo?'

'Thanks to Vanessa,' Bren replied with disarming honesty, saluting his wife with his coldie in its insulated holder.

'Is that so?' Stuart glanced speculatively at Bren's wife and when he spoke his voice had an edge to it. 'I wasn't aware that British theatre paid *that* well. I thought stars lived the high life and spent up to their earnings.'

'Don't believe everything you read in women's magazines, and especially not about this star,' Bren said with a chuckle. 'If Vanessa never took to the stage again or did another movie role, her financial position would be, shall we say, comfortable.' He looked at her for confirmation, 'Wouldn't it, hon?'

Vanessa didn't like talking about money and especially not about her money to Stuart Selby even though they were, technically, related. 'I guess so. Kerri's a good financial manager as well as a topnotch theatrical agent. She makes sure my investments do well.'

'I've a couple of ventures on the boil here. Perhaps you'd consider investing some of your much prized British pounds in them?' he asked, continuing to ignore Diane's disapproving glance.

'Sorry, Stuart, Kerri handles all my investments.'

'You could make a killing,' Stuart said, his tone changing to its persuasive best.

'Darling, please, not business,' Diane interrupted smoothly. She shook her head at her husband. 'Sometimes,' her smile towards Bren and Vanessa was apologetic, 'he doesn't know when to switch off. Besides, we've more exciting news to tell you.'

Bren and Vanessa waited expectantly.

'Our eldest daughter, Kim, is going to have a baby.'

'Little Kimmy,' Bren's open palm hit the table with a thud of surprise. 'I don't believe it, she's still just a kid.'

'Some kid. She's five months older than you, Bren. I despaired that she'd ever settle down and produce a family,' Diane, proud grandmother-to-be, advised.

'That's wonderful,' Vanessa said enthusiastically. 'Has Kim been married for long?'

'Four years. She and Tom are very excited about the baby. They work at the pearl farm Stuart has an interest in. Our other married daughter, Traci, is envious — she and her husband, Vance, have been trying for two years to have a baby. You'll meet them and their husbands at dinner tonight. But,' Diana's mouth quirked in a derisive half-smile that didn't quite extend to her eyes, 'I'm not sure Stuart is as thrilled as I am by the news.'

'I'm too young to be a grandfather,' he said gruffly, pouting. 'Walking a pram around town will spoil my image.'

'And what precisely is your ... image?' Vanessa asked tongue-in-cheek though she thought she had a good idea of what *he* believed it to be.

Diane supplied the answer before Stuart could speak. 'Oh, you know, the usual wealthy man-about-town image; the successful businessman who, when he thinks he can get away with it, tries to live the life of a bachelor half his age.'

Vanessa would have had to be slow-witted not to pick up Diane's undertone of rancour. She and Bren exchanged glances after which she made a mental note to discuss this new insight when they were alone. Apparently, and if she hadn't misinterpreted Diane's tone and expression, Bren's uncle and his wife were not as content in their 'Garden of Eden' existence as they purported to be. She was getting bad vibes — a barely subdued passive aggression from Stuart and thinly veiled tolerance from Diane who, with her tight-lipped expression, appeared to be not happy.

'That's bloody nonsense and you know it, Di,' Stuart remonstrated, his tone tense. He threw back his head and downed the remains of his drink in one long gulp. 'Anyone want another?'

'I will,' Bren said, hoping to break the edge of tension at the table.

'Soda water for me,' said Vanessa. As Stuart moved towards the bar she looked at Diane and asked, 'So, when is Kim's baby due?'

■　■　■

Later, in the professionally decorated guest bedroom with its own roomy bathroom which overlooked the pool and distant sandhills leading to Roebuck Bay, Vanessa subtly pressed Bren for information on the state of his uncle's marriage.

'It ... was a little awkward down by the pool,' she began as she applied her make-up, talking to him through the bathroom's open doorway. 'I had no idea that Stuart and Diane were, well ...' she paused, let the words hang in the air for a moment or two. 'They seemed happy enough in Darwin.'

Bren shrugged his shoulders. He was naked apart from a towel around his waist, and was waiting for her to leave the bathroom so he could take a shower. 'They've been like that for years. One day they're fine, the next they're snapping and sniping at each other like dogs. Curtis reckons ...' He stopped, suddenly distracted when she emerged from the bathroom, ready for dinner. She was wearing a shoestring strap black and white patterned frock that showed a tantalising length of shapely legs, accentuated by her high heeled sandals. 'You look gorgeous.'

'Thank you, kind sir,' she gave him a smile, 'and what does Curtis reckon ...?'

'Oh, yeah. He's of the opinion that their problems began a long time ago. They had to get married, if you know what I mean, and they had Kim and Traci pretty quickly and years later, Gillian and Anna. Stuart, well, frankly, my uncle considers himself something of a ladies man, which Diane does not appreciate. Over the years there have been whisperings of affairs all over the place — that

Stuart, supposedly, has a woman in every capital city!' He wriggled his eyebrows suggestively. 'Curtis believes Diane's stayed with him because of the girls. They all have a nice lifestyle here and, I guess, so long as Stuart's discreet about his extra-curricular activities, she chooses to turn a blind eye to his womanising.'

'Sounds a touch despicable to me,' Vanessa's tone was honest. 'Diane seems to be a nice person. She deserves better, don't you think?'

Bren shrugged again. 'Dunno, I try not to get involved with it.'

Oddly, Bren's disclosure about the state of his uncle's marriage should have satisfied her as to her feeling of being uncomfortable with his uncle, but it didn't. The fact that he was a womaniser was interesting but, in today's semi-promiscuous society, not unusual. No, there was ... something else, something she couldn't tie down to anything specific. A certain wariness towards him remained. When she'd been young her mother had said to always trust her instincts, that they wouldn't let her down and to date they hadn't. Around Stuart Selby, it would be wise to remember that.

During their four-day visit, she saw little of Bren because Stuart monopolised his time. Diane and her daughters went out of their way to make sure that Vanessa enjoyed her stay in Broome. While Bren and Stuart went golfing, to the pearl farm and did some deep-sea fishing in Stuart's boat, the women showed her the area. That included a trip to Stuart's pearl farming interest, to Cable Beach, where she rode a camel and later, to Malcolm Douglas's

Crocodile Park. In town she was given a behind-the-scenes look at, and instruction from no less than one of the directors of the fabulous Paspaley Pearling Company, the largest and most profitable pearling company in Broome.

'You should come over for *Shinju Matsuri*, the Festival of the Pearl. It's celebrated in August,' Diane said as they sipped cool drinks at an outdoor street cafe in Napier Terrace.

'It's the highlight of our year,' dark-haired Kim advised. 'We give thanks for the pearl harvest with a parade, and there's traditional Japanese ceremonies and fireworks.'

Vanessa smiled. She was learning so much about the country she had adopted as her own, finding it more diverse than she'd believed possible. 'I'd like to see that.'

'If you can tear Bren, or Curtis, away from Amaroo — they're usually busy at that time of year,' Diane said.

Vanessa looked up and down the street. It was a mixture of new and not so new buildings, the sign of a town in transition. Not overly affluent, but certainly moving forward. Young families, casually dressed tourists, four-wheel-drive vehicles, souvenir shops, organised tour shop-fronts too, permeated the streetscape together with tubs of bougainvilleas — which flowered practically all year round — in a riot of colours, from pale apricot to deep burgundy.

'I'll find a way.' There was determination in her voice. Besides, she had a plan — she intended to learn how to fly the chopper and if Bren couldn't bring her, she hoped that by then she would have her own licence and the expertise to fly herself to Broome. 'And we'll want to come and see your baby.' She smiled at Kim, to whom she had taken an instant liking. 'Two good excuses, no, reasons, to come, if you ask me . . .'

When the wet ended, for the first time in her life, Vanessa saw a wondrous transition in the land. Gumbledon Creek had overflowed its banks in several places and would remain a raging, uncrossable torrent for weeks. As ground water evaporated or was absorbed into the earth, shoots, then blades of fine green grass began to sprout. Certain wildflowers, bloomed on hitherto uninteresting shrubs and bushes, and a variety of gums sprouted shiny new leaves. The garden at the front of the homestead, which mostly consisted of a selection of native flora, brought forth a rainbow of colours that would blaze only once a year.

It took another week of unrelenting sunshine before the ground was solid enough for Vanessa and Nova to ride into the foothills — the first time in almost three months — to witness the rejuvenation of nature.

'I'm going to miss this when I go to South Australia,' Vanessa said wistfully. Tomorrow she was leaving to take up her movie role which was being shot in the Flinders Ranges.

They were giving their horses a rest, having dismounted and found a group of largish boulders next to the trail to sit on. The trail led to the Exeter Waterfall but they couldn't get close enough to see it because the fall was producing such an abundance of water that the usually dry creek that ran through the gorge had more than a metre-high flow racing through it.

'Be grateful,' Nova replied, 'if you stick around here, Bren will have you herding cattle from one end of the property to the other. We have to cut a third of the mature stock out for export. It'll be hard yakka here for a month or more.'

'Oh, I'll miss all the hard work,' Vanessa shot back with a pleased-as-punch grin. 'Acting is hard work too, you know,' she added after a moment's reflection. 'I know that what you see on the screen makes it look easy, but getting the desired result can be and often is tedious work.'

'I've always been fascinated by how they do films,' Nova admitted as she picked up a stick and began to draw patterns in the earth. 'Which do you prefer, movies or live theatre?'

'Live theatre. I think it's what I do best. Every performance becomes a little different because of how you feel at the time, and how each audience — which is also different — responds. That keeps it fresh for me. Some actors get bored doing the same lines night after night. I don't because it's my job not to.' Vanessa flashed her a speculative look and adroitly changed the subject. 'What about yourself, your career? You could have one, you know.'

Nova glanced at her then her gaze skittered away to the creek. 'I'm still considering it. Dad says I should give it a go but ...' she stopped, thought, then said, 'it would be a very different world to here. I'm comfortable with this place.'

'Sometimes you have to get out of your comfort zone to get what you really want. We only get one shot at life, Nova, and often just one chance to grasp what's being offered. That's how it worked for me with my acting. I've heard Kerri say that many live entertainers, singers, struggle for years to get what that Sydney manager offered you on a platter.'

'I know, but . . .'

Vanessa, wisely, chose not to pursue the topic. What was the point? She had her suspicions as to what was holding Nova back. Not a lack of belief in her talent or that she could make a success of it, but Curtis and the feelings she had — or thought she had — for him. Ironic, really!

'When I come back from South Australia I'm going to have Bren teach me how to fly the chopper. Do you want to learn too?' Vanessa enquired as she moved along the boulder into a deeper patch of shade.

'Uh huh, I'm happy to be a passenger. You're very brave to want to fly the thing.'

'It's the most efficient mode of transport out here. If I could fly I wouldn't feel or be isolated. I could go to Kununurra, visit Lauren and the boys more often, see Diane in Broome. And Amaroo should have another chopper for mustering — even hiring out to other stations. That's a possibility too.'

'They're pretty expensive.'

'I know, but why can't the property lease one instead of buying one outright?'

Nova looked surprised. 'I don't think Bren or Curtis have thought about doing that.'

'Before I go to Adelaide, they'll be more than thinking about it. If I'm going to fly I want a new or near new chopper — even if I have to pay for it myself.'

'Good luck with that. Bren, Dad and Curtis had to do a lot of study, theory and practical, and it costs. Over thirty thousand dollars, so I've heard. Dad reckons the station has to be able to justify such a cost otherwise it isn't economical.' There were times, Nova thought, when Vanessa's self-assurance irritated her. She always knew what she wanted and how she was going to get it, so much so that, occasionally, by comparison Nova felt inadequate. And she resented being made to feel that way, yes, definitely.

'That much?' Vanessa looked thoughtful. 'I didn't realise ... but I did think there would be study involved. A pilot's licence is a pretty responsible thing to have.'

'Of course, it can work out okay financially, once you get a licence. Curtis is a licensed instructor — he did that when he was younger and working on a station in the Northern Territory for a while. When he was there he used to hire out to do sky mustering for a couple of smaller stations around Tennant Creek. Dad says sky mustering is more cost effective than putting on several stockmen for a muster.' Nova grinned. 'But you know Bren. He can be a tight-arse when he wants to,' Nova said frankly. She stood up. 'Come on, we'll go out to Spring Valley. It's very pretty there after the wet.'

Still smiling at Nova's remark about Bren, Vanessa nodded. 'Lead the way.'

That same evening over dinner, Vanessa brought up the subject of her learning to fly and leasing a newer chopper. Much debate flew between Reg and Curtis, and Bren and Warren, the stockman, as to the merits and demerits. Then Bren brought the discussion to a close, he thought, by declaring that a lack of funds stopped Amaroo from making any such outlay until the loan from Vanessa was paid back.

'I can pay for the cost of the licence and, you know, routine test flights, medicals, and any qualified special instructor's fees, and fund a lease for two years with what I'll earn from the *Heart of the Outback* movie,' Vanessa countered.

The kitchen became startlingly quiet for thirty seconds or so.

Vanessa watched the men stare at each other, shaking their heads. 'Why not? Another chopper would be an asset to the station. Wouldn't it pay for itself, say, over a five-year period?'

'It might,' Curtis admitted, grudgingly.

'On an annual basis, it should cut casual labour costs too,' Reg said, scratching the stubble on his chin as he thought more deeply about it.

'Amaroo's a big station. Wouldn't using two choppers instead of one to muster stock be quicker and more effective?' Vanessa persisted.

'Perhaps, but ...' Though Bren lowered his voice everyone at the table could hear what he said. 'What you earn in your acting career is *your* money. I don't expect you to invest your earnings in Amaroo.'

Vanessa turned her head towards him, a certain light — people at the table knew it was the gleam of battle — flicked in her brown eyes. 'I know, but what if I want to? Am I going to be denied the opportunity to improve the situation here because I'm not a born and bred Selby?'

'That's not it,' Bren came back defensively, his expression showing that he wasn't pleased with the way the conversation was going, especially in front of their employees.

All at once Vanessa didn't care. She wanted everyone to know how she felt and that when she came up with a good idea, that idea shouldn't be put aside lightly. 'Isn't it? I can afford to do it, Bren. I want to be a real part of Amaroo, do the things Nova does — branding, mustering, fencing.' She glanced meaningfully at Curtis. 'I'll even tackle castrating the weaners. I don't want to be known around the Kimberley as,' her English accent changed to something that resembled the way Queen Elizabeth might speak, 'Vanessa Selby, oh, you know, the actress who queens it around Amaroo Downs in between acting jobs.' Her voice normalised. 'I want to be known as Vanessa Selby, a true-blue outback woman.'

Curtis couldn't help chuckling with amusement at the way she'd put it, which earned a scathing glance from Bren.

Reg thumped the table with his open hand and said to Bren, 'By George, I'm glad she's your wife and not mine,' he grinned conspiratorially at Fran, 'she's got too much ummm . . . spirit for me.'

Vanessa silenced the head stockman with a stormy look. 'I'm serious. And the sooner all of you take me seriously, the better.'

'I think she means it,' Curtis said to Bren and anyone else who might be interested.

'Bloody right, she does,' Nova affirmed, keeping the sourness out of her voice. Jealousy and envy were emotions foreign to Nova but Vanessa in full cry, while interesting to see, was also annoying. She wanted to be like her, in control, confident and successful, but at the same time — she'd been noticing the feeling more often of late — close and prolonged proximity to the mistress of Amaroo was making her grind her teeth with frustration.

'We can talk about it, learning to fly the chopper, when you come back from Adelaide,' Bren's tone was soothing, his change in demeanour meant to placate.

Vanessa would not be put off. 'No, I want a decision on it tonight.' She turned her attention to Curtis. 'You're the whiz in the family. I'm sure you can get some figures and do one of those cost benefit thingies you love to do.'

Curtis glanced at Bren who, after a sigh, gave an assenting nod. 'Okay, I'll get on to it after dinner.'

By the time Bren and Vanessa went to bed and made love, Vanessa had what she wanted — an agreement that she should learn to fly, and that they'd lease a Robinson 44 helicopter for two years — as well as a promise from Bren that he would give her some preliminary flying lessons.

On location in Adelaide to shoot *Heart of the Outback*, Vanessa stood in the open doorway of the trailer she shared with another female actress, letting the air conditioner cool the back of her body. She was aware that a percentage of the coolness was slipping out around her to merge with the outdoor heat, but for the moment, being blissfully cool, she didn't care. This was the last day of on-location shooting and inside she battled with a mixture of regret and elation. Regret that the shooting of the movie was over because she had enjoyed doing the role and working with the crew and the talented, new director, Ross Jaxson, and because she had a sense of pride as to how the movie was turning out. Reports from the movie's editor on the dailys were positive and her part in the movie was almost done, except for the final scene. The elation part came because Bren was coming to Adelaide to fly her home and she had missed him dreadfully.

Curtis Selby, his brightly coloured visitor's badge pinned to his T-shirt, stood on the periphery of the camera crew and other people who made up the production cast, watching Vanessa. Together with the star who played the leading role of Sara in *Heart of the Outback*, and the hero, she was about to play the final scene — they were saying goodbye to Vanessa's character, Annie, who was returning to England.

It was the fifth take and Curtis had expected to be bored by now but, curiously, he found the film-making process interesting and was staggered by the number of people who worked at different levels to make a scene work. But mostly what captured and held his interest was Vanessa's performance as Annie Brompton. How she managed to do it, he had no idea, but every time she played the scene she brought a new vitality and believability to her lines and expressions though she had done them several times before.

A spark of admiration for her ability began to force its way through the impenetrable wall Curtis had erected in regard to her. Since she had come to Amaroo he had tried to maintain his dislike of Vanessa, silently belittling her efforts to assimilate to station life, believing it was an act to impress Bren and others. However, as much as he might like to continue that line of thought, he couldn't any longer. Unconsciously, because he knew she didn't care much for him either, she was whittling away and dismantling every reason he thought he had to dislike and distrust her.

When the director called, 'Print that,' everyone cheered and the cameras and work ground to a halt. Curtis moved forward to catch Vanessa's attention.

'Curtis? What are you doing here? Where's Bren?'

'You ... you were great,' Curtis said with a lopsided, can't-we-be-friends grin. 'Bren's okay, but he had an accident, that's why I've come.'

'What? What's happened?'

He watched her eyes darken, her features tighten with concern. 'He's all right,' he stressed as, taking her elbow he moved her towards the edge of the crowd. 'He had a fall. Tripped over Sandy in the dark, in the living room. He's torn ligaments in his left ankle. Can't walk well and he's cranky as hell 'cause it hurts, a lot.'

'Don't go overboard with the sympathy, Curtis,' Vanessa gave him a mild rebuke. 'When did this happen?'

He shrugged a shoulder at her. 'A few days ago. I thought he'd broken a bone, maybe several bones, so I flew him to the hospital in Kununurra. They x-rayed him and diagnosed it as soft tissue damage. He'll limp for weeks.'

'Poor Bren . . .'

Something jolted inside his chest. What was it? A response to her tone, so soft, so concerned. Hmmm, it must be nice to know that someone cares about you so much. He'd once thought Georgia felt that way about him. Now, well, all he had was Regan.

'You should have let me know,' she remonstrated, but in a less outraged tone as they walked towards the trailer.

'Fran and I wanted to but Bren said no. He didn't want you to get upset, in case it affected your acting.'

'How sweet of him, but if anything similar happens in the future, Curtis, I want to know. Straight away, okay?'

'Sure, if that's what you want,' he agreed readily enough. 'When will you be ready to leave?'

'I'm packed. My bags are in the trailer, but first I have to change and take clothes back to wardrobe.'

'I've hired a car for the day, to take us back to Adelaide, and booked overnight accommodation near the airport. If you haven't got anything else you want to do in town we can fly home first thing in the morning.'

'In . . .?' she arched an eyebrow.

He smiled, understanding the question perfectly, 'In the almost new, only six-months-old Robinson. You can have your first lesson if you want to, on the way back. We'll stop once to refuel.'

Vanessa's eyes lit up. 'I can? But I thought Bren . . .'

'With his ankle, he won't be up to teaching you for a few weeks. Besides, I'm the one with the instructor's licence, but, if you want to you can wait till he's one hundred per cent again.' He stopped, waiting to see if she'd take the initiative.

Suddenly she remembered what Nova had said on her first day at Amaroo — that Curtis would make a better chopper pilot instructor than Bren because he was more patient. By now she knew her husband well enough to know that patience was not one of Bren's virtues, and that they'd most likely have many heated 'discussions' if he instructed her.

'Are you saying that you're prepared to teach me to fly?' she asked straight out, because straight talking was something Curtis appeared to prefer.

The question jolted him into a momentary silence. Was he? Did he want to be bothered? Would they fight? She had a quick fuse temper and oddly, around her, his own patience was, at times, in short supply. Then came the careless shrug, which wasn't careless at all, but more of a mannerism. 'Why not, I have more flying hours up than Bren.'

'Great.' She took his odd answer as a yes. Curtis was a strange man in many ways but if Nova thought the sun and moon shone out of him, she guessed there must be finer points to him that, so far, she had missed. 'Give me half an hour to say my goodbyes, change, and get this goop off my face then we'll go.'

'Isn't there a party or something happening here?' he asked. 'Don't rush off on my account.'

'I'm not. I'm thinking about Bren. The sooner I get home to him the better.'

He couldn't argue with that and again the niggle of ... What was it? His gut tightened inexplicably. Was it admiration for her or envy towards his brother for having a beautiful, caring wife? Damn it, he didn't know, but whatever it was it made him feel somehow ... out of sorts.

# CHAPTER TEN

It took months of lessons twice a week, and a lot of study done via correspondence, during which Vanessa notched up the legally required number of flying hours, before Curtis decreed her competent to sit for her pilot's licence. Initially, and to her irritation, he insisted she not only know how to fly the chopper, but that she be able to do routine maintenance on it as well. This had resulted in a fair share of broken nails, grease deposits around her quicks and many bruises and several small abrasions — due to stubborn tools and an uncooperative engine. Still, now she could do elementary mechanical work on the motor, should she ever have to, and she understood why the chopper engine and the rotor blades worked the way they did.

Bren, at present leaning against a workbench near the hangar's entrance, watched Curtis put Vanessa through the normal safety checks before they flew to Kununurra where she would do her test. He was proud of what she had achieved in the time she'd been at Amaroo. There wasn't a task she wasn't prepared to tackle and master, some — like branding and castrating the weaners — he knew she found distasteful. But she'd gritted her teeth and done them because they had to be done, and because she was determined to prove to all and sundry that she was up to doing just about anything.

His gaze moved to Curtis and he was barely able to suppress a smug, I told-you-so grin. His brother, known for his seriousness, rarely found reason to complain about Vanessa these days. Not that he heaped praise her way though. He simply didn't voice many negatives which meant, in his book, that she was doing most things right.

Vanessa got down from the cockpit and came towards Bren for a good luck hug, saying, 'We'll be gone most of the day, I expect.'

'Why's that?' Curtis queried.

Without looking at her brother-in-law she answered him. 'I want to do some shopping while I'm there.'

'Don't hurry back on my account,' Bren said. 'Stuart rang a while ago. He's just taken delivery of a twelve metre, six-berth cabin cruiser and I'm flying the Cessna to Broome to see it. He wants to give it a shake-down run, see how it performs, and we'll do some deep-water fishing.' He purposely didn't look at Vanessa as he added, 'I won't be back for a few days.'

'Have you forgotten that we planned to start the winter muster tomorrow?' Curtis reminded him, not bothering to hide his annoyance.

'Start it without me. I'll be back by the end of the week, in time to help you load the stock into the transports.'

'Without you we'll be shorthanded.'

'No you won't. Vanessa will help out on the ground. Won't you, hon?' She nodded that she would. 'We decided that she has enough experience now to work the mob.'

Vanessa, slightly gobsmacked by the news Bren had just delivered, that he was taking off for Broome and wouldn't be coming with them to Kununurra or on the muster, hid her hurt as she said to Curtis, 'You and Reg can fly the choppers, chase the strays. Nova, Warren, Tony and I will move the mob.'

Curtis, tight-lipped, nodded. 'Fine. I see that the two of you have everything worked out.'

'As Nova would say, bro, "it's cool. It'll work out".' Bren glanced at his watch. He only wore it when he was going away from Amaroo. 'You'd better get airborne if you want to beat the mid-morning turbulence.' He kissed Vanessa. 'Good luck, hon. Radio me after you've passed the test.'

'I wish I had your confidence that I'll be passing it.' He didn't even notice that her tone was cool, her expression stony-faced. He was already looking forward to being with his uncle and on his new boat.

'You'll do just great,' Bren assured her. He looked at his scowling brother. 'Won't she?'

'I wouldn't let her take the test if she wasn't ready to solo,' Curtis replied dourly. He moved towards the chopper and got in on the passenger's side, saying to Vanessa as he belted up. 'You might as well fly us there.'

'All the way?' She got in and belted up too.

'Sure. If you're going to fly the Kimberley and beyond you'll need stamina for distance flying. Your test isn't till midday, which gives you time to shop and to rest up. Start her up.'

Vanessa pressed the starter button and the overhead rotors began to whirl as the engine fired. When the revs were high enough, she manoeuvred the joy stick and the chopper rose, leaving in its wake a flurry of fine red dust. Once airborne, she executed a half turn to bring the nose around and slightly down, checked the direction of the compass and headed north-east.

Diane Selby answered the phone when it rang.

'Diane, it's Vanessa. Is Bren there?'

'You've missed him and Stuart by half an hour. They've gone off on the boat, like kids with a new toy.'

'Oh . . .'

'Something wrong?'

'No, I said I'd let Bren know I passed the pilot's test. I thought he'd still be there.'

'That's wonderful, Vanessa. Congratulations. I'll radio him if you like.'

'Can't I talk to him?' Speaking into the receiver at the pay phone in the restaurant's foyer, she hid her disappointment. Out of the corner of her eye she saw Curtis at the table, drumming his fingers on the tablecloth.

'The boat's out of range but I'll be able to contact it on the ship-to-shore wave length tonight. Stuart said we should take it in turns to call each other after they anchor for the night.'

Vanessa suppressed the urge to sigh. 'Then that will have to do. Please tell him for me.' A percentage of the delight at having passed with flying colours began to evaporate. She had so wanted to tell Bren personally. But, as she glanced at Curtis again, the thought came to her that it was due to his patience and skill that she'd done so well, not her husband's! *Oh*, almost immediately she banished the disloyal thought as she heard Diane say . . .

'Be sure I will, Vanessa. And now that you can solo I'll expect a personal visit soon. Kim and Tom are dying to show off baby Justine.'

'Of course. As soon as the muster's over. Bye.' Vanessa replaced the phone's receiver in its cradle and took a moment to compose herself, and to put aside her disappointment, after which she made her way back to the table.

As she sat opposite Curtis, she said brightly. 'Let's have a slap-up, best on the menu meal to celebrate my success.'

'Why not? I've already ordered champagne,' Curtis advised as he unfolded the cloth serviette.

'Should we be drinking if we have to fly home before dark?'

'You can drink. I'll just have a sip, make the congratulatory toast and I'll fly us home. You did very well, Vanessa. What did Bren say?'

She smiled. Praise from Curtis! A doubly memorable day. 'The champagne, it's a grand idea.' Then she confessed. 'I couldn't contact Bren, he's somewhere out of range, with Stuart. Diane's going to tell him for me.'

Then a thought embedded itself in her mind and wouldn't go away. Bren, not Curtis was the one who should be here, sharing her success. He could have delayed taking up Stuart's invitation. *And* he should be here for the entire muster, she added, amazed that she could be thinking such thoughts. She had never considered Bren selfish but his behaviour in this regard was just that. And the more she deliberated over it the more she realised that, increasingly, Stuart Selby was exerting a stronger influence over Bren. They had similar personalities, she acknowledged — though Bren didn't have his uncle's prickly nature — and similar outdoor tastes, such as snorkelling and big-game fishing.

As she made a pretence of studying the menu, Vanessa tried to justify the uncle and nephew's closeness. Was it because Bren missed his father, and in his mind and emotions Stuart had assumed the role of a substitute father figure? Oddly, Curtis didn't feel a similar closeness to his uncle. If anything, her brother-in-law was quite anti-Stuart, resenting his tendency to involve himself in Amaroo's business affairs, and his belittling of the modest improvements being made at Amaroo, especially those suggested by Curtis. She and Curtis didn't see eye to eye on many things, but surprisingly, though neither of them had openly discussed Stuart, they were united in not quite trusting Matthew Selby's younger brother.

To take her mind off the peculiarity and disloyalty of her thoughts she tried to focus on the hotel restaurant's menu. 'What about Lobster Newburg?' It was the most expensive dish on the menu but ... weren't they celebrating? 'Where do they get lobsters around here?'

'They truck in seafood, mostly prawns, from Wyndham on the coast, I think. Wyndham's about one hundred kilometres north. It was once an important seaport with a huge abattoir processing plant. Nowadays most cattle trade around here is shipped live overseas from Derby.' He gave her a penetrating look that seemed to gauge her mood. 'So, it's lobster for two?'

The glint in Vanessa's eyes was nothing if not determined as she smiled at him, and it coincided with the waiter arriving with the champagne.

'Most definitely.'

It was the last day of the muster. Reg and Curtis, using the choppers, had rounded up the strays in the hills and the numbers had swelled to roughly more than a thousand head: a large mob for four people to control on the ground as they drove them towards better pasture. This year the dry period had been excessively dry and on Amaroo good grazing areas were becoming increasingly rare. So much so, that with the wet still months away, they'd soon have to drop bales and salt blocks to sustain the herd. One intention of this muster was to separate a percentage of mature stock, drive them to holding yards then and truck them to Derby to be sold for the best price possible. Trade to the Middle East was down but stable and slowly recovering. They would realise less profit by selling cattle early, but that was preferable to having a percentage starve to death because of lack of feed.

In earlier days Vanessa had thought she'd never get used to the noises the Brahman and Kimberley Shorthorns — the latter were gradually being bred out — made as they were driven. Their mournful lowing never ceased, even when the mob was stationary, but she had become so used to the sounds that they failed to register with her anymore. Neither did the constant red dust kicked up by their hoofs as they ambled along choke her as it first had, because she wore a bandanna to keep the dust out of her mouth and nostrils. She reached into her saddlebag for the flask of water. Staying hydrated in the heat — though it was winter everywhere else in Australia it remained hot in the Kimberley — was essential to one's survival.

For a while, lulled into a semi-stupor by the movement of her horse Runaway, her thoughts wandered to Bren, then to England. It was the month of July and Wimbledon finals time, arguably the best summer month in England. If Londoners were lucky, the weather would be fair, if a little cool. *Cool!* A trickle of sweat slid down her spine. Out here 'cool' was a four letter word that didn't occur very often. Sometimes she daydreamed about being in Antarctica, surrounded by penguins with cool, white-blue ice dominating the terrain as far as the eye could see. She chuckled as she urged Runaway to chase a steer trying to separate from the mob. Kerri would be impressed with the skills she had acquired and she was looking forward to seeing her. She and Yannis were coming to Sydney for the premiere of *Heart of the Outback*.

As she brought the steer back to the fold, she remembered something Nova had said to her. Reg now considered her a 'qualified' jillaroo, since she had assisted in the birth of a Brahman calf whose mother had been having difficulties pushing the overly large calf out. It had been a life and death tussle, and being involved in seeing a new life come into the world, watching the calf stand in the scrub and stumble instinctively towards its mother's nipples had been an experience she would never forget.

Every day she was gaining a deeper insight into what living in the outback, being one with it, was about. And to think she wouldn't have had these experiences had she not met Bren and fallen in love. But ... she was still cross with him for not being contactable after she'd got her pilot's licence. When she had more experience she hoped to participate in the sky mustering. Getting her licence a few days ago had been an important step and, though she didn't like to admit it, Bren had let her down. She wouldn't let his casual behaviour gnaw at her insides when, most of the time, he did everything right.

She screwed the top back on the flask of water and shoved it into one of the two saddlebags which contained items she'd brought on the muster and not carried by the support truck — a change of clothes, underwear, toothpaste, lipstick, comb, soap and toilet paper. God, she'd be first in the shower when they got back to Amaroo, to wash the grime and grit off her body and out of her hair.

'Vanessa ...'

Over the noise of the mob she heard Nova's yell. It made her rein in as she watched Nova gallop towards her. Cattle, spooked by the fast riding, scattered in three different directions. Then she looked past Nova and saw a cloud — a strange, reddish brown, swirling cloud — that had materialised out of nowhere.

Nova pointed to the cloud as she pulled up beside Vanessa. 'It's a dust storm.'

'I didn't think the Kimberley got that sort of thing.'

'We don't get them often, but there's no time to explain the weather pattern or how it occurs. Forget the mob. Ride for cover.' The urgency in her tone was unmistakable. She pointed south. 'Over there. Try to ride out of the storm if you can, and go south, not west. Due west from here, a few kilometres away, there's an escarpment with a sheer drop. Stay away from it. Go due south to where there are rocks and boulders. They'll give you some protection.'

'You're coming too, aren't you?'

Nova shook her head. 'I have to warn Warren. He's driving the truck at the back of the mob and with the dust they kick up he won't see the storm coming.'

'But ... the cattle?' All the work they'd done mustering them! As Vanessa asked the question she was adjusting her bandanna, tightening it around her mouth, and ramming her Akubra down hard on her head.

'Don't worry about them,' Nova said impatiently, 'they'll scatter but the choppers can round them up again. It's more important for us to find cover. Gotta go.' Nova nudged her horse's flanks and changed direction, racing away at full stretch to the back of the mob.

Vanessa took a moment to eye the ominous red cloud. In the space of their conversation, less than a minute, it had moved closer and had begun to look menacing. She had never seen anything like it and deep inside a ripple of fear stiffened her back, making the muscles go rigid. She didn't waste another second. Turning Runaway to the south she began to canter, then she gave the horse its head, moving into a full gallop to cover ground as fast as the sturdy Australian stockhorse would go.

Vanessa rode and rode, hoping she was still heading south, swerving around the occasional gum and clumps of low bushes. Her gaze narrowed to slits as flying particles of red dust caught up with her, stinging her skin from the velocity of the wind that carried them. The wind screamed and squealed like a hundred banshees as it rushed headlong at her, around her and over her.

She couldn't gauge how long she rode Runaway. Time seemed meaningless. It might have been minutes but from the lather gathering on her horse's neck and flanks it was more likely to have been over an hour. As she neared exhaustion, she coughed and choked as the dust storm enveloped them and cut visibility almost to zero. She sighed with relief as she glimpsed a clump of rounded boulders. They were close and might afford her and Runaway some protection.

The next instant, on her left, an updraft of wind blew up and it was so powerful that Runaway shied with fright. Instinct made the horse jerk to a stop, then rear. Unable to adjust to the suddenness of the braking horse, Vanessa was tossed to the ground. Her left shoulder hit the earth with a thud that jarred her torso. The pain was excruciating and she cried out and, instinctively, rolled off her back onto her un-injured side. Oh, no, *I've broken my arm, or my shoulder.* A secondary wave of pain made her shudder then, as it intensified, with a quiet moan she passed out.

A contrite Runaway neighed and lowered her head to inspect the woman who'd ridden her. Animal curiosity caused her muzzle to prod the inert body as the dust storm enveloped them both. She neighed again and pawed the ground as the dust storm thickened. Then, as if sensing that her rider needed protection, Runaway did what horses don't normally do. She got down awkwardly, on all fours, near the unconscious Vanessa, and tucked her head in close, in her own way providing what protection she could with her solid body.

When Vanessa came to, all was quiet. The dust storm had wreaked its havoc and moved on. She found herself covered in red dust, as was Runaway who lay beside her. 'Yuk,' was the most expressive word she could think of. As she moved to sit up a shaft of pain travelled from her shoulder down her left arm. It made her remember the fall. The arm was useless. Tentatively she wiggled her fingers and they responded. Maybe the arm wasn't broken. Protecting the injury as best she could, she sat up and looked around.

She wasn't wearing a watch but she could gauge what time it was because the sun was low in the western sky. It would set in about an hour, she reckoned. She studied the land around her and began to wonder where she was. In a panic, to escape the storm, she had ridden the living daylights out of Runaway. Looking at the horse a wave of guilt rushed through her. The lather on her coat had dried, and clumps of congealed dust hung from it because Vanessa hadn't been able to wipe or shower her down. Continuing to study the land and distant, low hills, she sought to recognise landmarks. Nothing, her heart lurched depressingly, looked familiar. And ... the silence, so absolute it hammered home the fact that she was very much alone.

*Think, don't panic. Yet! What are your options?*

Runaway stirred, stood up and nuzzled her. Vanessa tried to stand but the injured arm and shoulder made that difficult. By grabbing the saddle's stirrup she managed to pull herself upright. With great care, because she felt awkward and lopsided, she climbed to the top of a boulder in the hope that being higher would give her a better view. She prayed to see someone riding towards her, or something she might recognise. Nothing.

Damn! Her shoulder was aching like the devil — the slightest movement set off a wave of intense throbbing that made her cry out in pain. She took her bandanna off, shook it free of dust and, being one-handed, it took her several frustrating minutes to retie the cloth around her neck to form a rough sling into which she put her left arm. It helped, a little. The pain kept coming, especially when she moved so, she reasoned it made sense not to move about too much.

*Face it*, the thought found its way into her head, *the light is fading and you are going to be stuck here till morning*. Facing west, she realised that she hadn't ridden due south as Nova had advised her to. Somehow, in the drama of trying to outrun the storm, she had veered off course and headed south-west. That would mean that those at Amaroo would take longer to find her.

Turning full circle on the boulder she then saw how perilously close the escarpment was, the drop being less than three metres away. Vanessa blanched under her tan. That's why Runaway had shied — the updraft from the valley below had warned the horse of danger. Dear God! A sickly feeling came over her as she saw how close she and Runaway had come to going over. By the time she got down from the boulder her legs were trembling with reaction. Taking Runaway's reins, she led the horse five to six metres further away from the edge. Relief, fear, apprehension inside, made her long to scream but what was the point — who would hear her? The situation was bad, but only temporarily, she assured herself. What she had to do was make the best of it. Okay — she tried to perk herself up — get organised before the sun sets.

With easy access to Amaroo's library, housed in Curtis's cottage, Vanessa had read a good deal about the pioneering men and women of Australia, about their privations, failures and successes in settling the less hospitable areas of the country. This had led her to greatly admire the fortitude of the women who'd accompanied their men in earlier times. If those women could do it tough for years, some even a lifetime, she, who'd never roughed it in the bush alone, could do so overnight . . . Of course she could!

Working one-handed was a handicap and, grunting with the effort it took, she loosened the saddle's girth strap and pulled it off Runaway's back. She used the saddle blanket to rub the mare down as best she could, fearing the horse would take a chill overnight if she didn't. Doing that task sapped most of her energy but, soldiering on, she then emptied the contents of her saddlebags. Not much joy there, and no food. There was some water in her flask, but it was less than a third full. No matches to light a fire either because that was Warren's area of expertise. All of which meant that she was going to be bloody cold, all night. Daytime temperatures in July could reach a pleasant thirty to thirty-five degrees centigrade, with low humidity, but inland, at night, the mercury could fall to almost zero because, technically, it was winter.

As she looked up at a darkening, cloud-scattered sky, she knew that at least she wouldn't get wet. Some consolation, she supposed. Moving awkwardly, gritting her teeth against the pain, she put on the extra clothes lying on the ground — a T-shirt and a lightweight zip-up jacket. She could only get one arm in her jacket and had to drape the other side over her left shoulder. It wasn't going to be very warm because it was cotton with a light interlock lining. Her gaze fell upon Runaway's saddle blanket. Her nose wrinkled at how it would smell but, she sighed, it was better than nothing.

Tether Runaway, she reminded herself. Taking the reins she roped them over a low bush, under which lay a patch of yellow grass for the horse to feed on. She didn't want the mare to wander off during the night because she was her only company. As twilight darkened the area around the boulders she looked at Runaway. She made a miserable picture. Parts of her coat remained covered in dollops of red dust — almost as if she had chickenpox. Vanessa giggled. The thought was ridiculous and it made her wonder if she was becoming delirious. She could well imagine Curtis's expression if she said that out loud — about the chickenpox. There were times when he wasn't blessed with a great sense of humour, not like Bren.

Bren ... Thinking about him made her remember their talks about being lost in the bush. He had, quite cheerily, told her several harrowing stories. Don't think about that now, she thought. She would remember the survival rules he had drummed into her. Like staying put, conserving energy and water, and in the day, finding and staying in the shade. Her stomach grumbled and her mouth watered at the thought of the meal Warren had promised to serve that night. A rich beef stew and ... there would be fresh damper and golden syrup to pour over it.

She stared at the setting sun, a ball of red fire that dulled the clear blue sky and tinted the clouds a soft, baby pink. Most days she tried to watch the sunset, if time and work allowed, because more often than not they were so special, as was tonight's sunset. Once the ball of fire slipped over the horizon, twilight didn't linger. One minute towards the west came a final splutter of light, then a blackness so dark that Vanessa couldn't distinguish her hand in front of her face, other than by feeling her breath exhaling onto it. It was going to be a very long night

. . . but she expected a half moon to rise later on. She wouldn't feel so alone then, she told herself, with the moonlight shining down.

Dear God, but she was tired. She ached all over from the fall and it was worse, damned near unbearable, around her shoulder. In the dark she fumbled around until she found the blanket, then she curled her body into a ball. Finding a comfortable position took ages, but when she did she pulled the blanket over her, closed her eyes and willed sleep to overtake her.

Nova, Warren and Tony sat disconsolately around the camp fire staring, trance-like, into its warming glow. They had managed to locate each other before sunset and make camp. Vanessa not being there had them all concerned.

'She's a smart lady, she'll be all right,' Warren said. An hour ago he had thrown ingredients — diced potatoes, carrots and sun-dried tomatoes, dried bacon pieces, thick, juicy cuts of beef, and two cans of beans, then added water — into a large skillet over the open flame to make the stew. Freshly rolled damper, wrapped in silver foil was cooking in the outer embers of the fire and water was bubbling in the billy.

'When the moon comes up, one of us has to drive back to Amaroo and tell Curtis,' Nova, who'd automatically taken charge, decreed gloomily.

Why hadn't she told Vanessa to follow her when she'd ridden off to warn Tony? Vanessa being lost out in the bush wasn't going to show her in a good light. Those who lived at Amaroo had expectations of her, especially Curtis. Bloody Vanessa, she cursed her roundly and silently, because she knew she would receive everyone's censure for Bren's wife being lost. Damn it all to hell, this was something she didn't need, now or ever.

'That'll take all night. Why not wait till morning? We might pick up her trail before we have to alarm everyone,' Tony suggested.

'What if we don't?' she threw back. 'If Amaroo doesn't know till half way through the morning there'll be fewer daylight hours for the choppers to search. It's better that they know tonight.'

'It's my fault, I suppose. I'm the fool who lost the uhf hand-held, racing to get away from the storm,' Tony admitted. He grimaced as he rubbed his thigh, because the leg he'd broken a while ago ached after a full day in the saddle.

'That was an accident, mate. We were all trying to outrun the storm. No one's gonna point a finger at you for that.' Warren tried to make Tony, who shared the stockman's quarters with him, feel less guilty. 'Could have been any one of us.'

'Reckon Curtis and Bren mightn't see it that way,' Tony muttered, his craggy features glum.

An impatient Nova interrupted their debate. 'That's not important now. We have to concentrate on informing Amaroo, quickly! As I have the best idea as to which way Vanessa went, I'll go back. Agreed?' She looked at both men, one eyebrow raised, waiting for their reply. They both nodded in agreement.

As soon as Warren dished the stew out she tucked into the hot meal. She ate in silence, but all the while she worried about the development with Vanessa. The woman was capable — hadn't she watched her grow and develop new skills since she had come to Amaroo — but being alone in the bush, unsure of what to do, would really test the Englishwoman's fortitude.

# CHAPTER ELEVEN

'Hell's bells, I don't believe it. Stuart and his bloody boat — they're out of hf range,' Curtis told Nova as he sat at the desk in the office. He clicked the microphone off and threw the pencil he'd been doodling with onto the desk's mahogany surface, frustration evident in his gesture. 'Diane said she's been trying to contact Stuart since last night because he didn't call in as usual. She can't raise them and this isn't the first time he's gone off the air. Some problem with the electronics equipment. Damned annoying.'

Nova had driven most of the night and arrived at Amaroo after sunrise to raise the alarm. She looked and was, exhausted. 'Fran can keep trying to contact Bren. It's more important that we get the choppers up and locate Vanessa quickly.' She glanced at him, saw his anger, and her gaze skittered away again. 'Should we ask Simon at Linford Downs to join the search?'

'Good idea and time is of the essence, so they say,' he agreed. 'I'll call Simon now and ask him. Reg can take the older Robinson, I'll take the newer one.' He pulled open a drawer and took out a map of the station's perimeters. 'Let's go over this again. Where do you think she might have gone?'

Nova pointed to where they'd been herding the mob and where the dust storm had blown in. 'I'm coming with you. If she isn't found today ...' Nova began but then hesitated. She didn't want to finish the sentence but she didn't have to — they both knew. Vanessa could be injured, and if that were the case she might be in a bad way physically and mentally if she wasn't found today.

Curtis stared, his glance raking from the top of Nova's head down to her boots. 'Like hell you are. You're done in.' He shook his head firmly. 'You need several hours sleep, Nova, four at least.'

Nova's shoulders slumped forward as she sought to plead. 'But ... '

His words came out as a half growl. 'No buts. The state you're in, you're no good to me or anyone else. Get some sleep. Later, you can relieve Fran and take over the hf.' He saw tears in her eyes and his voice softened as he added, 'You know I'm right.' A muscular arm went around her shoulder and he gave her a brotherly hug. 'Reg and I will find Vanessa and we'll do it today.'

Nova watched him stride out of the homestead's office, and when he was out of sight she collapsed into the desk's chair and, overwrought, burst into tears. Curtis hadn't laid any blame on her, Tony or Warren, but as she'd driven through the night, a sense of guilt regarding Vanessa's disappearance had multiplied, not so much because Bren's wife was unaccounted for, but for what Curtis would think of her. That he would be disappointed in her was something she couldn't bear to think about. What she had done had been done with the best of intentions and in hindsight — a wonderful but useless attribute — she should have had Vanessa ride with her instead of directing her south. Vanessa wasn't like the rest of them, not yet. She didn't know the country as well as others at Amaroo, she lacked experience to survive with bush know-how!

Curtis, when he took the time to analyse what had happened would realise that and apportion some blame for this situation to her. Christ, she didn't need him to think badly of her when she wanted him to fall in love with her. She didn't need that at all.

Bren sat harnessed into the padded, rotating chair at the back of Stuart's boat. They were in deep water, approximately forty kilometres off the coast and roughly level with the town of Derby though they couldn't see it. Stuart's sonar, his 'fish finder', had picked up a school of large fish which possibly included marlin, and they were cruising at a low speed in the middle of them waiting for a bite. He squinted as he stared at the deep blue ocean. The sun had been up for an hour, the swell was smooth, conditions perfect for the kind of fishing they planned to do. Stuart had said that all he had to do was hook one and play the fish till it tired, then haul it into the boat.

He grunted to himself. Stuart made it sound easy but he knew it wasn't. They had gone deep-water fishing when he and Vanessa had been in Broome and he had loved the challenge of it. Real man stuff and very different to herding cattle. He should be feeling guilty for being here, enjoying himself, instead of being on the muster, but he didn't. Sometimes a man needed time off, away from the tedium of doing the same chores year in, year out. That was something his uncle understood but he knew Curtis didn't.

At times he envied Stuart's kind of life. A successful businessman and recognised as such, he had so much money he didn't know what to do with it; hence this toy — the twelve metre cruiser with its powerful twin engines, capable of taking the six-berther wherever he chose to direct it. Thinking of boats, and being on the water, made him recall the time he and Vanessa had taken her friend's barge to Oxford. That had been his first experience on the water. It was different to what he was doing now, but, Christ, he had enjoyed it. He smiled as he released several more metres of line, trolling the lure. The best part had been being with Vanessa and them making love for the first time.

*Vanessa.* Where would he be without his clever wife? His grin widened as he thought about what she had achieved since she'd come to live at Amaroo. She was becoming quite the outback woman and relished the challenges that came with living in a rough, inhospitable land. Now she had her chopper licence — she'd passed the test — that would make her more independent. She could visit Lauren and her boys, get to know her sister-in-law better. His wife continued to surprise him with her ability to learn new skills, and she surprised Curtis too! He chuckled under his breath as he thought that. His brother was, grudgingly, amazed at how she'd settled in, even if he remained unwilling to admit that she was doing well.

The index finger of his right hand, lightly touching the line, felt it go taut then the tip of the rod bent downwards. Something had taken his bait and it was big. He braced his feet against the bar bolted to the deck, put there for that purpose, and gave his quarry some slack then he reeled in, a little at a time. Suddenly there was a splash and about forty metres south-west of the stern a fish jumped clear of the water — a blue marlin. It was a bloody beauty.

Stuart came to the stern and put his hand on Bren's shoulder. 'Don't rush. It has more strength than you do. You have to tire it out, play it, reel it in a little at a time.'

'Yeah, I hope I can do that before it tires me out.'

Stuart laughed. 'By the way, the ship to shore's still on the fritz. Bloody thing's probably short-circuited.'

Bren threw him a glance. Stuart was a better than average handyman who could fix most mechanical problems. 'Should we be worried?'

Stuart shrugged his shoulders. 'No, before we left I told Diane where we were going and how long we'd be. She'll be cranky that I didn't call in last night, but she knows that sometimes boats get out of range. We'll have another day here, then put what we catch in the boat's freezer and head back. Okay?'

'Mmm, Curtis will be pissed off. I'll miss the muster.'

Stuart's gaze hardened. 'So what? He can handle things and you need some R and R. Surely he doesn't begrudge you that? There's a lot of pressure running a station the size of Amaroo.'

'True,' Bren was quick to agree. His uncle understood the pressures, much better than Vanessa and Curtis did. He tossed aside the thought of Curtis's annoyance. Vanessa's too. He'd make it up to them both by bringing back a stack of marlin steaks for Fran to do a seafood cook-up. The marlin surged out of the water again and flopped back down, creating a foamy splash. He forgot about Amaroo, forgot about Vanessa, and concentrated on landing his catch.

Shivering almost uncontrollably from the cold — it had seeped into her bones during the night — Vanessa saw the sun rise over a scrubby plain. Her expressive eyes bleak, she watched shadows under low bushes shrink away as the sun rose in a cloudless sky. Weatherwise it was another perfect day. However, as far as she was concerned matters were far from perfect! The night, even after the moon came up, had seemed interminable. The pain in her shoulder ranged from excruciating to almost but not quite bearable, and the foreignness of being outdoors with no camp fire, the chill as the temperature dropped dramatically, and the sound of a pack of dingoes howling in the distance, had heightened her sense of aloneness.

Things always appeared worse at night. It made her remember the night in Guy's Hospital in London when doctors had tended to David. That had seemed to take an eternity. But with the sun up now and its warmth defrosting her bones, she felt more optimistic and hopeful that her ordeal would soon be over.

By now *they*, Nova, Warren and Tony, would have assumed she was lost and informed those at the homestead. And, she knew it wasn't the first time Amaroo had had to mount a rescue. Bren had told her about one of Stuart's scrapes. When in his teens, Stuart had had a monumental row with his father and had ridden off into the night, and remained missing for three days. A group of wandering Aborigines found him near Sandy Plains Paddock, the driest area on the property. Horseless, he had two broken ribs, was dehydrated and was going in and out of delirium. The rescue party found him at the Aborigines' camp.

She disliked having anything in common with Stuart, but at the moment her situation was similar. She moistened her lips with her tongue but resisted the urge to reach for the water bottle. Right now though, she would kill for a glass of cold water. She was trying to take just an occasional sip to make the liquid last as long as possible.

Vanessa did her best to glean some comfort from Bren's story about Stuart, that all had ended well, but as the day wore on and the temperature moved into the mid-thirties, her confidence crumbled. She glanced at Runaway who, like her, looked miserable. Her horse wasn't even bothering to forage. She felt guilty about not sharing what water she had but Bren had been very insistent at pointing out that a person's survival was more important in the outback than an animal's. It made sense, but it didn't make her feel any better, nor any less guilty.

By midday all the shade was gone around the boulders and every time she moved a blast of pain darted through her shoulder and down her spine, making her cry out. Not that anyone other than Runaway heard her cries. The horse would raise her head, give a whinny and snort, then become silent again.

Weakened by the injury, lack of food and liquid, Vanessa dozed, woke, moved into a more comfortable position then dozed again. The next time she woke her mouth and throat were so parched she couldn't produce saliva, and her lips were beginning to crack. She should put some lipstick on: her lipstick with its small, attached mirror was the only piece of make-up she'd brought with her. Her right hand touched her cheek — it was hot and, increasingly, she found it hard to concentrate. Is this what it's like to die from dehydration? The thought made the thread of fear deep within her that she would be found too late — she had kept it at bay during the night and for most of the morning — grow disproportionately. Of course she would be found, she reprimanded herself ... soon.

Still, in spite of her attempts to gee herself up, her imagination drifted into overdrive. She had ridden off course so, would they assume she had fallen to her death over the escarpment like the exploring Frenchman, Guy La Salle, had done when he'd been prospecting? She had read an account about La Salle in a compilation of stories and facts, including a compact history of the famous Durack family, and legends and tales about those who came to the Kimberley to make their fortune.

What if they didn't find her? *Get a grip*, she told herself, frowning furiously to reinforce the order.

Curtis, Reg and Nova knew her capabilities as well as her shortcomings. They knew she wasn't equipped to survive alone in the bush, as they were. Bren ... he would be worried sick too. Her earlier irritability towards him disappeared as she thought about her husband. So ... he wasn't perfect, neither was she! She'd been cross because he was with Stuart, someone she had little time for. And ... she wanted him home because they were trying to make a baby and start a family. The frown left her forehead as she forced herself to contemplate how wonderful that would be; a little girl or boy, like Bren, to love and nurture and teach. She was looking forward to motherhood, very much.

After that she tried her standard pep talk routine. In the past it had helped when she was having difficulty adapting to a stage role. *Vanessa, my girl, if you want to be a mother, first, you have to get out of this situation!* And then she posed the question. If a chopper came along could the pilot see her in the scrub? Mmmm! A signal fire would be good, no, it would be excellent. Unfortunately, she had no means to make a fire — no matches and no Girl Guide expertise in that regard. Perhaps ... something to reflect against the sun's light!

Her gaze ran over the saddle, dissecting it inch by inch. Once the metal stirrups had been polished steel but they were now dull and coated with a veneer of surface rust. They'd never reflect the sun's rays. Still, there had to be something she could use. The stinging sensation from her cracked lips helped Vanessa find the answer: her lipstick with the mirror. She rummaged through the up-ended contents from her saddlebag until she found it. She had bought it at Harrods before they'd married because she had been taken by the idea of a lipstick that conveniently had a mirror attached to the top that lifted off. She applied the lipstick then put the top with the mirror attachment into her right hand and rolled it around in her palm, studying it.

The mirror part was small, three centimetres wide by about six centimetres high, oval shaped with a gold metal edging. Experimenting, she positioned the mirror towards the sun and after some adjustment was rewarded by a ray of light reflecting onto a boulder about eight metres away. It would work!

Then she studied the sky, looking so hard that after a while her eye muscles hurt, as she prayed to see a speck that would become an aircraft. Nothing, not even a cloud or a bird flew by. Exhausted, hungry and with her thirst growing, she let a dejected sigh escape. She raised her knees, cradled her head on them with her good arm and, finally, gave way to tears.

Curtis blinked, and blinked again. Behind the sunglasses his eyeballs ached from peering out the chopper's windows. He and Reg, and Simon from Linford Downs, were using the quadrant method of air search. They had been at it for hours, returning to Amaroo only to refuel and grab something to eat before returning to the sky. Hell's bells, where was she? He was considering flying over the escarpment towards Frenchman's Leap, though Nova had told Vanessa to go in the opposite direction. But, after several hours of searching, he knew one thing; his sister-in-law wasn't where she was supposed to be.

Fran and Nova still hadn't made contact with Stuart's boat. Damn his uncle and ... damn Bren too. He should be here. He should always have been at Amaroo instead of running off to play sailor with Stuart. Sometimes his brother's casual attitude to the property from which a small band of people derived a living, made him want to shake some sense into him. Clamping his anger down, he pushed the joystick forward then to the left and flew towards the escarpment.

Knowing they only had a few more hours of daylight left in which to search heightened Curtis's sense of urgency. He sweated profusely inside the chopper's, mostly glass, cabin and it reinforced in him how hot it was in the scrub. Reg and Simon had just reported in — stating they had found no sign of Vanessa but that the mob they'd been herding towards Spring Valley were straggling in that direction because the cattle could smell the limited water in Gumbledon Creek.

Because Vanessa should have been located by now, because Bren hadn't been informed that she was missing, a knot of anxiety was tying up Curtis's stomach muscles. He hated how his gut did that when he got tense. He was always uptight around Georgia but this feeling was different. Somehow, he felt responsible for Bren's wife. Nothing had been said to the effect that he was but instinctively he knew Bren had left her in his care, and the sense of responsibility weighed heavily on him. No-one was to blame for what had occurred, nature and the Kimberley being what they were. Commonsense told him that but knowing in no way eased the growing, anxious feeling inside him. Where the hell was she?

Curtis angled the chopper down into the escarpment where the gums were taller and the growth thicker because the area received more moisture. All of which made spotting anything not naturally there a matter of good luck rather than effective searching. An experienced bushman, he knew how easy it was to disappear without a trace in the Kimberley. He had heard and read many stories about such happenings, and could picture the British tabloid headlines if Vanessa wasn't found: RENOWNED ENGLISH ACTRESS MISSING, PRESUMED DEAD IN THE KIMBERLEY.

Another thought jumped into his head as he stared down at the dense bush. If Bren lost Vanessa, it would just about finish him. His brother had, over many years, exhibited an unwillingness to take things seriously, traits inherited from their maternal grandfather, Bernard Curtis, who had won and lost several fortunes in his lifetime. Marrying Vanessa had gone a long way to curbing that aspect of Bren's personality. However, knowing Bren as he did, that could change if he became unsettled. Then where would Amaroo be? An aggressive, moody Bren was capable of almost anything ... even selling up and doing something else. He shook the disloyal thought away. Bren would never do that, no matter what ...

Rising above the escarpment, he flew along the rim, about thirty-five metres above the ground. An upwards draft made flying tricky, and he kept both hands on the joystick to maintain control as he squinted against the sun's glare for clues to Vanessa's whereabouts. Then, a flash of light bounced off the windscreen, caused by something glinting on the ground. It disappeared then came back again. What was it? Curtis banked to the right for another sweep. There it was again, a speck, something bright and not very big, obviously metal or a mirror. Adrenaline coursed through him. Maybe . . .?

He dropped lower and hovered, trying to locate what was glinting. There, away from the escarpment's edge, on a clump of boulders, flicking on and off as it reflected the sun's rays. *Vanessa.* Hell's bells. She was flashing a piece of metal at him and raising a welcoming arm. Grinning as a wave of relief washed over him, the taut muscles in his stomach began to settle. He scoured the terrain for somewhere to set down and found a reasonable bare patch of ground after which, with more speed than grace, he landed.

Curtis grabbed a full bottle of water and a blanket, exited the cabin and sprinted to the boulders watching, as he ran, Vanessa climb down awkwardly. She collapsed onto her knees in the earth and bowed her head.

'Vanessa!'

She didn't have the energy to look up as Curtis closed the distance between them. It had taken the last reserve of her energy to scale the rocks on hearing the most wonderful sound in the world, the chopper's whirring blades.

'Thank God, you're all right.'

He knelt in front of her, taking in her state. She didn't look good. Beneath the sunburn he knew that her skin would be as pale as a ghost. Her left shoulder was unnaturally lower than the other one, and the bandanna she'd tied around her wrist wasn't doing much of a job supporting the dropped shoulder. She had to be in a lot of pain and he saw that she was when her head came up to look at him. Vanessa couldn't even manage a smile, feeble or otherwise, she was too done in.

He put the bottle of water to her lips, let her have a few sips then took it away. When she tried to get it back he suggested, 'Drink just a little at a time, otherwise you'll puke.'

'So ... thirsty ...' Her tone was faint, thready. 'Can't be sick, there's nothing in my stomach.'

He thought that she could bring up bile but he didn't bother to tell her that. 'You've injured your shoulder. Anything else wrong?'

Vanessa shook her head. Her eyelids drooped with fatigue and her breathing was shallow. Curtis gauged that she might be going into shock. She had kept herself alert for so long, but now she was running on empty. Her shoulder injury was one he was familiar with. Curtis had seen more than one stockman dislocate a shoulder; he knew what had to be done. Vanessa wasn't going to like his treatment, but getting her to Amaroo would be intolerably painful for her if the shoulder wasn't put back in place.

He gently removed the bandanna and after she'd had more water, laid her back on the ground. 'I'm going to have to, umm, attend to your shoulder, make you more comfortable ...' Trying not to telegraph his intention, he took her arm, straightened it and before she could ask why he was doing that, gave the arm a single, mighty jerk downwards.

Her eyes went wide. She screamed as loud as exhaustion allowed her. 'You bastard ...' was all she got out before her eyes glazed and she passed out.

Curtis grimaced. He felt awful about doing what he'd done but it was for the best and, with luck, she wouldn't come to until they were at Amaroo. He glanced across at Runaway. The mare was a curious animal and had whinnied on hearing Vanessa scream. 'I know. It was a mean thing to do but she'll get better more quickly now, girl.' Talking *and* justifying his actions to a horse! Was he crazy? He shook his head as he got up and walked towards the horse with the water bottle in his hand. He poured water into his peaked cap and let Runaway drink her fill.

'I'll have to leave you here tonight, girl. Reg will drop someone off in the morning to ride you home.' He gave the horse the rest of the water then walked back to where Vanessa lay.

For several moments he stared at the unconscious woman at his feet and a rush of sympathy went through him, its emotive quality surprising him. As knocked out as she was, injured and sunburnt, dishevelled and dirty, Vanessa still looked ... magnificent.

Bren was a lucky bugger. Born first, he'd inherited the station. He was better looking, more robust, *and* he had Vanessa. A muscle at the side of Curtis's jaw tightened. He looked away and stared at the nearby boulders for maybe thirty seconds then he sucked in a breath and pushed several peculiar, disquieting thoughts from his head. Twilight was almost upon them and he had things to do. Like letting Amaroo know that he'd found Vanessa so . . .

Move, damn you, and get her home.

# CHAPTER TWELVE

The first thing Curtis did after he, Fran and Nova got a semi-conscious Vanessa into bed, was to contact the Flying Doctor Service to find out how to help her. The dislocation had caused a lot of bruising and inflammation but with the shoulder back in its socket, the FDS advised that what Vanessa needed most was re-hydration and several days of bed rest, with periodic cold compresses to reduce inflammation around torn ligaments and tissues. Strapping the area was deemed unnecessary but her arm would have to be supported by a sling for several weeks.

'She won't be a happy camper when she wakes up,' Nova gave her opinion from the foot of the bed. Having watched one stockman convalesce from a similar injury, she knew Vanessa was going to be in pain and uncomfortable for several days.

'Why should she? She's been through a dreadful ordeal,' Fran said as she straightened the sheet around their patient.

At her return, Sandy, Vanessa's dog, had taken up residence on Bren's side of the double bed and refused to move. He would growl ominously if anyone tried to dislodge him, and his intelligent gaze followed everyone's movements as his mistress was attended to. Periodically he would lick Vanessa's hand and whimper with disappointment when she failed to reciprocate by patting his head.

'At least we contacted Bren — heavy seas caused him and Stuart to end their voyage prematurely. He's on his way home. He'll be here tomorrow morning,' Fran said.

'Shouldn't have left Amaroo in the first place,' Curtis responded, his tone quietly critical.

The two women glanced at him, surprised by his words and his tone. Nova raised an eyebrow at Fran, because neither could remember a time when Curtis had so freely criticised his older brother.

*What's got into him?* Nova wondered as she glanced at Curtis. He appeared out of sorts and annoyed. He could be prickly at times but usually that only happened when the problem concerned Georgia, or if the station wasn't running smoothly. Maybe he was tired — he'd been in the chopper all day. Or, the thought came to her, was he putting the blame on Vanessa for getting lost? If so that would be good because it would take the pressure off her feelings of guilt. But, cunningly, she stuck up for the Englishwoman. 'Getting lost wasn't Vanessa's fault.'

'I know that,' Curtis looked at her. 'If Bren had been around and on the muster as he should have been, he would have looked out for her and the situation wouldn't have come up.' He paused, thought about it again, then changed the subject. 'Now we have to regroup the mob and move them to Spring Valley.'

'They're meandering that way by themselves,' Nova told him, 'because there's still water in Gumbledon Creek.'

'Most are but there's always stragglers to round up. Tomorrow, we'll locate them in the chopper and drive them towards the others.' He glanced towards Fran who had moved and was hovering near the bedroom's doorway. 'Will you be able to care for Vanessa by yourself? I'd like Nova to be on the range with Warren and Tony.'

'Of course. Vanessa will be no trouble. I expect she'll sleep around the clock.'

Vanessa moved suddenly, and moaned. Her eyes opened and she blinked twice, then smiled as she recognised Fran and Nova. After that her gaze fell on Curtis. The smile disappeared. 'You ... hurt ... me ...' she accused. Her eyes closed again.

Curtis gave Nova and Fran a guilty, lopsided grin. 'I'd hoped she wouldn't remember me putting her shoulder back in.'

Nova gave him a droll look. 'How would Vanessa forget that? She's going to be in pain for days.' Which would be a reminder of what he'd done. *She* knew Curtis had done the expedient thing but she wasn't sure that Vanessa would see it that way. Men were funny creatures! 'It might be best to give her a wide berth for a while, till she's feeling brighter.'

'Guess so,' he agreed.

After giving them and their patient a sweeping look he left the room and headed towards his haven, the old stone cottage. His dog, Ringo, sat patiently on the verandah, waiting for him. Curtis pursed his lips and gave a shrill whistle whereupon Ringo bounded up to him, tail wagging expectantly. Taking a torch off a hook attached to one of the verandah posts, he addressed the blue heeler. 'Come on buddy, let's check the chicken coop. Fran reckoned she saw dingo tracks there this morning.'

It took months for Vanessa's shoulder, with regular, gentle exercises, to be back to normal, which was just as well because the end of her convalescence coincided with the opening night, the premiere, of *Heart of the Outback* in Sydney.

The night before Vanessa, Bren and Nova, were to fly from Amaroo to Australia's largest capital city, a party atmosphere existed on the homestead's stone-flagged patio. A barbecue provided a sumptuous outdoor feast for the Selbys and Amaroo's employees, plus Stuart and Diane, and Lauren and her family, who had all flown in that afternoon.

One person was not in a festive frame of mind. Nova, sitting alone at the end of the long, timber barbecue table, was going through the process of admitting as she watched Curtis talk to Stuart, Marc and Reg, that the romance she hoped to develop with the man she was in love with, was not happening. And, worse, she had exhausted all ideas as to how to make it happen.

Since Vanessa's episode in the bush she had made a concentrated effort to capture and hold Curtis's attention, to let him see her as a desirable woman. Dressing in obscenely short shorts and midriff tops or singlets to display her body to its best advantage, wearing perfume and make-up, drawing him out in conversation. Nothing worked. She'd even taken up regular correspondence with his kid to let him see that she would make a good stepmother. As well, she cornered him alone whenever possible, hoping their closeness would ignite a spark of attraction between them but ... it was as if Curtis Selby was made of granite. It was so ... frustrating.

And she knew that had she turned a similar effort on Tony Wells, one of the stockmen, he'd have been eating out of her hand in next to no time, but not Curtis! What was wrong with him? Or ... was there something wrong with her? Did she have to lie naked in his bed to create a reaction? She gave that due thought then dismissed it. What if, instead of turning him on, it turned him off?

Lauren's youngest son, Guy, came running up to her. 'Nova, will you push me on the swing, please?'

Banishing her black mood she answered with forced cheerfulness. 'Of course, mate.' From the play area, which included a set of swings, a slippery dip, a see-saw and a sandpit with a cover, she could watch Curtis and he could see her too. After a while, when he saw her miming that her arms were about to fall off from fatigue, because Guy kept wanting her to push him higher and higher, he came and took over.

'Guess your bag's already packed?'

She nodded. 'I can hardly wait. The premiere's going to be too much.'

Curtis grimaced at her phrasing. 'Too much. Really? Not my scene, I'm afraid.'

'You love to hang around Amaroo and do outdoorsy things. I bet, if Regan wasn't living in

Sydney, you wouldn't step off station land unless there was some kind of emergency.'

He shrugged as he gave Guy a harder push. 'Amaroo gives me what I need, a sense of achievement. Three square meals a day, and work I love to do.'

'There could be more to life than that, you know.'

'For some, yes,' Curtis didn't argue, 'not for me, though I understand others wanting more.'

'Like ... Vanessa?'

He frowned. 'I guess so. My mother too. Over the years she needed more than Amaroo could offer — station life can be hard on a woman. She's making a good life for herself in Darwin.'

'And Bren, sometimes he needs more than Amaroo.'

'Bren's always been like that, needing other stimuli. There's nothing wrong with this life but it isn't for everyone.'

Guy, who'd got bored with the swing, hopped off and ran off to play with his brothers, Cameron and Lance. Nova and Curtis, continuing to talk, meandered away from the playground to the shadowy area of the tennis court. Nova looked back at the brightly lit patio where Vanessa was trying to teach Lauren some Spanish dancing steps. In a gesture of camaraderie Curtis's arm went around Nova's shoulders as they watched the women dance. After a minute or so Diane Selby joined the dancers.

'Vanessa, she's good, isn't she?'

'Good? I wouldn't know. I'm not into Spanish dancing,' he answered non-committally.

'You don't have to be into it to see that Vanessa's good at it. All you have to do is look,' Nova replied, then asked, 'Why is it that you try not to give her credit for anything?'

'That's not true,' he retorted, his glance moving off the women on the patio. 'I've said it before, Vanessa has learned a good deal. She ... she ...' he stared at his sister, aunt and sister-in-law, and couldn't quite tear his gaze away. 'Vanessa is ...'

'What?'

He shrugged his left shoulder, a mannerism he adopted when he felt pressured. 'An asset to Amaroo.' His tight-lipped expression betrayed his irritation. 'Satisfied?'

Nova was a long way from being satisfied with him! Slanting an upwards glance at his face, she made a decision. If Curtis wasn't going to make a move then she would test things by making a move ... on him. She turned to face him, and threw her arms around his neck. Then, standing on tiptoes, she planted a kiss on his mouth. He stiffened against their sudden closeness, his hands finding her narrow waistline with the intention of pushing her away. Nova refused to be pushed away. She locked her fingers behind his neck and clung determinedly to him.

When they separated he asked in a gruff voice, 'What was that about?'

'Just a little something to remember me by, while I'm gone,' she whispered, refusing to be put off by his lacklustre response. It felt good to be so close to him — his hands on her bare skin were burning their mark on her. She never wanted to let him go. If only she could see his features, but the light was too poor to gauge his reaction. Was he moved, intrigued, attracted? Did he want her? ... A little bit would be enough to begin with. Desperate for a reaction, she kissed him again, this time putting all her feeling into it, until she ran out of breath. She broke away and stood back, waiting for him to say something!

'What on earth's got into you? Have you been drinking or something?' Curtis asked, confused. He shuffled back, putting an arm's distance between them and dug both hands into the pockets of his jeans.

'You ... you didn't like it?' Her question was hesitant, almost shy now that she realised the import of her actions. What a foolish thing to do. Had she blown it? Turned him off completely?

'I wouldn't say that,' he drawled. 'What red-blooded male doesn't want a pretty girl like you kissing him? I just don't understand why.'

'Oh!' Fighting for composure, she said the first thing that came into her head. 'It seemed like a good idea at the time, but ...' He hadn't taken the hint and, while he hadn't rejected her, the reaction she had yearned for had not occurred. Patches of colour warmed her cheeks, she felt embarrassed, mortified even. 'M-maybe I have had one drink too many.'

Unable to bear his quizzical expression a moment longer and dreading the thought of facing him in the cold light of day, she gave a loud sniff and pushed back the threatening tears. Eager to save face, she turned on her heel and walked back to the party knowing that because of what had just occurred, and his lukewarm response, she had a lot of thinking to do.

■ ■ ■

The premiere of *Heart of the Outback* at the Hoyts Theatre complex in George Street, Sydney, was a resounding success. The audience and the critics loved the movie because it was a mixture of adventure and drama, with a little comedy mixed in for good measure.

At the Park Hyatt Hotel, over a late breakfast the following morning, Kerri Spanos and Vanessa conducted a post-mortem on the event, something they did as a matter of course after first nights. Bren had taken Yannis, a first-time visitor to Sydney, on a tour of the city, which would include a ferry ride to Manly and a sortie to Darling Harbour — the men would be gone for most of the day. That suited the women because now they had time for a leisurely, catch-up talk. Nova, who'd had a ball at the premiere and the after-show party, was enjoying the luxury of sleeping in before contacting friends and going out for the rest of the day.

'I heard good things about you last night,' Kerri confided over toast and marmalade. 'Jaxson, the director, is being inundated with new material, scripts, etc and a producer from Channel Ten wants to meet with me this afternoon to discuss a part for you in a movie pilot of a police-cum-detective series. If the pilot works the series will be shot in Melbourne.' She lifted an eyebrow. 'Interested?'

'You bet,' Vanessa said, repeating one of Bren's favourite phrases. 'Providing it doesn't conflict with other commitments.' She picked up her coffee cup and took another sip. Time to tell Kerri what she had been doing while convalescing from her ordeal in the bush. 'I'm working on a script. It has an

Australian historical setting, with most of the story set in the outback.'

'Really.' Kerri's dark eyes locked with Vanessa's. 'That's something you've never done before. What's it about?'

'The idea for the plot came after reading quite a few Australian stories. Amaroo has a library with many books about the pioneer men who opened up the outback, but little about the women who came with them. Women rarely get a mention in official histories, yet their roles, the support they gave their menfolk were important to settling the land.' Enthusiasm had her leaning forward in the chair. 'While convalescing I had time to do a lot of thinking and one day a story line just popped into my head. I've been working on it ever since, whenever I had some spare time.'

'How much have you done and what's the plot about?'

'I'm about half way through. It's a serious drama set in the 1870s, about a family of five that come from England to start a new life. The story centres around the lives of Emily and Charlotte Whitfield and their repressive, ambitious father. It isn't lighthearted like *Heart of the Outback*.'

'I'd like to see what you've done so far. When can I?'

'You are on holiday,' Vanessa reminded her friend.

Kerri gave her a piercing, typically Kerri look. 'Did you bring it with you?'

'Yes, but . . .' Vanessa smiled and gave in. 'It's in our room.'

'Good. I have no problem mixing business with pleasure. Makes everything all the more tax deductible.'

Vanessa laughed and shook her head. Kerri was always mindful of the pound value in everything she did. If there was an angle to be exploited she did so and last night Kerri had been on the job, making sure she was introduced to the wheelers and dealers in the Australian theatrical world, people it might be important to know. 'Working the crowd,' Kerri called it . . . But now she'd talked about her script, there was one more personal thing she wanted to share . . .

'I'm not sure you're going to like hearing this, but there is one more thing,' she paused, then charged on, 'I think I might be pregnant.'

'You *think*.' A black eyebrow rose querulously. 'Don't you know?'

'It's early days. I'm only a week and a half overdue.' Vanessa's smile was radiant with expectation. 'I haven't told Bren yet, 'cause I don't want to disappoint him.'

Kerri gave Vanessa a hard-eyed stare for a moment or two and sucked in her cheeks as she pondered this news. The fingers of her left hand drummed a staccato beat on the pristine table cloth. The dining room, which was almost devoid of diners, seemed suddenly, oppressively quiet.

'Well,' Kerri finally said, straight-faced, 'I wondered how long you'd take to reproduce. You've been married for more than a year. Is it what you want?' she asked. She smiled as Vanessa nodded that it was. Her fat, be-ringed fingers reached across the table to pat Vanessa's hand. 'Congratulations, luv.'

Vanessa blinked, recovered her aplomb. 'You approve?'

'I wouldn't say *approve*. A child will make a difference to your career, to what work you can do. I've been expecting, shall we say, *something*.'

'Could we keep it to ourselves till I'm absolutely sure?'

Kerri winked at her then touched the side of her nose, her smile widening, 'Pardon the pun but, "Mum's the word!"' She glanced towards the dining room's windows through which a view of part of the harbour could be seen. Outside, it was a sunny morning. 'Sunshine. Bloody wonderful, isn't it? If only I could bottle it and take it back to England with me. Come on, we've got things to do. Let's have the hotel do a copy of your script then, guess what?'

Vanessa grinned and her brown eyes twinkled. 'We're going shopping?'

'Spot on. Our fifteenth wedding anniversary's coming up. I want to get a string of black pearls, like the strand you had on last night.'

Vanessa chuckled at Kerri's well known love of fine jewellery. 'You're incorrigible.'

During the five days Vanessa and Bren spent in Sydney, they saw little of Nova. When they enquired she was out with friends, unavailable for dinner most nights and, generally, a will-o'-the-wisp. They discovered why the night before they were due to go home, when Nova knocked on the Selby's suite door.

'Hi, everybody,' Nova said as she came into the living area. 'Packing, I see.'

'I assume you've done yours,' Vanessa said. Over the five days they had been there she had been disappointed by Nova's behaviour. At Amaroo, she was always around helping, chatting, showing her how to do various tasks, whereas here, after attending the premiere, she couldn't help but think that the younger woman had decided to give Bren and herself the flick. Busy with promotional commitments, and Kerri, she hadn't spent a lot of time assessing Nova's behaviour, but when she had thought about it, it niggled at her sense of rightness.

'I'm not going home,' Nova announced without preamble. 'I rang Ansett and cancelled my ticket. The booking clerk said they'd send a refund to Amaroo in due course.'

Bren looked up from the television show he'd been watching, his jaw slack with surprise. 'What?'

Vanessa studied Nova for about ten seconds before asking quietly, 'Why not?'

Nova didn't make eye contact with Vanessa as she replied, 'I need a change. There's lots of different stuff to do in the city, you know.'

'Such as?' Vanessa enquired. She beckoned Nova to follow her into the bedroom so they could talk without the distraction of television.

'The club scene, a wider variety of jobs. I've several friends here too. It's been cool to catch up with them this week.'

'And ...?' Vanessa probed as she sat on the side of the bed.

'I've been talking to that artists' manager, Anthea Dennison,' Nova admitted. 'She heard me sing a while ago and is keen to get my singing career going.

I thought, why not. I'll never know if I can do it if I don't try.' Besides, after the embarrassing scene with Curtis, she needed to put a little distance between them for a while.

'Can't argue with that.' That was why Nova had been elusive, she deduced, other fish to fry. 'Does Curtis have anything to do with your decision?' Vanessa asked incisively. Too many times she'd seen Nova's longing looks, the love in her eyes, the tell-tale pining sigh. Curtis must have been as blind as a proverbial bat not to have noticed Nova's preoccupation with him but obviously he hadn't.

'What do you mean? What makes you think my decision has anything to do with Curtis?'

'Nova, I've seen how you look at him when you think no-one's watching you. I know how you feel.'

'Oh . . .' came out in a small voice. Nova flopped into the only chair that didn't have anything draped over it. 'You know then. Does? . . .' Her gaze moved towards the living room where Bren had his eyes glued to a sports program. It annoyed the hell out of her to think that Vanessa was perceptive enough to have guessed her feelings for Curtis. *Her* knowing, more than anyone else only enhanced Nova's sense of discomfort — because Vanessa was so happy and so close to being perfect.

'Your secret is safe with me, and I don't think anyone else has twigged.' Vanessa smiled commiseratingly at her. 'I'm sorry things didn't work out.'

'Me too.' Nova's sigh was dramatically forlorn. 'I need time away from Amaroo, to think about what I should do with my life.' She managed a self-derisive grin. 'I'll be singing the blues with real feeling for a while, that's for sure.'

'Curtis is an obtuse fool. It's his loss not yours.'

Nova blinked several times, holding back the urge to cry. 'Is it?'

'Yes,' Vanessa's tone was positive. 'Now you go off and become a terrific country and western singer, win several Golden Guitars, and end up famous.' She waggled a finger at her. 'I expect nothing less.'

'I promise to give it my best shot.'

The two women moved towards each other but it was Vanessa who initiated the hug.

'You'll keep in touch?'

'Of course,' Nova assured her.

Vanessa was going to miss Nova. They'd become friends, if not intimate friends, over time. The station was, of necessity, a male-dominated domain but it had been good to have a woman other than Fran, who was in her fifties, around to talk to. Still, she acknowledged that being self-reliant was partly what outback life was about, and that Nova had helped her achieve a satisfactory degree of that. Besides, she had other matters to occupy her, such as finishing the script — Kerri thought that what she'd done so far had potential — as well as preparing for a baby.

She smiled a secretive smile as she waved goodbye to Nova at the suite's door. A new life was coming to Amaroo and because of it, her life was going to change . . . forever.

# CHAPTER THIRTEEN

All the books Vanessa read about pregnancy and childbirth stated that the last month, towards the end of the third trimester, was the most difficult for expectant mothers to bear. She believed it. A shade over eight months pregnant hers had been an exceptionally healthy pregnancy but she was too large to ride and now she couldn't fit behind the chopper's controls or the driver's wheels of any of the station's vehicles.

It was a plus that the nursery was ready. She and Bren had organised the room several months ago, opting for neutral colours because they'd chosen not to know which sex their child would be. Often Vanessa would stand at the nursery doorway, studying what they'd done with a sense of contentment wafting through her. Decorating it had been fun and everyone on Amaroo had made a contribution. Bren and Curtis had resurrected Regan's bassinette from one of the storage areas and spruced it up. A tallboy of 1930s vintage had been repainted and decorated with nursery rhyme stick-on characters, as had the walls. Fran made curtains and sheets for the bassinette and, later, the cot. Reg and Warren contributed by making a sturdy change table and had covered it with padded vinyl. As well as the essential baby paraphernalia a selection of toys stood on shelves above the bassinette. Kerri and Yannis mailed four, dressed teddy bears from England, and other family members, mostly Lauren's boys, parted with some of the toys they'd outgrown for the nursery.

Now all that was left to do was wait for the 'blessed event' and, with at least fifty per cent of Spanish blood running through her veins, patience was not one of Vanessa's finer points. When she wanted something she wanted it immediately and waiting nine months for the birth was a real test of what patience she had. An ongoing regret was that there would be no family of her own to share the wondrous event with, and that her and Bren's child would only have one grandparent: Hilary, someone she still didn't feel comfortable with.

As she eased herself into bed beside Bren, she knew that little could be gained by getting melancholy over what could not be changed, or improved. And ... at least they'd agreed on names: Kyle for a boy, Amanda for a girl.

'You okay, hon?' Bren asked on the downside of a yawn as he slipped an arm around her voluminous waistline.

'Yes,' she sighed, 'but I feel like a blimp.'

'A very beautiful blimp,' he whispered as he kissed the side of her neck.

She gave his arm a playful punch. 'Oh, thanks. You know how to make a woman feel better about herself.'

Unabashed, he chuckled as he cuddled up to her. 'Isn't that what husbands are for?'

Vanessa didn't dignify that statement with a reply. Instead, she listened to his breathing deepen. In less than five minutes he was sound asleep. Yawning, she tried to do the same ...

... Something didn't feel right!

Vanessa lifted her head to check the bedside clock. 3.10 a.m. As she became more awake she realised what had happened. Her water had broken. Then she got a contraction — her first. *Oohhh*. She gasped as the pain built to a crescendo then slowly ebbed away. It's too soon, three weeks too soon, the thought ran through her mind. After the second contraction she nudged Bren.

'Wake up, Bren, wake up.' When he didn't respond she grabbed his shoulder and shook him till he stirred. 'The baby's coming, Bren. For God's sake, wake up.'

'Wh-at?'

Holding onto her stomach — though she wasn't sure that would help — Vanessa struggled out of bed. She flicked the light switch on and started to dress. 'My water's broken, it's the baby, Bren. We have to get to the hospital.' The agreed upon plan had been — when she had two weeks to term — for her to go to Kununurra and stay there till she went into labour. It had been a sound plan but 'Junior', so it appeared, was deciding to come early.

Bren sat up. He supported his upper body weight on one elbow while his free hand rubbed his eyes. 'The hospital?' he said dully, still unable to comprehend the situation. 'You're too early. It's a false alarm, hon.'

'Don't "hon" me and we're not having a debate, we're having a baby. Now. Quickly, get up and get dressed.' She watched his eyes open wide, his back straighten. The message was getting through.

'Shit! Really?'

'Yes, darling, really.'

Nova walked onto the stage with the air of someone who'd already claimed the space as her own. One hand arced wide in a wave to the audience as they began to clap while the other hand gripped the microphone. Two spotlights followed her as she moved centre stage and hooked the mike into its stand. The audience hushed and an air of expectancy hung over the club's auditorium. Adrenaline charged through her body, vitalising her. That always happened before a performance and she loved the feeling it gave her of being different, admired, envied. She half turned to give the leader of the band, Leo Muller, a smile.

She and Leo had become close over the six months she'd been with his band, touring and working gigs along the eastern seaboard. Leo's attention and affection had helped take the edge off her disappointment over Curtis and, so far, the relationship was working out. She was professionally and romantically involved with someone who understood what she was about — the singing, and songwriting, a new talent she had discovered within herself, partly due to Leo's encouragement. Anthea, her manager, expected great things of her, and said she had the talent and the ability to make the grade as a top country and western singer.

She smiled confidently at the audience. That was precisely what she was going to be — the best — rivalling Vanessa in *her* chosen career. Her chin tilted upwards with determination as the lead guitar played the intro chord. She moved closer to the mike, her lips almost touching the metal. She would show Curtis and all the Selbys that she was special. One day she would be a star, like Vanessa, only *she* would be bigger and better.

Nova was half way through the set when the club's manager, standing in the wings, beckoned her over. He thrust a note into her hand, muttered that the message was supposed to be important, then shooed her back on stage.

Nova opened the piece of paper, read what was written and suddenly whooped into the mike, after which she shared her news with the audience because audiences liked that sort of thing, making them feel more involved with the artist on stage.

'A friend of mine, actor Vanessa Forsythe, has just had a baby boy, Kyle Matthew.' She motioned the audience to give the announcement the traditional round of applause. 'I'm going to dedicate my next song, one of The Judd's hits, 'Young Love', to Vanessa, Bren and baby Kyle.'

Grinning, Nova began to sing the lyrics. *'She was sitting cross-legged on the hood of the Ford, filing down her nails with an emery board ... '*

During a lull in the constant rain — the wet was on its way out — everyone who lived and worked on the property sat clustered around the television set watching an excerpt from the Tamworth Country

Music Festival. The presenter was about to announce the starmaker award for best new country and western talent and had read Nova Morrison's name out as one of the five nominees.

Reg was so nervous he couldn't sit still. He fidgeted, sipped his beer, and tugged, semi-constantly, at his right ear lobe. Tony and Warren sat on the floor, their fingers curled around beer cans. Curtis perched on the arm of one of the chairs and Vanessa, Fran and Bren were sharing the sofa.

'Nova has to have a real chance,' Tony remarked as he watched a clip of one of the nominees, a young man strumming an electric guitar. 'Geez, he's singing off key.'

'Nerves,' Reg sympathised gruffly. 'Even the best get nervous.'

Nova's image came onto the screen and Bren let loose a piercing wolf whistle. 'Doesn't she look fantastic!'

Vanessa stared at Nova and made her own silent assessment. Fantastic? Different maybe, but not fantastic by her yardstick. Nova had lost a considerable amount of weight and her black, straight hair was curled and wild-looking. She had developed an air of sophistication though, which was reflected in the clothes she wore. A short, fringed black leather skirt with a tantalising side split, a white body hugging top with an open V neckline and filmy scarf-like sleeves — very funky — and long, dangling earrings that matched the choker pendant around her neck. Embossed black and white leather, calf-high boots completed her outfit.

Listening to her sing, Vanessa gave credit where it was due. Nova was good. Better than good, she decided, and that the song was her own composition — Reg had said it was — was another plus in the talent stakes. Still, she wasn't sure, though she wouldn't say so, that her performance was professional enough to take out the top award. The first nominee, a tall, constantly smiling young girl with blond hair, had exceptional talent and that rare attribute, television charisma. She would be stiff competition for all of them.

'Nova's pretty damned good,' Curtis gave his opinion honestly. 'I watched her audition in Sydney. She's improved one hundred per cent since then.'

'I wouldn't want to be the judges,' Fran was nothing if not diplomatic. 'They're all terrific.'

'Nova's a shoo-in,' Bren said confidently. He held up his empty can. 'Anyone for another?'

The presenter's face returned to dominate the screen. 'And the winner is ...' He paused, grinned maddeningly to lengthen the tension, 'right after the break.' His image faded as an advertisement came on screen.

'Bloody annoying. They always do that,' grumbled Reg.

Vanessa smiled at his nervousness. 'They call it a dramatic pause.'

As if on cue, Kyle began to cry lustily from the nursery.

'Talk about timing,' Bren muttered. 'My son has an absolute talent for crying at the wrong times.'

'Is there a right time for a baby to cry?' Fran asked dryly.

'He shouldn't be hungry, I fed him an hour ago,' Vanessa said as she got up to check on him. As she did her glance included Bren and she saw his annoyed look. As a new father, he wasn't coping well with the crying: it got on his nerves and made him irritable. He didn't like to change nappies either or help to bathe their tiny son, much to her disappointment. She made excuses for him, to Fran and the others. He wasn't used to a baby being around but then neither was she, yet she accepted that babies cried and when they did they were attended to. Bren said she was spoiling Kyle, giving him too much attention and that she should just let him cry and, unfortunately, Kyle cried a lot.

Quelling her irritation with Bren's impatience she went to the nursery. Kyle was wide awake, and he smiled as she spoke to him. She picked him up, changed his nappy and took him out of the room. He was a sociable baby who enjoyed being with other people and when thus occupied, he usually stopped grizzling for a while. The Flying Doctor nurse had said he had colic, lots of babies got that in their first three months and it didn't bother him all the time, thank goodness, but struck mostly at night, and when it did he took a lot of pacifying before he settled.

Even so she wasn't entirely satisfied. She believed there was something more — she just hoped that a serious problem wasn't developing. There was something else about him too, his skin tone ... When he'd first come home from the hospital he had been jaundiced. The doctor said that would fade quickly but it hadn't. He was now four months old and, though she hadn't mentioned it to Bren because he'd think she was being paranoid, she was becoming concerned. If he was no better in a month, she intended to take him to Darwin to have him checked out thoroughly.

As she held Kyle up over her shoulder and made her way down the hallway to the living room, her niggling disappointment because of Bren's attitude accelerated. He had been considerate and affectionate during her pregnancy but since Kyle's birth, little quirks — impatience and even an immature sulkiness — were emerging. Fran believed he was jealous of the attention she gave Kyle but Vanessa found that too incredible to be true. He was a grown man, albeit one who'd been indulged by his mother and probably his father, more so than Curtis and Lauren had. He should understand that babies had needs. That he didn't was beginning to seriously irritate her.

She sat on the sofa as the presenter returned to the screen and announced: 'And the winner is ... Chelsea Talbot.' The blond. 'And 1992's runner-up is Nova Morrison.'

Amaroo's living room erupted in a noisy cheer. Kyle, frightened by the sudden noise, began to cry in earnest.

'For God's sake,' Bren turned towards Vanessa, 'can't you shut him up?'

'The noise everyone made scared him,' she defended staunchly, attempting to placate Kyle with his dummy. He spat it out and kept on wailing.

'A man can hardly think with all that commotion,' Bren continued to rant.

'Oh, I don't know,' Curtis tried to diffuse everyone's embarrassment at Bren's cranky display.

'You're making as much noise as your son, and you're a grown up.'

Bren glared at his brother. 'You're the one with the baby experience, you keep him quiet.'

Incensed by her husband's outburst, Vanessa rose and moved towards the kitchen with Kyle in her arms and Sandy trotting faithfully behind. She went through the kitchen and because the rain had stopped she continued on to the back verandah. She sat and stared at the outbuildings and, beyond to the wide open paddock that blurred into the horizon as twilight deepened. The most marvellous sunset she had ever seen was occurring.

Set against the near-black silhouette of a large gum tree and the boundary fence, the roiling clouds were dusted with the fiery red and orange of the setting sun. Smudged and temporarily lightening the clouds, which were heavy with impending rain, the sunset stretched across the sky in a superb panorama of colour. For a little while Vanessa held her breath at the magnificence of it, then began to talk quietly to Kyle, pointing out the spectacular colours. His little body was stiff with pain caused by the colic. There was little she could do other than try to distract him until the pain passed.

She wasn't there long before Curtis joined her. 'You okay?'

'Of course. Isn't it a wonderful sunset?'

'Yeah, you only see that kind of sunset during the wet, when the clouds are laden with rain.' Then he cleared his throat and said, 'Bren doesn't mean it, you know,' trying to excuse his brother's behaviour. 'He loves Kyle. Talks about him all the time when we're working, ad nauseam, in fact. What he's going to teach him, how he'll groom him to run Amaroo as he grows up.'

Vanessa glanced up at Curtis, who was leaning laconically against one of the vertical verandah posts with his thumbs hooked into the waistband of his jeans — a habit both he and Bren had in common. 'The way he carries on about Kyle's crying, I find it hard to understand.'

Curtis shrugged. 'Some men never get it. They don't understand that that's what babies do. Eat, cry, poo and sleep. Not necessarily in that order.'

The straight-faced way he said it made Vanessa chuckle. She and Curtis, since she'd come to Amaroo had, over time, come to a silent understanding of sorts, based on growing, mutual respect. In many ways they got along well now, were in some ways better tuned to the running of Amaroo than Bren, and they had similar tastes, in reading and music.

'Let me have him for a while,' Curtis offered.

He took Kyle off Vanessa and went and sat in one of the wooden armchairs scattered about the verandah which doubled as a sleep-out when the weather was abominably hot. 'Regan was a fussy baby too and Georgia didn't have a lot of patience with her.' Resting Kyle across his lap, he turned him onto his stomach, supporting his head and neck with one arm, while the other hand massaged his back, from his shoulders down to his tiny hips. 'Sometimes this helps.'

After a couple of minutes Kyle's cries became less frequent, his arms and legs stopped flailing. Seeing the change, Vanessa's eyebrows lifted in surprise. 'Amazing. He's settling.'

'Can't promise that it always works,' Curtis admitted, 'but it's worth a try.'

In the night's silence beyond the lights of the homestead and the stockmen's quarters, it was pitch black. A dingo began to yip and was answered by another dingo. Sandy, dozing at Vanessa's feet, stirred. His small head went up, his ears twitched. He stood, trotted to the edge of the verandah and began to growl, then bark.

'Shush, Sandy,' Vanessa ordered, concerned that Kyle would start to cry again. Sandy's response was to race down the steps and into the blackness, barking as he disappeared into the moonless night.

'Get him back, Vanessa. Those dingoes aren't far away, around the hangar from the sound of them. We've found dingo tracks around several buildings, including the chicken coop. I've put Ringo on a long chain to guard the coop at night, in case they try to burrow under the wire,' Curtis told her as he changed Kyle's position. 'If Sandy gets near those dingoes they'll make minced meat out of him.'

Hearing that, Vanessa didn't hesitate. She flicked on the floodlights that illuminated the wet ground and puddles as far as the breaking-in fence and raced down the steps into the darkness, alternatively whistling and calling Sandy to her. She had to chase the Jack Russell as far as the large machinery shed before he came to heel.

'You're a bad dog,' she scolded and, before he could shoot off again, she scooped him up in her arms. Sandy, she had discovered, had a problem.

The little dog believed he was as big and fierce and as brave as Bubba, Kimbo and Ringo, the station's dogs.

When she came back to the verandah Kyle was asleep in Curtis's arms.

'You must have a way with babies,' she whispered, her tone a mixture of amusement and admiration.

'I do. Kids, dogs and old people love me. But I strike out with young, beautiful women.'

She looked him up and down. 'You're not so bad, and I have seen you in a suit. You scrub up okay.' And, she reminded herself, there was at least one beautiful woman — Nova — who was more than willing and able to accept his attentions. Curtis simply wasn't aware of her adoration, more's the pity. Nova had tired of waiting and had embarked on a new life with a lover named Leo and was, one assumed, over Curtis. The outback man would never know what he had missed. Her mouth quirked in a smile as she thought that it was funny how things worked out.

'I'll put him to bed, if you like,' Curtis offered.

He stood up with Kyle and, with Vanessa following him, they returned to the nursery and put the sleeping baby down . . .

Vanessa studied the face of her seven-month-old sleeping son. Kyle was curled up in his seat with the seat belt fastened, with airline blankets and two pillows around his small body to support him. The commercial flight from Kununurra to Darwin was relatively short but she couldn't nod off. She was too uptight, in more ways than one. The argument with Bren over Kyle's declining health had started it all off. Her husband couldn't or wasn't able to see that their baby boy wasn't the healthy bouncing child he should be. His skin tone had remained yellowish since birth, he had problems with his bowels and with digesting food. Finally Vanessa had had enough and insisted they take him to the doctor they saw in Kununurra, Dr Adam Strong, for a consultation.

She glanced at Bren who sat across the aisle. His eyes were closed, but she knew he wasn't asleep. After Adam had examined Kyle, his expression and words had been the wake-up call Bren needed and now, like her, he was intensely concerned about their child's health.

Adam thought Kyle might have a viral infection that was affecting liver function which was why he was jaundiced, but the doctor hadn't sufficient paediatric expertise to correctly diagnose it, hence the referral to a specialist paediatrician in Darwin. Hmmm! At times, Vanessa thought cynically, doctors tended to label some ailment that wasn't easy to diagnose as a virus, in the hope that the patient would be satisfied. After the surgery visit, Bren had phoned his mother and she'd insisted they stay with her while they were in Darwin . . . a mixed blessing as far as Vanessa was concerned.

As Vanessa's hand reached out to smooth the short, fine blond strands of her baby's hair her heart swelled with love but simultaneously, a frown creased her unlined forehead. Kyle was not well and she could no longer rest or allow herself to be fobbed off by any doctor who implied — as Bren initially had — that she was being paranoid and over-protective. A sensible mother knew when something was wrong with her child and, for months the signs had been growing and could no longer be ignored. What was affecting Kyle was much more serious than a mysterious virus that he would eventually get over ...

Vanessa watched the white-coated doctor shuffle then tidy up the papers in the file, and adjust the gold-rimmed glasses on his nose. He cleared his throat and, finally, began to fiddle annoyingly with the pen set on his desk. She was at the end of her tether! She, Bren and Kyle had spent a week in Darwin. Kyle had seen three specialists — a paediatrician, an immunologist and an oncologist — and undergone a plethora of medical tests — blood tests, x-rays, a CT scan and an MRI, a sophisticated electronic test that showed bones, organs, tissues ...

'Well, Dr Klemski? ...' Vanessa encouraged the doctor to speak while at the same time she ignored Bren's frown implying that she should wait for the doctor to get the ball rolling. A listless Kyle lay in her lap. Every day he became more listless and less the Kyle she knew and adored. Something was very wrong with her son and she wanted answers — now.

'Well, Vanessa, Bren, as you know, we've run lots of tests. Tested young Kyle for practically every disease we could think of. Coming up with a diagnosis has posed some difficulties but ...'

'That's obvious. Doctor, surely you must have reached some conclusion as to what's wrong with him?' Vanessa insisted. She gave Dr Klemski her no-nonsense-now look.

'We have.' Klemski's features set. He nodded his head at her, knowing that he could no longer delay telling them. 'Your son has what is known as biliary atresia. It's a rare, congenital condition and is usually discovered when a baby is very small, just a couple of weeks old. It's amazing that it has remained undetected in Kyle for this long.' He paused for a few seconds to let that sink in, then he continued. 'With biliary atresia what happens is that the flow of bile from the liver becomes obstructed. We don't know why it occurs, but when it does the consequences are serious. Kyle's liver shows signs of cirrhosis which is why, though he inherited his olive skin from his mother, the skin tone has now become distinctively yellow, the colour of jaundice.'

'Shit,' Bren muttered under his breath, forgetting his manners.

Vanessa called on all her acting skills to appear calm, and to control the wave of shock and fear threatening to overtake her. The doctor had explained it succinctly enough but she had little real understanding of what it meant to her son. It was his tone — nothing uplifting or hopeful — that chilled her heart. Somehow she rallied and refused to be shaken by the fear threatening to overtake her, and asked what had to be asked.

'What can you do to make him better?'

'As I said, it's a serious illness . . .'

250

'We understand that.' Impatience won over politeness. 'I want to know how to restore Kyle's health, Doctor. We'll do whatever it takes.' She glanced towards Bren, 'Won't we?'

'Of course.'

Dr Klemski made a steeple with his fingertips and his mouth skewed into a sympathetic smile. 'For a small number, about ten per cent, medication corrects the problem. We started medicating him yesterday and will be able to see in a few weeks whether it works in Kyle's case. For the rest who don't respond to the medication there is no cure to halt the progression of biliary atresia. If Kyle doesn't respond to medication the best chance he has is,' he paused to look straight at Vanessa, '*a liver transplant.*'

# CHAPTER FOURTEEN

'*A liver transplant*,' Vanessa repeated weakly.

'Yes. A healthy, compatible liver will give Kyle a very good chance for a reasonably normal life,' Dr Klemski went on. 'Survival rates for such transplant patients currently run at ninety per cent for the first year and eighty per cent over five years. Medically speaking, that's reasonable odds.'

Vanessa's head was spinning. How could she take it all in? Her son's life was at risk. Dr Klemski wasn't talking about a transplant as an option, he was saying that if medication didn't fix the problem, it was the only option for Kyle's survival. She glanced at Bren again who, like her, appeared struck dumb by the news. The only person not concerned was Kyle who, bored, had fallen asleep in her lap.

'The operation could be done in Brisbane — where the world's first transplant took place back in 1989, or in Sydney at the Camperdown Children's Hospital,' Dr Klemski added gently. 'I'm sorry. I know it's a lot to absorb in one go but I have to be frank, looking at the long-term situation and that, as it's taken so long to diagnose your son's problem, it's most likely that the medication won't work and that he will need a transplant.'

'Assuming that's so, don't we have to wait for a donor organ to become available?' Vanessa asked. The thought of having to wait like a hovering vulture for that to happen through someone else's death was abhorrent to her, but if that was the only way . . .

'That used to be the case, but often it isn't these days. Liver and kidney transplants, while rare in Australia have, arguably, the highest success rates of all transplanted organs. Often the transplant team finds a match within the family and at Kyle's age, his liver is quite small. No more than twenty per cent of a healthy liver could be taken from an adult donor and transplanted into Kyle. I've already taken the precaution of seeking advice from the head of Sydney's transplant team, Dr Frank Samuels, that the entire procedure, from donor to Kyle, takes about fifteen hours. And,' he added, 'according to Dr Samuels, it's a more unpleasant operation for the donor, with a risk of complications, than for the recipient.'

'My God!' Bren, couldn't sit still any longer. He stood and began to pace the doctor's office.

'So Bren or myself could donate part of our liver to Kyle?'

'Whoever is the most compatible. Dr Samuels and the recipient's family usually decide that. I suggest we continue the medication on Kyle. He should be admitted to hospital where we can observe if there's an improvement.' He paused to shuffle a few of the papers in his folder. 'But, we should also do blood tests and biopsies on close family members to determine which liver is the most compatible so, in the unhappy event that he needs a transplant, the best possible donor will be available.' Bren's restlessness distracted the doctor for a few seconds. 'Sometimes it's neither parent but a cousin or a grandparent.'

'And the sooner the better, before Kyle deteriorates further?' Vanessa heard herself say the words. How could she come to terms with the awful fact that her darling son's life was in danger. She didn't want to, couldn't think about a life without her son, how bleak and devoid of meaning it would be.

'Right. In Kyle's case, time may not be on our side. While we wait to see how he responds we can do the family's tests here, send the results to Dr Samuels, and if needs be, he'll schedule a date for the operation,' Dr Klemski informed them matter-of-factly.

Vanessa looked the doctor squarely in the eyes. 'Dr Samuels, is he the best?'

'The best and the most experienced with regard to this speciality in the country,' Dr Klemski confirmed with a nod of his head.

Vanessa looked across at Bren who was standing side on, staring out the window. His outdoor tan had paled and his hands were trembling. He planted them in the pockets of his trousers to hide that they were. Like her he was shocked and distressed and, she feared, not coping well with this dreadful news. She ran a finger across her forehead to wipe away the sheen of cold sweat — it was fear. Never in her imaginings, when she had insisted Kyle be checked out had she expected this dire news. Her brain was in a whirl, a mass of tangled thoughts and anxieties dominating, and she had to blink several times to force the tears back. Now was not the time. Later, when she was alone, she could and would cry her heart out over her baby's plight.

Keep focussed, she told herself, now was the time for action, for being positive, and for keeping her fears buried deep in her subconscious. 'Very well. When can the tests be done?'

'Tomorrow and the day after. I'll organise appointments with a pathologist I know, and have my secretary call you. The results will take several days. You'll stay in Darwin till then?'

'Yes. You have our Cullen Bay address.' She tried to smile but it was an utter failure. 'Thank you. Having to give this kind of news can't be easy for doctors.' Awkwardly, with Kyle in her arms, she got up. Bren came and took their sleeping son, cradling him in his strong arms. She could see tears in her husband's eyes and was hard pressed not to give way to them herself.

Shaking his head in sympathy, Dr Klemski watched the Selby family walk out of his office . . .

As they waited to see whether Kyle responded to the medication for biliary atresia, the family, including Hilary, Stuart, Curtis and Lauren, had blood tests, with Bren, Vanessa, Hilary and Curtis also having biopsies. After the results were collated, it came as a surprise that Curtis was the one with the highest compatibility rate, having an eighty-five per cent compatibility, with Bren and Vanessa at sixty-three per cent. Once Curtis knew, he offered himself as

255

the donor and while Bren, pettily, wasn't pleased that Curtis had the higher compatibility rate, Vanessa convinced him that if it were necessary, Curtis should be the donor because by then their son would need the best chance the higher compatibility rate would give him.

Luck did not go Kyle's way ... The medication did not improve his condition and, with time running out as Kyle's health deteriorated, the transplant was scheduled to take place in Sydney, within two weeks ...

Night time humidity hung in the air like an invisible fog. Day time temperatures were close to unbearable and, in the evening, not much better.

Vanessa tiptoed into Kyle's room. Wearing only his nappy — that's all he wore day and night in the heat — he was fast asleep, with the overhead fan rotating at full speed to keep him cool. Poor darling, he slept a good deal these days because he had so little energy. She looked at the change table. His case was packed and ready but not zipped up. It contained clothes plus several of his favourite toys. Tomorrow they would 'hike' to Sydney, a trip of approximately four and a half thousand kilometres which would take, with waiting time for connections, the entire day and part of the night.

For several minutes her gaze browsed over the contents of his room, as if memorising how the contents epitomised her son's emerging personality. He loved soft toys and had a large collection of various sized teddy bears on a shelf. And he was almost sitting up, so his car collection appealed to him. He especially loved his Tonka cement mixer. Over near the window was the sports collection he would play with as he grew — a much used and dented cricket bat that had once been Curtis's, a soccer and rugby ball, a tennis racquet, and paddles to play shuttlecock.

She blinked back tears as he rolled onto his side. She tried not to speculate on the next few days and how awful they were going to be. Walking to the window she looked out. A light in Curtis's cottage was still on. Undoubtedly, he was finding it hard to sleep too. His generosity in offering a portion of his liver to save Kyle was something for which she would be eternally grateful. He was giving her son the gift of life and that made her feel closer to him.

She left Kyle's room and moved down the hall towards her bedroom but stopped when she heard a voice in the office. She went to see who it was. Bren was on the phone. She managed to catch a few words before, on seeing her, he said a quick goodbye and hung up.

'Talking to Stuart? A bit late in the evening for a chat, isn't it?'

'Just catching up,' he said evasively, his gaze unwilling to meet hers.

'Really?'

Her unconvinced tone made him retort, 'Talking to others, like Stuart, about Amaroo's problems helps me to deal with Kyle's problem.'

'I have serious doubts that Stuart knows too much about what happens on stations these days. Hasn't he been off Amaroo for over thirty years?' She could have added but didn't, that she and Fran were the ones who'd done most of the caring and worrying about Kyle. Keeping a sick baby amused and interested, trying to stimulate his appetite, was no easy task. As well, she had the sneaking belief that Stuart put strange, unworkable ideas into Bren's head because he was such a nosy, annoying man, and she objected to his sly attempts to interfere with the management of Amaroo. She and Curtis were aware of Stuart's undue interest in the station and didn't like it, but they trod warily around Bren because he didn't consider Stuart's input a problem, and would have been offended had the suggestion been made that Stuart was influencing his decisions.

'The timing isn't appropriate, Bren. You could have been more helpful with Kyle instead of wasting time chatting to your uncle ...'

There, she had said what she had wanted to say for several weeks without worrying if it bruised his feelings. At times he became so self-absorbed that he could block out everything other than what interested him and when he did, it hurt. She expected more compassion and caring and his lack of it reinforced an opinion she was coming to of late, that in many ways Bren's nature was close to his uncle's. Stuart, according to gossip, appeared to care little for Diane's feelings or sensibilities and Bren was developing similar traits.

'Well, that's great!' It only took an instant for his tone to turn aggressive. 'You think I don't care about our son being ill.'

'I didn't say that,' she retorted, her spine tightening with tension. 'I said you could have been more helpful. That's not quite the same.'

Bren dropped the pen he'd been fiddling with and thumped his fist on the desk. 'Damn it, Vanessa, I'm doing the best I can to deal with ... Kyle. It ... it isn't easy, seeing him so lethargic, disinterested. He is usually such a lively, scrappy baby.' He ran frustrated fingers through his hair and shook his head as he admitted. 'I don't know how to handle it.'

'Do you think it's easy for me?' she threw back. 'It's torture but somehow one makes the best of it.'

He reached for the whisky glass standing to the right of his hand, and took a swallow. 'Women are better at that sort of thing than men.'

'I won't argue with that.' Her disdain evident, she watched him down the last drop of whisky. 'Go easy on the alcohol, Bren. We've an early start tomorrow and it's going to be a long day travelling.'

'Christ,' he exploded again. 'Can't a bloke have a drink without being made to think he's an alcoholic?'

Stung by his irrationality, and knowing it wasn't his first drink of the evening, she hit back. 'I would think you'd have more important things on your mind, such as Kyle's health, than choosing to get sozzled.'

In a defiant gesture and expressly to annoy her, he picked up the bottle of Johnnie Walker and poured another generous measure into the glass. 'Oh, leave me alone, Vanessa. Just ... go away.'

She didn't say anything but stayed in the room long enough to stare him down. When he dropped his gaze, feigning interest in the drawings on the desk, she turned on her heel and left.

Coldly furious, Vanessa showered and got into bed, lying on top of the sheet. If she lived to be one hundred she would never understand men and in particular, Bren. There was something lacking in her husband, a sensitivity of feelings. She had once thought him sensitive but as time passed she was learning otherwise. Curtis, surprisingly, showed more of an emotional response to things and circumstances, than his older brother. Anxious and irritable, she lay listening to the whir of the overhead fan for a long time before she drifted into a dreamless sleep ...

The week following the Selby family's arrival in Sydney flew by in a flurry of activity. Admission, tests, more tests until, finally, the day for Kyle and Curtis's surgery arrived.

Not a moment too soon for Kyle, Curtis observed as, in his theatre gown, he stood at his nephew's bedside while Bren and Vanessa murmured encouraging words to the drowsy baby. The youngster's skin tone had become quite yellow because his condition was deteriorating quicker than the doctors had expected. And it was obvious to anyone with reasonable vision that he was a very sick baby. Curtis glanced at his brother and his heart went out to him. He could only imagine what Bren was suffering mentally — the worry, the anxiety. His gaze moved on to Vanessa, the courageous one. Talk about stoic! She was shedding a few tears now but this was the only time he had seen her cry. Oddly, her sorrowful features didn't seem to make her any less beautiful.

'Mr Selby, Curtis,' a sister came up to him. 'You should be in bed. You've had your pre-med,' she tut-tutted at him. 'We don't want you falling down and injuring yourself before surgery, do we?'

Sister Bennett was a good-looking woman, around forty, he guessed. 'I wouldn't mind, Sister, if you're the one who'd be picking me up,' he answered flirtatiously.

'No such luck, Curtis. The male sisters get to do that and they're not half as gentle as the female ones.'

Taking note of that, Curtis scooted back to bed. If he were honest with himself, he wasn't looking forward to surgery. Dr Samuels had explained in great detail that he might have considerable post-op discomfort, possibly more than Kyle. But he accepted that because he knew the cause was right. Besides, had the situation been reversed and Regan been ill, Bren would have done whatever he could to return *his* daughter to good health.

He would have plenty of time to think while he recuperated, he realised as he stretched under the hospital sheet, about where life was taking him. Of late he had been doing a bit of that and as a consequence a strange restlessness hung over him, something he had never before experienced. He was sure as to what he wanted from life, wasn't he? If he saw more of Regan it would make a difference; he'd be more involved with watching her grow, and helping her to learn things, which would give his life a certain purpose but he was coming to believe that he wanted more — someone to *share* his life. But ... who and where and how could he meet women, isolated as he was on the station? Still, when this — the operation and convalescence — was behind him he would make a sincere attempt to find that special someone.

As he put his hands behind his head he could feel his body relaxing, the pre-med injection finally kicking in. His eyes drooped, closed. He opened them and saw Vanessa standing in the room's doorway. She came up to the side of his bed and gave him an encouraging smile.

'I know I've said it before but I'll say it again before you nod off. Thank you for what you're doing. We'll see you when you wake up,' she said softly.

Curtis drifted into oblivion with the image of her face in his mind . . .

The next twenty-four hours, then thirty-six hours were a stressful time for Bren and Vanessa who had been briefed by Dr Samuels and his team as to what to expect by way of Kyle's recovery rate.

When her baby son opened his eyes for the first time, a few hours after the operation, saw her and smiled, Vanessa had to exert all her self-control not to burst into tears. The transplant team had deemed the operations on both Kyle and Curtis a success but she couldn't accept that Kyle's was until her son's smile. Her baby boy was still smiling, weakly, but Bren wasn't there to see it because he was with Curtis. They had been taking turns to sit with each of them as both became more alert.

The intensive care sister, checking several of the monitoring machines above his hospital cot, grinned at Vanessa. 'That's a good sign,' she said, patting Kyle's head. 'It's a little too soon for liquids like water or milk but you can give him a little crushed ice. I'll go get some.'

Vanessa smiled with relief as the sister walked away. Instinct, love, desperation or perhaps a mixture of all three emotions told her he was going to be all right. The relief wended through her body and into her soul, diluting the worry, the fears that had caused her so many sleepless nights. Her imagination had been working overtime from that day in Dr Klemski's rooms when they'd learned of Kyle's condition, conjuring up all kinds of dreadful scenes. All she had been able to think about and concentrate on, was her baby, how sick he was, and that he might die. It was an experience she prayed never to go through again.

The scope of Curtis's generosity, given unstintingly in his no fuss way, strengthened her respect and liking for the man she had once loathed. They had travelled a long way down the friendship road from the day of the wedding reception in Darwin. It hadn't always been easygoing between them with differences of opinion aplenty, but of late they were very much in agreement, with regard to Amaroo, and Kyle. She wasn't religious but on occasions she said a prayer and when she did she would remember Curtis for the gift he had given to her son. It was interesting too, that while being uncle and nephew, the bond was now a lot closer because they both shared part of a vital organ.

As she spoon-fed a sleepy Kyle pieces of crushed ice, she thought how this crisis had taken its toll on

Bren and was still doing so. He'd been distraught after the operation, fearing the worst, unable to lift his morale or to be optimistic. She knew he couldn't help it because sometimes he became either hyped up or depressed. However, while she felt sympathy for him, she also experienced waves of frustration. Her husband was a man of strength and determination in many ways, but Bren hadn't been dependable in this regard, and that he hadn't been, confounded her. It would have been a comfort for him to be her 'rock', but too often she was the one with the stiff backbone who was leant on rather than vice versa.

Five days after Kyle's transplant operation Dr Samuels advised the family that his prognosis was a positive one. His small body hadn't rejected the donor organ, something that often occurred within thirty-six hours of receiving it, and if he continued to recover at the present rate he could go home and lead a reasonably normal life within weeks with the proviso of regular medical checks for several years and having to take anti-rejection drugs, probably for the rest of his life.

For Curtis, the recuperation period took longer and was hampered by him suffering a blood infection that kept him in hospital for another week after Kyle's release.

Kyle and Curtis's return to Amaroo was a good reason to throw a welcome home party. Those attending were close neighbours, the Johns from Linford Downs Station, plus the Selbys from Broome, Lauren and her family, and Hilary, who'd brought Regan with her. It took place during a lull in the annual wet, before Christmas, which made it a double celebration for everyone.

Curtis, with his fifteen-centimetre scar, was still too weak for normal duties and had been relegated to attending to the station's paperwork. Kyle, amazingly, was almost back to normal, and had begun to crawl, getting into lots of mischief, and trying to copy the antics of his cousin, Guy, who at four was the closest to him in age.

However, if any one person could be regarded as the happiest, it was Bren. He liked nothing better than a party and having family around. He knew that he had been less than one hundred per cent supportive of Vanessa during Kyle's illness and his inability to cope depressed him as much as his son being sick. Children, Bren had come to see, were a huge, ongoing responsibility and he couldn't help it that he disliked the 'baby phase,' and had little patience with their crying, their puking and the demands made on the mother. Vanessa, having to spend more time with Kyle, meant less time for him. *You're a selfish bastard, Bren Selby.* He was but he couldn't and didn't want to change and that was that.

Sipping his beer, his gaze followed Vanessa, good hostess that she was, as she mingled with everyone. She was the best thing that had happened to him and, damn it, why wasn't he more appreciative of the fact? It amazed him, when he took the time to think about it that she, with her personality, talent and charm, could love someone as ordinary as himself. A bloody miracle, he reckoned. He watched

Vanessa fuss for a few minutes over Curtis, who was sitting in a comfortable wooden chair near the barbecue.

His brother wasn't bouncing back to good health as quickly as he'd have liked to, and like Bren, Curtis hated to be inactive. This made him recall some of the injuries that had landed him on his back over the years. Broken ribs from a horse he had been breaking in. Later, he had fallen off one of the artesian bore towers and cracked his skull, and there'd been the sprained ankle when Vanessa had been making the movie, *Heart of the Outback*. He had loathed every minute of being incapacitated and had some sympathy for how Curtis felt.

Vanessa spent considerable time, tending to Curtis's needs in the cottage. It was good that the two of them got along well now, when once they'd spat insults at each other. The specialist had said Curtis could be the slower one to recover and Dr Samuels was being proven right.

His gaze moved to Regan, who was having a rare visit to Amaroo with his mother, and Lauren's eldest boys, Lance and Cameron. They were all getting along well. Outback kids usually mixed well, because there were fewer choices for company than in the city. They were presently playing a game of shuttlecock before it got too dark.

Stuart came up behind him and slapped him soundly on the back. 'Good to have everything back to normal, hey?'

'Not quite normal. Curtis isn't one hundred per cent yet.'

'And he won't be in a hurry to get back to full

strength either. Look at the attention he's getting from the women. Fran, Lauren, Vanessa, Diane, even Hilary. They're all making a fuss of him.'

Bren shrugged his wide shoulders. 'A little spoiling won't do him any harm. He's lacked a woman's touch and caring for a while,' he commented as he watched Fran and Vanessa try to entice his brother with several plates of nibblies.

'Now you can start to plan the home-stay development, the one we talked about on the phone a while ago.' Stuart changed the subject, though his gaze remained fixed on Curtis and those dancing attention on him.

'Not yet, I want to keep it hush-hush for a while. I'm not even telling Vanessa or Curtis till I've done some preliminary planning. They won't be keen for the station to go into debt again,' Bren said quietly. 'Knowing Curtis, the first thing he'll want to do is a damned business plan, projecting costs and profits for the first five years. I'm not ready for that yet.'

'Bren, Bren,' Stuart scolded. 'The home-stay plan can't fail, believe me. I know the tourism business. Well-heeled tourists will jump at the chance, and pay handsomely to stay several days on a working cattle station, *your* station. Look at the El Questro Ranch up north, it's top of the line. There are a few other good ones too. You're not the only station thinking of making a move in this direction. You'll see what I mean and,' he nudged Bren in the ribs, 'it's good business to get in on the ground floor, before others do. Trust me.' He paused for a brief reflection then added slyly, 'Besides, it is *your* station. You're the boss.'

Bren kicked a small rock as he hooked his thumbs into the belt loops of his jeans. 'Maybe.' His uncle was a smart businessman with a proven track record. It made sense to believe him rather than be swayed by what his wife and brother might say. 'When Curtis is fit, in about a month, we'll do a few trips, check out several places.'

'Good. In the meantime, have Fabian do a cost-effectiveness chart or whatever it is that accountants do. That's sound business too.' Stuart smiled as Bren nodded agreeably, confident of his influence over his nephew.

'I will.' Stuart was right. He was always right! The home-stay plan called for boldness, for enterprise and if told prematurely, Curtis and Vanessa's caution could strangle his vision. A muscle flexed in his jaw. He wasn't going to allow that.

'It's time to diversify, to give the property a double income stream,' Stuart went on encouragingly. His gaze, still focussed on Curtis, narrowed as Vanessa, who was standing next to him with a hand on his shoulder, laughed at something he said. Curtis looked up and smiled. Stuart's mouth thinned speculatively for a moment or two then a knowing smile lit his still good-looking, lightly lined features.

'Do what you think is right, but just don't leave it too long, that's all I'm saying,' Stuart said, his tone quietly conspiratorial.

Reg banged his barbecue fork on one of the saucepan lids signalling that the steak and sausages were cooked. Bren and Stuart meandered first to the trestle table that bore an array of alcohol — spirits in bottles and cans of beer in old, scoured-out oil barrels, packed in ice flown in from Kununurra that afternoon — then to the table laid with a variety of food.

His uncle was right, he was the boss, and when he was ready he'd announce the home-stay plan as an accomplished fact, even if it took more than a year to get his head around the whole idea; he wasn't going to let it come over as a pipe-dream. Amaroo was his and if he decided that's the way they would go then Vanessa and Curtis had to accept that. He tilted his glass of whisky and brought it to his lips ...

# CHAPTER FIFTEEN

The next year was a disastrous one for Amaroo because the wet did not come.

The normal wet weather pattern bypassed their station, Cadogan's Run and the Linford Downs Station entirely, a phenomenon that had only occurred twice in living memory. The land, the cattle, the flora and fauna in that part of the Kimberley stood as if in suspended animation, desperate for rain to revive them and bring new life, and hope. It became so dry that the bloodwoods, gums and willow barks down by Gumbledon Creek began to shed leaves in an effort to survive. The cracks in the dry creek bed widened, the banks eroded further and fell away to expose more of the trees' roots, which put the trees under more stress.

And little by little, what capital reserves Amaroo had stored, after working the accounts into the black again, became as empty as the creek bed. The Selbys were forced to pay an exorbitant fee for an engineering company to come and drill for new bores, hoping to tap into additional underground water sources.

The seriousness of the downturn had an effect on everyone at Amaroo. Bren decided that they could get by with just one station hand, so Tony was reluctantly let go. Then, as finances and the drought wore inexorably on, more cattle were rounded up and all but the best of the breeding stock were trucked to Derby to be sold for ridiculously low prices. Bren's level of confidence suffered. He became plagued by doubts as to whether they could tough it out for almost two years, till the next wet, though it was a situation over which he had little control. As a consequence of this his irritability soared, and he began to seek solace in alcohol, as he had done once before early in their marriage.

Vanessa was at a loss to know how to shake him out of his depression, a state for which she had great sympathy. She too was devastated by having to watch what had been built up — the breeding stock, improvements to the property, their funds — go backwards. The coup de grâce was the repossession of their near-new helicopter because they could no longer afford it.

As well, at the end of the month Vanessa was leaving for Melbourne, with Kyle, to take up the role of Detective Kim Clancy, in the television police series titled *The Twenty-first Squad* being filmed at a Melbourne production house. The thirteen weeks had been organised long ago; accommodation was booked and a nanny employed to care for Kyle when she was on the set. She hated to leave the station in the condition it was but, contrarily, the survivor within her acknowledged that it would be good to be away from Amaroo and the day-to-day tension.

Admitting this as she bathed her son, doing her best to elude the splashes of his rough-housing in the bath which she'd rationed to less than forty centimetres deep — he loved water and would stay in it half the day if she let him — gave her no joy. As she got him out, protesting loudly, and wrapped him in a fluffy towel, Vanessa had a moment's regret for the atmosphere in which Kyle was to celebrate his second birthday. Adding unnecessarily to the strain was the expected arrival of Hilary, Stuart and Diane Selby. They were expected any time now, to participate in Kyle's birthday celebrations. He was now a healthy, happy and active child after his earlier ordeal.

Vanessa thought the timing unfortunate. Bren's moodiness had extended to and enveloped Curtis, making her brother-in-law more acerbic than usual. Reg, an outback man through and through, kept his own counsel and went about his chores without murmur or complaint, as did Fran. The only one who didn't understand how tough things were, but had begun to know what birthdays were all about, was her bundle of joy.

A doting mother, Vanessa constantly marvelled at how much her son had grown and learned in just two years of life, especially after being so ill, and her only ongoing disappointment was Bren who continued to show some irritability towards him. Fran, though she'd never experienced motherhood herself, was of the opinion that some men weren't good with small children though Vanessa knew, from Fran and Nova, that Curtis had been wonderful with Regan when she'd been small. It was difficult but she was having to accept that in Bren's case, that was probably so. But ... she didn't have to like it.

Vanessa was dressing Kyle in his usual day-time attire, a nappy, because it was too hot for other clothes, when Fran poked her head around the open doorway. 'Reg said to let you know, the Selbys are about fifteen minutes away.' She gave a disdainful sniff. 'Trust Stuart to arrive in time for morning tea. The man has an uncanny knack of timing his arrival around food or refreshments. It's a wonder he's not the size of a house.'

'It's not Stuart that concerns me, it's ...'

'Hilary.' Fran gave an understanding nod. 'She's all right once you learn not to be fazed by her condescending stares.' She thought for a moment then added. 'Don't think she didn't have her problems with the isolation, the solitude of Amaroo. Matthew, so I've heard via camp-fire gossip and such, was, in the early days of their marriage, often away for extended periods. Did you know that Hilary even had a nervous breakdown after Bren was born?' One eyebrow lifted as she delivered that information. 'No one knows exactly why because his was a regular, run-of-the-mill labour. Then she had Curtis and Lauren pretty close together, and that kept her too busy to be lonely, until Bren went to boarding school in his teens.'

Vanessa gave Fran a grateful smile. 'I didn't know that. She gives the impression of being totally unfazed!'

'She is, now! Over the years Hilary perfected the mistress of Amaroo role to a 't'. But you're its mistress now and don't let her forget it. She's the kind who, if she sees a weakness, will take advantage of it.'

'You're probably right. Still, I'd feel happier about her visit if the station was doing better.'

'Don't worry about that,' Fran said offhandedly. 'She's been around long enough to know that properties in the Kimberley have their ups and downs. Just show her how well you fit in. Once she sees that, and that Bren's happy — she's always been over-protective of him for some reason — she'll be closer to accepting you as Amaroo's mistress.'

Vanessa shook her head in admiration of the older woman's advice. 'You are a wise one.'

'Reg and I have been here almost eighteen years. People don't stay in one place if they're not reasonably content. I learned a long while ago how to get around Hilary. In time you will too.' She put her arms out to take Kyle, and suggested, 'Go make yourself beautiful for your in-laws.'

What Vanessa expected to be an ordeal, initially, turned out much better than anticipated. Hilary, on arrival, had masked her ongoing disappointment that she had another grandson with the statement that it was important for Amaroo to produce a male heir and that there was plenty of time for more children. Diane, whose second daughter, Traci, was expecting her first child, clucked and cooed over Kyle and even Stuart, whom Vanessa believed to be one of the most self-centred men she had come across, paid her son undue attention. Perhaps he did due to the novelty of Kyle being male, because his offspring, including his first grandchild, were female. The attention pleased Bren and brightened his mood for the length of their stay.

Although ... with her penchant for observing people, as they ate, dining casually in the kitchen, and even as they played night tennis, Vanessa made several interesting, and curious observations. Below the surface camaraderie a subtle animosity existed between Hilary and Diane, the latter being three or four years younger than her mother-in-law. And more curious still, it wasn't the sharp-tongued Hilary who'd slyly deliver the occasional sniping remark and the veiled criticisms, but the milder mannered, pleasant Diane.

'What are you doing about the drought, Bren?' Stuart asked from his position at the end of the long table where everyone congregated for Kyle's birthday dinner.

'Like everyone else, we're waiting it out, just surviving. We've cut back, haven't we, hon?' Bren glanced towards Vanessa for confirmation, which she gave with a nod of her head. 'CT Engineering have dug four more bores, found water in one.'

'That must be costing you plenty,' Diane said. She had grown up in suburban Adelaide and knew little, apart from what Stuart told her, about the hardships of life on the land.

'The earth,' Curtis contributed dryly. 'But if the drilling finds another water source it will help our situation a lot — see us through till the next wet.'

'I presume you're dropping feed,' Hilary asked. She looked at Bren for her answer as she dandled a sleepy Kyle on her lap. It was almost his bedtime.

'Yes. We've managed to maintain a percentage of the herd,' Vanessa informed her on Bren's behalf, 'and have brought the stock in closer to bore water to make feeding and watering easier. We can monitor them better that way, too.'

Everyone at the table knew several more months would pass before the next wet broke the drought. Vanessa, personally, had grave concerns as to how they'd manage till then, but if the situation became borderline and money was needed fast, she would sell the property she had bought — when Bren paid her back the money she'd loaned him — as an investment in Darwin. Her chin firmed as she made the mental decision, that she would do so with or without Bren's approval. She was determined to ensure Kyle's inheritance though such a situation was many years away.

'We put in several underground water tanks before the last wet, so the homestead and buildings close by won't run out of water.' Bren glanced towards Vanessa and grinned. 'At Vanessa's suggestion.'

'Really!' Hilary's gaze spun towards her daughter-in-law. 'How innovative.'

'Vanessa's done several things around Amaroo since she's been here,' Diane said. 'Spruced up the stockman's quarters.' She darted a narrowed glance at Hilary. 'Not before time either. As I remember them they were pretty revolting. Put in a new bathroom, a common room with an updated kitchenette, including a freezer, a new television and expanded the video library.'

'That's right. Amaroo's set a benchmark for other

stations to aspire to,' Curtis added, unaware of the current of tension between his mother and Diane.

'Stockmen tend to come and go with the seasons, and sometimes they don't look after things,' Hilary fired back but her expression showed that Diane's comments had hit their mark.

'The blokes who've been here have appreciated the effort,' Reg threw in, helping to give Diane's words further weight.

Vanessa had already gleaned, from conversations with Fran, Reg and Curtis, that when Hilary lived at Amaroo she preferred to spend money on herself, or in refurnishing the homestead but Diane's not-so-subtle criticisms caused a ripple of tension to radiate around the table.

Still on the attack, Diane went on. 'A few less overseas holidays and lavish parties when Matthew was alive and there would have been the wherewithal to make similar improvements to Amaroo. Wouldn't there, Hilary?'

Hilary gave Diane a dagger stare as she ashed her cigarette in the ashtray. 'I recall that you never knocked back the opportunity to attend any party we gave.'

'I came because my husband wanted to. After all, Amaroo is where he grew up,' Diane tossed back without apology.

'Diane!' The suppressed anger in Stuart's tone added to the unease. 'That will do. Sorry, everyone,' he glanced at those around the table, 'after two glasses of wine, my wife tends to get stroppy.'

'The hell I do,' Diane retorted as she saluted him with her wine glass before downing the last drop.

Fran happened to catch Vanessa's eye, and an eyebrow lifted. She intervened to break the tension. 'Don't know about anyone else, but I'm ready for another cup of coffee and a second slice of birthday cake.'

'Me too,' Vanessa was quick to agree. She pushed back her chair and moved towards Hilary. 'But first, it's past Kyle's bedtime and a certain young man looks sleepy,' she said as she scooped Kyle out of Hilary's lap.

'Mind if I come too?' Hilary asked, staunchly refusing to look at Diane who sat opposite her.

'Of course not,' Vanessa replied. She was embarrassed by Diane's undiplomatic behaviour though it confirmed what she had been thinking, about the animosity between them. Something was wrong between the two women, and she'd come to believe that the situation had been gathering malice for years. She cast her mind back to other family gatherings and could remember, now that she thought about it, the occasional stinging remark from Diane, but nothing as pointed as what had been said tonight. What was the problem?

Jealousy or was it a personality clash? No, it seemed deeper than that. Perhaps ... could Diane think she'd been wronged or in the past, intimidated by Hilary? Whatever the reason, it was all very ... interesting. And because the battle lines had been drawn tonight, she would puzzle over the cause until she knew why. But who could she ask? Bren? No. He knew his mother's shortcomings but he was a loyal son. It would have to be someone else. Curtis or Fran? Maybe ...

· ■ ·

Filming of *The Twenty-first Squad* in Melbourne was kept to a tight schedule and Vanessa often worked twelve to fourteen hour days, but not Sundays which, due to Kerri's contractual organising, she had off to spend with Kyle. She missed the life at Amaroo very much. The station had become familiar, it was home and she revelled in the freedom, the open space and though they had their ups and downs she missed Bren too. Still, isolated from home and her husband, as well as spending hours learning scripts, planning scenes then acting them out, Vanessa still had time to deliberate on their marriage.

The rose-tinted glasses had come off a long time ago and there were times when she surprised herself by how dispassionately she could view their relationship. Theirs wasn't the perfect marriage her parents had enjoyed. But when she cast her mind back to Edward and Rosa Forsythe's marriage, she admitted that her memories could have been enhanced by a romantic youthfulness on her part. She and Bren had a good, working marriage. Most, but not all the time, there was give and take and they both compromised, well, at least she did. It was just that ... When she took the time to consider the details of their relationship, and reminisced on their first days together, she wondered what had happened to *that* Bren.

Initially, she had been attracted to him because of his lighthearted, easygoing ways. Something had made him change, and he was still changing. She didn't know if she was to blame, whether it was because of Kyle or was it the pressure of running Amaroo? All she knew was that his lightheartedness and easygoing manner were being replaced by periods of aggressiveness and, on occasions, an irrational moodiness.

Adding to that, sometimes she even questioned the sense of some of his decisions, such as selling off most of the herd because of the drought. She and Curtis had argued against selling the stock, preferring to take out a loan for feed till the wet rejuvenated the land, as was being done on Cadogan's Run and Linford Downs. But no, Bren had been adamant that *his* way was right so she and Curtis had, with reservations, given in. She also suspected that Bren was listening to advice Stuart gave about managing Amaroo, though he refused to admit that he was. The two were very . . . cosy with their regular phone calls, the more than occasional reciprocal visits. Obviously Bren admired Stuart's business acumen and wanted to emulate his uncle's success on the land but, she questioned Stuart's capacity, despite him being raised on Amaroo, to understand that what worked in tourism didn't necessarily translate to success on a cattle station.

She glanced at her script and tried to regain her concentration. They were halfway through the detective series and she was enjoying her first experience at working on a television drama. It was different to anything she'd done before and more demanding than live theatre, where one might do the same role and dialogue for several months. Suppressing a yawn and after marking the page she was up to, she accepted that she wasn't in the right mood to learn lines.

Vanessa rested her head against the sofa's back and closed her eyes. She knew that Sandra Long, the live-in housekeeper who cared for Kyle while she was on set, was out shopping. Kyle hadn't woken from his afternoon nap either, and after he did she planned to take him to the park down the street. He loved the park known as Darling Gardens because it was so green and bordered the Yarra River. He liked to watch the occasional boat and racing skiff train — something foreign and fascinating to a small child growing up hundreds of kilometres inland.

A knock on the apartment's front door prevented Vanessa from slipping into the doze she had been anticipating. After a sigh, she got up and went to see who it was. Her eyebrows flew up in surprise as she opened the door.

'Nova. I don't believe it! How did you find me?' She stepped back to let Nova enter the living room.

'Rang Amaroo. Bren gave me your address. I've been working in Geelong and Bendigo.' Her slanted eyes darted around the large, furnished living room with its floor to ceiling windows that, being in South Yarra, had a partial view of the city. 'Nice place,' she said as she walked to the window and took it all in. 'Great view.'

'It's good to see you.' Vanessa masked the inclination to frown. Something was wrong, Nova didn't seem herself. She appeared agitated and trying to hide it. As if she were uncomfortable.

'Where's Kyle? I'd love to see him.' Nova thrust a parcel at Vanessa. She liked to appear to be doing the right thing. 'I brought him something, seeing how I missed his birthday party. He's well now?'

Vanessa smiled. 'How thoughtful. He's terrific, healthwise. He's taking a nap but he should wake soon. How about a cup of tea, coffee?'

'Do you have anything stronger?'

Again the urge to frown. Vanessa controlled it. 'Are you kidding? With production staff and actors dropping in at all hours I have to keep a supply of grog in the fridge,' Vanessa admitted with a smile. She went into the spotless, modern kitchen, opened a cupboard and took out two glasses. From the refrigerator she took a half-empty bottle of chardonnay and poured the wine into the glasses.

'So, tell me, are things going well? Lots of gigs, making plenty of money?' Vanessa asked, while at the same time she surreptitiously observed Nova over the rim of her wine glass. The younger woman had an air of — what? — recklessness about her. At first glance and studying her clothes, she looked very with-it. Clean jeans, T-shirt, leather jacket and heeled boots but it was her face and eyes that worried Vanessa because she looked as if she had been crying for a week. The corners of her well-shaped mouth were turned down and her skin had an unhealthy pallor to it. Probably not eating or sleeping properly, Vanessa concluded. But ... she couldn't help but question whether that was all.

'Couldn't be better,' Nova replied, too quickly. 'I have solid bookings for the next six months. The band and I are working on a new album and I'm collaborating with another country and western singer-songwriter, Jo Brooks, on several numbers. She's terrific at harmonising.'

'That's wonderful,' Vanessa was duly impressed. Still, if everything was so well why wasn't Nova happy? '*But . . .?*'

Nova stared at Vanessa. 'But what?'

'I can hear the "but" in your voice even if you didn't say it out loud. What's wrong?

Nova's gaze narrowed on the woman she had decided to make her role model, to be more successful than. 'You always were perceptive. I can fool most people but not you.' Shit, why had she bothered to look Vanessa and Kyle up? To listen to a lecture from Vanessa? Hell, no! Then why was she here? She knew she wasn't going to take much comfort from the answer. Because, odd as it seemed, she felt she could trust Vanessa. The actress was a good listener and really, who else did she have to talk to about her problems? Not Fran or her father or the busy Anthea. Vanessa, unpalatable as it might be, was the best alternative.

'Do you want to talk about it?'

Nova shrugged in an attempt to minimise the problem's importance. 'I should be happy, I'm doing well. Anthea is so pleased she's negotiating with an American recording company for an audition in Nashville. But' . . . she shook her head, 'I'm miserable and I don't know why.'

'Your boyfriend?'

Nova's gaze skipped towards the view again. 'M-maybe. I'm not sure. *The Smokehouse Five*, that's the name of Leo's band, were struggling before I hooked up with them. They did the backings for my album. Leo's a great arranger, but there are times when he resents *my* success. Sometimes, we argue and he ... he gets ... mad. He's hit me once or twice.'

Vanessa shook her head. 'You don't have to put up with that. No woman does.'

'I know. But I kind of provoke him and he reacts,' Nova admitted, rather shamefacedly. 'Afterwards, he brings me flowers and gifts, and all is forgiven.' She turned towards Vanessa. 'You see, it's like ... We need each other.'

Vanessa understood about the mutual need. 'He needs you to keep his band in work and you think he's the best musical arranger you can find. But do you love him?'

'I guess.' Nova still couldn't make eye contact with Vanessa. 'As much as I'm capable of loving him.'

Aahhh! Of course, Vanessa had her measure. Nova still had feelings for Curtis. It was evident in her guarded expression, her less than wholehearted avowal regarding Leo. 'You know, if you ever need a break away from music, you'll be very welcome at Amaroo.'

Nova smiled for the first time. 'I know. Thanks. I will take time off in a couple of months to come home, after the wet.'

'Yes, well, the way things are at Amaroo, we're praying for an early one. It's so dry there.'

'I'd heard that you were doing it tough.'

'Yes, we're not alone, others are too. What is it about the Australian outback?' Vanessa struggled to produce a smile. 'It's either feast or famine, no in-between.'

'It's a bugger,' Nova agreed, her grin sympathetic in spite of her being more concerned with herself than the state of Amaroo.

From the second bedroom came a plaintive cry. 'Mumma. Up.'

Vanessa grinned at Nova, delighted that Kyle was awake because she loved to show him off. She stood, then pulled Nova out of her chair. 'Come and meet my son.'

Kyle was a hit with Nova and vice versa. With his father's grey eyes, his sturdy build, Vanessa's blond hair and olive skin, he was a miniature whirlwind, playing, gabbling to himself and generally responsible for creating disaster zones wherever he went. They took him to the park and bought him an ice-cream treat, half of which he spilled down the front of his clothes.

Later, Nova was easily persuaded to stay for dinner.

That night as Vanessa lay in bed, her thoughts focussed on Nova Morrison. She genuinely liked Nova but she could tell that the woman was troubled. The thought came to her . . . was she doing drugs? So many young people did these days. It was, sadly, fairly commonplace in the entertainment business. Artists should have been satisfied with achieving what they achieved but many weren't, and a percentage took a cocktail of drugs to keep themselves on a high and to disguise a range of complexes. With the success she was having the world was Nova's oyster now, but happiness for her seemed . . . an elusive element.

Her thoughts moved to Curtis and, unable to drift off, she began to wonder what her brother-in-law wanted from life and why he was so anti-women? She knew he had been hurt by his ex-wife but, did that mean one gave up looking for a partner forever? Stretching under the covers, she rolled onto her side. No matter how right it might be for Nova, she couldn't see Curtis falling in love with her. The chemistry wasn't there and she doubted Nova's ability to create it. But what kind of woman could Curtis fall for? Not another Georgia type nor, she suspected, someone like Nova.

Not that it was her concern, she assured herself with a sigh. Curtis could fall for whoever took his fancy. Then the fact that she was even thinking and worrying about his non-existent love life annoyed her. Why was she? Cranky with her thoughts, she screwed her eyes up tight and tried to fall asleep. She was expected on the set at 5 a.m. so she had no time to speculate over Curtis's love life. Yawning, she thumped the pillow and rolled onto her stomach ...

Bren Selby twirled the whisky around in his glass; he liked to listen to the sound the ice made as it clinked against the sides. He enjoyed drinking his mother's Johnnie Walker export quality whisky. The Darwin evening was oppressively hot, the much-awaited wet about to arrive. Everything steamed, everything appeared abnormally still, which made you more conscious of the heat. You got used to and, perversely, never got used to it. Tomorrow Vanessa and Kyle were flying up from Melbourne. The thirteen episodes of *The Twenty-first Squad* were 'in the can,' as Vanessa said and she was coming home. Not soon enough, as far as he was concerned. He had wallowed in a series of moods since her departure, missing her and the little feller who had, thank God, gone through the messy baby stage and was becoming more interesting. His son! How much would Kyle have grown in thirteen weeks?

Vanessa reported that he was getting into lots of mischief — a typical Selby male. He chuckled at that, he could recall some of the scrapes he and Curtis had got in to as kids — even his father and Stuart had had their share of misadventures as they'd grown up on Amaroo. As he sipped his drink Bren admitted that he was growing to dislike the periods Vanessa spent away from Amaroo. He wanted her where he could see her, talk to her, make love with her. A ripple of jealousy made his stomach muscles tighten as, belatedly, he realised that her stage and now screen career hadn't suffered because she lived in the Kimberley. She was such an accomplished actress that, as her reputation grew, she was becoming more in demand, with Kerri passing on job offers on a regular basis.

Grudgingly, he conceded that what she earned made a difference to Amaroo's surviving the drought. His pride had compromised in that regard. They'd not had to borrow from the bank, though there had been belt-tightening exercises, for everyone. That's the way it was on the land: a couple of good years followed by a few bad years and so it went on and on, interminably. He shifted restlessly in his chair. His uncle didn't have any such problems. Stuart's business was going from strength to strength, and he was rolling in the green stuff.

Bren pushed the copy of the several days old *Melbourne Age* newspaper to the far side of the table. His mother had left the entertainment page open because it showed a picture of Vanessa and the cast of *The Twenty-first Squad,* including the producer, Martin Pirelli, toasting its expected success. He didn't care for the familiarity of Pirelli's arm draped around Vanessa's shoulders. Shit, he didn't care for that at all. Producers, directors, actors, in his opinion were for the most part a scummy lot. His forehead rippled into a frown.

Some would have seen Vanessa, a woman alone with a child, as fair game. How often had a man tried to come on to her, he wondered? He would never know the answer because she was too wise to tell him due to his tendency to react aggressively. Well, she was his, and if any man laid a finger on her ... Damn it, why was he worrying? She loved him and he was a lucky so-and-so because she did. With her looks, talent and personality, Vanessa could have any man she wanted — the miracle was that, after almost four-and-a-half years of marriage, she continued to want him.

Downing the remains of his drink, he got up to pour another from the traymobile-cum-bar in a corner of the living room. His mother was in the kitchen making dinner, cooking one of his favourite dishes, barbecued baby octopus in a creamy sauce which would be served on a bed of salad greens and side vegetables. It was a dish Fran would never do and he smirked complacently, pleased that his mother enjoyed spoiling him — more than she did Curtis or Lauren.

'You'll stay a few days, won't you?' Hilary asked as they sat, eating dinner on the patio.

'Depends on Vanessa. She might want to go home straight away.'

Hilary reached across to cover Bren's hand with her own. 'You're a persuasive man. I'm sure you can convince her to stay a while. I'd like to see more of Kyle, he's growing so fast.'

Bren gave his mother a considering look, unsure whether it was Kyle she wanted to see or whether she liked having him around so she could try to dominate him; Hilary Selby was like that. Just to be difficult he made her wait for his answer. 'I'll see what I can do.'

Vanessa, Kyle and Bren stayed at Cullen Bay for three days then, pleading the need to get back to the station, they returned to Amaroo.

# CHAPTER SIXTEEN

The arrival of the wet to break the drought was a good reason to throw a party at Amaroo, even if only six people attended. Fran outdid herself with the food, whipping up a special meal from what was considered a much depleted pantry. There was also plenty to drink. Bren and Curtis, no matter how tight finances were, managed to keep a supply of alcohol about the place. Vanessa, who for the most part drank little, was silently perplexed by the Australian males' propensity for beer and the consequences of over-imbibing.

Reg, who became merry after four stubbies, would periodically burst into song, much to Fran's embarrassment. Warren, after a few, liked to find a wall to lean on and grin inanely at everyone. Alcohol, unfortunately, made Bren aggressive and he'd want to challenge people to silly dares — such as swimming across Gumbledon Creek, now a raging torrent. And Curtis, well, he barely changed at all, other than becoming quieter than usual.

'Hey, bro,' Bren yelled to Curtis across the living room, 'you're not keeping up,' he said, raising his can of beer in a challenge.

'Not in the mood. Besides, I can't compete in the grog stakes with you,' Curtis retorted. 'No one on Amaroo can.'

Bren grinned, pleased by what he considered to be a compliment. 'Piker!'

Curtis responded with a rude gesture. Everyone laughed, well almost everyone. Vanessa didn't. She didn't want to appear a nark but Bren's behaviour — he was no longer a teenager with a need to prove his manliness — was disappointing. She didn't mind that he drank, it relaxed him, but why wasn't he mature enough to know when to stop? Some evidence of what she was thinking must have shown on her face . . .

'Wifey doesn't approve, do you, hon?'

An eyebrow lifted as she queried him, 'Approve of what?'

'Me getting pissed.'

Vanessa tried to make her reply sound lighthearted, 'What I don't approve of is you being hung-over and grumpy for the next twenty-four hours.'

'Doesn't matter, not much to do in the wet anyway. Might as well be drunk as sitting around watching the rain. Gets bloody boring.'

'It might be boring but we'd be cactus here without the wet,' Curtis threw in.

'Too right,' Warren and Reg chorused and raised their tinnies in a silent salute to the rain.

'I love the rain.' Vanessa said. 'The sound it makes on the tin roof, its awesome power. It reminds me of . . . '

'Bloody England, I suppose,' Bren retorted, turning nasty.

'Amaroo, not England, is my home, Bren,' she pointed out quietly, now aware that her husband was working himself into a thoroughly disagreeable mood. When he had too much 'brew' he would argue over anything and nothing.

Curtis tried to attract attention. 'I will have another, bro. I need the practice 'cause one of these days I will drink you under the table.'

'The hell you will!'

Vanessa's smile thanked Curtis for his intervention, and like a co-conspirator he grinned back at her. They had a good, mutual understanding of each other nowadays, seeming to know when to join ranks against Bren's more outlandish, unworkable ideas, and when to jointly encourage him. They made a good, if silent, 'team'.

'Wazza, mate, fancy a game of soccer in the rain?' Bren challenged the lone stockman the station had retained. They could get away with a lean, mean working crew of just five, including Vanessa, because all were experienced in handling stock and other situations.

'If I can have Curtis on my side,' Warren responded after some consideration.

Bren looked questioningly at Reg. 'We can do 'em mate, can't we?'

Reg shook his head. 'You're mad as a cut snake, Bren.' Then he gave his boss a crooked smile. 'Why not?'

A few minutes later Fran and Vanessa, while Kyle was having his afternoon nap, stood on the verandah, peering through sheeting rain as the four men kicked Kyle's soccer ball around the front yard.

In seconds they were soaked and being covered in mud. Ripe language and insults rent the sodden air and with Curtis and Warren more lithely built and better coordinated than Bren and Reg, they ended up with the lion's share of the ball, a fact which infuriated an overly competitive Bren.

'They're not coming inside wearing that mud,' Vanessa muttered to Fran. However, in spite of her schoolmarmish tone she had to laugh at the sight they made. Every other time one man kicked the ball, he more or less ended up on his backside. 'At times like this I wish I had a video camera.'

'That wouldn't be good, they'd be inhibited. Besides, the lads are just letting off steam. No one can get used to days, then weeks of inactivity during the wet,' Fran said, by way of excusing the rough-housing. 'Silly Reg, he'll be so stiff tomorrow he won't want to get out of bed.'

'Men,' Vanessa chuckled. 'I'll never understand them.'

'Mmmm, isn't that what men say about women?' Fran replied tongue-in-cheek. 'They can shower the mud off in the stockmen's quarters. I'll make a pot of coffee to go with the madeira cake I took out of the freezer earlier on.'

Vanessa watched for a few more minutes, then she left them to it to check on Kyle . . .

It was late in the evening, the wet had come and gone and the flooding creeks and puddles were drying up. The Morrisons had retired for the night, Kyle was in bed and Vanessa, Bren and Curtis sat around the kitchen table, discussing finances.

'The idea's laudable, Vanessa, but I don't see how the station can afford it,' Bren said as he dropped the piece of paper onto the kitchen table.

'*I* don't think the station can afford not to. We should look at ways to drought-proof Amaroo.' She tapped the paper with its rows of figures. 'Each year a sum of money should be set aside — perhaps two or five per cent of the station's net profit — in a separate, untouchable account for when it will be needed.'

This was a scheme Vanessa had thought up while working in Melbourne. She would rather Amaroo have less disposable income each year than go through the privations they'd recently suffered. Their cash reserves had been expended and in the end she had had to sell the property in Darwin to keep the station's figures in the black. There had to be a better way . . .

'I don't agree. Droughts here are as rare as hen's teeth,' Bren pointed out. 'We probably won't see another one in our lifetime.'

'I hope we don't,' Vanessa said with fervour, 'but if we do I'd rather be prepared — surely it's good management. It's going to take a year, probably two years, for us to become financially comfortable again. As well, we have to rebuild the breeding stock we sold.' She stared directly at him. 'A downturn in overseas sales, such as what happened during Desert Storm in '91, could finish us.'

'That isn't likely,' Curtis intervened. 'The export beef trade is booming in the Middle East and Asia. I've heard that some stations in Western Australia can't fill their prescribed orders.'

Vanessa's chin tilted determinedly. 'Maybe so, but where's the harm in being prepared for the worst?'

'Vanessa has a point,' Curtis conceded to Bren. That he did made his brother scowl at him.

'Ganging up on me, are you?' Bren retorted. He was becoming increasingly irritated by Vanessa's obsession with finances. After all, she was a relative Johnny-come-lately to the outback, what did she really know?

'No, but it is worth considering,' Curtis refused to be intimidated by his brother's churlishness. 'Why not run the idea by Fabian, see what he thinks of it?'

Bren stared first at Curtis, then he turned an angry gaze on Vanessa. '*I own Amaroo* and I'll make the decisions, thank you both.' And so saying, he scraped his chair back, got up and strode from the room.

Annoyed by his display Vanessa got up, her intention to go after him. As she did she silently acknowledged a growing frustration at the way Bren dealt with confrontations and matters he didn't like, by ignoring them or walking away, instead of talking things through. That it was happening more often with regard to Amaroo and their personal relationship concerned her. Just recently she'd said she wanted another child and they'd argued unsatisfactorily about it without reaching an agreement because Bren had walked away.

Curtis touched her hand. 'Let him cool down.' For a moment or two he studied the fieriness in her eyes, the rapid breathing, signs that her temper was on the rise. 'You know Bren, he doesn't like to be *told.* He likes to think "suggestions" regarding Amaroo emanate from him. I wouldn't bring the savings plan up again. In a week or two — when he's mulled it over — it's likely that he'll raise the matter as if it were his own idea.'

Vanessa stared at Curtis, admiring his ability to read Bren so well. Fleetingly, she wondered if he had studied psychology when he attended university. 'Your brother can be very . . . annoying. I only want what's best for Amaroo, we all do. Why can't Bren see that?'

Curtis gave her a slow grin. 'Stubbornness, it's a Selby trait. You should know that by now. He'll come round, wait and see.'

'But . . . You do think it's a good idea, don't you?'

'It has merit,' he agreed. 'As you know, there'll be years when our profits will be low due to a variety of reasons. Most stations experience that.'

'Then, in the years we make good profits, we put aside twice as much.'

His grin widened. 'You're a hard woman to get around, Vanessa Selby.'

Delighted that he saw the merit of her plan, Vanessa's anger abated and her eyes suddenly twinkled at him with mischief. 'That I am, Curtis. *You* should know that by now,' she paraphrased what he'd said earlier. 'Living in the outback has taught me to be determined.' She rinsed their coffee cups in the sink then walked to the hall doorway. 'I'll say goodnight.'

Left alone at the kitchen table, Curtis did his best — and failed — to erase from his mind that cheeky look of hers before she'd left. Vanessa Selby was turning out to be a woman of some substance. Feisty, intelligent, talented. He brushed crumbs off the table with his left hand and let them fall onto the floor. Then he closed his eyes and shook his head as a panoply of memories assailed him, from the first time he'd laid eyes on her. How she had dug her heels in and been determined to learn everything she could about outback life, embracing the good things and the hardships with equal vigour. How brave she'd been after the dust storm. Yes, she was turning out to be a true-blue, modern pioneer woman though she didn't have a drop of Aussie blood in her, which made her character and behaviour all the more admirable.

His swing from dislike to admiration, to respect and liking, had occurred subtly, he realised, because he had been almost unaware of the change. He squinted at the sheen on the stainless steel kitchen sink, wishing ... What did he wish? That Bren would appreciate the treasure he had in Vanessa. She, not his moody brother was becoming Amaroo's strength, its heart, its soul. But in the next breath he scoffed at his musings — they were too fanciful — as he stood up and went outside. Tilting his head back he looked up at a star-studded night, doing so was a ritual with him, before he went to bed.

Christ, he slapped his thigh as he walked towards the cottage, his brief talk with Vanessa had put him into a strange mood. What he needed was to get away, to go and see Regan. He'd go whenever Georgia was off on a photo assignment in Europe. That way they wouldn't need to see or trade insults with each other.

297

Regan was almost twelve. That thought jolted him. Where had the years gone, and how quickly they were passing. His daughter was almost a teenager, and he'd been alone, without a woman for almost seven of those years. He'd never done anything really about trying to find a woman, as he'd said he would do before Kyle's transplant. *Maybe that's how it was meant to be.* Not every man in the outback ended up happily, or even unhappily, married. That made him spare a fleeting thought for Nova and the night she had kissed him — such un-Nova like behaviour had been a shock. He shrugged a shoulder, dismissing her action as coming from someone who'd had a few too many glasses of wine. Nova didn't fancy him, he was sure of that. She was in a full-on relationship with Leo, the guy in the band. After a last look at the stars, and a long sigh, he opened the cottage door and went inside.

Vanessa typed the words 'the end' into the computer, sat back and breathed out in a satisfied sigh. The script provisionally titled *North of the Nullarbor* was finished, at last. The work had taken considerably longer than anticipated and she knew that Kerri was anxious to receive the final draft because she had two potential backers. They were interested in an overall production package which, if negotiations went well, might include Toni Collette, veteran actor Jack Thompson in the role of Rufus Whitfield and Andrew Clarke as Rupert. With the possibility of Jane Campion, a talented director from New Zealand — if she liked the script — directing the film. The project was getting to the exciting stage and seeing the script through to the end had given her a sense of fulfilment. However, having limited experience in the ways of film and stage proposals, Vanessa knew the project was a long way from being a done deal.

Bren came into the office and stood behind her. His strong hands began to massage her tight shoulder muscles. 'Finished. That's great, hon.'

'I don't know about great, but it was a relief to type "the end".'

'You've devised a wonderful, pioneer story, Vanessa, about Emily Whitfield and her family,' he assured her. 'There's passion and privation, greed, murder, a cattle stampede and the bad guy gets his just desserts in the end. I'm no expert but I reckon it's top movie material.'

Vanessa chuckled at his praise. 'Maybe you should go to London and try to sell it to the backers.'

'Your agent wouldn't like that. I'm still not sure that Kerri fully approves of me.'

She turned around in the chair to look at him, couching her words so she didn't hurt his feelings. 'Nonsense, Bren. If Kerri didn't like you, believe me, you would know it in no uncertain manner. She doesn't hide her feelings, her likes or dislikes unless it's prudent for her business to do so.'

'If you say so.' He spun the chair around once and when it came full circle he pulled her out of it and imprisoned her with his arms. 'Coming to bed?'

She blinked coquettishly at him. 'Will you make it worth my while?' She had gone off her contraceptive and, whether Bren liked it or not, they were going to have another baby. She was confident that he'd come around and be happy about the idea once she became pregnant.

'You bet.' He kissed her, gently at first, then, with growing passion. His hands roamed across her back, fitted around her waist and then slid down to cup her buttocks and pull her hard against him.

In response, Vanessa's arms crept around his neck and she arched against him seductively. They'd been married almost five years and despite some ongoing difficulties in their relationship, the excitement between them remained strong, perhaps even stronger because they were periodically separated due to her work. Lovingly, the fingers of her right hand traced down his recently shaved cheek and across his chin.

A discreet cough made them leap apart, almost guiltily.

'Sorry,' Curtis drawled from the doorway. 'Thought you should know. Reg had a call from Nova. She's coming home. He's going to pick her up from Kununurra in the morning.' Having delivered the message, and with a slightly embarrassed grin, he disappeared.

'Too many damned interruptions around here,' Bren grumbled as he patted Vanessa's bottom. Hand in hand they went and checked on Kyle then walked towards their bedroom.

After they'd made love, Vanessa lay on the bed listening to Bren's even breathing as she snuggled up to him, still too wide awake to fall asleep. It was good that after a few weeks thinking time he had agreed to go ahead with Amaroo's savings plan. Curtis had been right about his brother's need to chew things over then make out that it was his idea. She didn't care who took the credit for it as long as Amaroo's future was assured.

And, at least they'd made love without arguing about another baby. Why wasn't he keen to have more children? That he wasn't puzzled her. Being an only child, she wanted a big family, three at least but Bren, disappointingly, appeared content with just one. She didn't want Kyle to go through the loneliness of being an only child, as she had. And while she wasn't entirely comfortable with deceiving him about going off the pill, she desperately wanted their son to have a brother or sister to play and grow up with. It would tie her down more and she'd do less stage and film work but that was, she had decided, an acceptable trade-off. And Bren would be happy about her doing less work as he didn't like her to be away from Amaroo for long periods of time.

Her thoughts shifted to London, and her next engagement. In three weeks she and Kyle were flying to the United Kingdom where she would have several weeks of rehearsal before appearing in the drama, *The Women's Room* at the Lyceum Theatre in the West End. She and Kyle would be gone for almost five months. Vanessa was looking forward to it, yet, at the same time she dreaded being away for such a long time even though there was appeal in the fact that it would be super to catch up with old friends and to show off her beautiful son.

She sighed and stretched like a sated cat. Tomorrow *she* would go and pick up Nova. She had to do several things in Kununurra and she didn't think Reg would mind if she took his place. Moving her body close to Bren's warmth, she let sleep overtake her.

The young woman Vanessa met at Kununurra Airport mid-morning was sombre and dull-eyed. Not even seeing a bouncing, energetic Kyle again lifted Nova's obvious depression. The chopper's engine made talking difficult, even with headsets and attached mikes for communication, so on the return trip Vanessa wisely said little, though internally she was concerned. After landing the chopper and switching off the motor, she reached across and laid her hand over Nova's.

'When *you're* ready,' she said as she watched Reg and Fran drive one of the station's utes towards them, 'we'll talk.'

Nova, understanding, nodded then asked, 'Where's Curtis?'

Vanessa schooled her features to show nothing of her thoughts, a technique she had mastered for television because there were times when her face was too expressive. 'He and Warren are on the slopes, due west and past the old quarry, should you think of riding out that way.'

Nova regarded Vanessa for a few seconds, and then gave her a weak smile. 'Thanks.'

It was three days before Nova felt sufficiently settled in to seek Vanessa's company. There were things she wanted to tell everyone but couldn't, as yet, bring herself to mention even to her father or stepmother. She didn't think they would understand that for her the last three months had been hell! She had sunk to the depths, lower than a snake's belly slithering on the ground — that's what she likened it to. Now she was in the throes of clawing her way out of the hole she had dug for herself then willingly fallen into, but she knew she had a long way to go before she got to the top.

Nova and Vanessa went for a bike ride down to Gumbledon Creek, while Fran took care of a disappointed Kyle, who'd wanted to go with them.

Propping her bike up, Nova got off and wandered close to the creek's bank. Gathering her thoughts she looked across the creek and saw a row of barrels lined near a fallen tree on the other side, 'the shooting range'. 'Do you still practise shooting?'

'Bren insists that I do, once every three months. He says it's easy to lose your eye if you don't practise regularly.'

'He's right. I suppose you're a better shot than me by now.' Probably better at just about everything, except singing, she thought disconsolately.

Vanessa gave Nova a wry smile. 'You'll understand if that's not something at which I want to be better.'

There was a little silence between them then Nova said as she leant against the trunk of a willow bark. 'You're so lucky, Vanessa. You've got it all together.' It was hard to keep the envy out of her voice but she managed to. 'Shit, I wish I could say that about my life. I've ...' she shook her head and blinked back the urge to cry, 'messed up.'

Vanessa put her index fingers behind her ears and wiggled them. 'I'm all ears,' she said with an encouraging smile. 'Unburden yourself.'

'I've been, umm ... *sick*. I didn't tell Dad, didn't want him to know. For the last six weeks I've been in a sanatorium, drying out.' She raised an expressive eyebrow and pre-empted the expected question. 'Uppers, downers, alcohol.'

'Hard drugs?'

'Shit, no. I might be stupid but not that stupid. I started taking uppers because I wanted to perform at my best. Leo introduced me to the habit. Then I needed downers to come off the highs and to relax. The boozing started when our relationship started to go down the tube. We busted up, you know.' She made brief eye contact with Vanessa. 'His fault, not mine. Leo couldn't stand me being more popular than he was. His bloody ego couldn't cope with it.'

Vanessa nodded as she absorbed that information. 'And there's no man in your life now?'

'No one serious though I've dated a few since. I've gone solo and I'm on the road a lot. That makes relationships difficult.'

'Sounds like you've had a nervous breakdown,' Vanessa made the obvious conclusion though Nova hadn't said she had, 'or gone close to it. How did it happen?'

'You know,' Nova tilted her head to one side as she thought about the question, 'I think some people have a self-destruct mechanism inside them. I think that's what I have. Everything was going well, I was coping without Leo. Mind you, he was good to have around in many ways. Great sex.' She wiggled her eyebrows. 'And he could cook and keep track of the money, that sort of thing. I still miss him for those things.'

'Really? Is it Leo you miss or the fact that he made your life easier?'

'The latter, I guess,' Nova's reply was honest then, uncomfortable with the admission, she changed the subject. 'I went to Nashville, did the big-time audition. A small, on-the-move recording company, Reece Records, signed me up. That's when everything started to come unglued.' She kicked a fallen tree branch into the water and the sound of the branch's splash scared off two jabirus on the other side of the creek. Screeching their annoyance they spread their long wings and took off to settle further down the creek where it was more peaceful.

'I had it in the palm of my hand — international success — and I let it slip away. Couldn't hack the pressure. I guess I am a stupid bitch. Reece pulled the plug on the album. The reason they gave was that putting the tracks down was taking too long; costing too much from a labour point of view was what they really meant, because I wasn't happy with the backing tracks. We were recording late one night and I took a break. An executive of the company, a damned born again Christian vice-president no less, caught me taking stuff.'

She glanced meaningfully at Vanessa, 'Smoking a toke. He went right off and that was that. No recording contract, exit stage right! Anthea's pissed off with me. Jo, my co-composer who was doing some harmonies with me, got pissed off. *Everyone* got pissed off and I ended up in the funny farm.' Failing to see any criticism in Vanessa's features, she continued the sorry tale. 'Anthea flew me home and had me admitted to a sanatorium north of Sydney to dry out. Afterwards, she told me to go somewhere quiet and pull myself together. That's why I'm here.'

Now she didn't bother to stop tears of self-pity from trickling down her cheeks. 'A-nd, a-nd ...' she began to hiccup, 'I'm scared shitless that I won't be able to hack it.' Not only was she scared, secretly she was angry with herself for letting the opportunity to eclipse Vanessa, by becoming an international recording artist, turn into a failure. That hurt more than anything, more than Anthea's reproachful attitude, more than Jo Brooks's disgust ...

It was galling to have to confess her shortcomings to Vanessa — *Miss Perfect* — she had dubbed her, but she had an ulterior motive, sympathy. Vanessa was a soft-hearted woman, a bit of a do-gooder like Fran, and getting her on side would make it easier to tell her father and Fran what had happened.

Vanessa, who'd been standing beside the bikes, came over to Nova and drew her into her arms. She hugged her. 'You poor thing, you have been through the mill.'

'Hah! That's the rub, I'm not poor. Anthea's a terrific financial manager. She took over my finances when Leo walked out. I have a very healthy bank balance.'

'That's good, you can be miserable in comfort.' Vanessa tried a lighthearted remark but seeing Nova's distress she became serious. 'You know, the thing about nervous breakdowns, according to what I've read and heard, is that most people, with good advice and treatment, get over them. You're in a trough, a downer, but it won't last forever. Your therapist probably told you that.'

'The shrink did. He also said that I'm the only one who can get myself out of it.' A rogue muscle twitched at the side of her mouth as she spoke.

'With help,' Vanessa encouraged. She found a pocket pack of tissues in the back pocket of her jeans — she kept them there because of Kyle — and offered them to Nova. 'Did the psychiatrist also say that you need to decide where you want your career to go?'

'He said lots of things, half of which I don't remember because I was strung out.' Oh, yes, she was laying it on a bit thick but she knew that Vanessa was enough of a sucker for a sad tale to believe her wholeheartedly, *stupid bitch that she is*, a thought, no, a strange little voice suddenly popped into her head. She was, Nova agreed with it.

Vanessa was quiet for a little while. 'Well, be assured that you're welcome to stay at Amaroo for as long as you need to. And whenever you want to talk, I'm here.'

Nova gritted her teeth. Vanessa being nice, being sympathetic, only rubbed more salt into her over-emphasised wounds. 'I know,' she said in a piteous tone. 'You, Bren and Curtis have been wonderful. I won't forget it.'

'Come on then,' Vanessa pulled her towards the bikes. 'Let's go for a real ride. We'll brush the cobwebs away with some fresh air and a bit of speed.'

'I guess you now ride a bike better than I do too,' Nova retorted, her mouth turning down glumly.

Vanessa straddled her bike and gave Nova a wink, challenging her with, 'Come on, let's find out.'

Fresh air, blue skies, rest and being around normal people, worked wonders on Nova's problem. It had been good for her inner soul to confess what had happened to all and sundry one night at dinner, leaving none of the gory and sometimes embarrassing details out. Good therapy. Vanessa had said it would be beneficial and it was. As well, she'd managed to gain everyone's attention and sympathy, especially Curtis's, though other people's reactions varied. Her father was shocked. Fran remained her non-committal self but she saw a glimmer of understanding and sympathy in the older woman's eyes. Bren, who had some personality difficulties of his own showed a surprising understanding, and Curtis was his usual kind, supportive self.

Afterwards, Nova began to compose again and it was a surprise to her that the source of her inspiration was the young, energetic Kyle who followed her everywhere, when she wasn't out on the range. It was something of a nuisance the way he interfered with her plan to be with Curtis whenever possible. But, the up-side to him tagging along was interesting because she could observe him and take on board the way toddlers thought and acted.

As a result, his innocence, energy and delightful personality became the basis for several compositions. She wrote three songs geared towards small children, recorded them on audio with a guitar backing and talked to Anthea who encouraged her to continue. Having Vanessa to talk to, and to a lesser degree, her father, Fran and Curtis helped to exorcise the demons within her, though occasionally, that strange, inner voice would pop into her head involuntarily, criticising Vanessa and the things she did.

Nova welcomed the return to feeling strong, mentally and emotionally, almost her old self, until one night . . .

At the barbecue Bren and Reg organised and were in charge of the cooking, Nova studied Curtis as he in turn watched Vanessa play with Kyle. All at once, seeing his concentration on mother and son, something, a certain realisation hit her with the force of a ten tonne Mac truck. Shit! She could hardly believe it, but neither was she imagining it. Because Bren and Reg were occupied, Curtis was giving his undivided attention to his sister-in-law and his expression could only be described as, she wasn't mistaken, rapt.

It was sickening. The man she had been in love with for years couldn't take his eyes off Vanessa as she chased a squealing Kyle around the sandpit, scooped him up in her arms and deposited him on the swing. *And, damn it, doesn't Vanessa look good; so healthy, vital and beautiful*, the voice said. And it was true. Amaroo's mistress rarely got sick; she didn't have any mental problems or a drug dependency. *Almost, bloody perfect*, the uncharitable thought ran through Nova's head.

Several muscles twisted inside her chest, around the region of her heart, squeezing, tightening, until a bubble of bile rose in her throat as she stared at Curtis. Shit a brick, why hadn't she cottoned on to Curtis's preoccupation before? Was she blind? *Yes, it's clear that Curtis has, or is developing feelings for his brother's wife*, the voice sniped subtly.

Nova shook her head, wanting to deny what she'd seen and the thoughts tumbling around inside her brain but the proof was there before her very eyes. No, maybe Curtis wasn't aware of his forbidden interest — she sought excuses. *I suppose that's possible, yet ...?* The insidious voice planted the uncertainty into her head. Angry with Curtis and with the unsuspecting Vanessa, the nerves at the side of her mouth began to twitch. She glanced towards Bren Selby ... If he knew he would kill Curtis. Bren was a possessive man and more than once he'd implied that if any one tried to crack on to Vanessa he would enjoy pulverising them.

A deep, spiralling depression began to engulf her, but the sensation was different to her recent breakdown though as intense and all-encompassing. The more she thought about Curtis and Vanessa the more physically ill she felt. Everyone at Amaroo knew Curtis had changed his opinion about Vanessa. At the beginning he had scoffed at her capacity to fit in but over the years, as she'd proven herself, the dislike had softened. *To what?* The voice in her head asked, *infatuation, love?* Her head shook from side to side again as she sought to clarify her thoughts. For a start she didn't believe that Vanessa reciprocated in any way. No way. She hardly knew that Curtis was alive, except as a brother-in-law and a business partner. *But ... that doesn't matter*, the voice inside drummed over and over in her brain, *Curtis is yours, he belongs to you — he just doesn't know it yet*. Yes, she agreed with the voice, with all her heart.

Being at Amaroo, seeing him almost every day, doing chores together, sharing jokes, talking with him had confirmed the love she felt for him. His kindnesses, his consideration and his gentleness were, to her, proof that given the right encouragement, over time, his feelings towards her would change and intensify. Now, this ... complication. Staring hollow-eyed at Curtis, then at Vanessa, made a nerve near her mouth begin to flick more erratically as a silent, frustrating fury flowed through her. It wasn't fair, shit, it was not ...

Her now thoroughly jaundiced gaze narrowed as it focussed on Vanessa, beautiful, talented Vanessa, and an anger so strong it made her tremble, came over her. *She's not really your friend, you know, she's the enemy,* her inner voice insinuated. Even if Vanessa had done a hundred things for her in the past, even if Nova had once considered her an idol to live up to and measure her own success by, none of that counted anymore. By God, it didn't. A powerful and vicious jealousy was making her stomach muscles tighten as she tried to think what she could do.

The next instant her features took on a feral slyness. She had to do something about *her* to attain her goal — Curtis. Her gaze swung towards Sandy. The dog was barking excitedly at Kyle being pushed on the swing. Hmmm, her thoughts were starting to tick overtime now, planning, scheming. The object of her anger was going to London soon and ... *Wouldn't it be good if she didn't return,* came the venomous thought. Mmmm, yes, that would be very good.

A cunning smile tilted the corners of Nova's mouth. There were ways to make life unpleasant at Amaroo, *things* could be done to encourage Vanessa to spend more time away from Amaroo than on it which, she believed, would effectively lessen Curtis's fascination for her. Her brain began to work double-time as an assortment of ideas, heightened by contributions from the internal voice that dominated her thoughts ...

# CHAPTER SEVENTEEN

Stepping out of the shower, Vanessa towelled herself dry. It was still early in the morning and she didn't have to rub hard; the warm air dried her body in a few minutes. She began to comb her wet hair. The strong, Australian sun had streaked it almost platinum on the top of her head. She gazed critically at her features. No freckles, yet, because her skin tone was too olive, still she dutifully moisturised her face twice a day and applied a fifteen plus suntan cream because she didn't want to look like a dried-up prune. Some outback women, Fran included, who hadn't taken care of their skin, aged prematurely because of the outback's harsh effects.

Her thoughts turned to Bren. He was out on a muster with Reg and Warren, rounding up and moving part of the herd to better pasture. They would be away for three days. A frown creased her forehead as she thought about her husband. It was hard not to, occasionally, when she found time to think about it, to compare the Bren of today to the man who had courted her in England. Oh, he could still be charming when it suited him, but he could also be aggressive, childish and moody. She had come to know the warning signs, usually triggered by restlessness. He would become short-tempered with everyone, then drink excessively, to relax, he said. But alcohol had the opposite effect on Bren, it made him *more* aggressive. And he would want more sex. She accepted that, but at such times he wasn't always a considerate lover, being too absorbed in his own pleasures. Then the restlessness would escalate until he took off in the plane or chopper to Broome or, less frequently to Darwin to be pampered by his mother. A change of scene helped because he came back the old Bren, the man she knew and for the most part, still loved.

Vanessa moved to the wardrobe to take out her favourite shirt, a pink cotton that was lightweight, perfect for the hot day ahead. When she pulled the shirt off the coat-hanger, to her consternation there was a large brown stain down the front.

'What the ...?' she exclaimed, frowning. The stain, across both sides of the shirtfront was brown and looked like machine oil or chocolate. Ruined, she thought. But how? Disappointed, she pulled out another shirt and put it on and, when dressed and with the ruined shirt in her hand, she went looking for Fran.

'Is something wrong with the washing machine?' she asked Fran as the latter came out of the pantry with an armful of groceries.

'Not that I know of, why?'

'Look at this.' Vanessa showed Fran the pink shirt. 'Any idea how that could happen?'

Fran studied the shirt, brought the material close to her nose to smell it. 'Smells like machine oil. I washed it the other day, ironed it and put it in your wardrobe. There was no stain on it then, I'm sure of that,' she affirmed then, scratching her head, added, 'I don't know how this could have happened.'

'Another mysterious happening on Amaroo, I suppose,' Vanessa said tongue-in-cheek. She didn't want to make a big deal out of the shirt, but she was puzzled. The other day, when she'd gone to dust ornaments in the living room she had found a photograph of herself — one taken when she'd been on stage doing *The Glass Menagerie* — smashed on the floor and the photo oddly torn, almost in half. No one knew how that had happened either — and it had been positioned on a shelf too high for Kyle to reach! And then, two days ago there had been another incident. She had been about to go out on a trail ride with Nova and Curtis and as she'd mounted her horse the saddle girth had snapped and she'd fallen onto the ground and bruised a hip. All very odd . . . she concluded.

'I'm sure it's not the washing machine, but I'll get Reg to take a look at it to be sure,' Fran offered.

Vanessa sighed. 'Okay, thanks.'

Nova, standing in the hallway, out of sight, smiled as she turned away and moved towards the homestead's office. She had more plans to unsettle Vanessa before she went off to London. Oh, yes, indeed she did.

The phone rang precisely at 8 a.m., disturbing the morning's silence in the kitchen. Fran looked expectantly at Nova who was closest to the receiver. When her stepdaughter made no move to answer it,

315

she clucked her tongue loud enough to show her irritation and picked up the handset herself.

'Hello.' Pause, 'Yes, she's here.' Fran wiggled the receiver at Nova. 'It's for you. Your manager.'

Nova, her eyes suddenly sparkling, a smile on her face, took the receiver. 'Anthea, hi. How are things in the east?'

'Chilly, love. Eight degrees this morning, but then it is the middle of winter in Sydney,' Anthea answered dryly. Then, business-like as usual, she got straight to it. 'About those children's songs you sent me. I have an interested party, a very keen party who wants you to do video clips of them and, if satisfactory, they'll follow it up with a local recording contract. It's the foot in the door we've been looking for, Nova.'

'Really?' Nova's smile widened. 'That's fab.'

'It is. The production company doing the clips is keen to do them straight away. There's even the possibility, it's a long shot, love, but if all goes well, there could be a children's show presenter's job for you, which wouldn't do your country and western singer image any harm; wonderful publicity. Look how well Monica Trapaga's done.' She let that sink in. 'How soon can you come to Sydney?'

Nova's smile faded. Leave Amaroo. Leave the safety, the peacefulness. *Leave Curtis?* came the thought in her head.

'I ... I'm not sure.' Her head and heart began a battle royal. She was making progress with Curtis, well, she believed she was. But then, the next instant the lure of fame and a celebrity status she'd only dreamed of tugged at her ambitious side. Anthea, in spite of the Nashville fiasco, was offering her a second chance to be the success she knew she could be. She was realistic enough to know that another such opportunity would not come her way but to take advantage of it meant she had to leave Amaroo. Shit, how could she decide? Who could she talk to? Dad and Fran would tell her to do what she thought best. Vanessa? No, she couldn't stoop to ask the person she now considered her nemesis. This was a decision she had to make by herself.

'Nova, I'll be frank with you, you know my thoughts on windows of opportunity. This deal won't be available for long.'

'I ... know, Anthea, and I do appreciate it.' She recognised the matter-of-fact tone and that she couldn't stall Anthea Dennison for too long; the woman was too astute. 'I'll check flight availability and stuff, and call you tomorrow. Is that okay?'

There was a momentary silence on the line. 'Very well, Nova. I'll expect to hear from you then or ...' the threat — this is your last chance with me, kiddo — was implicit in her voice. 'Got to rush, love. 'Bye.'

Nova replaced the receiver then went and sat at the kitchen table, cradling her chin in her hands. Bugger, bugger, bugger, but already the tug of adrenaline was pulsing through her as she thought where this opportunity might take her. To the top? Maybe.

'Sounds like good news,' an obviously curious Fran said.

Nova looked at the tall woman standing with her back to the sink. She was the only mother she remembered, but Nova had never been able to accept or call her Mum. 'It is.' After which she rabbited on for ten minutes about the opportunities and where they might lead.

'Is it what you want, Nova?' Fran asked in that quiet, commonsense way she had.

Both women knew what she was getting at. What did she want most — fame or Curtis? The problem was, she wanted both. She scraped her chair on the vinyl flooring as she stood up. *You want it all, and you deserve it all,* her inner voice said simply as she walked out of the room towards the office. Could she have a career *and* Curtis? That was the question she posed to herself as she sat at the desk and turned on the computer.

After all, Vanessa had a career and a good home life. Could she go to Sydney and make her mark, then return to Amaroo and Curtis? Maybe, and then the tantalising thought came to her. If she left for a while he might realise how much he missed her. The nerve at the side of her mouth began to twitch. Annoyed, she rubbed the offending tic, trying to make it settle. Damned thing acted up when she got into serious thinking mode. Mulling things over while she made flight bookings via the Internet, her skewed thinking came to the conclusion that she didn't have much to lose by going to Sydney.

Vanessa was going to be away for months, limiting Curtis's exposure to her, which would allow Nova time to establish herself as a children's presenter — if that part of the deal came off — as well as a country and western singer, especially with exposure from the video clip. She did want both, she decided. Curtis *and* a career and with luck, while Vanessa was in London the woman would have second thoughts about spending so much time at Amaroo. Her eyes narrowed as she mentally debated the pros and cons: if Vanessa had it all, so could she . . .

It was too hot to sleep even in the verandah's fly-screened sleep-out. Vanessa tossed and turned, unable to settle. She glanced at the clock: 2.03 a.m. Getting up, she went to the kitchen to pour a glass of water from the fridge, then she checked on Kyle. He was sound asleep, as was Bren. Somewhere outside she heard a dingo call to his comrades, another mournful howl following. The noise they made always chilled her blood. She hated their light, high-pitched sounds.

Recently, she'd read an account of Lindy Chamberlain and the dingo that had taken her baby Azaria and, though Lindy had later been exonerated of her child's death, as a consequence of reading about it, Vanessa couldn't relax when the heat brought dingoes close to the station and because Kyle was an active youngster who loved to roam as far as the outer paddocks, she had asked Bren to eradicate the animals but Bren said she was over-reacting. Kyle, he'd said, was now almost three and was too big and that the animals foraged at night — when Kyle was safely asleep in his bed — and slept during the day because day-time temperatures preceding the wet were stultifyingly hot.

She gazed through the fuzziness of the fly screen. A quarter moon shone dully on the side yard and the station's buildings and now wide awake, she stared at the sky, blacker than black, trying to distinguish specific stars. Curtis, who had an interest in astronomy, was attempting to educate her about the various galaxies and constellations. She was pleased when she, finally, recognised The Southern Cross, the Big Dipper and Venus. One by one she studied them as she sipped the water.

A different sound disturbed her concentration — barking. She looked around for Sandy and couldn't see him. He usually slept in his basket in the sleep-out, with them. When the dingoes prowled she kept him on a lead at night to stop him from running off and getting into trouble. In the low glow of a night light she found the lead, went over and checked it. The little devil. Sandy had chewed the rope through and escaped. Why hadn't she put him on a chain, as Curtis did Ringo? She gave an annoyed sigh. Sandy, the rotten little monster, was roaming free and, if he got close to the dingoes . . . Her heart started to race. She didn't want to think about what a pack of wild dogs would do to her dog if they got close to him.

She shook Bren by the shoulder. 'Wake up, Bren. Sandy's got loose.'

'What?' he muttered.

Wearing a long singlet top, she pulled on a pair of shorts and found her boots. 'Sandy's out. Get up, Bren.' She shook him again but he was in such a deep sleep that he couldn't be roused. 'Oh, stay asleep then,' she said crankily. She would find Sandy herself.

Leaving the house via the back verandah, she had the commonsense to pick up the Winchester 30/30 rifle kept high — out of Kyle's reach — on wall brackets near the back door in case of emergencies, not like the station's other rifles which were locked in a cupboard in the office. She flicked the switch on, and two floodlights lit up the ground as far as the breaking-in yard. Whistling and calling Sandy, she checked the chicken coop. All was well there with Ringo guarding the sleeping chickens. She moved past the breaking-in yard towards the hangar, picking her way carefully as the light faded. Sandy wasn't barking anymore so ... where could he be?

Vanessa turned the hangar-workshop lights on. Dingoes had been there. A couple of oil barrels lay on their side, the contents rifled through. She noted a T-bone from a steak picked clean. Who, on the station, had been silly enough to leave food scraps there? Everyone knew dingoes were on the prowl. She shook her head in consternation and her right hand tightened around the rifle. The beat of her heart increased the further she moved away from the established buildings.

'Sandy,' she yelled at the top of her voice. 'Come here, boy.'

He answered with a series of furious barks. Thank God, he wasn't far away. Then she heard the dingoes howl ... Alarmed by their closeness and what followed — a sudden, high-pitched squeal from Sandy, then a long whimper — she picked up a torch from the bench. It was a big one, the type used to check the plane and chopper's engines. She began to run towards the first paddock fence ...

When Vanessa saw the first pair of yellow eyes in the torch's beam, then a second and third pair, her courage almost failed her. She moved the light, spraying the ground and low bushes until she found Sandy. Her darling little dog, so brave and utterly foolish, stood with his back to a low, scrubby bush, facing the dingoes. One front paw was bent and off the ground — obviously a dingo had nipped him — but he was otherwise stiff-legged and defiant. His cropped tail stood high in the air, his ears aggressively at attention. He barked defiantly for all his worth, then growled deep in his throat as his attackers closed in.

Vanessa didn't have the luxury of time to be frightened as, without hesitating and awkwardly one-handed, she trained the rifle's barrel at the closest dingo. She squeezed the trigger. Bang!

The torch's glow showed a cloud of red earth rising where the bullet, missing the animal, rammed into the soil. The dingoes yipped with fright then just as quickly snarled in unison as they turned their attention to her. Though the night was steamy a chill snaked down Vanessa's spine and her heartbeat quickened. How many bullets were in the rifle's magazine, she wondered? Four? five? she hadn't taken the time to check. Undaunted, she squeezed off another round. One animal gave a high-pitched squeal. She let off two more shots and within seconds the animals with their yellow eyes had slunk back, disappearing into the darkness to leave a still growling, triumphant Sandy to have the last bark.

'Come on, boy, come to me.'

The Jack Russell limped towards her. He tried to leap into her arms but couldn't. Sliding the rifle under one arm, she bent down and picked him up, cradling him close. She could feel a stickiness on one of his front legs and when she trained the torchlight there she saw blood. 'Oh, Sandy, one of them bit you. What am I going to do with you, boy?'

Within a minute or two she and Sandy were joined by Bren, Curtis and Nova, torches in hand, who'd come to investigate the rifle shots.

Bren took the rifle from Vanessa, Nova took the torch. 'Why didn't you wake me?' Bren asked with a frown, his tone more than a little critical.

'Are you okay?' Nova asked with feigned sincerity. Secretly she was pleased by Vanessa's shaken demeanour. *Good,* Nova's little voice giggled inside, *a little going away present.* In a solicitous gesture she put her hand on Vanessa's arm.

'I will be,' Vanessa confirmed. She could feel Sandy trembling against her as she held him to her chest. She was trembling too, as reaction to the drama set in. 'Bren, I tried to wake you but you were fast asleep. You couldn't be roused.' Her comment made Bren scowl. He didn't like it, but too bad, sometimes the truth hurt and Vanessa was becoming increasingly weary of having to couch her comments in terms that, because he could be so prickly, didn't offend him.

Bren glanced at Curtis and they gave each other meaningful nods. 'The baits don't seem to be working so I guess we have to do something about the pack now. Vanessa managed to nick one,' Bren said as he trained the beam of light from his torch on a puddle of blood that trailed off into the bush.

'First thing tomorrow.' Curtis's gaze was focussed on Vanessa. He gave her a strange, assessing look, as if concerned as to whether *she* was all right, but didn't ask it aloud. 'Warren and I will pick up their trail at first light and finish them off.'

'Come on, hon, let's go back.' Bren tried to take Sandy from Vanessa but she wouldn't relinquish him. He sighed and shrugged his shoulders. 'All right, but we should tend to Sandy's wound quickly. Bloody dingoes carry all kinds of germs. The little feller will be lucky if he doesn't get infected.'

In silence, the four began the long walk back through the steamy night to the homestead.

The early morning air, half an hour after sunrise, was refreshingly cool. Nova, as she stood inside the hangar watching Bren load Vanessa and Kyle's luggage into the plane, pulled up the collar on her sleeveless, zip-up vest. It hadn't been necessary for her to get up to see them leave but she wanted to, even though she too was leaving the next day for Sydney, energised by the prospect of resurrecting her career. She needed to see Vanessa leave with her own eyes. A smile flicked across her mouth as she remembered the image of Vanessa's pinched features as she'd boarded the plane. The 'episodes' she had created had sunk in and affected 'Little Miss Perfect,' and Nova believed, possibly because she desperately wanted to, that the consummate, cool actress's nerves had been severely rattled.

Nova knew Vanessa liked to analyse things through and to mull matters over in her own time before she acted. That suited Nova perfectly. Vanessa had the next five months to contemplate her future and whether Amaroo was the best place

324

for herself and Kyle to spend long periods of time. The only negative was that she wasn't sure if she had put enough fear into the actress to make her think seriously about spending perhaps half her time at Amaroo and the other half in London or wherever else she chose to live. If she hadn't, other episodes could be arranged to encourage Vanessa to her way of thinking.

As she watched Bren do the instrument check before take-off, in her mind she reviewed the dinner table talk last night, about the movie Vanessa might become involved in because she had written its script. Nova hoped, she'd even prayed — and wasn't that a novelty — that the deal would go through because it would keep Vanessa away longer. She had also noted Bren's mouth turn down sourly when Vanessa and Curtis had talked about *North of the Nullarbor. Bren doesn't like his wife and son being away for so long,* Nova's inner voice piped up with. *Whereas you don't care if you never see either of them again!* The admiration Nova had once felt for Vanessa and the desire to emulate her career success had been eclipsed by a growing jealousy, bordering on unreasonable hatred because Curtis liked her.

As she straightened to her full height and stretched her arms up over her head in a wave, the plane taxied down the packed earth runway. *Good riddance. Now you're free to concentrate on Curtis and make him forget that Vanessa exists.*

That same evening, after dinner, which was a quiet affair because Vanessa and Kyle were absent and

Bren was unusually quiet because he was missing them, Curtis was the first to leave.

'Night, everyone,' he said as he left the homestead's kitchen and headed for the cottage. He opened and closed the door then leant against its solid timber, and shook his head in confusion. He stayed there for a while, his thoughts stuck on Nova ... Hell's bells, she was driving him crazy but, thank God tomorrow morning she was leaving.

Her leech-like behaviour towards him had been going on for weeks. Every time he turned around she was at his heels. Wherever he went on the range or around the paddocks, doing various chores, she would wheedle her way into accompanying him even when he didn't need help. What was he to make of it? At first he had thought she was lonely for company, anyone's company but it had gone past that and her 'devotion' was damned annoying. What was the matter with her? He scratched his chin as he pondered the irritation of her constant presence. She had been through a lot and mindful of that he had wanted to be understanding, accommodating and patient, but his patience had worn dangerously thin.

And if that wasn't bad enough, he hadn't a clue what to do about her. His brother thought her attentions amusing and reckoned she had a crush on him. Curtis closed his eyes for a moment and shook his head emphatically. A possible romance between himself and Nova? No way. Besides, she didn't flirt or come on to him she was just ... there.

Seven years older than her, he had watched Nova grow up and change from child, to girl, to woman.

As a person, and accepting of her character shortcomings, he liked her but he wasn't sexually attracted to her, not in the least, despite Reg's occasional joke — he'd assumed it was a joke — that one day he and Nova might get together. Not in his lifetime. Still, there remained a reluctance to hurt her feelings by telling her to bugger off and leave him be. His parents had taught him too many good manners to do that, but he was fed up with her shadowy presence.

Continuing his disgruntlement, he moved away from the door towards his bedroom. If she hadn't been going tomorrow he'd have invented a reason to visit Cadogan's Run. *That's running away, mate*, his conscience prodded him. So what? Wasn't that better than a confrontation in which he might say things to upset Nova's delicate mental balance? Yes, he believed she was still fragile mentally because most of the time it didn't take much to get her upset. Now thoroughly out of sorts, he moved to the bathroom, stripped, turned the shower on and stepped under the lukewarm spray. As he did, another disquieting thought teased his mind. Was it Nova he wanted to be rid of, or was he suffering from withdrawal because Vanessa and young Kyle would be away for months, and that he'd miss them?

Oh, shut the hell up, he told himself, and lathered up . . .

# CHAPTER EIGHTEEN

'What do you think she wants?' Bren asked. He was watching Curtis throw clothes into a duffle bag on his bed.

'With Georgia, who knows. She wants to meet me at Mum's on the seventeenth. She, ummm, didn't care to discuss it on the phone but I'm sure it has something to do with Regan.' Curtis's reply was distracted. He had been going over and over various scenarios since Georgia's phone call. What did his ex-wife want? More money? Well, she could whistle in the wind for that.

'So you drop everything to be at her beck and call. Bro, she still has you by the short and curlies, hasn't she?'

The look Curtis gave Bren was cutting. 'I couldn't care less about Georgia, I'm going because it concerns Regan. Maybe she's sick or Georgia could be having problems with her. Hell's bells, Bren, I don't know and I won't until she tells me.'

'Okay, okay,' Bren backed off in the face of Curtis's growing irritation. 'You'll keep me posted?'

Curtis closed the bag and slung it over one shoulder as he headed for the doorway. 'Of course.'

Curtis had plenty of time to think about what Georgia might be up to as he flew the chopper from Amaroo to Darwin. Time to worry if Regan was all right, time to consider what options he might have, time to school his dislike of his ex-wife and, because of the things she'd done to him, get that dislike under control. It was interesting that she'd wanted them to meet in Darwin instead of making him fly to Sydney. Throughout the course of their separation, divorce and afterwards, his mother had played a non-committal, sitting on the fence role, neither condemning Georgia nor siding with him simply because she wanted to maintain contact with her only grand-daughter. Hilary did that by having Regan spend school holidays regularly at her Cullen Bay home.

In the early afternoon, at his mother's home, Curtis stood by the floor to ceiling windows, looking at the view but not really seeing it. Like him, Hilary had no idea why Georgia had requested the meeting but had, diplomatically, decided to be out when she arrived. Curtis glanced at the clock on the chrome and glass wall unit. She was late, another Georgia-ism that annoyed him. He believed she did it on purpose to create an effect. Well, the effect it had on him was to make him irritable. He believed himself to be a patient man but where his ex was concerned, most of the patience had dissipated a long time ago.

The doorbell rang. Curtis went to answer it.

'Hello, Curtis,' Georgia's blue eyes gave him the mandatory once over. 'You're looking well.'

'Thank you.' He deliberately didn't return the compliment though she looked her usual fantastic self: perfectly groomed, coiffed and dressed. In that way only did she remind him of Bren's wife. Vanessa, whether she was riding a horse, helping with the branding, or fixing a bore pump, somehow managed to look ... almost immaculate. Except once, when he'd been trying to explain the rudiments of a bike's engine, he'd seen a smudge on her nose and ...

'Hilary not in?' Georgia enquired politely.

'Shopping,' he explained succinctly. 'Would you care for a drink?'

'No, I'm fine, thanks. So polite, so cool, Curtis,' she teased, smiling as they gravitated towards the living room, then she changed the subject. 'I love what Hilary's done with this place. She has put the stamp of her personality into the house, don't you think?'

A muscle began to twitch in Curtis's cheek. He knew what Georgia was up to — keeping the conversation trivial long enough to goad him into a terse response. 'I suppose,' he said easily, to annoy her in return. 'I've never thought much about it.'

Then, almost with a sense of guilt, his gaze swept the room, taking in the décor which was very modern. Leather lounges with a variety of coloured cushions, marble and glass tables, tiled floor, strategically placed pot plants, a few oil paintings of Australian scenes. Not his cup of tea but, yes, it looked tasteful and expensive — very Hilary Selby.

'You called this meeting, Georgia. I presume to talk to me about Regan,' he said pointedly.

'Aaahh, yes.'

He watched her lick her lips, a dead give-away that beneath the veneer of sophistication, she was nervous.

'A, shall we say, delicate matter has arisen . . .'

As he waited, he noticed that she was fidgeting. Georgia didn't fidget. Very curious. 'She's not sick, is she?' That had been the first and foremost concern on his mind, that their daughter wasn't well.

'No, Regan's as healthy as a horse. You see it's . . .' she pursed her lips, took a deep breath. 'How can I put it? Umm . . . I'm getting married again.'

Curtis stared at his ex for perhaps twenty seconds, during which time his gaze managed to, for the first time, fasten on the diamond ring on the third finger of her left hand. It was obscenely large. 'I guess I'm supposed to say congratulations. Congratulations.' His tone was flat, patently uninterested.

'Yes.' Her expression changed, becoming rapt and dreamy-eyed. 'To a wonderful man. Gregor is a publisher. He has a string of lifestyle and women's magazines in several European countries.'

'Then Gregor is mega-wealthy, I imagine?'

'He is. His name is Gregor Farber, he's German. We'll live in Berlin most of the time though he has an apartment in New York for business purposes and a holiday villa in Cannes.'

He resisted the urge to say, *doesn't everyone*. 'You've done well, Georgia,' Curtis couldn't resist the tongue-in-cheek remark. 'Guess those German language tapes you bought years ago have paid off.' She was remarrying, great. He couldn't care less that she was. In fact he kind of pitied what was his name? Gregor — the man was welcome to her.

'So, what's the problem with Regan?'

'Regan doesn't want to live with us in Germany. Gregor says she should go to boarding school, in

Switzerland, but I think she's too young. Regan's being ... very difficult about everything. Rude to Gregor. Stubborn as a mule.'

Curtis's grin was almost gleeful. Well, she was a Selby. 'Regan's only eleven. She shouldn't have to go to boarding school if she doesn't want to, in a country where she doesn't speak the language.'

Curtis's brows knitted together as the full impact of her words sank in. If his daughter went to live in Europe, how and when was he going to see her? Another thought quickly followed. Could he legally stop Georgia from taking Regan overseas? Hell's bells, there had to be something he could do to keep her here.

'What about your parents? They mind her a lot when you're on assignment.'

'Mum and Dad are getting on. It's asking too much to expect them to care full-time for an energetic girl who'll soon be a teenager. As much as they adore Regan, it would be too much responsibility.'

She was right. Georgia's parents, Ben and Marje Stephens, had married late and they hadn't had Georgia till Marje was almost forty. Both were in their early seventies now. He stared at Georgia for a long time but all he could concentrate on was the thought that he might be losing his daughter forever. He wasn't going to take that lying down. If he had to fight her through the courts, he would.

'I don't want to rain on your parade of happiness regarding your engagement,' his tone was sarcastic, 'but I'm telling you straight out, I'll fight to keep Regan in Australia. I believe that's best for her.'

Georgia's mouth pulled into a thin line, and her stare became openly assessing. 'I agree ...' she said slowly, as if she had given the matter a lot of thought. 'Regan's best interests would be served by staying here.'

Curtis, who'd been sitting on the edge of the sofa, almost fell off it from shock. 'What did you say?'

'I agree with you. Is that so hard for you to believe?' A plucked eyebrow rose questioningly. 'Regan would find adjusting to European life, very ... trying. She would hate it, and in the end, hate me. You might not think I've been a good wife or mother, but I don't want to alienate my daughter like that.'

'Then don't marry Gregor. Surely Regan comes first.'

Georgia shook her head from side to side, then flicked a stray lock of red hair off her face. 'Are you crazy? Not marry Gregor?' She looked at him as if she hadn't heard right. 'The man's loaded. Only a fool would pass up the chance to be Mrs Gregor Farber. And ...' a cunningness swept over her features. 'I may be many things but I am not a fool.'

'So, it's not wholly true love,' he drawled, enjoying the chance to niggle her. As well, he was beginning to believe that, finally, the pendulum of fairness was about to swing in his favour.

'Of course I love him, Gregor's a charming man. We're going to have a sophisticated, very social kind of life, a life that ...'

Curtis got the message. 'Regan wouldn't fit in with. She would be in the way.' He was rewarded when she had the grace to look embarrassed.

'Frankly, yes.' Georgia shifted in her seat, uncomfortable with his incisiveness. 'Look, Curtis, what it comes down to is this: I'm prepared to give you full custody of Regan subject to visiting rights, that is, having her twice a year during school holidays.'

'If it fits in with your social calendar.' There was bitterness in his tone as he spoke. My God, she was a selfish, self-centred bitch! Had she given any but the barest amount of thought as to how her decision would make their daughter feel? That Regan would feel as if her mother was discarding her. He doubted it.

'Being bitchy doesn't become you. Are you interested in the deal or not?' Georgia spat the question at him.

Curtis didn't answer straight away. He wanted her to stew for a while, but already he was thinking how great it was going to be to have Regan at Amaroo. As a small child she had loved the station and now that she was older, he could show and teach her so much. 'Of course. But this isn't the kind of deal we just shake hands on. I want everything done legally, signed and sealed.' *So you can't change your mind some time down the track if your marriage goes belly up.*

'Naturally. We both know solicitors in Darwin. That can be done tomorrow.'

'You are eager to be rid of her.'

Her cheeks flushed guiltily, and she looked away. When she looked back at him again there was a hardness in her eyes. 'Gregor is a popular man and, all I'll say is that I don't want our plans to go awry. The wedding date's set for the fourteenth of next month, in Berlin. I'll fly Mum, Dad and Regan over for it and afterwards they can bring her to Hilary. You can pick her up from here and take her to Amaroo. Agreed?' She held out her hand.

He looked at her outstretched hand but refused to shake it. 'Let's wait till the paperwork's done. Then it will be a deal.'

'Bastard ...' she muttered, loud enough for him to hear.

'Thank you, but I believe that after this you have the dibs on moral bastardry. And, what's more, I think it's important that I be there when you tell Regan. I'll fly back to Sydney with you. Poor kid,' he shook his head. 'She's probably going to feel like a package being pushed from one person to the other.'

'I ... Don't think it was an easy decision, Curtis, it wasn't,' Georgia said, and had the audacity to produce a few tears. 'After all, she is my daughter, and I do love her ...'

'Give me a break. You love her but not as much as you love the thought of Gregor's money. I hope being rich makes you happy.'

Georgia, realising that he wasn't going to bend, wiped the tears away. She stared at him as she got up and smoothed down her skirt. 'Do you, really?'

He shrugged his shoulders. In truth, he had reached the point where he couldn't care less whether she was happy or not, but if she were it would make life easier for him and Regan because then she would leave them alone. 'Sure. Why not.'

Kerri's sixth sense was always alert where Vanessa was concerned and she could tell that her friend was down in the dumps but disguising it as they celebrated Kyle's third birthday in Vanessa's Belgrave Square flat. Seven children from the pre-school kindergarten Kyle attended three days a week, plus an accompanying parent for each child, were there for the party. Present also were Yannis, Melody Sharp, Vanessa's long-term friend and Melody's partner, Joe Vasengi, all there to enjoy Kyle's special day.

*The Women's Room* only had one month left to run. The play had been an outstanding success but, unfortunately, negotiations regarding the production of *North of the Nullarbor* were drawn out and had stalled which meant Vanessa would have to stay in London until the deal was finalised. Possibly that's why she appeared glum, Kerri thought or, more likely, she was missing that husband of hers. She *made* herself think charitably about Bren, and Amaroo.

Before Vanny married Bren Selby, Kerri had been wracked by serious doubts that the marriage would last and that her friend wouldn't cope with the privations and loneliness of outback life, of which *she* knew nothing. But, contrarily, having read the script and deduced that a percentage of the text touched on difficulties Vanny herself had experienced, she had a greater insight about how much her friend had grown and matured. Still on the sunny side of thirty-five, Vanny remained a striking-looking woman who had grown into a superb actress and a true Australian outback woman.

'Buck up, Vanny,' Kerri whispered as she watched Yannis, who adored kids, supervise the 'Pin the Tail on the Donkey' game in the living room. 'You won't be stuck in London forever. Charles Pittman promised to get back to me by tomorrow with a compromise deal. It's just that he was disappointed that Jane Campion wasn't available to direct. Still, Martin Pirelli's list of credits is impressive.'

'Patience isn't one of my virtues. There are times when I don't know why I'm keen to have another child — the nine months waiting thing almost drove me crazy.' Vanessa's brown eyes misted. She had that far-away gleam again. 'I should be at Amaroo. They'll be starting the muster soon. I should be there to help.' She half expected that when she did fall pregnant Bren would throw a mini tantrum before he accepted the situation. When he knew how much she wanted the baby, how good it would be for Kyle, she was sure he would become enthusiastic. Kerri's voice cut through her thoughts.

'I'm sure Bren and his brother will manage well enough without you.'

'They will,' Vanessa agreed. 'It's just that *I* enjoy being a part of it. You can't imagine how it feels. The starkness of the land, the heat, the way of life, gets into your blood and when you're away it's like a part of you has gone missing.' She looked at her son who was waiting his turn to play the game. Tallest of the seven children present, Kyle was huskily built like his father. 'Kyle's starting to fret too, he's gone off his food. He enjoys kindy well enough but he misses Bren and Curtis.'

Kerri clicked her tongue and shook her head. 'You worry too much. One week kids love food; the next week they hate everything you put in front of them. Besides in a month he'll be home, and isn't Curtis's daughter, Regan, at Amaroo?'

'She is, but Kyle's only three and she's almost a teenager.'

'You watch, I reckon the two of them will get along really well, even with the disparity in their ages,' Kerri prophesied.

The doorbell rang and Melody's partner, Joe, went down the hall to answer it.

'*Daddy, Daddy . . .*'

Vanessa glanced from her son to the hallway. Standing next to Joe was Bren, a jacket over one shoulder, one hand behind his back and a bag in the other. Her hands flew to her lips with shock. What was he doing here? 'Oh, Bren . . .'

Wife and son ran at Bren and engulfed him in a huge hug, while the children and other people in the room smiled and looked on.

Bren kissed Vanessa and hugged her till, embarrassed, she whispered that he should let her go. Pleased surprise added a tremble to her voice as she asked, 'What? How . . . what are you doing here?'

Bren gave her a wide grin. 'Curtis got tired of looking at my miserable face. He suggested I come and see you, that I might as well because I was pretty useless on Amaroo.'

She smiled back at him. She could well imagine Curtis saying just that. 'Your brother is a man of infinite wisdom. We've both missed you, especially,' her eyes darted to where Kyle stood, his arms wrapped around one of Bren's legs, 'you know who.' Then, still slightly breathless, she asked, 'How long can you stay?'

'A week. We're starting the muster early because we got an additional order for one thousand head for the Middle East — an exporter let an Arabian livestock importer down. Mustering starts in just over a week.'

Vanessa had hoped he would be able to stay longer. 'Oh, of course. Well, some time is better than no time,' she said brightly, hiding her disappointment.

Bren bent down and, one-armed, picked up his son. 'Mate, you've put on weight and got so much taller. Happy birthday, Kyle.' From behind his back he showed Kyle that he was holding, a large, brightly wrapped parcel.

With his smile as wide as his father's, Kyle insisted on being put down so he could open the present straight away.

Melody, who'd been busy in the kitchen with Trudy, the night time baby-sitter, heating up sausage rolls, cocktail frankfurts and making fairy bread, came over to them. 'Food's ready. Just tell me when you want it on the table.'

'When the game's finished,' Vanessa said as arm in arm, she introduced Bren to those who didn't know him. Bren, keen to blend in, went over to Melody's partner, Joe who was half Nigerian, half English. Joe was having a hard time keeping three children, boys, from getting hyped up and wrecking Vanessa's elegant living room. She rolled her eyes as Bren, with his wide frame and commanding voice, got the boys under control. If she could be assured that her and Bren's next child would be a girl, she would be overjoyed.

Kerri's mobile rang and she drifted away to a quiet corner of the room, near the balcony, to take the call. Vanessa, coming down from the shock of her husband's sudden arrival, watched her agent's face. Kerri's mobile features changed as she conversed with whoever was on the phone. Vanessa saw her eyebrows fly up, then she frowned and ran a hand through her abundant mop of black hair. After that Kerri waved the same hand about, gesticulating wildly. Finally came the triumphant smile. Whatever the topic of conversation, it was going Kerri's way.

The last child had her turn at pinning the tail on the donkey and received a prize, all the children received a small gift, then the joint chant began as fourteen little eyes spied plates being put on the table.

'Food, food, we want food.'

Vanessa then had little time to wonder who Kerri had been talking to as the children converged like starving beasts on the party food. Even Kyle forgot his manners, she noted. Well, he was no angel. Her son got into his share of mischief — he was used to being outdoors. Amaroo Station as far as the first paddock had been his backyard. Here, the flat and the courtyard garden out the back, which was delightful in summer but drearily cold in winter, forced her to keep him inside more than her son appreciated.

After the children sang 'Happy Birthday' and the cake was cut into generous portions and devoured, one by one, children and their parents began to leave. Kerri sidled up to Vanessa who was standing at the flat's front door saying goodbye and voicing her thanks for them having come.

'More good news, Vanny, though I doubt it will eclipse Bren's arrival,' Kerry said dryly. 'I've been speaking to Charles. The deal is looking positive and the contract should be drawn up next week.'

'That's wonderful,' Vanessa replied, though her concentration was off. She was watching Kyle show Bren the presents he'd received. Her son's face was aglow with excitement from the party and his father's arrival. If all went according to plan she and Kyle could be on the plane home within twenty-four hours of the final curtain coming down at the Lyceum. Home — Amaroo. The friendly faces of those who worked there, the camaraderie between herself and Curtis. The stretching-forever land. She could hardly wait ... and now that Bren was here, the week was going to be hectic but they could be together, a family again.

Bren and Vanessa stood at the open doorway of Kyle's bedroom checking that their son was asleep. Bren's arm was around her shoulder.

'He's had a big day,' Vanessa whispered.

'He has. I can't believe how much he's grown. The four months has seemed like forty months to me.'

She turned into his arms and smiled up at him. 'Oh! You've missed us, *me*, have you?' Her arms crept around his waist to pull his body against hers.

'You bet.' His hands cupped her face and for a while he studied her features, as if it had been more like four years than four months since he'd been this close to her. 'I hope you don't intend to go so far away, or for so long again. I don't like it.'

'I don't like it either.'

She had decided that and told Kerri so one day, even if she forfeited work because of it. The Kimberley was her home and she wasn't prepared to take long breaks away from the place she had come to love so much. There was another reason behind her decision too. She worried over some of the things Bren was doing ... The occasional letter from Curtis had pointed out that he wanted to build an American-style dude ranch on Amaroo, labelling it as home-stay accommodation — a tourism set up that was gaining popularity in parts of the outback. Tourists would come to Amaroo and be involved in station life for a short period of time.

Curtis had pointed out the dangers of the idea, that the project would need an infusion of capital for several years until it was in profit mode, and that without careful management and advertising it could flounder. Reading between the lines of his letters she was certain that Stuart had put the idea into Bren's head. Now her husband was determined to see it through, though he had, in phone calls and letters, said very little about his new project.

His lips found hers and their kiss projected the pent-up passion of months of separation. It was good to be in his arms again, to feel the thrill of his hard body against hers, his energy, the wanting in him. All thoughts of his project, that Amaroo would be put into the red again, fled Vanessa's mind as she responded wholeheartedly to the powerful physical attraction that arced between them.

'I hope your baby-sitter, Trudy, sleeps soundly,' he said quietly as, arms around each other, they walked down the wide hallway to the large bedroom.

'She does, like the dead.'

'Good, because,' he chuckled throatily, 'hon, I don't think I'll be letting you get too much sleep tonight . . . I'm not used to being on a sex starvation diet, and I decided months ago that I didn't like it.'

'Me neither.' A delicious shiver of anticipation ran down her spine. With a little luck and a lot of loving, she might get pregnant while he was here. She didn't like being underhanded or secretive, but she was determined to have another child — Kyle needed a brother or sister to play with, and for company. She didn't want him being a lonely, only child as she had been. And if she got her wish this week, she would keep it to herself until she was sure.

Nova Morrison sat at a table in the upmarket Perth restaurant waiting for Glen Latimer, the publicist assigned to her by the video company, to return from the men's room. She had completed the last leg of a promotional tour for her children's music video — the tour having taken her to every capital city in Australia — and both the tour and the video had been spectacularly successful. Who'd have thought it, she happily queried as she waited. She now had two separate vocal careers — country and western, and composing and recording songs for children. And with the exposure from the children's show she now co-presented with the personable Andy Crenna, her video was selling like proverbial hot cakes.

A woman's high-pitched, out-of-control laugh on the other side of the restaurant, distracted her thoughts. She twisted her head, curious to find the culprit and her eyebrows lifted in amazement as she recognised Diane Selby accompanied by two other women. Diane was the one laughing uproariously. Experiencing a niggle of irritation at Glen's long sojourn in the loo, Nova got up and made her way over to Diane's table to say hello.

'Nova. What a lovely surprise.' Diane welcomed the younger woman like an old friend, giving her chic, business-like appearance a cursory once-over. 'You look fabulous. Sit down, please. Let me introduce you to Toni and Nicki, from Adelaide.'

'Hi, everyone.' Nova directed her next remark to Diane. 'Where's Stuart?'

Diane giggled, made a face and took another sip of her wine. 'We had a row. How very unusual.' Her mouth quirked cynically. 'He apologised and sent me to Perth on a no-limit shopping spree. Whee!' Her voice rose gaily. 'My friends, Toni and Nicki, decided to join me and help me spend obscene amounts of money.'

Nova grinned. 'Sounds like the perfect arrangement. Stuart makes it, you spend it.'

'Yesh, lovey. What else are wives for if not to spend their husband's hard-earned dollars? The bastard deserves whatever it costs him,' Diane said with a wink. 'Him and his affairs. He thinks I'm overly suspicious but I know my husband and his cheating ways.'

'Are you *the* Nova who does the children's television show in the mornings, *Grandma's Gingerbread House,* with Andy Crenna? It is you, isn't it?' Toni asked. 'I saw your video clip the other day. It was terrific. Chloe, my three-year-old grand-daughter, loves it.'

'Nova's done very well,' Diane was slurring her words more noticeably now but that didn't stop her from taking another swallow of white wine and lolling back in her chair.

'I have, thanks to young Kyle. If I hadn't been at Amaroo a while back and spent time with Kyle and Vanessa, I might not have written those children's songs. Kyle inspired me with his cute, funny ways,' Nova admitted. She glanced towards her own table. Glen hadn't returned so there was no need for her to hurry back. Besides, she liked Diane Selby, more than she liked Stuart.

'Poor little mite,' Diane said, sniffing. 'He's well now, and he should have a little brother or sister to play with in a few months time, but when he was a baby,' she told Toni and Nicki, 'Kyle almost died. Had to have a liver transplant and now he's doing well, thanks to his Uncle Curtis.'

'I agree,' Nova was quick to remark. *In so many ways.*

'It was hell for Vanessa and Bren.'

'And Curtis,' Nova added. 'He's the one who donated a percentage of his liver to save Kyle.' She threw that information in for the other women.

'Yes, our Curtis is quite a man,' Diane agreed with a sigh. 'It's a shame he hasn't found anyone to share his life since ... the divorce. Georgia did a real job on him, turned him into a woman-hater.' She reached for the wine bottle in the ice bucket and poured wine into each of the glasses.

Toni and Nicki, as if silently cued to, suddenly excused themselves to visit the ladies' room.

After they'd left, Nova's dark eyes made a sly, clinical study of Diane. She really was quite tipsy. More than tipsy, halfway to being drunk. When she offered her a glass of wine, Nova declined. 'I don't drink in public. It doesn't go with my squeaky-clean children's presenter image,' she said with a smile. Naturally she didn't add that when she needed to she drank in private and continued to indulge in popping uppers and downers, but only when they were *needed*, she assured herself.

'Smart girl. You know, lovey, you'd be just right for Curtis.' Diane quirked an eyebrow. 'Interested?' When Nova didn't answer, she went on, as if musing to herself, 'Mark my words, he's been badly done by, has our Curtis. In more ways than Georgia screwing him for every penny she could get. If you ask me, that Hilary has a lot to answer for.' She stared into Nova's eyes and wiggled her eyebrows conspiratorially, as if the younger woman knew precisely what she meant.

Nova had enough experience with people who were on their way to drunkenness to know that it paid to be a good listener. Besides, what Diane said stirred a certain curiosity. What did Diane mean? That Curtis had been badly treated by his mother, or was she referring to the commonly known fact that Bren was Hilary's favourite? Everyone, including Curtis and Lauren, knew that and they had, presumably, accepted it years ago. No ... She had the distinct feeling that *it,* whatever Diane was alluding to, had a different meaning. *Ask her, you want to know, don't you?* The little voice said in her head.

'You mean about Bren being the favoured child?'

Diane gave her a bleary-eyed glance. 'No, lovey. That's not why she treats Bren the way she does. Hilary does it out of guilt!' She took another sip of wine, more than a sip — she downed half the glass's contents in one long swallow.

Fascinating. Nova sensed she was on the brink of an important discovery about the Selby family but was Diane's tongue sufficiently lubricated to reveal it before Toni and Nicki returned? Out of the corner of her eye she saw Glen wave to her. Stuff him. He could wait. Her heart picked up its beat and her breathing became more rapid. *What is Diane implying about Bren and Hilary?* Unable to work it out herself she focussed her attention on the older woman, and waited.

'Her and *my* bloody husband should be ashamed of themselves. What they did ...' Diane began to hiccup. She lifted her hand to her eyes to blot away a tear. 'Did you know that when I was pregnant with Kim and we weren't even married, he had the hots for Hilary?' Her voice dropped to a whisper. 'Mind you, Hilary was beautiful enough when she was young and Matthew, trusting fool that he was, made the mistake of leaving her alone for too long. Young, beautiful women used to men's attention don't like being left by themselves for months and months. Hilary was like that.'

'And ...?' *This is interesting. Wait. Subconsciously she wants to confess all to you.* Nova chewed her lower lip as she tried to make sense of Diane's disclosures. All at once she appeared to be very drunk. Then, as if a veil lifted, her ramblings became clear. Of course. 'Did Stuart have an affair with Hilary?'

'Yesh. Rotten bastard. Should never have married him, but what could a girl do? I was four months preggers back in 1955.'

Containing her delight and giving Diane a mock solicitous look, Nova murmured, 'At the time I'm sure you did the right thing. It wasn't done to have children out of wedlock back then, was it?'

'Too right, and not in straitlaced Adelaide. My parents would have freaked.' The next instant Diane sat bolt upright and blinked several times with shock, realising what she had said. She gave Nova a lopsided frown. 'Now, lovey, what I just said, all of it, it's just between the two of us.' She tried to look serious but with her eyelids drooping and her mouth slightly open, all she did was look comical. 'Okay?'

Nova tapped the side of her nose and grinned at Diane. 'Naturally. My lips are sealed.' *What a coup, Nova,* her little voice chortled. Hilary and Stuart had had an affair. Which meant ... Oh, bugger! Toni and Nicki were wending their way back through the tables. She stood and patted Diane's shoulder. 'It was lovely to see you, Diane. Enjoy your spending spree.'

As she walked back to her table and Glen, Nova didn't find it hard to read between the lines of Diane's confession. Stuart's wife may not have spelt it out in so many words but there had been a definite level of animosity directed at Hilary and Stuart, which made only one conclusion possible. Diane hated Hilary because of the affair with Stuart, in spite of the fact that he'd had the grace to marry her and legitimise their first child. *But, lovey, the fascinating thing is, this isn't all* said the voice in her head. *Unless you've read the information incorrectly it's possible, more than possible, that Bren Selby isn't Matthew's son.* Nova knew that Kim, Diane's eldest daughter, and Bren were only five months apart in age. Stuart could be Bren's father. Wow! What a discovery.

When she put the pieces together it made sense. Stuart, who had four daughters, was openly fond of Bren but he didn't give a tinker's damn about Curtis and Lauren. And Hilary, by making Bren her favourite over her other children, could be compensating for her guilt for being unfaithful. Shit, what a bombshell. Her gaze narrowed as she sat opposite Glen. She smiled at him as if nothing momentous had just taken place. But ... if Diane's admission was true and could be proven so, Curtis was the rightful heir to Amaroo. Of course. That's what Diane's comment, 'Curtis being badly done by' meant. *The man* you *love has been cheated out of his inheritance*, came the voice again.

Hmmm! Was there a way she could use this information to help Curtis and to give him what she knew he wanted — and what was his birthright — Amaroo? A cunningness, which had developed as she'd matured, told her that she would have to be careful how she used this information because it had the potential to blow Amaroo and the person she cared for — Curtis — apart. With an enormous effort she masked the excitement Diane's *faux pas* had brought her way, and extended her smile at Glen.

'Sorry I took so long,' the publicist apologised. 'I bumped into a couple of friends in the foyer. We haven't seen each other for years.'

'That's okay. I caught up with someone I know too.' She looked at the menu. 'Let's order. I'm starving.'

'Glad to hear it. I've noticed that usually you eat like a rabbit.'

'Not tonight. I've something to celebrate and I intend to order the most expensive dish on the menu.' She saw his quizzical glance and gave him her most winning smile, 'To commemorate the winding-up of a successful promotional tour.'

Glen raised his glass of beer in a salute. 'I'll drink to that.'

Kerri and *North of the Nullarbor's* producer, Heather Clarry arrived at Amaroo after the wet when the weather, being summer all over Australia, was stupefyingly hot. The days were dry again and the nights pleasantly warm. This was Kerri's first visit to the outback and Vanessa, flying the women in from Kununurra in the chopper, intended that her friend should go away with a memorable impression of life in the Kimberley.

Heather, based in Melbourne, was a forty-five-year-old redhead with freckles, originally from Glasgow, who planned to stay at Amaroo for a week. She and Vanessa took to each other straight away and while Kerri slept off the residual jet lag from her international flight, they went over the proposed scenes and location possibilities.

'If July and August are the best months,

weatherwise, that's when we'll shoot the local scenes,' Heather said, after checking the stockmen's quarters. 'From the point of logistics, because of the remoteness, we'll truck or fly in most of the equipment and the crew, probably for about five weeks. Having adequate accommodation here is a bonus too. Then there'll be approximately two weeks in Fremantle using outdoor streetscapes to depict the family's arrival from England. Other scenes, such as sailing from England will be filmed on board *The Bounty* in Sydney Harbour and the interior scenes are pencilled in to be shot at Movie World's lot on the Gold Coast.'

'At a stretch we should fit most of your crew in the stockmen's quarters, do some doubling up in the stone cottage and there will be rooms in the homestead for Martin Pirelli and the camera crew,' Vanessa told Heather. And with Bren dead keen on his home-stay accommodation plan, it would be an effective dry run to see if the station could cope with the extra numbers. They'd also have to bring in assistant cooks so Fran wouldn't be run off her feet.

'We'll truck in vans for make-up and wardrobe.' Heather stopped to study the front of Curtis's cottage, on their way back to the homestead. 'Would it be okay to see inside?' she asked, pointing to the cottage. 'With proper lighting we might be able to shoot a few interiors there and, because of its rustic appeal, an outdoor shot or two on the front verandah.'

'Don't forget Gumbledon Creek. Several scenes — the camping scene, the fight between Rupert and Thomas, cattle crossing the river etc — could be filmed along the creek. There's a lot of dappled shade though so someone in the camera crew, or a lighting technician, should check that the light's adequate and for the best time of day to shoot,' Vanessa suggested. Then she asked, 'Getting around to the various spots I want to show you will be easier if you ride. Do you?'

Heather grimaced. 'Not as well as I'd like to but, yes, I can, so long as the horse is a placid beastie,' she said in her Scottish accent. She gazed towards the distant foothills and the line of gums that denoted the route of Gumbledon Creek. 'I think we'll get some wonderful scenes here to suit the script, Vanessa.'

'You will. I've a list of places for us to check out over the next few days.' Vanessa was proud of every inch of Amaroo but she intended to save the ride to Exeter Falls for the last day so Heather would leave with its memory solidly implanted in her head.

Heather glanced pointedly at Vanessa's stomach. She was almost five months and beginning to show. 'It's okay for you to ride?'

'Goodness, yes. I rode when I was pregnant with Kyle till I was seven and a half months.' Remembering the difficulties of that, she chuckled. 'One day I tried to mount Runaway, my horse and couldn't, not even with help. I was a blimp. Couldn't even drive a ute ...' she shook her head. 'I've resigned myself to going through that again but at least this time I know what's ahead for me.'

Over the following days Vanessa enjoyed showing Kerri and Heather many of the places she loved on Amaroo ...

■   ■   ■

For the ride to Exeter Falls Fran packed them a picnic lunch, plastic cups and a bottle of white wine.

Heather was rapt in the scenery and clicked off an entire roll of 35-mm film before they reached the falls and the gleaming, inviting pool of water the falls dropped into.

'Aren't you glad I suggested you bring bathers?' Vanessa reminded a perspiring Kerri as they dismounted and tethered the horses near a patch of yellow grass. She took the wine from her saddlebag and sank it up to its neck in water to keep it cool.

'This place is magic,' Heather enthused, her tone noticeably awed. 'It will be perfect for the love scene between Emily and Rupert, the escaped convict.'

Vanessa beamed, 'I thought so too.'

'Speaking of escape, can we escape into the water? My body's so hot I think I'm going to spontaneously combust,' Kerri complained good-naturedly. Ripping her bathers out of her backpack, she was about to go into the bush to change, when Vanessa spoke.

'Let me check the area for snakes. This is where one almost bit me not long after I'd come to Amaroo.'

Hearing that, Kerri and Heather gravitated towards a clump of rocks and stood on them, happy to wait for Vanessa to check the surrounding bushes.

'All clear,' Vanessa gave the go ahead, giving them a maddeningly cheeky grin at their apprehensive expressions. 'Should have brought Sandy with us. He's a great snake catcher.' Then, the water being too inviting, she threw down her Akubra, stripped off her clothes — having her bathers on underneath — and waded in. The water was cool against her heated skin as she breast-stroked to the centre, where it was deepest and coolest, to wait for Kerri and Heather.

'Vanessa, it's-it's bloody cold,' Heather said through chattering teeth.

''Cause your body's hot. You'll adjust in a little while,' Vanessa advised with a laugh. 'It's more pleasant here than paddling in Gumbledon Creek, even though the creek's flowing well after the wet. Sometimes,' she added for their information, 'if the wet's particularly heavy, we can't get in for a month or two, till the flow eases. I had Bren fly the area yesterday to check that it was okay to come up.'

'What about crocodiles?' Kerri asked tentatively. Her black eyes darted suspiciously around the shoreline.

'It's croc safe.'

Kerri sighed, her features relaxing. 'Thank God for that.' She rolled onto her back and began to float. 'It is beautiful here, quite starkly beautiful,' she said as she floated towards Vanessa. 'After some time here it's easy to see why you fell in love with the place. There's a raw strength to the land, a sense of timelessness about it.'

During her visit, Kerri had been quietly observing everyone on Amaroo, and Bren got special attention. She still had reservations as to his worthiness and over the years, as far as she was concerned, he hadn't done enough to make her opinion change. Bren Selby was, she referred back to when they'd been courting, the affable, hail-fellow-well-met type of man, but whether Vanny was aware of it, in her opinion there wasn't a great deal of substance to the man. It was, she believed, a tribute to Vanny's highly developed sense of loyalty that the marriage had lasted as long as it had and, now, with a second baby on the way. She sighed, well ... To her credit, Vanny never complained or said anything that reflected badly on Bren. But knowing her as she did, she sensed a tension between them, enough to guess that the marriage was going through a bad patch.

The three were ready for lunch after spending an hour in the cooling waters of Exeter Falls. Vanessa spread a lightweight rug, which had been strapped to the back of her saddle on the ground, and they sat cross-legged on it to devour every morsel of food, including the wine and a thermos of iced, but now lukewarm tea.

'Not so primitive, after all, hey?' Vanessa quizzed Kerri because, occasionally she had taken verbal pot shots at the remoteness of where she lived.

'No. Mind you, it isn't as civilised as a picnic in Hyde Park, with vendors hawking ices and soft drinks, but here is ... quite acceptable.'

'There's another plus. No hordes of tourists trampling about the place either,' Heather voiced her opinion.

'Above the flood-water line there are several Aboriginal cave paintings. If you don't mind a half-hour hike uphill,' Vanessa suggested.

'Oh, lovely! Just what I need to work off Fran's lunch,' Kerri said tongue-in-cheek.

'We can go up in our bathers and boots, have a look, then come back for a quick dip before we head home,' Vanessa said. 'First though I'll sluice the utensils off in the water.' Of necessity they travelled light but because Heather and Kerri were guests, Fran had packed plastic plates, cutlery and glasses.

Afternoon shadows disguised a cover of moss clinging to several rocks as Vanessa, barefoot, hopped from one rock to another to get to the water's edge. She didn't see the wet patch of green that had been dampened when they'd exited the water, until it was too late ...

Her left foot slipped on the moist area, and unable to regain her balance, her legs went from under her. She landed squarely on her bottom, hard. Instantly the jarring travelled from her coccyx all the way up her spine. The air whooshed out of her lungs. She dropped everything and used her hands to stop from pitching forward onto more rocks, then into the water. As she righted herself a sharp, breath-catching pain stabbed low in her stomach. The baby. Oh, *noooo* ... !

# CHAPTER NINETEEN

Heather and Kerri rushed to Vanessa's aid, helping her to her feet.

'Are you all right?'

Vanessa shook her head. 'I don't know. I felt ... something.' Another pain grabbed low in her midriff, making her double over.

'The baby,' Heather whispered, looking at Kerri, who nodded back gravely.

'Vanny, you shouldn't move, or walk,' Kerri said, taking control.

'How will we get her back to Amaroo?' Heather wanted to know.

Vanessa, who had collapsed on the ground again, the fingers of both hands spread protectively over her stomach, looked up, wide-eyed, at Kerri. 'There's a two-way radio in my backpack. Get it for me. Bren can fly the chopper in to where the gorge begins, but we'll have to ride out and meet him there.'

'I'm sure you shouldn't move. You could lose the baby,' Kerri interrupted, her dark eyes full of concern. She bit down on her lower lip as she was wont to do when anxious.

Vanessa shook her head. The pains were turning into something she recognised, mini contractions. They made her fear the worst. 'It isn't a matter of choice,' she said. 'The gorge is too narrow for the chopper to land in safely. I have to ride Runaway to a pick-up point. Get the radio and I'll make the call.'

By the time they reached the rendezvous point, which took a good hour or more, Kerri, who'd stayed close to Vanessa as Heather rode ahead, towards the chopper, spotted the dark stain — blood — on the loose, cotton shorts Vanessa was wearing. She knew her dear friend was holding the pain and the hurt in, and the knowledge that she could be miscarrying.

Bren shouted over the whirr of the rotor blades as he lifted Vanessa, who was barely able to contain her emotions, into the chopper's cabin. 'I'll take her to the hospital in Kununurra. They're expecting us.' Fran had given him towels and blankets to keep Vanessa warm. Settling her, he turned to Kerri and pointed to Amaroo's foreman. 'Reg will take you back to the homestead. I'll phone as soon as there's news.'

Kerri and Heather stood back as the spinning of the rotor blades increased in tempo with the revs of the engine. The chopper took off and angled north-east, and in silence as profound as the bush around them, the two women followed Reg, on Runaway, back to the homestead ...

The first thing Vanessa saw when she opened her eyes after having a curette to clear away what remained of the foetus — she had haemorrhaged, losing huge clots during the helicopter flight — was a large bunch of flowers. It was an outrageously extravagant gesture in a town of roughly six thousand people who lived far away from mainstream civilisation. She knew, without having to read the card, that Kerri had ordered them through Interflora, and had them flown in expressly to cheer her up. She smiled weakly at the precious, colourful blooms, aware that it would take more than a floral arrangement to do that. Tears welled in her eyes, overflowed and ran down her cheeks. She'd lost the baby she had longed for so much, especially after the trials and tribulations over Kyle's health.

The door opened and Bren came in. He had a box of chocolates in one hand and he placed it on the bedside table. His eyebrows lifted when he saw the flowers. 'From Kerri, I suppose,' came the comment in a less than enthusiastic tone. He sat on the chair beside the bed, took her hand and squeezed it. 'How are you feeling, hon?'

'I've had better days, *many* better days,' she said bravely, without smiling. 'I did so want a brother or sister for Kyle to play with.' She had miscarried a little girl, she'd been told.

'I bet. It was bloody bad luck all around. But,' he shrugged his shoulders, 'accidents happen and,' he paused to clear his throat then said, 'perhaps it's for the best.'

*For the best?* How could losing a baby be for the best? His words made little sense to her and, she noted that he hadn't said anything about them trying again when she was back to normal. She threw a baleful glance in his direction and, still overwrought by the experience, muttered, 'You never wanted the baby anyway so, now, I suppose you're happy.' To her annoyance, and amazement, he shrugged his shoulders again.

'I wouldn't say that, exactly. It just wasn't meant to be this time round, that's all.' When she continued to stare at him he shifted uncomfortably in the seat. 'The doctor said you could go home tomorrow. And, umm, Kyle's missing you.'

'Give him my love. I . . .' she sighed, 'I'm so tired . . .'

'Of course you are, hon, you've been through an ordeal. I'll push off so you can get some rest, and come in tonight. I've put the hard word on Fabian to stay at his house tonight.'

'That's good, see you tonight then,' she murmured so softly Bren hardly heard the words as he left the room.

Hurt beyond measure by his cool, almost callous acceptance of her miscarriage, Vanessa turned her head on the pillow to stare out the window. Outside the air-conditioned room, dusk was encroaching, turning the cloudless sky a hazy, yellowish-mauve. It would be another magnificent sunset.

At least Bren wasn't pretending that he cared. That would have been truly detestable of him. A band of pain circled her heart and squeezed till she could hardly breathe. She couldn't bear to look at him, nor did she want to deal with what she was beginning to feel, or not feel! But she had to. As the pain began to recede a kind of numbness replaced it but she was still able to think, to evaluate . . .

What was wrong with him, and of more importance, what was wrong with their marriage? Something had dissipated, diminished and she knew the answer as surely as she knew that very soon the sun would set. The tears began trickling again and she let them flow unchecked as she lay in bed. What had happened to the gentle giant she had married, the caring, fun-loving considerate man? Had it all been an illusion? Was it her fault, hadn't she tried hard enough to keep their love alive and vibrant? She thought she had, but how could she when he responded as he had a few minutes ago, with little real affection. For some reason known only to Bren, them having another child hadn't suited him. Why? She puzzled over that for a while until she came up with a possible reason. It was as if he were too involved with himself and what affected him to care deeply about anyone else. And that had started even before they'd had Kyle ...

Vanessa tried to pep herself up, decide what she had to do to address the problem. She would do more, she decided, try harder, be more understanding, more ... more conciliatory, if that's what it took, but the truth of it was that she couldn't do it all! Bren had to meet her halfway ...

Bren was happy because he was involved with his new project. Sitting at the desk in his office he studied the rough plans he had drawn up. He was no architect but he had managed to draw a rudimentary plan that showed a layout for up to ten tourists in four-to-a-room, bunk-style accommodation, two bathrooms, a large kitchen and an outdoor eating facility.

He had yet to decide on the best site — and expected Curtis to help him with that, but his brother had been no help at all. He was still trying to wear down Vanessa and Curtis's resistance to the project. Both were urging him to go slowly and carefully, when he wanted to gallop away with the idea and get things started. He found their reluctance to 'come on board' a continuing source of irritation.

In particular he resented Vanessa's caution because, most of the time she was a forward thinker capable of embracing new ideas. He believed that the miscarriage she had suffered had made her unduly careful, about everything. She had changed, become clucky and protective of Kyle because he was their one and only. His son was a rip-roaring, energetic kid who wanted to be treated normally, not coddled, and, as far as he was concerned, Vanessa had become too cautious.

They had argued last night, and the night before about the timing of the pregnancy, *and* his home-stay project. Of late, they were always at loggerheads with each other over one thing or another, so much so that every person on Amaroo would suddenly find something they had to do when a discussion about the pros and cons of the project came up.

If only he could talk to someone sympathetic about his own doubts, the uncertainties that concerned him. He couldn't talk to his mother. She would relish the thought that Vanessa wasn't being supportive, so he was too proud to mention his misgivings to her. Stuart? His uncle was a very successful businessman, an understanding man, who'd been through several ups and downs in his own marriage, Diane accusing him of several affairs over as many years. Could he confide in him?

With his elbows propped on the desk, he massaged his forehead with his fingertips. He had to talk to someone, he had to. But first ... He got up and closed the office door, assuring himself of some privacy. He sat again and reached for the phone, then stopped.

Putting one hand on the desk he drummed rhythmically with his fingertips for maybe half a minute, staring around the room. In his head he still referred to the room as 'my father's office,' not his, because much of Matthew Selby's presence remained, in a subtle, almost shrine-like way. There was a huge set of long-horns; he'd brought them back from a trip to the United States of America. A framed, glass-protected map which detailed the original perimeters of Amaroo hung on one wall and a selection of photographs, black and white ones, hung on a timber-panelled wall. They were photos of his father with famous people, mostly Western Australian cattlemen. There was one with the legendary Lang Hancock, and several with past federal politicians.

Bren felt close to his father when he was in the office, here more than anywhere else on Amaroo. He sat up and stopped drumming his fingertips as the realisation came to him — his father was no longer around to counsel, to chide, or to compliment him on a job well done. The only person who did that regularly was his uncle.

He reached for the phone, picked up the receiver and dialled Stuart's number ...

* * *

Warm winter sunshine warmed Bren's back and he grinned as Kyle ran full pelt towards him after his ride to the old stone quarry with Regan, Vanessa and Curtis. His son loved the pony they had given him when he and Vanessa had returned from London. It was good to see his son active and normal again. Dr Samuels, at his recent, annual check-up, said the transplant was a continuing success but Kyle would have to be watched for any sign of rejection or infection. Vanessa did that, too well, as far as Bren was concerned.

'Hey,' Bren ruffled his son's hair. 'You smell of horse. Phew!' He held his nose as if there was a great stink under him.

Kyle grinned up at him. 'Yeah, Dad, cool, isn't it? Ruby's a beaut horse. I galloped her all the way to the quarry.'

Regan, a few paces behind, said, 'Kyle's riding very well, Uncle Bren. He didn't even look as if he would fall off.' Then she reminded her charge, 'What did your mum say, Kyle? To hit the bath straight away, I think.'

Kyle grimaced. He hooked his small thumbs into the belt loops of his jeans, copying his father's and uncle's habit. 'Do I have to, Dad?'

Bren made a big thing out of sniffing the air. 'You do, mate. Definitely.'

He smiled again as Regan generously gave Kyle a five-metre start and chased him towards the homestead. They got on well, the two cousins, in spite of the several years difference in their ages.

He turned in time to see Vanessa stumble as she got off Runaway. Curtis was there quickly, his arm extended to steady her. He watched the two of them laugh, as if her awkwardness was funny. And, mercurially, his mood changed, the fine line on his temper tightened. Why? Because Curtis could make time to ride with Vanessa and the kids but he was too busy to help him find a suitable site for the home-stay project. What was it his uncle said when he had confided that Curtis was being evasive and difficult? Confront the situation head-on, that's what Stuart had said: bring it out in the open. He would!

'Damn it, bro, you piss me off. Here you are, wasting time with my wife and the kids, on trail rides, when I need you. When will you get it through your head that I'm the boss around here? That I call the shots,' he said in a loud voice as he strode towards Curtis and Vanessa.

'What are you talking about, Bren?' Vanessa queried, her features pinched with annoyance because of his tone. 'Curtis was just helping . . .'

'I know what he was doing,' Bren barked at Vanessa, 'not doing his bloody job, that's what.' He had been holding down a growing anger towards both of them for weeks and it was high time they understood who was in command at Amaroo.

Vanessa glanced towards Curtis, whose expression was one of consternation. Her gaze then flew back to Bren to interpret his body language. Amazingly, she saw that he was spoiling for an argument. Could it be that he didn't like Curtis coming to her aid or was he put out because they hadn't meekly fallen into step with his plans?

Prudently, she decided to give him the opportunity to apologise, or calm down. 'Curtis stopped me from falling on my backside, which wouldn't have been very pleasant.'

'Yeah. Sure! Since your miscarriage you've become obsessed with yourself, Vanessa. That you have doesn't become you,' Bren criticised out of the blue.

'Steady on, Bren. There's no need for that kind of talk,' Curtis said, taking up Vanessa's defence. Automatically he stepped in front of her, as if to shield her from his brother's temper.

'Get out of the way,' Bren ordered, his anger now more directed towards Vanessa.

'I will, when you calm down.' Curtis stood his ground. 'What's wrong with you anyway? Feeling liverish over your precious home-stay project because we haven't fully embraced it? Is that your problem, Bren?'

Bren stared at him, silently amazed by his brother's incisiveness. 'Frankly, yes. I'd expected loyalty from both of you, but it seems that you've joined forces against me.'

'Oh, for goodness sake,' Vanessa's own quick temper rose in response to his words. 'We've only suggested that you be cautious. Your plan to borrow a great deal of money will put Amaroo into debt again. It makes sense to be careful,' she said, talking around the side of Curtis's body.

'So,' Bren's jaw jutted stubbornly, 'I don't have any sense, is that what you're saying?'

'Oh, grow up, mate. Stop acting like a kid who isn't getting his own way,' Curtis taunted. 'Our advice is just to be sensible about the whole thing.'

He stared back at his brother who was standing with his legs apart, less than a metre away. Of old, he knew the signs; Bren was spoiling for a fight. His chest had puffed up, his hands were balling into fists and he was balancing forward slightly on the balls of his feet. Commonsense told him that the smart thing to do would be to walk away. He turned sideways, towards the horses.

'Hey, I'm not finished talking to you,' Bren shouted at him.

'It's pointless trying to talk to you in this mood. We'll talk later, when you've settled down.'

'Damn you, Curtis, I want to talk now.' Bren stepped forward. He was close enough to reach him so he grabbed Curtis by the shoulder and spun him around to face him. His gaze ripped from him to Vanessa then back to his brother. 'You and Vanessa are plotting something, aren't you? Did you think you could fool me, bro?' Breathing heavily, rational thought forgotten, his muscles bunched with tension and the urge to beat the living daylights out of his sibling strengthened. His index finger jabbed again. 'Are you going to 'fess up?'

'You're crazy. There is no plot against you, it's all in your head. Go and skull a few beers, that'll cool you off.'

'Bren, stop this, you're sounding ridiculous,' Vanessa implored.

'Shut up, Vanessa,' Bren shouted at her, 'and get out of my way.' He reached across with his other arm and gave a none-too-gentle push that caught her off guard. She stumbled backwards, hitting the breaking-in yard's fence.

Something flicked in Curtis's eyes, the gleam of battle. It made him change his mind about walking away. Bren's temper was, quite oddly, spiralling out of control but for once in his life Curtis didn't care. He wasn't going to stand by and let his brother manhandle his wife; Vanessa deserved better treatment than that. His gaze narrowed on Bren as he squared up to him. 'Stop pushing your wife around,' he said. There was quiet menace in his tone.

Bren's fingers closed more tightly around Curtis's denim shirt. 'Make me, bro. Make me.' Grey eyes glared at him, and before Curtis could answer, Bren's right arm bent at the elbow, swung back and his fist flew forward into his brother's face. He knocked Curtis off his feet. 'Come on, get up. I'm going to enjoy beating the shit out of you.'

Curtis, lying on his back, tried to push himself up. He stared at the man towering threateningly over him. Since childhood he had never been able to beat Bren in a physical fight — that was something they both knew. Already the fall had jarred the healed scar where a section of his liver had been removed. Hell's bells. He knew he didn't have time to think about the irrationality of Bren's behaviour, about his apparent frustration. Such thoughts would come later, in hindsight. Right now what he had to do was to diffuse his brother's growing rage. He rolled away and bounced back to his feet to stare challengingly at him.

'Are you both mad?' Vanessa screamed as they circled each other. 'Bren, Curtis saved your son's life. Is this how you repay him? For God's sake, think about what you're doing.'

Bren jabbed towards Curtis, testing the distance. 'Stay out of it,' he snarled at Vanessa as he closed in with a confident smile. 'Come on.' He raised his chin provocatively at his opponent. 'Maybe this time you'll be lucky and show me what you're made of . . .'

Curtis feinted with his left and received a fist to the side of the head. Shaking his overly long locks because his vision blurred for a few seconds, he managed to deflect a right to the stomach as he back-pedalled. He knew that would frustrate Bren because he was lighter on his feet, and over the years had developed an in-built ability to elude serious blows.

'Come on, you pansy, fight.'

'I don't want to hurt you,' Curtis had the temerity to tease, trying to joke his way out of what was going to be a pretty one-sided contest.

'Hurt me? You've never laid a glove on me and you know it.'

Bren's concentration, askew because of his ill-temper, gave his opponent the opportunity he needed — one good punch. Balling the fist of his right hand Curtis crunched it into Bren's solar plexus. It connected with a dull thud. With one eye closed, due to the first punch, Curtis, not seeing well, followed with a left to Bren's jaw, making him stagger backwards.

Infuriated, Bren rushed in, close enough to deliver a blow to Curtis's nose which started to bleed. Then he began to attack his ribs, one punch following another.

Stockhorses in the yard close by pigrooted and whinnied nervously at the disturbance on the other side of the fence. Vanessa stood open-mouthed, watching Curtis land a glancing blow to Bren's shoulder. He was taller but eight kilos lighter than his older brother who, now almost forty, had put on several kilos during their marriage. She couldn't believe she was watching them fight, over what? Bren's skewed imagination. Grown men, two brothers who loved each other were trading blows because one had spoken his mind and the other had taken offence to it. It would have been laughable if it wasn't so serious. Why was Bren reacting so aggressively? It made no sense. Being an only child Vanessa had little concept of sibling rivalry, especially that which might exist between two strong-minded males.

'Damn you, Bren, you'll kill him,' Vanessa yelled though she knew she was wasting her breath. Her husband was beyond reason, beyond comprehending commonsense. For some peculiar reason, known only to him, he seemed intent on pummelling his brother into unconsciousness.

Desperate to stop the un-equal battle, she saw Warren jogging from the stockmen's quarters towards the melee but she had to do something *now*. Looking around, she saw an implement that might help — the hose they used to shower horses down after a hard ride. Could that be of use? She ran to the end of the hose, picked it up then, holding it, raced to the fence where the tap was attached to a fence post. She turned it on as hard as she could.

First came a disappointing trickle then, thankfully, a strong spray of water gushed from the nozzle. Vanessa was about two metres away from Bren, facing him and she pointed the stream of water straight at his face. As she did so she saw Curtis, hurt, drop to his knees. The blast of water was enough of a surprise to divert Bren.

'Turn that bloody thing off,' he shouted, using his hands to ward off the bore water's force.

'Come and make me,' she said gamely, hosing him all over, then back again in the face. 'Water is the best thing to cool down a hot temper like yours.' As he advanced towards her, his features screwed up with anger, she retreated until her back came up against the yard's fence and she could go no further. He grabbed the hose off her and threw it to the ground.

He looked so angry that she thought he would strike her. Her brown eyes, dark with anger at his behaviour, dared him to touch her. Then, via her peripheral vision she glimpsed Warren trotting up to them.

'Aahhh, Warren. Good to see you,' she said through clenched teeth as she eyeballed her husband. 'I think Curtis needs help.'

Vanessa watched Bren's features contort as he tried to regain control over his temper. And then, through her own anger at his disgraceful behaviour, came an unexpected rush of pity. Her hand, steady as a rock, reached out and touched his face. A small miracle happened. His features settled and he stared at her as if, suddenly, he was able to see her and himself clearly. Her eyes began to brim with tears as the enormity of what had taken place between the brothers set in. It made her own anger die quickly and emphatically.

'Bren,' she whispered, as if she were speaking to a child. 'What's the matter with you? *With us?*'

# CHAPTER TWENTY

Early next morning, after learning from Fran that Curtis and Regan were packing bags to take to Darwin, Vanessa went to the stone cottage. For an instant or two, when Curtis opened the door and before she said a word, there was a moment of acute embarrassment between them over what had erupted yesterday.

Vanessa spent five minutes pleading with Curtis not to leave and winced mentally as she visually catalogued the damage Bren had inflicted. Curtis looked dreadful. He had a black eye, a swollen nose and a bruise along his jawline, and his knuckles were bruised and skinned.

After listening politely to her plea Curtis had been adamant that the best thing to do until they both cooled down was to put a thousand kilometres or so distance between himself and Bren. He and Regan left soon after, taking the old Cessna, ostensibly for Regan to spend time with her grandmother. However, the small community on Amaroo knew the real reason. A rift, possibly one that could not be mended, had occurred between the Selby brothers — and between Vanessa and Bren as well.

■ ■ ■

Dressed in tourists' garb — cap, sunglasses, shorts and singlet top, and sandals — Curtis wandered along The Esplanade, the road that bordered part of Darwin's harbour and on which a multitude of three to five star high-rise hotels were built. Half an hour ago he had left his mother and daughter in the CBD, to indulge in a shopping spree. He had been walking around aimlessly ever since. He knew the city of Darwin almost as well as he knew every hectare of Amaroo, having spent his teenage years on holidays here. It was the largest city within reasonable flying distance of the station.

A park fringed the road down to the shoreline and he found a shaded bench to sit on and stare at the greenish blue waters of the Arafura Sea. He had been at Cullen Bay for a week now and Regan was revelling in the pampering his mother was giving her. It pleased him to see how well they got along. His daughter, he realised, and not for the first time, sometimes needed a woman's touch and interest now that she was a teenager. Understanding that brought his thoughts to Vanessa. Regan got along well with Vanessa too.

He touched his nose gently. The swelling had gone down and he could breathe through it again, and even smell the slight saltiness coming from an onshore breeze. His sunglasses masked the leftover bruising from the black eye as well as the bleak expression in his hazel eyes as he studied the harbour's smooth water. Hell's bells, what was he going to do? The rare opportunity of being inactive was giving him time to think, too much time, during which he was being forced to admit a truth he'd been hiding from for months.

*He was in love with his brother's wife.*

Why hadn't he realised the depth of his feelings for Vanessa before the fight? And why had the fight been the catalyst that made him aware of how he felt? Had it been because of the way Bren had treated her, his roughness? He nodded. The fight had brought everything to the surface for him, with an amazing clarity, making him see that he had been blocking the admission of his feelings for ... He pulled a face. How long? Months, perhaps years! A sardonic smile lifted the corners of his mouth. He was in love with Vanessa Selby. Clever, talented, courageous Vanessa, who'd taught him several lessons in fortitude, in being good-natured, in showing strength of purpose, over the years he had known her. How could he ever, once, have thought her lacking in substance and being too soft? He slapped his thigh in rebuke. And ... how had he managed to let such a stupid thing — falling in love — happen?

When had it started ...?

Had it been the first time he saw her ride? Seeing her mastering the mustering or teaching her how to fly the chopper and her joy at getting her licence? Then there was her devotion to Kyle, her kindnesses towards Nova. The way she always knocked, so politely, on his cottage door when she wanted to borrow a book. Their discussions afterwards as to the merits of such books and the authors' skills. Hell's bells, there were so many instances. Like her interest in astronomy, and ... seeing her on location that last day of filming *Heart of the Outback* and realising how much talent she had.

When had admiration deepened to *love*? Had it happened so slowly and subtly that he hadn't recognised it until the fight? Was being decked by Bren the action that had dislodged the wall around his heart to set the truth free? He shook his head, wondering and at the same time marvelling over the revelation of his love.

For a while, longer than was sensible, he let the admission of his feelings for Vanessa filter through him like the savoured appreciation of a splendid wine. He loved everything about her. The way she walked, how she curled a lock of hair around her index finger when she was thinking about something, a curiously childish trait. Her laughter. Oh, yes, her laughter. The tinkling, glorious sound it made as it rippled through a room and came back to envelop you in its warmth. Her compassion. He chuckled when he recalled the episode about castrating the weaners and her English outrage. Then there'd been her bravery, being lost after the dust storm and a little while ago, taking on those dingoes on her own.

No wonder she had been able to write a compelling script about a colonial, pioneer family. She was a modern-day reincarnation of that type of woman. He could feel his body becoming aroused as he thought about her, and for several moments he gave in to the joy of wanting her ... so very much. But then came reality and the frustration that went with the wanting, heightened by the sobering knowledge that he could never have her. That had a similar effect to a cold bucket of water being thrown over him.

All right, it had happened, he loved her. What was he going to do about it? A growling, unhappy sound, half sigh, half exclamation forced its way through his lips. Absolutely bloody nothing.

Bren had phoned him and apologised profusely, said he was all kinds of an idiot, which he was, so, in a few days he'd return to Amaroo and pretend that nothing monumental had happened. But something had and things would never be the same. He had to think ahead and ... what he was thinking was that he couldn't stay at Amaroo. He wasn't enough of a masochist for that. Once Bren sorted out the development thing he and Regan would leave. There were always cattle stations in the Kimberley or the Northern Territory looking for competent managers. Or, if Lauren and Marc agreed, they could buy out his share of Cadogan's Run. That would give him the wherewithal to start his own, small station, somewhere far away from Amaroo. It wouldn't be the same, but it would be a starting point for him and his daughter. Yes, that's what he would see if he could do ...

The utility Nova had driven from Kununurra, one of two that belonged to her father, squeaked and bounced along the dirt road as she headed towards Amaroo. In the rear-vision mirror she saw a cloud of red dust in her wake, and to the left and right of her the land was scrubby and flat. In the distance, on the right, stood a row of light green trees bordering

Gumbledon Creek as it wended its way through Amaroo to join up with the Chamberlain River. Further back was a range of low foothills and right now, in the late afternoon light, they were a soft, mauvish-blue and a reddish-sandstone hue. How familiar and comfortable she was with the land around her, because she knew it so well. Still, she would be pushing it to reach the station before dark. She didn't slow down and the Holden shuddered over another cattlegrid.

From the time she boarded the plane in Sydney she had been telling herself to contain her excitement, that she had to wait for the right time to tell all to Curtis. She had heard, via her father that, while Curtis and Regan had returned to Amaroo, things were still cool between himself and Bren. Thick-headed Bren and his temper — he'd always been a hot-head. Spoilt by his parents because he was the eldest, coddled by Hilary. He didn't have Curtis's strength of will or his character. Shit, she wished she had been there for the fight. She would have loved to see Vanessa's reaction, though she was the one who'd been clever enough to break up the ruckus.

A wicked grin spread across her lips as she checked her reflection in the mirror. Damn, even if she thought so herself, she looked fantastic. New hair-do, new clothes and an air of confidence that came with being successful. This was the 'new' Nova. And with regard to Bren and Curtis's fight, it was only the preliminary round. She chuckled as she thought that. Wait till the main event, when Curtis told his brother, correction, half-brother, that Stuart was his real father. *There will be fireworks, big time*, her internal voice chuckled. *Vanessa is going to be out on her arse*. The truth would force her to forfeit her position as one of the most respected women in the Kimberley — with her public profile she had become that over the last several years. Vanessa and Bren would end up with nothing if she had any influence, though she supposed Curtis, being the loyal, honest man he was, would give Bren a fair financial settlement.

She stopped the ute about five metres from the rough-hewn, wide timber posts with their painted sign that straddled them, declaring it the boundary of Amaroo Downs — the homestead was another fifteen kilometres due west. Feeling for the water bottle on the seat beside her she unscrewed the top and took a long drink, after which she reached into her bag to pull out a small bottle. She put two pills into her hand. For a few seconds she stared at the pills, mentally debating whether to take them. She shrugged her shoulders. Why not? They calmed her, made her feel in control and, besides, now she had her image as a personable TV presenter to live up to. That's what they expected at Amaroo and that was what she intended to show Vanessa — that she was as good if not better. She swallowed the pills with more water then got out for a minute to stretch her legs.

Underneath the station's name, in smaller letters were the words:

'Proprietor: Brendan Selby'.

Standing with her hands on her slim hips, Nova stared at the sign, then, in a slow pirouette, she did a full circle. Her gaze took in the three hundred and sixty degree view of what could be seen for a distance of about twenty kilometres. A sly, confident smile, made her appear quite beautiful. Her gaze returned to the proprietor's name and her expression became vindictive. The smile widened as the inner voice chanted for Nova's benefit, *not for much longer, Bren Selby, not for much longer ...*

Nova's return to the fold, so to speak, was sufficient reason for Fran to cook up a celebratory dinner which was waiting for her when she roared into the yard behind the homestead and brought the ute to a bone-shaking halt.

During dinner in the large, friendly kitchen where everyone ate except on special occasions, it was gratifying to be welcomed like a long-lost member of the family. In all honesty, the Selbys were the only family Nova had ever known, having spent almost all her growing up years on the property. She had gifts for everyone.

Kyle loved his set of model cars and the video of her latest children's song. Regan, with whom she kept up an occasional correspondence, loved the clothes she'd bought her. Her father, who collected records, almost got teary-eyed when she presented him with an original Vic Damone vinyl. Vanessa got her favourite perfume, Curtis received several books and Bren was pleased with a leather-bound whisky decanter. Warren liked his new CDs and Fran wasn't forgotten either, receiving slippers and several new kitchen aprons.

'You'd think this was Christmas,' Fran remarked as she gave Nova a peck on the cheek. 'Thanks, love.'

'And thank you for the delicious dinner,' Nova responded.

'What are your plans now that the TV series is finished?' a curious Warren asked.

'I've an option for another series. Anthea's negotiating with the channel for a better financial deal.'

'Good on you, love,' Reg said with a chuckle. 'I'm looking forward to you keeping your old man in luxury in my declining years.'

'Hah. You mean like now,' Fran shot back and everyone laughed.

Nova, smiling, let her gaze rest on Curtis. Both he and Bren, who was usually the gregarious one when a party atmosphere evolved, were subdued. The strain of the recent squabble — an understatement if one believed Reg's version — was evident in their polite, guarded remarks to and around each other. Vanessa, superb actress that she was, behaved as if nothing untoward had occurred but, Nova, as she quietly appraised everyone at the table, knew better. An undercurrent of tension in the room was obvious.

After dessert, and feigning tiredness after a long day's travel, Nova was first to leave and go to the tidy apartment at the back of the stockmen's quarters to unpack. Her nerve ends tingled from the excitement of anticipation — the same feeling she got before she performed. How in hell was she going to sleep? Very soon she would be dropping the biggest bomb on those who lived at Amaroo — and the repercussions had the potential to shatter the lives of half the people who lived there. Yet she felt no remorse about what she planned to do. She saw it as a means to an end, her way of assuring Curtis's undying gratitude.

Oh, boy. She lay on her single bed in the bedroom whose walls were still covered with the posters of country rock stars she'd been crazy about in her teens. It was going to be spectacular.

Vanessa was supervising Kyle and Regan as they did their School of the Air lessons in one of the bedrooms that had been turned into a schoolroom. Curtis had organised things so that Regan and Kyle had separate desks, and there were bookshelves for school and project books, a computer and printer too. One wall contained several maps thumb-tacked to the wall and on a separate table near the window stood the radio used to contact the School of the Air. After their turn at the microphone, where they spoke to their teacher, Debbie Franklin, she watched the two heads, one blond, one ginger, bend studiously over their books.

Vanessa should have been working but her concentration was poor, and she was doodling instead of checking the final script draft for *North of the Nullarbor*. The movie was scheduled to start production in a few months' time. Her thoughts kept drifting ... She should be pleased and relieved because Curtis had returned to Amaroo. She was, but ... things were different between them. The fight had changed everything, including her feelings for Bren, what was happening to them and how, frighteningly, she had been a hair's breadth from walking away from their marriage.

Something indefinable had been lost between Bren and Curtis, and herself and Curtis, and she doubted that, while Bren had taken the blame for the fight, the special, unspoken camaraderie between her and her brother-in-law had become a thing of the past. The balance had somehow shifted and she doubted that there would be a re-adjustment. Since his return she had been aware of a distance between them, as if he were uncomfortable when he looked and spoke to her. She had tried to figure out why but had been unable to come up with an answer.

Resolutely, because thinking about it got her nowhere, she turned her thoughts away from Curtis, to Nova's return. Nova had come a long way, with her share of ups and downs, and was now a success. She had found her niche, and exuded an aura of confidence that had been lacking before. Despite all of that, the question rose in her mind — was this the real Nova or was her confidence and personality being assisted by ... drugs? Hmm, she wasn't sure. Her heart wanted to believe that Nova had outgrown the need, but niggles of doubt prevailed. She had read that addicts usually did something to give themselves away and only time would tell if that were so. Nova had returned because she still dreamt of a relationship with Curtis, and if such a situation came about everyone on Amaroo would breathe a sigh of relief.

Nova would be happy. Reg and Fran would be happy. Vanessa's thoughts turned to getting and keeping them together, in the hope that doing so would strike a romantic spark. For one thing, the seven sub-artesian bores throughout the far-flung property were due for checking and who better to do the chore than Curtis and Nova? She hadn't dabbled in matchmaking before but it was something that would take her mind off her problems with Bren. She believed Kerri would be amused, but, if that's what it took to get things started then so be it.

The ride to and from the last bores in Spring Valley, so named because of its profusion of wildflowers in spring, had been accomplished in half a day. Inspecting the last bore Curtis and Nova found the remains of a bird impaled on the metal. It had slammed into the blade's propeller at the top of the windmill tower, bending it out of shape and useless. Because the windmill wasn't pumping the water up, they had to start the diesel engine and pump water into the tank which filled the circular cement trough to service several hundred head. They cooled their heels till quite a few Brahmans ambled up to drink their fill, then they refilled the trough as they discussed the repairs to the propeller.

'We'll need to put a new one in if we can't fix this one,' Nova said as she looked up at the bent shaft of the propeller.

'The cattle have enough water for a couple of days, but with evaporation and use, it'll have to be fixed by the end of the week or we'll have some very thirsty Brahmans on our hands.'

'We could do it Thursday.' For Nova, spending the day working with Curtis had been like old times. They made a good team, each knowing what the other wanted or needed without having to be asked. That's how it was between them, Nova assured herself, they were so compatible.

Two hours later, with the homestead and other buildings in sight, they gave the horses their head and galloped through the bottom paddock towards the stockyards. They dismounted outside the saddle room to remove saddles and bridles, after which they washed, then rubbed the horses down.

'You haven't lost your deft touch with a diesel motor, you got it started first go,' Curtis praised, giving her a wink as he spoke.

'You and Dad taught me everything I know about motors, and about Amaroo. I can still fix my share of things about the place.'

'And it's good that you don't mind getting your hands dirty.' He gave her a cheeky glance. 'What with you being the successful TV star and all,' he added as he washed his hands under the hose.

'Do go on,' she responded, batting her eyelids and joining in with his lightheartedness.

At that moment Nova, prodded by her inner voice hissing dictatorially, *tell him, tell him, now,* made her decision. Now was the time to tell him because he appeared contented and at ease. They'd been working together for two days and he was like the Curtis of old, teasing, sharing a joke or two, friendly. It was time he knew the truth so he could realise his full potential, to step away from and out of Bren's shadow.

'Curtis,' she began, 'I've been trying to find the right moment to tell you something. It's important.'

He bestowed a quizzical glance on her then continued to rinse his hands. 'About you or me?'

'About you.'

'What? Have you been making a list of my character flaws?'

'No, silly. Be serious.' She turned to face him. 'I am.'

Studying her in that quiet way of his, he leant against the stockyard's fence and hooked his thumbs into the waistband of his jeans. 'Okay, fire away.'

Nova had rehearsed, over and over, what she intended to say, how she was going to tell him but with the moment upon her, in delivering the words she got tangled up. 'It's about your mother, and Stuart,' she blurted out. 'How they cheated on your father and, and ... had an affair. She got pregnant and ...' she had to take a breath before she said it. 'Bren is Stuart's son, not Matthew's.' There, she'd said it.

With her heart pounding inside her chest, she exhaled slowly, and not daring to check his expression, waited ...

# CHAPTER TWENTY-ONE

'Are you insane?' his usually quiet voice rose dramatically. 'What the hell are you talking about, Nova? Who told you such a stupid story?'

'It's true, Curtis, every word. I swear.' She had expected him not to believe her at first, that he would take some convincing. 'I found out, several months ago in fact. I bumped into Diane Selby at a restaurant when I was in Perth. She was a touch under the weather and we talked. During our conversation Diane said several things and, when she realised her slip of the tongue, she swore me to secrecy but,' her shoulders shrugged with indifference to Stuart's wife's problem, 'I think you have the right to know.'

Curtis's gaze narrowed on her sharply, his features taut with controlled anger. He asked through thinning lips, 'What did Diane say? Tell me, word for word.'

Her confidence rising because he hadn't laughed at her, or turned and walked away, she began to relate the details of what had been said that night at the restaurant ... When she finished, he shook his head in disbelief. *He's in denial, we knew he would be at first.*

'You know Diane. She's had it in for Stuart for years because of his indiscretions. She lied and you bought the lie.'

'At first I thought that but, Curtis, her story makes sense. Think back: remember the stories we've heard over the years. How Matthew was often away for long periods of time and that Hilary used to get lonely. How she had a nervous breakdown after Bren's birth and that her cousin, Claire, came and helped out for two months. Why did that happen when Bren's was a normal birth? Was it guilt because of what she and Stuart had done? And why was Bren her favourite — more guilt over her affair with him?' She was on a roll now and though she could tell that he wanted her to stop, she kept going. 'Also, look at Bren. He doesn't resemble your father at all but he does look very much like your uncle. They *could* be father and son.'

'Of course they're alike,' he retorted with forced amusement, 'they are uncle and nephew, after all.'

'All right, something else.' She let that one go, she had other points to bring to his attention. 'Remember when Kyle was ill and you had the highest compatibility rate for the transplant. Why wasn't Bren more compatible?' She saw a shadow of doubt creep across his features but it was gone in an instant.

'The specialist explained that. Sometimes a more distant relative, for no logical reason they know of, can be more compatible.'

'There is one way to find out,' she challenged, 'ask Diane. If she confirms my story, you could then ask your mother.'

'Why, Nova?' He stared at her as if she had suddenly developed two heads. 'Why are you telling me this?'

*Tell him why, Nova,* her little voice hissed through her brain. 'Because I believe that Amaroo is rightfully yours. The station doesn't belong to Bren.'

'Jesus ...' All at once the ramifications of Nova's disclosure began to sink in. Curtis passed a hand across his forehead and ran it through his sandy coloured hair.

'Curtis, all this,' her hands swept encompassingly around the shed, the breaking-in yard, to the paddocks and beyond, 'could be yours.'

His mouth tightened and he put up his right hand, palm raised like a stop sign. 'Don't say another word. *Don't.*'

She was bewildered by his reaction; she had expected doubts even anger, not dismissal. 'I ... thought you'd be pleased. You can have Amaroo. It's what you've always wanted, isn't it?'

'At the expense of turfing my brother and his family out?' He shook his head. 'What kind of monster do you think I am?'

Confused, she blinked owlishly at him, unable to believe that he couldn't see what he was on the brink of. 'B-but you will talk to Diane, and Hilary, won't you?'

He turned on his heel away from her, his answer coming in a half growl. 'Yes, damn it, I'll check it out. But don't expect me to thank you for the information. In one fell swoop you've effectively made my mother an adulteress and my uncle an adulterer, my brother a bastard and me the worst bastard of all if I take advantage of what might be the truth.'

Nova watched him stalk towards the stone cottage, his spine stiff with anger. Her cheeks were coloured spots of embarrassment and no small amount of disappointment. *So, it hasn't quite gone to plan*, the voice soothed. *Curtis is angry with you now, but that will pass.* Yes, it's the shock of it, she assured herself. He needs time to absorb the consequences of Bren's illegitimacy and what that means. Then ... then he will thank me and see what a wonderful team we will make.

She touched the tic at the side of her mouth and frowned. Damned, uncontrollable thing. It was beating double time, and she didn't need a mirror to know that it made her look as if she had a peculiar, lopsided smile. Curtis would be indebted, she strove to re-affirm her belief, because she had played her hand and now she had to wait until he acted. She bit her lip as a wave of anxiety stiffened her muscles. And, of course he would ...

Dinner that evening in Amaroo's roomy kitchen with its long, refectory timber table was, as usual, a noisy affair with everyone who worked on the station present. But two, Nova and Curtis, only paid lip-service and barely contributed to the conversation. Curtis wore an expression of preoccupation, as if he had his mind on other things, which he did, and Nova said little but she watched everyone ... and listened.

'Tomorrow, I've an architect and a builder coming from Darwin to discuss the home-stay accommodation scheme. They'll be arriving about 9.30,' Bren informed everyone, and his smile implied that he was inordinately pleased with himself.

'Isn't that premature? The loan hasn't been approved yet,' Vanessa, who'd said her piece several times as to her opinion on the project but had deferred to Bren because the property was solely his, asked. The truth of that and him reminding her of that fact had left a bitter taste in her mouth especially when she knew that she had contributed mightily and financially to Amaroo's well-being over the years of their marriage. They were often 'at each other' these days and she could see no end to it ... because the chasm between them was widening, almost on a daily basis.

'I don't think so,' Bren responded testily. 'They've given me a rough estimate but I need to finetune the details to get a firm cost.'

Curtis, more often than not undiplomatic, put his knife and fork together noisily on the half-eaten plate of food, and then stood up. 'Don't expect me to squire them around or keep them entertained. I'll be off at first light to Lauren's.'

'Okay, but take the chopper, will you. I might need the Cessna,' Bren said accommodatingly.

Curtis looked at Regan and forestalled her question. 'No, love, you can't come this time. It's purely business.' He gave a little salute with his index finger to those at the table. 'Goodnight everyone.'

Fran gave him a peculiar look and followed up with, 'What, not waiting for dessert?'

Curtis's gaze swept the table, resting for a few seconds on Vanessa, who was trying to get Kyle to eat his vegetables, and finishing at Nova. 'Not tonight, no appetite for sweets. Don't forget to do your homework, Regan,' he reminded his daughter as he strode towards the kitchen's back door and disappeared into the night.

'He's in a mood,' Bren muttered dismissively, a hint of amusement in his voice.

Vanessa's expression was thoughtful as she stared at the empty kitchen doorway. 'It's not like him to be quite so ... abrupt. Perhaps he isn't well.'

'We did a lot of work today, hard yakka, most of it. He's probably just pooped,' Nova made the excuse to Vanessa.

*What a bitch! Making out that she's concerned about her brother-in-law. Playing a role. Oh, yes, she's good at that.* The muscles in Nova's stomach tightened as she recalled Curtis's parting glance at *her* nemesis. What was she to make of it? Did he have deep feelings for the bitch or was it more a case of non-sexual male admiration? Well, she attempted to comfort herself, that didn't matter. Neither of them would have to look at her or Bren and Kyle for much longer. When Curtis assumed his rightful position *they'd* make it clear that Bren and his family were not welcome on Amaroo.

*That would really put Vanessa out, having to leave and start all over again somewhere else.* Nova stared at the actress's trim again figure. Pity about losing the baby. She had received lots of sympathy but, apparently, not much from Bren. She'd overheard Fran telling her dad that Bren hadn't been pleased about them having another kid. Just as well the miscarriage had happened naturally or something might have had to be done to ... kind of encourage Vanessa to believe Amaroo wasn't a safe place for her to be for long periods of time. She didn't have to worry about Vanessa anymore though. When Curtis claimed what was his and they were together ... the actress would become no more than an unpleasant memory ...

Curtis Selby was not a happy man. In fact, he couldn't remember ever being as miserable as he was at this moment, not even when Georgia declared their marriage over. Sitting in an armchair, the phone cradled in his lap, he held onto the receiver after having disconnected the line from Diane in Broome.

Shit. Shit. Shit! Resting back on the chair's material, his head shook from side to side as he tried to deny what Diane's confirmation of Nova's story meant. No longer could he discount it as the venom of a jealous, two-timed wife. He had something even more unpleasant to do now — talk to his mother. He glanced at the clock on the wall, it was sandwiched between the book-crowded shelves — she would still be up but ... it could wait till morning, couldn't it? No, Hilary liked to sleep in and he was leaving for Lauren's at sunrise. And ... it would be better to have their 'talk' before Regan came in for the night.

Hell's bells, what a predicament. He shut his eyes for a moment or two, squeezing back a threatening moistness. His upper lip curled derisively and he blinked the moisture away. Outback men didn't cry. Be it surviving on the land or personally, they took whatever was dished out on the chin and got on with life. What a load of bullkaaka that was!

His world as he knew it had been turned upside down by Nova's revelations. So far he hadn't bothered to analyse the reasoning behind her tale, there would be time for that later. Maybe he'd make a cup of coffee before he called. No, a whisky would be better. He shook his head. You're procrastinating, my lad. Get it over with. He stared at the phone and began to dial the Darwin phone number, but stopped half way through. Christ, how could he baldly ask the questions he had to ask over the phone? The phone was too cold a medium, too impersonal. He had to front his mother and ask her face to face. Yes, that's what he had to do. Damn, that meant a trip to Darwin. He'd call Lauren and tell her there had been a change of plans, and leave a note on the kitchen noticeboard telling everyone he was going to Darwin.

His throat tightened and he could hardly swallow at the thought of confronting Hilary. He was concerned by how she would react but, it had to be done, and no matter how unpleasant the answers might be, he had to know . . .

Next morning Bren and Vanessa read Curtis's note on the kitchen noticeboard, about going to see Hilary instead of heading for Cadogan's Run.

'Wonder what he wants to see dear old Mum about?' Bren asked idly as he sat at the table, ready for breakfast.

Nova, sitting between Regan and Kyle, didn't bother to disguise her boredom. She smiled and said nothing.

'He probably just needs a break,' Vanessa said, but she was frowning. Curtis had been acting strangely since his return after the fight with Bren. Clearly something was on his mind but, as was typical with the Selby men, they only discussed what and when they wanted to. Obviously he didn't want to.

'Maybe. He chose not to be around when the architect and builder arrive. Curtis can be a stubborn bastard at times.'

Vanessa gave him a hard-eyed stare, clearly unimpressed by his criticism. 'And you're not?'

Bren shrugged. 'What can I say, it's a Selby trait.' His previously genial expression became serious. 'You are with me on this development, aren't you?'

Vanessa heard the anxious note in his voice. She spent so much time re-assuring him, bolstering his confidence. 'You know my reservations but, if it can be done economically ...' She didn't finish the sentence, instead she changed the subject. 'With the new breeding program only half complete and you know that more bores need to be sunk, finances are tight.' In spite of her low enthusiasm she dredged up a softening smile. 'Fabian told you that. My only proviso is that the development shouldn't run us too deeply into the red. Red, on an accounts ledger, is not my favourite colour.'

Since Bren had first talked about the project she had given a lot of thought to the advantage of Bren being involved in something he was passionate about because it made him easier to live with.

Which was why she hadn't strenuously objected, as Curtis had. Bren was Bren and what was becoming more obvious was that when he wanted his own way regarding something, that was all he could focus on, *his* goal, with little concern for commonsense, money or reality.

'So, Fran, what are you going to give our guests for lunch?' Bren asked as Fran emerged from the homestead's room-size pantry.

'Don't expect *haute* cuisine from me, Bren Selby, that's not my style. Your guests will get a platter of cold cuts, fresh potato salad, a bowl of salad greens and dessert followed by cheese and crackers.'

'That sounds just right; it's going to be a hot one today,' Vanessa said as she wiped her brow. The overhead fans in the kitchen were rotating though it was still early in the morning. She moved about the kitchen, clearing the table while Nova sat and did nothing. Afterwards, she checked the week's mail — a dozen letters of varying sizes sat on the kitchen dresser that housed the crockery and cutlery. There was a letter and contract from Kerri for her role in *North of the Nullarbor*, plus a note that the film's producer, Heather Clarry, would fax a list of preferred shoot locations on Amaroo to her in a couple of days.

She slit open an envelope and pulled out a brochure that advertised a new type of electricity for remote stations, using solar panels to generate power. Interesting. They should look into that, she decided as she tucked the paper into the pocket of her loose, floral skirt. Perhaps she would ask the visiting architect a question or two about its possibilities.

Glancing at the kitchen clock, Vanessa saw that it was almost time for school. 'Kids, School of the Air starts in two minutes,' she said to Regan and Kyle. 'You should be in the schoolroom.'

Regan, an eager student, jumped out of her chair straight away, but Kyle's scowl reminded her of Bren. He was still grappling with the concept of learning and having to do 'work'. Vanessa knew he would rather be out helping with the cattle or assisting Reg or Warren with maintenance work around the property — what young boy wouldn't? She pretended not to see his down-in-the mouth expression for, not only did it make him look like his father, it reinforced the fact that he was like him in many ways. Bren, too, had not had an affinity with the three Rs, so Curtis had once told her.

Thinking about her brother-in-law again, her gaze moved thoughtfully to Nova. There was something different about her. She had changed, again, become more ... distant, less friendly. Almost as if she didn't like her anymore! What nonsense, she scolded herself. But ... she couldn't halt the thought and was unconvinced as to whether she was *using* again. At times Nova appeared sluggish, particularly in the mornings and sometimes she was over-the-top cheerful, as if she were hyped up.

You're imagining things, she rebuked herself. Nova was all right, she was just too focussed on trying to work her way into Curtis's heart. And in that respect she admitted to a certain curiosity about the budding romance and if Nova's strategy of trying to be with him as much as possible, was working. Once she would have asked but this new, determined, super cool Nova had her thinking twice, and made her decide to remain a silent observer. If Nova wanted to talk about it, she knew where to find her.

Jolting herself out of her analysing mood, she gave Kyle another reminder.

'Come on, don't dawdle. Off you go before Miss Franklin gets on the airwaves. You know she has a lot of students to talk to and she doesn't like to be kept waiting.' Hiding her smile, she watched Kyle, feet dragging, follow Regan out of the kitchen and down the hallway to the schoolroom.

During the chopper flight to Darwin, which took several hours — not landing till almost midday — Curtis had time to go over what he wanted to say, how he wanted to phrase the questions he felt honour-bound to ask his mother.

As he stood inside the air-conditioned living room, by the windows, waiting for his mother to join him — she was outside giving the gardener instructions as to what was to be planted in a freshly turned garden bed — Curtis had never felt so uncomfortable. Hell's bells, how do you ask your mother whether she had an affair with her brother-in-law and fell pregnant to him? Even before he asked what he knew he had to, he was steeling himself for her response. There could be anger, disdain or tears. Maybe she would throw all three reactions at him at once. God, it was going to be unpleasant.

After a few opening pleasantries and when they'd become comfortable on the sofa, Curtis got right down to it. 'Mum, some disturbing information has come my way and it's, well, difficult to put into words that don't offend so, forgive me if I don't try.'

Hilary gave him an imperious look. 'What are you talking about, Curtis?'

'About you and ... Stuart.' He shifted uneasily on the leather sofa which squeaked as his weight moved. 'Old stuff, really. That ...' he plunged straight in, 'you and he had an affair before he married Diane.'

Hilary sat up straight, as if she had been stung by something sharp. Her gold-rimmed bifocals almost fell off the bridge of her autocratic nose. '*What?* What person told you such ... lies? Tell me, who was it?'

Succinctly, he explained that Nova had passed on information from Diane and that he had checked with his aunt who had corroborated it. He watched her reach for her pack of cigarettes and lighter, and light up. She didn't answer straight away and he gauged from her closed expression that she was holding her anger down while she attempted to come up with an answer that would satisfy him and save her pride.

'Is it true?' The question was asked with gentle insistence. It was significant that his mother refused to look directly at him. Her gaze was set on a potted palm to the left of and behind him. A long moment's silence pervaded the room. Then —

'Yes,' she said, her lips compressed together. She did that when she wasn't happy or at ease. 'It ... it happened a long time ago.' The fingers of one hand held the cigarette while the other moved aimlessly on her lap, smoothing out imaginary creases. 'I did something very foolish and have regretted it every day of my life since.'

'Do you want to tell me about it?' Curtis asked, believing that because the matter was out in the open, she would want to unburden herself.

Hilary stared at him strangely almost as if he had asked her to commit murder. 'It isn't easy to tell a son that you had an affair, but now that you know, I suppose you should know how it happened.' An eyebrow arched meaningfully. 'If only to counteract the innuendos and lies Diane's probably told.'

'Diane gave me the bare facts, that's all. No details.'

She took another drag on the cigarette, exhaled and watched the smoke spiral up and evaporate before she spoke. 'Matthew and I hadn't been married long, about a year, I think. He was away a lot and I, well, I wasn't used to being on my own so much, having come from a busy social life in Brisbane. I had spent holidays on my grandfather's property on the Darling Downs but I didn't know very much about the realities of station life.' She looked at him. 'How you have to occupy yourself — there's always plenty to do anyway — so you don't get bored or lonely.'

'At the time, Stuart was engaged to Diane and working on a pearling lugger. He came to Amaroo for a week's break. There was no one else around other than Dulcie, the part-Aboriginal woman who cleaned and cooked. No-one stimulating to talk to. We started off doing things together, riding, checking the bores, listening to music at night, sharing meals etc ... One night, well, we both had too much to drink and ...' she shook her head, 'I'm sure you don't want the lurid details, but *things* happened. Next morning we woke up in bed together and ...'

'Stuart got you drunk so he could seduce you?'

Hilary gave him a self-deprecating smile. 'I'd like to be able to say that but in all honesty I can't. I was lonely for companionship, for affection. Matthew had been gone for almost three months, droving along the Canning stock route to deliver cattle to a station in the Flinders Ranges. I was a willing participant, I'm ashamed to say.' Her tanned, lined cheeks stained pink as she admitted her guilt.

'Then Diane called. She told Stuart that she was pregnant and he'd better come to Adelaide and marry her before her parents got wind of it.' She shrugged her shoulders. 'He went.'

'Bastard ...'

She rolled her eyes. 'You know Stuart. He isn't big on compassion or things that don't serve his best interests. Diane's family had money, and a business interest in tourism. That's how Stuart got started in the business, he learnt it from Mike, his father-in-law.'

Now for the big question. Curtis took a calming breath. 'And Bren. He was conceived that night with Stuart, wasn't he?'

Another, longer silence. 'Diane said that?' Her tone was very cool, contained.

'She implied it.' He thought for a moment. 'No, more than implied. I believe that's partly why she's ticked off with both of you. You had the son she longed to give Stuart and wasn't able to.'

'What a stupid woman.' Hilary's tone held no pity. 'Diane never knew how to handle Stuart, she still doesn't. That's why she puts up with his extra-curricular activities, because she doesn't have the guts to leave him. I would if I had a man who played around as often as Stuart does.'

Hating himself for being a relentless bastard, Curtis reminded her, 'Mum, you haven't answered my question about Bren?'

'Do I need to? I can see in your eyes that you've made up your mind as to the identity of Bren's father.'

So she wasn't going to confirm it one way or another, unless forced to. 'There's a lot of evidence pointing to that being more than a possibility.'

'Is there?' she challenged.

'You always told us that Bren came early, that he was an eight-months baby. His birth weight was big compared to myself and Lauren, and we were full-term babies. I believe Bren was full-term and that he was conceived a month before Dad came back from droving. Then there was your nervous breakdown. No-one could understand why it happened when your pregnancy and the birth were normal.' He gave her a swift look, but her inscrutable expression gave nothing away. 'Guilt, perhaps? That's why you've treated Bren differently to Lauren and myself, you feel guilty because he isn't Matthew's son.'

'And there's the physical likeness between Stuart and Bren — they could be father and son. Which is why Bren and Stuart are close, because Stuart *knows* he's his father. And more recently, there were the compatibility tests to give Kyle a new liver where

I was the more compatible of the two of us. The transplant team were surprised by that . . .'

Hilary smiled for the first time during their conversation. 'Son, you're drawing a long bow with some of those claims. You have no concrete proof of anything, other than Diane's accusation.'

He didn't want to mention paternity or DNA tests, he wasn't going to go that far. 'Possibly not, however, there is enough to give one pause to think, don't you agree?'

Hilary studied her son for several moments, and it was obvious that she was trying to gauge how he felt about what he'd said. 'A hypothetical question, Curtis. What would you do if I told you that it was true, that Bren isn't Matthew's son?'

'Do?' Though he frowned, deep down he understood the question. He sought a moment's respite to formulate his answer. 'What do you mean?'

'*If* Bren isn't Matthew's son, it alters the question of inheritance, as no doubt you're aware. It makes you Matthew's legal heir. If that were so, what would you do about Amaroo? Would you claim your inheritance?'

He had been mulling over that possibility ever since Nova had made her claim. 'What? Toss Bren and his family off Amaroo?' He shook his head and, fleetingly his gaze moved to the window and the bay beyond. 'I wouldn't be much of a brother if I did that. I love Bren and it would hurt him too much. As far as I'm concerned, nothing would change. It's just that now that the matter has come up, I have to know the truth. Besides,' he took a breath, 'I've been thinking it's time for Regan and myself to move on. In the long term, there's nothing for me at Amaroo.' He had already made that decision because of his feelings for Vanessa. There was no way he could stay there, loving her as he did and not being able to have her.

'Moving on, to where, doing what?' a surprised Hilary asked as she lit a second cigarette.

'Lauren and Marc have done well at Cadogan's Run. They want to buy out my share of the property. That would give me a deposit on something smaller, somewhere else.' Curtis saw tears beginning to form in his mother's eyes and looked away so as not to embarrass her. He felt sorry for her. The years of guilt, of compensating and hiding the truth from his father and the family. It was little wonder she had become so ... difficult. Years of piled up guilt could do that to a person, he imagined.

'You'd do that, give up Amaroo to keep Bren happy?' She smiled in wonderment as he nodded, and leant across to pat his hand. 'You're quite a man, Curtis. Your dad would be very, very proud. Damn it,' she sniffed noisily and added, '*I'm* very proud.'

'It's the best thing for all of us.'

Continuing to hold his hand, she pressured him to know how he really felt about her. 'I suppose you ... hate me, now that you know I'm not the perfect mother I purported to be?'

'No, Mum, you're like everyone else,' he grinned at her, 'human. Things happen. "Shit happens", as Nova would say. One error in judgement doesn't make a person worthless. You made Dad happy, you were a good mother to us and a capable mistress of Amaroo. I don't have anything to complain about.'

'Then for the record, and just between us, I'll tell you the truth. Bren is Stuart's son. Everything you said earlier was true. Stuart knows, which is why he pays him so much attention. That's why he makes a fuss over Kyle too.'

Curtis nodded gravely, pleased that she'd had the guts to admit something so unpalatable. Now everything made sense. 'Stuart must have had a good laugh when he found out that he'd got you pregnant. It was the perfect revenge for not getting a share of Amaroo, to know that *his* son would inherit Amaroo, not Matthew's. That's probably why he comes around so often, to silently crow over his achievement.'

Hilary gasped as the full import of what he'd said sank in. 'All these years, I've never thought of it in that light. For a long time, afterwards, it was difficult. Having to be friendly towards Stuart, Diane too, with the knowledge that if either of them wanted to hurt Matthew they could tell him what we'd done. It was a strain.' She gave him a tentative, unsure smile. 'So, *all this* ... stays with us?' She shook her head, her features tightening with concern. 'If Bren found out ...'

Curtis understood, perfectly. 'He won't learn the truth about his birth from me. That's a promise.'

'Good, but what about Nova?'

Nova might be a problem but he didn't want his mother to know that. He forced a note of confidence into his voice. 'She'll be right. I'll make sure she understands that it's our secret.'

404

'Well, after this ... chat,' she laughed nervously, 'I think we've earned a drink. I certainly need one,' Hilary said with feeling.

The ordeal was over, Curtis thought as he moved towards the large traymobile with its ample stock of liquor. A gin and tonic for his mother, a whisky on the rocks for himself. He was sure they would both be having more than one ...

Nova stared at the fluorescently illuminated numbers of the digital clock on the bedside table: 11.20 p.m. She couldn't sleep, her nerves were all a tingle because she was almost jumping out of her skin with anticipation and excitement. Curtis was back from Darwin. He had talked to his mother and she was in a lather of anxiety to learn what had been said. Hilary could have denied Diane's story because she had more to lose than Diane — both of her sons' love and respect.

She shrugged her shoulders in an I-couldn't-care-less attitude as, in the darkness, she fished into her top drawer, found a bottle and took out a couple of pills. She swallowed them with a mouthful of water taken from the glass on the bedside table. So what if she had a habit, she could control it. Those dickhead psychiatrists at the sanatorium said she wouldn't be able to but what did they know? Bloody nothing. Then she spared Curtis's mother a moment's sympathy — it was too bad about Hilary, but the woman had played around, had her fun and now the truth was out and she just had to wear it. What she cared about was Curtis, about him getting what was rightfully his so they could share it together.

Amaroo would be Curtis's, and hers, and how bloody marvellous that was going to be!

For a minute or two she listened for any noises in the flat. Her father and Fran had come in about an hour ago. Through the plasterboard walls she could hear Reg's gentle snore, and Fran would be out for the count. The old duck got pretty tired these days. Amaroo days were long ones and helping Vanessa with Kyle guaranteed that she went to sleep as soon as her head touched the pillow.

It was too hot for even a sheet so she got up, and without switching on the light, peered through the window. Curtis's cottage was fifty metres away and she could see that the lights were on — he was still up. Dressing in shorts and a singlet top, she pulled on her daggy, elasticised boots, took her torch from the chest of drawers near the door before leaving her bedroom and tiptoed outside into the night's steamy silence.

On the walk to Curtis's cottage Nova stopped twice and almost turned around, curiously undecided as to whether she should push the issue to find out what Hilary had said. *Go on*, her inner voice encouraged, *you want to know what the old crow said, don't you?* She moved forward, using the torch to light up the ground in front of her. What if Hilary had denied everything? That would make her look a dill and a half, and destroy any credibility she had with Curtis. Still, in spite of that possibility, she itched to know what had happened; she wouldn't rest until she did.

Nova knocked gently on the front door, then turned the handle and opened it. The room reeked from the essence of liqueur whisky, Wild Turkey.

She had to search the room to find Curtis. He sat slumped in an armchair facing the bookcase, only his profile was visible. A small table stood by the chair with a bottle and an empty glass on it. She thought he was asleep until, suddenly, his head and shoulders swivelled towards her.

'Oh. It's you . . .' he said, his tone was gloomy in the extreme. He turned his head away.

Nova's eyebrows shot up and she looked at the half empty bottle. Not a good sign. Curtis liked a drink or two though he wasn't a patch on his brother, but he rarely touched Wild Turkey unless his intention was to get drunk quickly. She remembered that he'd got drunk a lot after Georgia had left and taken Regan with her. Standing inside the door she almost turned to leave, until she remembered that she had a stake in knowing. Her future happiness hinged on what Hilary had confessed to and what Curtis planned to do about it.

'So,' gathering her courage she sauntered towards him, pulled out one of the dining table chairs and sat opposite him, 'How did it go in Darwin?'

The expression in his eyes was stormy. 'It wasn't a picnic.'

Good. She leant forward, eager to catch every word. 'Tell me, what did Hilary say?'

Curtis didn't answer straight away, deliberately taking his time. First he filled his glass again, picked it up and took a long swallow. 'She corroborated what you said.' He stared balefully at her. 'Everything.'

'Then you are Amaroo's rightful heir.' There was satisfaction in her voice. *We've won, lovey, we've won.* 'Curtis, I'm so happy for you. Now we, I mean, you can do the things you've always wanted to do on the station. The improvements, herd diversification, so many of the things Bren vetoed.' Almost unable to believe how easy it had been to manipulate the situation and put Curtis where she wanted him to be, she moved her chair closer, until their knees almost touched. 'It's going to be wonderful. You and me, and Amaroo. We'll turn it into the best station in the Kimberley.'

Brows knitting in a frown at her choice of words — *you and me* and *we'll*, he made no comment but said instead. 'That's not how it's going to be. Bren's a family man, and I have no intention of usurping him from his position at Amaroo. Mum and I decided that was for the best, that Bren's confidence would be shattered if he knew the truth about his birth.' And before she could comment on that he added in a serious tone, 'I expect you not to tell anyone what you know. It'll be our secret.' He stared pointedly at her again. 'I'd be very unhappy if, somehow, Bren found out about Stuart and Mum.'

Shit! *Is he mad? Maybe we didn't hear him right.* The muscle at the side of her mouth began to jerk erratically. What was all this mumbo jumbo about Bren's confidence being shattered — who cared a fig about that? She didn't. *And keeping what you know a secret! Doesn't Curtis realise that you've done everything for him because you love him so much?*

Breathing heavily, anger building inside her, she shouted, 'To hell with pandering to Bren's lack of confidence. I don't give a rat's arse about hurting his feelings.' *Tell him you've handed Amaroo to him on*

408

*a platter and so far you haven't heard a word of gratitude from him*, prodded her little voice.

Nova nodded in response, her belligerent gaze narrowing to slits. 'What's in it for me, Curtis? What do I get out of your stupid, magnanimous gesture?'

# CHAPTER TWENTY-TWO

Curtis looked at her steadily, his features impassive as he scolded, 'Keep your voice down. I don't want Regan to hear anything. What were your expectations, Nova?' He didn't wait for her answer. 'Did you expect me to thank you for being the catalyst that has the potential to tear my family apart? Did you? That isn't going to happen.' He shook his head firmly. 'Bren will stay at Amaroo and I'm making plans to start my own station, somewhere in the Northern Territory. All I ask of you is that you keep what you know to yourself.'

'B-but what about me, about *us*? I ... I thought that when you knew, that we, I mean, you ... you'd ...' What had she thought? That he'd be so overjoyed and so grateful that he would realise what a great team they made, and want to marry her. Yes, that was precisely what she had thought, dreamed, expected.

'Aaah!' He nodded, understanding. 'That's why you used the words *you and me*, and *we'll* so easily. You thought I'd reward you for the information. What did you want, Nova, money or perhaps a financial interest in Amaroo as your reward?' There was an edge to Curtis's tone now and his expression hardened as he stroked his jaw contemplatively.

Stung by his tone she didn't think the words through before she spoke. 'I ... I hoped that you'd appreciate me more, like me more and that *we* ...' Agitated, she began to clasp and unclasp her hands. Oh, shit, this wasn't going well, not at all as she had planned. He was angry with her because she had caused trouble between himself and Hilary, and while he now knew that Amaroo was rightfully his . .. *It's obvious he doesn't have the will to reach out and take it. What a fool your Curtis is.*

'You're too soft, Curtis,' Nova lashed out at him. 'I've given you the power to take what you want but you're too ... too ...' there was no other word for it, 'gutless.'

'Gutless, am I? Has your brain become so warped by the stuff you've put into your body — I have noticed that you still have a habit.' His eyebrows lifted meaningfully, 'That you can't see that it takes real guts to walk away from the place you've cherished all your life and start from scratch somewhere else. That takes courage, Nova, *courage.*' His tone was scathing as he added, 'Or are your brains too stuffed up to work it out?'

She didn't want to listen to what he was saying, the harshness in his voice, the criticism, the flint-like expression in his eyes — hurt too much. The inner voice was getting louder and more insistent, making her head spin and something — anger, frustration, disappointment — was pounding in her head, driving her crazy, making her say things she knew she would regret but she couldn't stop them.

Everything was unravelling, she was unravelling, inside. Her love meant nothing to him; he wasn't interested. Her plans, dreams, hopes were shattering into a million pieces. Oh, God, she hurt all over, a deep dark hurt, the kind of hurting that would never go away. Her arms went around her torso and she hugged herself in an attempt to contain the pain.

'You're not running off because of Bren, it's because of *her*,' she spat at him. *That's right, tell him that you know about her.* 'You're in love with Vanessa and you can't stand it 'cause she doesn't care one iota for you. That's the real reason you're leaving.' A tense silence enveloped the room before he spoke and she knew he was mentally adjusting to the fact that she knew.

His cool expression gave nothing away as he said, 'Who I love is none of your business. All I want from you is a promise to keep your mouth shut about what you know.'

'Why should I? What do I care if everyone in the Kimberley knows? People in the outback like a good scandal as much as anyone else.'

Curtis rammed the glass down on the table next to him with so much force that it broke into several pieces. 'Because if you do, some of the muck will stick to you. People don't like scandalmongers either, people who manipulate things to better their position. If you spread this information around I'll counteract it with a rumour of my own: that you did it because you expected me to be so grateful that I'd marry you.' He noted her sharp intake of breath before he continued. 'That wouldn't look good in the media, with you being a nationally known TV presenter and a country and western singer.'

She gasped. 'How did you know that I ...?'

'Blind Freddie could work it out. I'm sorry you thought there was a chance that might happen but I could never be in love with you,' he shook his head sadly, 'even if I didn't care for someone else.'

She winced as if he had hit her. *The rotten bastard. He's a mean, heartless man. He doesn't deserve your love, Nova.* He didn't, she agreed, but Curtis was right about one thing, she thought, her instinct for survival taking over. If she couldn't have him and Amaroo, the only thing she could count on was her career, on being the best she could be and eclipsing Vanessa's fame and good fortune. Unable to look at him, she jumped up from the chair, unmindful of the noise it made as it scraped against the stone floor.

She gave him what she hoped was a look of utter loathing, and whispered, 'I hate you, Curtis. You've destroyed my dreams but at least I have the satisfaction of knowing that you will never attain yours.' Her laugh was short, and venomous. 'You'll never have Vanessa. Never.' Straightening her spine and with considerable aplomb considering how upset she was, she let herself out of the cottage and began to walk back to her parents' flat.

Curtis stared at the broken glass, the droplets of Wild Turkey lying on the table, then he ran a hand — it was a little unsteady — across his eyes and through his hair. Try as he might he couldn't erase the memory of the crazed way Nova had looked when she'd understood that he wasn't going to

413

respond as she wanted him to. It made him wonder ... was she unhinged? Possibly. He had had his doubts about her since she'd returned to Amaroo because she had become almost manic, needing to be near him, trying to please him. His head shook in consternation and realisation. Hell's bells, he should have been smarter, seen the warning signs and done something before it got nasty and personal.

He leant back in the chair and tried to get his thoughts into some kind of order, which wasn't easy. The last few days had been awful, and he wouldn't want to repeat them. When he got back from Cadogan's Run tomorrow, he would talk to Nova again. She would be calmer and more sensible then, he hoped. He would suggest she go back to Sydney because it would be best for everyone if she did, and not return to Amaroo for a very long time.

Nova didn't go back to her room in the flat she shared with Reg and Fran. She was too het up, too devastated to sleep. She wanted to smash things, to hurt something because she was hurting. For a while she wandered around the property, shone her flashlight around the yard where they kept the horses, the chicken coop, poked her head into the saddle room. She couldn't settle. She was so furious she wanted to scream for a very long time but couldn't because the noise would wake everyone. Damn Curtis Selby. He had ruined her life, trod on her dreams, her feelings, told her how unimportant she was to him. *It's all right to hate him,* her little voice said dispassionately to her, *you're too good for him anyway. He'd never fully appreciate someone like you, not like I do . . .*

Her meanderings took her to the hangar where all kinds of machinery in various stages of repair or improvement were kept, including the bikes and a reconditioned engine Bren had bought to revitalise the Cessna. Tears of frustration and of loss, streamed down her face and onto her chest as she sat in the darkness on a wobbly stool, with only the flashlight to illuminate her surroundings.

It was over. Curtis didn't want Amaroo badly enough. *In his own way he's as weak as Bren.* She sat up straight, nodded in agreement with the voice inside. *You should make him pay, big time.*

'I hate him,' she said aloud and listened to the words echo hollowly around the large space. 'I want to hurt him, like he's hurt me.' *You can do it, you have the power to.*

'If I can't have him no one will have him,' she muttered. *Then do something about it . . . You're good at manipulating situations to your advantage.*

'Yes!' Nova stood up so quickly the stool toppled over. Shining the torch on the Cessna then arcing the light towards the chopper parked outside the hangar, she smiled. Curtis was going to take the Cessna and fly to Cadogan's Run tomorrow. She knew he would take the plane because the chopper needed new spark plugs fitted before it went up, and he wanted to be off at sunrise. Her smile became sly, contemplative and, coupled with her nervous twitch, made her appear maniacal.

She knew what had to be done; the voice was as good as telling her to do it . . . And then, she

415

chuckled crazily, she had one more important thing to do before she went to bed ...

Bren was as cranky as hell and he had been that way for several days. Recently, Curtis had gone off to Darwin and done his own thing and Vanessa had been less than enthusiastic when Harvey Timms, the architect, and Rollo Venuti, the builder, had come to discuss the home-stay development. Why was he bothering with it when he was the only one who could see its potential? Sometimes ... He wished he could walk away from *everything:* from Amaroo, from his less than happy marriage, from the responsibilities that were growing, not diminishing, year after year. That was what he hated most, having to be responsible for it all. He knew he wasn't always a good decision-maker, not like Vanessa and Curtis.

Those two seemed to have an in-built antenna on what worked and what wouldn't work. Christ, the thought ran through his head and not for the first time either, perhaps he should sell the place and do as Stuart was suggesting, go into partnership with him in his tourism business. He sucked some more beer and, contemplating the possibilities, stared unseeingly at a boring television show.

It was well past midnight, he should go to bed. One eyebrow shot upwards ... not a lot of joy there though. Vanessa had gone pretty cold on sex since she had miscarried, cold on him too. He had made a mistake back at the hospital, implying that the miscarriage had been for the best and that he wasn't keen to have more children. It had been stupid to say so at the time, when she'd been distraught.

Vanessa hadn't forgiven him and a gut feeling told him that she never would.

He was finishing his beer when Vanessa, in her bed-time, over-sized T-shirt that fell to mid-thigh, came into the living room. Kyle had picked up a cold and because of the anti-rejection drugs he took, she worried about him and didn't sleep well. She got up to check on him several times during the night. He saw her glance at the coffee table strewn with the development plans and the floor where he'd thrown several empty beer cans. He watched the annoyed frown wrinkle her brow and knew why: because beer or something stronger was what he resorted to when matters weren't going the way he wanted them to. Without saying a word she was about to turn on her heel and return to bed when he touched her arm.

'I want to talk.'

There was a touch of impatience in her sigh. 'It's late, Bren. Can't it keep till morning?'

He shook his head. A dozen thoughts were tumbling around inside his head and he couldn't sleep so, why should she. He switched off the television. 'I'm thinking ... serious thoughts, about the future.' He gathered his courage and came out with, 'About selling Amaroo and moving to Broome. Stuart's asked me to go in with him as his partner, an equal partner.'

Vanessa blinked several times, her spine went ramrod stiff and for several seconds she was speechless. Staring at him, her dark eyes wide, she eventually found her voice. 'What? Are you out of your mind?'

It took a lot to shock her but this time he had managed to. She moved to stand in front of him and as Bren looked up at her from under his lashes he noted that she wasn't bothering to disguise the fact that she was stunned. 'Amaroo is becoming a bloody hard grind. I'm pretty fed up with — everything. The year-to-year struggle to stay in the black, the wet, the dry, the whole scene. Maybe it's time for a change.' He gave her a tentative smile. 'We could have a good life in Broome. Live in a mansion like my uncle's, have prestige in the community. Kyle could go to a regular school, have other kids to play with.'

'Your mother would kill you, so would Curtis,' she said, tight-lipped. 'What about tradition, Bren? A Selby has run Amaroo for three generations. And, what about Kyle? Amaroo is his birthright.' Her eyes glinted with disgust, her temper, often close to the boil these days when they 'talked', rose a notch, 'You want to sell out, to take the soft option. I thought Selby men were made of stronger stuff.'

'Not all of us, look at Stuart. He was born here but he's made a life for himself elsewhere, a bloody good life too.'

'So that's it, you want to copy Stuart, be his … clone.' Her gaze narrowed on him. 'Has he suggested this?'

Bren looked away, his answer quick, defensive. 'No, it's my idea. Besides, properties in the Kimberley, in fact all over the country are bought and sold on a regular basis. Some times people are ready to move on.' He ignored the angry shake of her head, how it made her blond hair sway attractively from side to side. 'And that's what I'm thinking, it's time for me to move on, to try something else.'

'Well, frankly, I think it's a terrible idea. It's . . . it's defeatist and unworthy of you.'

He winced at her harsh tone but in particular at the words she used. Vanessa wasn't bothering to couch her words diplomatically and that showed how much their relationship had deteriorated.

'I'll fight tooth and nail to keep Amaroo for Kyle. So will Hilary, Curtis and Lauren.'

Stung, Bren turned nasty. 'Well, you won't get far. I own Amaroo and I'll do what I like with it.' He got up, tossed the empty beer can on the sofa and walked towards the hall. 'I'll sleep in the guest room tonight,' he threw back at her grumpily as he marched off down the hall.

As soon as he was gone chain reaction set in. Vanessa's legs began to shake, then her torso, and after that her whole body. She reached for the side-arm of one of the loungers and collapsed into it. *Bren was serious about selling Amaroo!* He wasn't baiting her in retaliation for her lack of enthusiasm towards his development project, she realised. She sat very still, listening to her rapid heart beat, her panicked breathing. He had been thinking about this for some time, she knew it from the look on his face, the tension in his voice. She cast her mind back over the year; it hadn't been a good one.

There had been a marked depression in the Asian cattle market which had caused Bren and Curtis to fly to Perth and search out new markets. Quite miraculously they had returned with a contract for a shipment of stock to the Middle East where trade had returned to normal after the Gulf War. And, soon after that she had miscarried. Her eyes misted as she recalled Bren's remarks — they had shocked everyone on the station *and* had qualified Kerri's long held opinion of him.

Her friend was right, though it hurt to admit it, her husband was not a sensitive man. And now, with a decision looming on Amaroo, which would be catastrophic for the family, she could no longer delude herself about their marriage. She accepted that most marriages went through bad patches but theirs wasn't going through a bad patch it had sunk into an endless quagmire of unhappiness. She had begun to lose respect for Bren long before Kyle had his health problem but his behaviour then and since, the fight with Curtis, his petulance regarding his project, her miscarriage and now, wanting to sell Amaroo! As far as she was concerned, to coin an oft-used phrase, it was the last straw.

Vanessa tilted her head to one side as she thought of something. What had Kerri whispered to her the day she had left Amaroo. '*A wise woman knows when it's time to gather her courage and move on.*'

She had tried to make things work. Given ground, made allowances, believed that the grievances she had weren't important, that being together as a family made up for his shortcomings, and as the years passed, a successful marriage could become a series of compromises, on both sides. However, there came a time when compromises and excuses no longer worked because the resentment and the feeling of being let down became too strong until it overwhelmed all else.

Dry eyed, her expression serious as she stared at the blank television screen, she came to accept what she had known deep down for quite a while, that the love had gone, evaporated, died for want of emotional nourishment some time over the last few years. She couldn't pinpoint the beginning of its demise — it wasn't one situation but more a series of situations, hurts, each piling on top of the other and smothering the affection she had once felt for Bren until the flame of love was no more.

Despairing of the decision she knew she was about to make, she pressed her fingertips against her closed eyes. Amazingly, she couldn't cry, she was too empty for that, beyond tears. She had to concentrate on what she was going to do, how to broach her decision with Bren. In a way, she didn't think he would be too surprised or that he would fight too hard to make her stay.

Vanessa sat in the armchair for ... she didn't know how long, with little awareness of time passing as she mentally reviewed the last seven and a half years. From sublime happiness and joyful expectations, to disappointment, pain and ... desolation. The grieving process had already begun, she admitted — months ago — for what they'd had and for what no longer existed and for what she had to do. End it!

Dawn was still a speck on the eastern horizon when Vanessa, who'd barely slept, went to the guest room Bren was occupying at the end of the house, well away from Kyle's room. She wanted to get the pain over with but first she had to know if he'd changed his mind about selling Amaroo.

As she flicked the light switch on she saw that he was awake, propped up in bed with his hands behind his head. He refused to look at her as she sat at the end of the bed.

'Can't sleep?' he asked moodily.

'About as well as you, I guess. Last night you gave me a lot to think about.'

'I know. I've been lying here thinking about how great it's going to be. Stuart's keen to have me come in as his partner. Eventually I see us sharing the business fifty-fifty. Kyle will see more of his cousins, and their kids. He'll love that, and being able to go to a proper school. And now that Lauren and Marc are buying Curtis's share of Cadogan's Run, he'll have a big enough deposit to purchase Amaroo.' He grinned, confident that he had worked the problem out. 'Which means that Amaroo will stay in the family.'

She stared at him despite his own inability to make eye contact. If he thought she would be placated by his spiel he couldn't be more mistaken. She had grown up in a tough environment in Brixton but with the dream that one day she would be able to give something to her children. Now he wanted to take away Kyle's entitlement — Amaroo. How could he expect her to be happy about that?

'You're still firm about selling Amaroo?'

'Yes. Once I make up my mind about something I don't usually change it. You should know that by now,' he said testily. 'It'll work out well, you'll see. We can have a very good life in Broome.'

She arched an eyebrow. 'I thought we had a good life here.'

'It will be better in Broome. Kyle can grow up near the sea; he loves the water. I can teach him how to fish, to snorkel, to sail. We'll have plenty of money too.' He said, throwing that in because he thought it might tempt her. 'Vanessa, you won't have to work, not even do stage work if you don't want to. And, let's face it, Curtis will manage Amaroo better than I ever could. He'll jump at the opportunity to buy it.'

'Maybe, but what about tradition? Kyle won't inherit Amaroo. If Curtis owns it, Regan will.'

'Shit, Vanessa,' he shook his head in frustration, then his arms moved, folding aggressively across his chest. 'I'll build our son a business empire in tourism, he can inherit that.'

'But I enjoy acting, and the work keeps coming in,' she reminded him. She thought she had become accustomed to his self-centredness but while he talked about how good it would be for Kyle and herself, really, he was only thinking of how good it was going to be for Bren Selby. 'I can't imagine myself not acting, no matter where I live.'

'Fine, do all the acting you want to,' he replied. But then the last part of her sentence aroused his curiosity and made him ask, 'What do you mean by "no matter where I live"?'

It was the opening she wanted, the right moment to tell him. 'It means that even if you change your mind and decide to stay on Amaroo, or whether you sell and go to Broome, I won't be with you.' She saw his confusion, but didn't wait for him to absorb what she'd said. Taking a deep breath she went on. 'It's over, Bren. Our marriage is over. I think we're both aware that it's been teetering on the brink of collapse for some time. I believe we have to face facts, that what we once had, our feelings for each other, have gone, *died*.'

'Jesus!' He jerked upright in the bed as if something had bitten him. 'What the hell are you talking about, Vanessa? Is that your idea of a threat, to stop me from selling Amaroo?'

She shook her head emphatically. 'No, my decision is the same whether you sell Amaroo or not. What you said last night forced a sense of clarity to what I've been thinking for a long time. It's sad but, we've drifted apart, Bren, and it's clear that the things we each want out of life are quite different. We're both to blame, I suppose, but neither of us should point the finger of blame at each other.' She stared at him. 'I don't believe things, us, can go back to being the way we were.'

Visibly shaken, he ran a hand through his dark hair. 'You're my wife, we belong together.'

'If you're honest with yourself, you'll admit that we haven't been "together" for some time.'

'You're right.' Still, Bren sought to apportion blame and his gaze narrowed on her. '*You're* the one who has made that difficult, flitting around, off doing movies, working on the stage,' he accused. Then he grinned as he thought of a solution. 'What we need is a holiday, together, where we'll have plenty of time for each other. Let's go back to Hayman Island. We can make things right between us, Vanessa, I know we can.'

That he wasn't prepared to take any responsibility for the demise of their marriage, that it was all her fault, was typical. She had expected it. She shook her head. 'A year ago that proposal might have worked, but not now.' She paused to reflect. 'I'm sorry, I don't have anything left to give.'

He leapt out of bed and began to pace the room, and when he spoke his tone was belligerent. 'So we become a bloody statistic? Another broken marriage. People will snigger and whisper behind our backs, you know. They'll say, yes, we knew it wouldn't last.'

'Is that what concerns you, what people might say? I don't give a damn what anyone says,' she said, tossing her head proudly. 'Their opinions aren't important to me.' Her disappointment with him and her anger were growing. Why couldn't he accept what was clear to both of them, that it was over, instead of trying to shift any blame for the breakdown away from himself, *and* worrying over the image their break-up might project. His reaction wasn't winning him any brownie points with her!

'I don't want you to go,' he said, and there was suppressed anger in his tone. He continued to pace, touching ornaments, pushing the curtains open to show a lightening sky. 'We've had a lot of good times together, Vanessa.' He looked at her again. 'We could try ... counselling. See if we can work things out.'

She noted that not once had he said 'because I love you'. But she understood why he'd mentioned counselling. Bren was a possessive man and in a way he saw her as a possession, an 'ornament' he was loath to part with because her celebrity status allowed him to bask in her reflected glory. Kerri had said that about him once but she hadn't believed it then. She was becoming less and less impressed, and if he thought that could win her back he was as wrong as a man could be.

'I've gone beyond that. As far as I'm concerned, counselling would only prolong the agony for both of us because I don't . . .' she knew his feelings would be hurt but it had to be said, 'love you anymore. And, like your decision on Amaroo, *my* decision on us is firm.' She was silent for maybe thirty seconds, allowing her words to sink in. 'However, for now, I believe we should keep our problem to ourselves until we work everything out.' It was going to be hard telling Kyle. Naturally he loved his dad, but she hoped that he was young enough to adjust and not be emotionally scarred by their separation. There were financial matters to work out too.

'Do you agree?' She watched his shoulders slump with defeat, and listened to his sigh. He was, finally, accepting that she would not be changing her mind.

'So, we go our separate ways. I presume you'll take Kyle?' His tone was cool, the anger inside him tightly controlled.

'That would be best for Kyle, don't you think?'

'I guess. I'll want to see him regularly though.'

'Of course.' Her smile was gentle, and tinged with sadness. 'You'll always be his father, Bren. I want him to grow up knowing you and loving you.'

His expression glum, Bren nodded and without another word, left the room.

■　■　■

Nova's movements were sluggish as she dressed in her usual day wear of shorts, a midriff top and boots. She picked her hat up off the dresser as she left her bedroom, leaving the bed unmade, the room a mess. She was a mess! Her head throbbed from the cocktail of pills she had taken last night to assuage her anger, then her grief. She could hardly get her brain into gear, even first gear. Bleary-eyed, she glanced over at the hangar as she walked towards the homestead's kitchen. The chopper was gone but the Cessna still stood there so Curtis hadn't left yet.

How was she was going to face him, to look him in the eye? She didn't know. Stopping halfway to the homestead she tried to decide whether she could. Her body gave a little shudder then her spine straightened. Sooner or later she would have to. Nova continued walking ...

As she got close to the homestead's verandah, a vague memory of something she had done last night filtered through her brain. What was it? Last night, after their confrontation, she had been full of spite, wanting to hurt him because he had hurt her. In the cool light of a cloudless Kimberley morning, she was having second thoughts. But ... she had done *something* in her fit of pique, however, right now her brain was too fogged up to remember what it was. Desperate to gain some concentration she almost stumbled over one of two bikes propped near the verandah step as she went into the kitchen.

The kitchen was remarkably quiet, except for Fran banging pots and the frying pan around in the sink. She had glimpsed Regan and Kyle going off for an early morning ride before School of the Air began. Vanessa was nowhere to be seen, nor was Curtis, and Bren sat staring at his plate, seemingly not interested in eating his usual breakfast of sausages, steak and eggs.

'Fran, where's Dad?' Nova asked. She wasn't overly interested in where her father was, it was just something to say to get a conversation going.

'He and Warren and the new man, Bruce, have ridden towards Exeter Falls to check the herd. Reg said you're welcome to lend a hand if you want to,' Fran added tongue-in-cheek. She knew full well, as they all did, that Nova preferred to shadow Curtis on whatever work he was doing. 'Curtis has taken the chopper to Cadogan's Run. He said he'd be there till this afternoon.'

Nova absorbed that information with a nod of her head. So, she didn't have to face him right now and ... she had known he was going there. Why? She frowned, trying to remember. Absent-mindedly, she picked up a slice of toast, buttered it and nibbled at it. Can't think. *I'm supposed to remember something, it's important ... What is it?* She drank a mouthful of scaldingly hot coffee. The hot liquid managed to jolt her memory. Plane. The Cessna. Yes! What had she done ...?

She remembered. Panic began inside her, working its way into every nerve, muscle and tissue of her body until she recalled that she had seen the Cessna parked on the runway. Curtis must have put the new spark plugs in and taken the chopper. Relief washed over her and tears pricked at her eyelids. She blinked them away. Christ, was she crazy or something?

Covertly, she rubbed the moisture away, not wanting Fran or Bren to see it and ask questions. The twitch at the side of her mouth started to get worked up. Stop it. Oh, stop it, damn you. She put her finger against the erratically moving muscle in an attempt to disguise its flicker. What she needed was something to relax her. Her right hand dived into the pocket of her shorts and pulled out a small round bottle. Prozac, that would calm her down quickly. Making sure no-one saw, she popped the tablet into her mouth and took another swallow of coffee.

Bren scraped his chair as he got up from the table. 'I'm off,' he said tersely. 'If anyone wants me I'll be in the stockyard, a couple of horses need new shoes.'

In a visual haze Nova watched Amaroo's owner move towards the back door. As was his practice when going outdoors, he took his battered Akubra off one of the pegs on the wall. Half a dozen pegs were nailed onto a horizontal piece of timber for the express purpose of holding hats; that's where everyone put their hats when they came inside. Her hat was on the end peg, Vanessa's grey Akubra was usually in the middle — it was missing now — and Fran's Longhorn Akubra hung at the other end to hers.

As Bren went to put his hat on, a piece of paper fluttered to the ground. He saw it, grunted, picked it up and unfolded the paper. Nova, watching, saw his frame stiffen as he read the message. His tanned face turned a noticeable red then white. A muscle flexed along his jawline and the muscles in his arms, because he was only wearing a singlet top and cut off jeans so she could see them, tightened until the veins bulged like a weight-lifters.

'Jesus ... bloody ... Christ,' he growled, hoarsely. He turned on his heel and walked back across the vinyl floor of the kitchen, down the hall and banged the office door shut behind him.

# CHAPTER TWENTY-THREE

Fran threw Nova a questioning look. 'What was that all about?' When her step-daughter shrugged her shoulders carelessly and didn't answer, Fran, after a more searching once-over, made no further comment. As she came to take away Bren's half-eaten breakfast and put the remains in the scrap bucket beside the sink, she said to no-one in particular, 'The hens are gonna eat well today.'

Vanessa, who'd been outside checking as Regan and Kyle saddled up, came in via the back verandah. She put her Akubra on the middle peg of the hat rack. 'Morning, everyone.' She went over to the percolator — Bren had insisted they have percolated coffee, not instant — and poured a cup for herself. She sat at the far end of the table, away from Nova, and buttered a freshly made piece of toast though she was still too upset emotionally — after her confrontation with Bren — to eat more than a bite. It was going to be awkward facing the man who'd been her husband for close to seven years and pretending that everything was normal between them. She grimaced into her coffee cup. Just as well she was an accomplished actress ...

And then the noise began ...

The three women in the kitchen could hear Bren shouting periodically from the office for close to five minutes. Fran, frowning, was mystified. Nova, zonked out, waiting for the Prozac to kick in, showed only moderate interest. Vanessa, curious about the racket, got up and stood unashamedly in the kitchen doorway, listening.

'What's wrong, what's happened?' Vanessa asked Fran. Was Bren venting his anger on someone because of their discussion or was it something else?

'Beats me. He was pretty quiet this morning, didn't eat much. Then he got his hat to go out to the stockyards but instead, he turned on his heel and stomped off to the office. He's clearly unhappy about something,' Fran grinned wryly, knowing she was understating things.

'So it seems,' Vanessa confirmed. She continued to listen to his muffled shouting.

The next thing they heard was the roar of one of the bikes as it took off from behind the kitchen.

Vanessa moved to the kitchen window to see Bren astride the bike, gunning the motor full throttle. His hat was rammed down on his head and he was heading towards the breaking-in yard and the smithy's stall. He didn't stop there, he kept on, past the machinery and storage sheds, riding towards the hangar. Her curiosity piqued by his shouting, she went into the office and her eyebrows lifted with surprise, then bewilderment at the state of the room.

Papers normally on the desk were everywhere. They'd been thrown haphazardly across its surface, they were on the floor too, as were books, magazines, and the in-tray which contained the accounts and breeding program's paperwork. A family photo — one of Bren and all the family members, including Stuart and Diane and his father — had been smashed and the glass lay scattered across the timber boards, all evidence of someone having been in a dreadful rage. The phone was off the hook too so she automatically returned it to its cradle.

*What on earth has happened?* Vanessa stood at the front of the desk, studying everything closely, trying to work out what could have upset Bren so much. Was the broken photograph significant, she wondered? Then, by sheer chance her gaze settled on a screwed up piece of paper lying where it had been thrown onto a bookshelf. Later, when she thought back over the events, she could never understand why that scrap of paper more than anything else had stood out to her. Picking it up, she smoothed out the creases and began to read what was written on it.

*The owner of Amaroo doesn't truly own it.*
*He sits on the throne but isn't the rightful heir.*
*A mother and an uncle are guilty parties.*
*They have cheated the true heir of his birthright.*
*Do you dare ask those who know the truth?*
*H and S have all the answers ...*

What ...? Vanessa read the ridiculously cryptic lines three times before she understood what the writer was trying to say. One didn't need a genius IQ to work it out. The note claimed that Bren wasn't

Amaroo's true heir. *H and S* were obviously Hilary and Stuart and the 'son' who might be the true heir had to be Curtis. What was this all about? As she shook her head in puzzlement she recognised the handwriting of the person who'd written the note — Nova. About to confront her to find out what she knew about all this nonsense, the phone rang, startling her.

Hilary Selby was on the line.

'Thank God. Bren hung up on me then purposely left the receiver off,' she panted into the phone. 'Is he all right?'

Vanessa's expressive eyes would have answered her question had Hilary been able to see them. 'I don't think so. Was it you he was shouting at on the phone?'

'Yes. I don't know how he found out about ...' Long pause. 'He said something about a note. It ... Oh, dear, he was so furious. I could hardly understand what he said to me.'

'Hilary, I have the note in my hand. Is it true?' Vanessa asked the question with, almost, an absurd sense of calm. It would be several hours before the ramifications, true or otherwise, sank in.

It wasn't hard to fill in the blanks. The note implied that Hilary and Stuart must have had some kind of relationship and Bren had resulted from that relationship, but because Hilary and Matthew were married — and Stuart was engaged to a pregnant Diane — Bren had been passed off as Matthew Selby's son. If it were true then Curtis was Matthew's only son and as such, the one entitled to inherit Amaroo. Vanessa rolled her eyes towards the ceiling. Oh ... this was a lovely mess. That's why Bren had taken off in a fury and, who could blame him for being angry. To learn at the age of forty-one that the man he'd always thought of as his father, wasn't, and that Stuart was, would make any man's blood boil. Had everyone been hoodwinked by Hilary and Stuart? She had to wait a little while for Hilary's answer. It came, finally.

'Ummm. *Yes,*' came through the receiver in an emotionally choked tone. 'I, I feel so bad. Stuart, Curtis and I, we never intended Bren to know. Curtis said he wouldn't tell, and that he would make Nova promise not to tell either.'

Curtis knew, *Nova knew*! But how? The surprises just kept coming. Vanessa leant weakly against the desk as, minute by minute, the truth was unfolding like a nineteenth century melodrama. With an inward sigh, she said, 'You'd better tell me everything ...'

Several minutes later, reeling from Hilary's embarrassing and awkward disclosure, Vanessa, the note firmly in her hand, headed for the kitchen where Nova sat, head in hands, her eyes glazed, staring at nothing in particular.

Angry almost beyond words because she believed Nova was the one who had initiated the problem, Vanessa threw the sheet of paper down on the table in front of her and said through clenched teeth, 'That's your writing, isn't it? What's your game, Nova? What mischief are you trying to cause?'

Nova blinked twice as she saw the note. She looked up at Vanessa. 'W-where did you get that?' She was frowning, trying to recall ... Had she written it after the fight with Curtis, and if she had, where had she put it? The answer came to her as she blinked for the third time. The hat. She had put it in the inside band of Bren's hat, knowing it would fall out when he went to put it on. Ooohh . . . yes, it was all coming back to her now.

Through the drug-induced fog she made herself concentrate. She could remember everything: the fight with Curtis and what he had said to her. How she had reacted, wanting to hurt him, Vanessa, everyone, as she had been hurt. That was why she had written the note to Bren and put sand in the Cessna's fuel tank last night. She'd wanted to give Curtis a fright when he was taxiing down the runway and the plane's engine suddenly conked out.

*Curtis has to suffer,* her internal voice had agreed with her. She knew the sand would do the job and frighten the living daylights out of him. The engine would work okay for a while then, as the fuel line clogged, it would splutter and fuel flowing to the engine would eventually stop, making the engine stall. Her eyes closed but that didn't stop the thoughts . . . Why had she done that? Finally, the answer came — she had a petty need to give him a scare, that's why.

'Well . . .?' Vanessa demanded, her anger growing as each second passed.

Vanessa's voice cut through Nova's thoughts. She sat up straight, ran a hand through her boyishly short, straight hair. But . . . it was all right, Curtis hadn't taken the Cessna to Cadogan's Run, he had flown off in the chopper. Thank God. Relief mingled with a growing sense of remorse made her eyes sting with unshed tears. Shit a brick, what had she been thinking? She must be insane to have contemplated doing something ... so extreme. *No*, the voice slid into her thoughts and she welcomed her friend, *you were justified in doing what you did because he had disappointed you and he deserved your anger.*

'Nova, are you listening to me?' Vanessa asked, her tone more insistent.

Nova's head jerked up, she had been listening to the voice. She looked into Vanessa's eyes, as if she had only just heard what she'd said. 'What did you say?'

Exasperated, Vanessa drew up a chair opposite Nova, and sat down. 'This note. Why?'

Fran, who'd been watching the scene with interest, glanced out the kitchen window. She shook her head in consternation as she reported, 'Bren's a funny one. He must have changed his mind about shoeing the horses. He's taking the Cessna up.'

Hearing that, Nova continued to ignore Vanessa. She jumped up and ran to the window to see for herself. 'No. Oh, shit! No, he can't ...' She began to hyperventilate. 'He'll die. Oh, God, no, I can't let him.' *But ... Nova, if Bren dies that will make it easier for Curtis to inherit.*

'No,' Nova said, shaking her head vehemently as she answered out loud, 'I have no argument with Bren.'

'What are you babbling about, Nova?' Fran asked, staring with concern at her increasingly agitated step-daughter.

Vanessa turned to stare at Nova. One assessing look was enough to know that something was very wrong and whatever it was, Nova had something to do with it. 'Nova, what have you done?'

Nova didn't answer straight away, she was heading for the back door. She screamed back as she ran out. 'The plane. I put sand in the fuel tank. I . . . I . . . wanted to hurt Curtis, but he took the chopper instead of the plane. I have to warn Bren.'

Within seconds Nova had disappeared out the fly-screen door. She straddled the one bike left there and turned the key in the ignition. The motor fired and she took off, hurtling towards the hangar as fast as she could make the bike go. Vanessa and Fran rushed onto the back verandah. They stared questioningly at Nova as she roared off across the yard, then at each other.

'Did she say what I think she said?' Vanessa, her expression one of someone expecting imminent disaster, queried.

'About the sand. Yes.'

'Oh, my God . . .'

Vanessa wasn't as clued up on mechanical matters as others on the station, but she knew enough to understand that putting any foreign matter, such as sand, into a fuel tank wasn't good. 'Get Bren on the hf. Tell him to abort the take off,' she called to Fran as she began to run after Nova.

Why was it that when you wanted a bike to go fast, the accelerator cable got stuck at thirty kilometres and wouldn't go a kilometre faster . . .?

In the distance Nova could see the Cessna almost half way down the packed earth runway. She had done a good job on the plane. The harder Bren

438

pressed to get revs up for take-off, the quicker the contaminated fuel would flow into the engine. She had roughly estimated that the engine wouldn't get enough fuel to become airborne, that starved of quality aviation gas and with the clogging sand, the engine would splutter, lose revs and probably skew off the runway into the scrub until it was stopped.

She was pretty sure that's what would happen. Since she had been tall enough to see over the top of a workbench her father had taught her about engines. How they worked, what could go wrong with them and how to fix them. He said she'd have made a good mechanic, had she wanted to be one.

A light breeze blew hair away from her face as she raced towards the runway. The Cessna was already near the end of the runway and beginning its turn for take-off. She glanced at the wind sock, it was hardly moving so there'd be no difficult cross-wind to contend with. White painted rocks every five metres marked the length and breadth of the runway on both sides, and she was riding close to the near side where a ditch to take water run-off during the wet had been dug. The plane turned to face her and began to move forward. She watched it bump along as it came towards her.

Damn. Why wasn't Bren stopping? The sand should be doing its job by now. Okay, she would change course, ride down the middle of the runway. He couldn't miss seeing her then! Nova heard someone calling her name over the bike engine's noise. She half turned around to look. It was Vanessa. Bren's wife was fit and running as fast as she could but she was no Cathy Freeman and wouldn't reach the runway before the plane got enough revs up to attempt to take off.

*She,* Nova Morrison, was the only one who could save Bren. Nova smiled because it made her feel good to know she was going to do that, and neutralise the fact that she had been stupid and vindictive. Suddenly, she realised that the voice in her head had been instrumental in her actions. She had to stop listening to it before she hurt someone, or herself. She wouldn't, she decided with a nod of her head, listen to it anymore, not ever! She would make everything right by stopping Bren before the inevitable accident. By God, she would ... And if nothing else, Curtis would be grateful to her for that.

*What the* ... Bren frowned as he peered through the Cessna's windscreen. 'Aarghh, shit!'

Damned fool of a girl. What was Nova trying to do? Was she showing off or did she want to hitch a ride with him? Well, not today. He was bound for Broome and a 'talk' with Stuart, *dear Uncle Stuart* — his father! His lips pressed together in a grim line as, concentrating to keep the plane's wheels straight, he increased the pressure on the throttle. It responded sluggishly and he listened to the sound of the engine change, becoming more guttural, beginning to splutter as if it had a feed problem. Oh, great!

Knowing he wasn't Amaroo's rightful heir didn't hurt as much as the knowledge that his mother and Stuart had lied to him since birth. Damn them both. After that he spared a melancholy thought for the man that up to half an hour ago he had believed was his father, Matthew Selby, someone he had tried to emulate. No wonder he hadn't been good at managing Amaroo, it was obvious why. He had Stuart's genes, not Matthew's. His brother had known the truth but, according to his mother, wasn't going to press for his inheritance. Right now that didn't make him feel any better. Curtis was going to continue the lie ... *ad infinitum*. He growled under his breath, unsure as to whether Curtis's magnanimous gesture made him feel better or worse.

He watched Nova continue to race towards him. Christ, they were going to collide if she didn't give way. Hell, he'd chew her out good and proper over this foolishness. He pulled the throttle back and applied pressure to the brake pedal to slow the plane. Then it happened.

As if in slow motion, he watched the bike hit something on the runway, probably a small rock that had been missed when the surface had been re-graded. Nova flew up in the air, more than two metres off the ground as the bike propped. Her body twisted in an aerial somersault and she landed heavily on her back. She didn't move again. 'Shit, oh, shit. Bloody shit.'

# CHAPTER TWENTY-FOUR

Continuing to yell profanities, Bren altered the Cessna's course by spinning the wheel in a semicircle so that it skewed sideways, towards the runway's edge. He rammed his foot on the brake as hard as he could and slowly the wheels ground to a stop less than a metre away from the ditch.

He got to Nova as fast as he could, half tripping over in his haste to reach her side. His sweeping gaze missed nothing and staring, he dropped to his knees. One leg was bent unnaturally under her and her head lolled at an extreme angle. Bren had seen cattle with broken necks, but never a human being, but he knew ... *He knew.* Her breathing appeared shallow and blood trickled from the side of her mouth. Internal injuries — he made an educated guess. Probably a rib had punctured one of her lungs.

Amazingly, Nova was conscious. Her dark brown eyes were wide open. She recognised him and strangely, almost eerily, smiled. 'I ... saved ... you. I knew ... I would.'

What the hell did she mean by that, he wondered, but said instead, 'Don't talk. Don't move a muscle, love. I'll get the Flying Doctor Service to come pronto. You'll be okay, just stay still.'

She smiled at him again, a curiously knowing smile. 'Don't think so.'

Vanessa, panting from her prolonged run, reached them and collapsed beside Nova. As she looked at Bren her gaze pleaded for him to say something positive. In no more than an instant she saw he wasn't able to. 'Oh, no,' she cried, her tone of voice small, broken.

'What was she trying to do, the silly kid?'

'She said she did something to the plane's engine,' Vanessa told him. 'It's complicated. I'll fill you in later.'

'I'm going to the plane to call the Flying Doctor Service. Stay with her,' he said gruffly. By mutual, silent consent both put their marital problems on the back-burner to deal with Nova's accident. He got up and jogtrotted back to the plane.

Nova's hand fluttered towards Vanessa, beckoning her close. 'I wanted to be like you, you know. I . . . I thought if I were famous,' she began to cough and more blood dribbled from the side of her mouth, 'that would help to make Curtis fall in love with me. But,' her eyelids closed and she was silent for a little while. When her eyelids opened again, her eyes had difficulty focussing on Vanessa. 'He didn't because he . . . couldn't.'

'You shouldn't talk, Nova,' Vanessa pleaded as she wiped blood away with a tissue. She glanced towards the stockyards and saw Reg's ute being driven at a furious pace by Fran. She watched it rattle up the runway. 'It will only weaken you.'

'Got to tell you ... I caused those little incidents before you ... went to London. Sandy getting loose too. I was jealous. Wanted ... You were competition and I ... I ... wanted you to go away.' Nova stopped talking and her eyelids fluttered and closed again, her breathing was becoming more ragged.

Competition for what? Vanessa assumed that Nova was rambling. She took her hands in her own, holding them firmly, unmindful of the river of tears cascading down her face. But had Nova orchestrated those incidents: the soiled shirt, the broken photograph, the strap on her saddle and Sandy getting loose? 'It doesn't matter now, Nova. It isn't important.' And it wasn't. God, where was Bren, and what was taking him so long? She didn't know what to do, didn't dare touch or move her.

Nova's dark eyes made contact with Vanessa's. 'F-forgive me?'

Vanessa tried to smile but found that she couldn't. 'Of course,' she said softly. At that moment she would have said anything to make Nova feel emotionally and mentally comfortable.

Bren came back. He used his Akubra to shade Nova's face from the sun's rays as he told Vanessa, 'The doctor said not to move her, but to make her comfortable. They've got a plane in the air, they've diverted from Halls Creek. It should be here in less than an hour.' The look in his eyes, before he turned his face away, implied that he didn't think Nova would last that long. He continued to shake his head in bewilderment over the improbability of the accident, but he didn't ask Vanessa any more questions ...

444

Fran, pulling up, got out of the ute and joined them in the dirt. 'Oh, no ...' Within seconds shock turned her lined, tanned face white, her features crumbling because, being a woman of the outback, she knew the inevitability of Nova's fate. She clasped her hands together, as if she were praying, until the knuckles went white.

Nova rallied at the sound of Fran's voice. Her eyes opened. They moved from one person's face to another until she found and recognised her stepmother. Coughing between each word, she managed to whisper, 'Tell Dad I love him.' She paused, managed a weak smile. 'I'm sorry, for every ... Love you too, Fran ... *Bye.*'

Nova didn't open her eyes or speak again. Bren and Fran kept themselves busy while they waited for the Flying Doctor Service by building a rough lean-to over her from nearby fallen tree branches and a tarp they found in the back of the ute. Vanessa sat beside Nova, smoothing her hair, wiping the constant, and increasing, trickle of blood from her mouth, watching her breathing become more shallow, then in quiet, uneven gasps as life ebbed. When there was nothing left to do, Bren and Fran sat on the other side of Nova, in silence ... and waited.

By the time the Flying Doctor Service plane touched down it was too late. Nova was gone ...

The shock of Nova's death overshadowed Bren and Vanessa's drama, and the truth of Bren's parentage. It affected everyone at Amaroo. Then, after several weeks, when life returned to some form of normalcy, the repercussions of the marriage break-up, combined with Stuart and Hilary's affair which had resulted in Bren's birth, changed the dynamics of Amaroo forever.

First and foremost, everyone banded together to keep the truth behind Nova's accident from the press. Fran took an inconsolable Reg off for a few months holiday to mourn her passing as best they could, though all believed that Reg would never get over the loss of his talented, emotionally disturbed daughter. Curtis, in his own quiet way, worked through the unfounded guilt of not being able to love her as she'd desperately wanted him to, as well as the realisation that, legally, he was Amaroo's heir and that Bren insisted he assume his rightful position as such.

Bren, once he had calmed down and could see the past in a rational light, found forgiveness in his heart for his mother's *and* Stuart's indiscretion. In a way, he was relieved to finally understand why he was so much like the man he admired but would continue to, for the sake of propriety, call uncle. Time passing also allowed him to accept that his marriage to Vanessa was over and that their lives were moving in different directions.

Curtis who, for as long as he could remember had lived, breathed and loved Amaroo, was pleased when Bren convinced him to buy the property for a nominal amount — the profit from selling his share in Cadogan's Run. But Curtis, renowned for his fairness, made the sale conditional on Bren accepting an ongoing percentage share of Amaroo's annual profits, together with Vanessa who was to hold the amount in trust for Kyle until his twenty-first birthday.

And later, after the financials for Amaroo were settled, Vanessa and Bren formally ended their marriage with a legal separation.

Moving to Sydney with Kyle and her dog, Sandy, was not the trauma Vanessa had expected. Kerri had begged via several long phone calls for her and Kyle to return to England but Vanessa couldn't. After so long she had become too Australianised; the island continent with its rawness and vitality had become *home* and, besides, going so far away, though it might benefit her career, wouldn't be fair to Kyle or Bren. Instead, she rented a small house with harbour glimpses, in a leafy street in Rushcutters Bay, close to a seaside park and Kyle's school. The property had a bigger than average sized backyard so Kyle, who'd started to play soccer and cricket, and Sandy, wouldn't feel too contained. And apart from her acting engagements, her judiciously invested share portfolio, together with rent from her Belgrave Square flat afforded herself and Kyle a reasonably comfortable if not luxurious lifestyle.

She found a reputable agent to represent her for work in Australia, and maintained links with Kerri for international work, and while Kyle attended Cranbrook Preparatory School she got ready for her biggest role, as Charlotte, the character-driven role of Emily Wakefield's sister, in *North of the Nullarbor*, with the interior scenes for the movie scheduled to begin in March.

After several more months Vanessa began to have the occasional date, if only to convince herself that she was, from an emotional viewpoint, over Bren. She had no intention of becoming involved with any member of the opposite sex, not yet, no matter how attractive he might be. She needed the passage of time to mentally and emotionally work through the disappointment of her marriage, and lay the memories to rest ...

When the cast and production crew for *North of the Nullarbor* arrived to film scenes at Amaroo, it was a mixture of heaven and hell for Curtis to watch Vanessa act out the role she had created and developed. There had been subtle and not so subtle changes between himself and Vanessa since Nova's accident and he accepted, with regret, that the long-established camaraderie between them was gone. Seeing Kyle again was great too, because he knew that Regan had missed her younger playmate, and had even said in an unguarded moment that she was looking forward to attending boarding school when she turned fifteen.

The year since Nova's death had been a difficult one for Curtis. He had had to come to terms with many things since Nova's exposure of the affair between his mother and Stuart, and he'd discovered plusses and minuses to the unpalatable revelation. For one thing, he and Stuart didn't have to talk to each other or pretend they tolerated each other anymore: that was definitely a plus. The relationship between himself and Bren changed too. He no longer felt in Bren's shadow, as he had all of his life.

As a consequence of that and being several hundred kilometres away from each other, they became more independent as they pursued different interests, with Curtis able to manage Amaroo as he believed it should be managed.

Curtis thought it remarkable that Bren had adjusted so easily to the failure of his marriage, but he was pleased his brother had successfully become a partner in Stuart's business. Bren had taken to the tourism business like a duck to water. There were changes in Hilary Selby too, and over time she became more human and a nicer person to be with.

On the surface and to those who thought they knew him well, Curtis projected the image of a man who'd found his place in the scheme of things, and was content with that. To some extent that was true except for one thing. The woman he loved completely, to distraction, remained unaware of his love and beyond his reach. Being exposed to Vanessa on a daily basis again was heart-wrenching because he had no idea how he could breach the distance that had developed between them. She seemed serenely confident, in control of her life, and subtly asked questions of members of the production crew let him know that as far as anyone knew there was no permanent man in her life.

He took what comfort he could from that . . . and her parting words as, a month later, the crew and cast having shot the necessary scenes, prepared to leave Amaroo.

'You will come to the premiere of *North of the Nullarbor*, and bring Regan with you?' Vanessa asked just before she boarded the ten-seater, chartered plane, leased for the flight to Kununurra. As she waited for his answer she helped Kyle up and into the craft.

'You want me to?' Curtis returned in that laconic, laid-back way of his.

'Of course.' Her smile was genuine. 'Rest assured, you'll receive a gilt-edged invitation in, say, about ten months, according to the director.'

Curtis took that information in with a nod of his head. 'Regan will want to see it. She's fascinated with the process of filming, and she wants to be a director now.' He grinned reflectively as his gaze took in his daughter, astride her horse, Crusoe, on the far side of the runway. 'Last week she wanted to be a veterinarian . . .'

'You have to come,' Vanessa insisted. 'Don't you want to see how Amaroo looks through the camera's lens?'

'I guess so. Yes.' He gave in as he'd fully intended to. 'We'll be there, me in a monkey suit and all.'

Suddenly her dark eyes sparkled mischievously as she gave him a swift once-over. 'If I remember correctly, you scrub up very well.'

'Will Bren get an invite?'

'Yes,' she replied. 'I doubt that he'll attend, unless it suits him to take Kyle back to Broome for a holiday or something.' She went up on her tiptoes to kiss him on the cheek. He moved and her lips landed on the right-hand side of his mouth, leaving a lipstick smear. She reached up with her hand to wipe the lipstick away but he stopped her, his fingers closing over her wrist for several moments longer than was necessary.

'It's okay,' his tone was suddenly husky. 'You'd better go. I think the pilot's waiting on you, to take off,' he reminded her that it was time to board.

For the merest moment, a heart beat in time, he looked at her and as she stared back, her brown eyes clouded with some kind of reaction. Unfortunately, he couldn't define what the look held — a glimmer of, was it wariness or *awareness?* Occasionally, during the filming, he had caught her watching him with an odd, indefinable expression, as if she were seeing him differently. It was enough to give him hope that she was emotionally free of Bren and that she might ... what? Come to love him! His inward smile was derisive in the extreme. Fat chance of that.

Still, he knew he'd walk around for the rest of the day with her lipstick mark on him and the memory of her feather-soft lips against his. Christ, he was such a fool, pining for a woman he couldn't have ... He made a big show of helping her into the plane, and then closed the door. After which, shading his eyes from the morning sun, and trying to arrest the depression growing within him, he watched the plane taxi down the runway with Vanessa who was flying out of his life. Again ...

Over the hum of the plane's engine, Kyle got the message — her son could be a chatter-box at times — that conversation was just too difficult, and resorted to reading a book titled *The Blue Banana*. It was one of Regan's favourites and she'd given it to him before they left. Vanessa sat very still. She pretended to watch the view — a view she was very familiar with — from the plane's window but inside she was acknowledging that she felt ... strange. While they were airborne and before they reached Kununurra where they then had to wait for a connecting flight to Darwin and on to Sydney, there was ample time for serious reflection, on Amaroo and ... Curtis.

She had loved being there. The freedom, the space, the silence. So different from the bustle of Sydney and, in her mind, an overpopulated suburbia. After living in the outback, she still wasn't used to the cacophony and variety of noises that came with city life. Amaroo had been like a breath of fresh air to her. Seeing everyone again, including Fran, Reg and Warren, being able to ride Runaway almost every day too. Curtis had told her that in her absence the mare refused to let anyone else ride her, and would buck and pigroot anyone who tried to mount her.

A feeling of nostalgia lodged in her throat, making the muscles tighten. She missed the place and, strangely, the admission came that what she missed had little to do with Bren or their marriage. It was Amaroo and the challenge of living in the outback. The life had infiltrated her heart and soul and that was what she missed.

She had missed Curtis too. Curiously, she had been a little hurt when, after her arrival, he'd kept his distance for a week or more. His remoteness caused her to believe he might be uncomfortable in her company because of what had happened between herself and Bren. But then he'd become more sociable and she assumed his initial strangeness was because having a production crew that, with actors, fluctuated between fourteen and twenty people — stretching Amaroo's hospitality to the limits — had made him withdraw into himself. God alone knew he had reason to with what had happened over the last twelve months.

Still, no matter how she reflected on it the conclusion was the same — Curtis was different. Quieter and more self-contained, if that were possible, but she longed for the friendliness they'd once shared. Perhaps it had been foolish on her part to think their relationship could remain unscathed with what they'd been through. She had moved on, changed aspects of her life, and so had he.

But, she chewed reflectively on the inside of her lower lip, and wondered, why had it become so hard to dismiss him from her thoughts? The question hammered insistently in her brain, *and* why had he been startled when she'd kissed him goodbye? That was food for thought too. What was she to make of his reaction to her friendly gesture? What was she to make of her response? There had been one and it had nothing to do with them being in-laws.

If she was honest with herself it wasn't the first time she had been aware of feeling *different* around him. Her kiss had caused a tingling in her lips, a rush of adrenaline down her spine, a sense of attraction towards him, something she had never felt before, and which confirmed something rather strange. She was developing feelings for Curtis!

A perplexed frown marred her forehead as she gave free rein to her thoughts. She closed her eyes to feign sleep but she knew only too well that no such respite would come as she continued to try to make sense of what was going through her head, in particular *that* response ... and whether she harboured deep feelings for the man she had once, so long ago, loathed ...

# CHAPTER TWENTY–FIVE

June, 1998

Kerri Spanos fussed over settling the folds of Vanessa's fitted gold satin and sequined gown in her Sheraton on the Park Hotel suite prior to them making their way down to the waiting limousine. It was booked to take them to the Hoyts Cinema complex in George Street.

'It's fine,' Vanessa assured Kerri, amused because she was behaving like the mother of the bride minutes before the opening strains of Mendelssohn's 'Wedding March'.

'I don't know how you can be so *calm*,' Kerri grumbled good-naturedly. 'This is, potentially, the biggest night of your career. At *North of the Nullarbor's* preview people raved about it, and your acting. Once the film does the rounds in America you could be looking at an Oscar nomination. And you stand there as cool as a cucumber!' She clucked her tongue in disgust. 'Must be your English blood, it's certainly not the Spanish in you.'

'There's no need for me to be nervous, you're doing a superb job for both of us,' Vanessa responded lightheartedly, and chuckled at Kerri's feigned outrage. She might be coming across as serene externally but on the inside a tumult of thoughts, and feelings, were raging through her as they had for weeks. This movie was an important step in her career and Magnavid, the Anglo-Australian consortium that had put the financials for the movie together, had spent lavishly on pre-premiere promotion. This meant that Vanessa and an upcoming Australian actress, Rachel Griffin, had already done a considerable number of magazine, radio and television interviews to create people interest. But of more importance to her personally was that she would be seeing Curtis again, and the possibilities that might arise from that . . .

Martin Pirelli, *North of the Nullarbor's* director, stood near the suite door, waiting. He was forced to issue a polite hurry up. 'Come on, ladies, it's not smart to keep the fans waiting too long. Daniel, the promo man, just left a message on my mobile,' Martin informed them as he opened the door in expectation. 'He said we really should go. There's already a crowd outside the complex waiting to catch a glimpse of the VIPs invited to the premiere.'

Vanessa smiled at Kerri. They linked arms as she said, 'Okay, lead the way, Martin.'

When Kerri Spanos attended one of her large stable of clients' first performances, she wasn't able to relax and simply enjoy the show. She spent the two hours of movie time listening, with accentuated hearing, for a variety of nuances shown by the audience. The occasional, surprised intake of breath. Chuckles over clever dialogue. The silence at dramatic moments and the expectant hush as the film reached its climax. All of that helped her gauge the audience's response, and over time she had grown wise enough to know that some attendees would love the performance and others would not. What she strove to divine as the house lights went on and people began to file out of the theatre was the audience's general receptiveness.

Were they talking about the movie or were they discussing where they'd go for supper? She strained to catch anything positive ... and eavesdropped unashamedly ...

'Best movie I've seen in years.'

'The man who played Rupert was sensational. Did you catch his name in the credits?'

'Wasn't Vanessa Forsythe great? I heard her interview on radio the other day. Did you know that she wrote the movie's script?'

'I hated the father, he was so ... repressive.'

'I hope it does well at the box office. I'd love an Aussie movie to win an Oscar. Show those Hollywood types we've got what it takes.'

Kerri began to smile as, working her way up the aisle, she took note of the comments being made. People were talking about the movie and that was very good. During its running she had lost contact with Vanessa, but she wasn't worried because she knew Martin would have whisked her out of the theatre as the credits came on the screen.

She thought the director had a bit of a soft spot for Vanessa. Not that Vanny reciprocated. Since she and Bren had parted company, and been divorced, Vanny had steered away from emotional entanglements, though she'd dated several men on a casual basis. That was wise of her. She believed her friend needed to get her perspective straight and become heart-whole before she considered falling in love again.

Their limousine stood at the kerb, with Vanny and Martin already waiting inside. Kerri hurried towards it, containing her delight at the audience's response until she joined them. 'It's a hit,' she said enthusiastically. She slapped Martin on the thigh and blew Vanessa a kiss. 'They loved it.'

'That's the feeling I got too,' Martin responded, then he gave instructions to the limousine's chauffeur to move off ...

Magnavid had organised a post-premiere party to rival a Hollywood event, at the Royal Sydney Yacht Squadron's Club at Kirribilli for members of the media, the cast, VIPs and other special guests, one of whom was Curtis Selby ...

At the party, Vanessa was soon surrounded by guests proffering congratulations, but all the while she was waiting for Curtis to appear. When she saw him hovering just inside the door she excused herself from the group around her to go and welcome him. She had searched the packed audience for him during the running of the movie but hadn't been able to locate him.

All the hoo-ha over the movie, the ringing endorsements, the congratulations were forgotten when, as he saw her, he smiled. Vanessa experienced something instantly — it was as if she had been kicked in the chest, and the muscles around her heart tightened. All the thoughts, doubts, wonderings, the analysing she had done over the last several months crystallised into one sentence: *Vanessa, you love him.* She couldn't fool herself any longer by thinking otherwise.

As he waited for her to reach him, standing composed and not intimidated by the glamour and glitter around him, he looked handsome, even urbane in his rented, well-tailored dinner suit. He was wonderfully special in so many ways and she freely accepted the feelings that were spiralling through her mind and soul, as love, a deep, abiding love. In fact, she didn't know how she was going to hide how she felt, after keeping her emotions subdued for so long.

Over the last year or so she had come to believe, on recalling a number of events during her years at Amaroo, and with the baggage of a failed marriage behind her, that someone special was missing from her life and, that someone was Curtis Selby. Even after several exhaustive soul-searching sessions she couldn't pinpoint the precise moment in which the shift in the emphasis of her feelings had occurred. She only knew that the sense of awareness had begun when she'd filmed at Amaroo and the emotional pull had built from that time, despite only seeing each other once in the interim when he had brought Regan to Sydney for a week to stay with her maternal grandparents. Now she was wondering where these feelings she had discovered inside herself might lead. And, if Curtis felt anything other than friendship for her. She had to know ...

It took considerable acting skill on her part not to betray exactly how pleased she was to see him. As they took each other's outstretched hands, a frisson of excitement slid down her spine then curled through and around her stomach muscles, making them tighten and be very much aware of her physical reaction to him. She prayed that he wouldn't see the fast-beating pulse at the base of her throat — it would be a dead give-away.

'Where's Regan?' Oh, damn. Did she have to sound so breathless?

'She was exhausted from the long flight today and too much excitement. I had Ken, her grandfather, pick her up after the movie. She's going to spend the night with them.' His smile widened as his gaze ran over her in open appreciation. 'Regan said to tell you that you were *too much*.' A sandy eyebrow lifted with amusement. 'I believe that's teenager's talk that translates to high praise.'

'Curtis, I'm so glad you came. It's good to see you.' She relaxed a little, pleased to be exerting better control over her vocal chords. 'How are things at Amaroo?'

'The station's doing well.' His grin proclaimed more than his words; the confident smile implied that the property was running the way he liked it to. 'The movie was terrific, Vanessa. I was very impressed.' Respect, even awe was evident in his voice.

'Thank you. It's a shame Bren couldn't come,' she said, then felt duty-bound to ask, 'How is he?'

Curtis's smile became less buoyant. 'Good. Very busy. He and Stuart called in last week. Bren seems,' he paused for a few seconds, 'contented and enthusiastic over what he and Stuart are doing.'

460

'I'm pleased for him,' Vanessa responded, and she meant it. As far as she was concerned there was no ill will between them — just a lingering, but dissipating sadness for a marriage gone wrong. She then considered it diplomatic to change the subject, besides, it wasn't Bren she wanted to talk about. 'I'm glad you enjoyed *North of the Nullarbor*. Didn't Amaroo look stunning? The film's camera crew and the editor did a marvellous job bringing out the best scenes and the colours.'

His gaze swept around the room, taking in its array of star-studded guests. 'I guess Hollywood might soon beckon, once the big time execs at a few studios see *North of the Nullarbor*.'

'I'm not fussed about Hollywood. My Sydney agent is getting me enough work to keep me gainfully employed — stage performances, television ads, voice-overs. But you know Kerri, she and Martin believe the movie has Oscar-nomination potential written all over it. I'm more conservative and would rather adopt a wait and see attitude.'

Vanessa was surprised by the wave of frustration that suddenly moved through her. She didn't want to talk about the film, or Bren, she wanted to talk with him, about them! About the possibility of there being a 'them'. But to her chagrin, out of the corner of her eye she saw Kerri and a media troupe bearing down on them. 'It's going to be too hard for us to talk tonight . . .'

Curtis understood straight away. 'Regan would love some time with you. Are you free for lunch tomorrow?'

She wasn't. She and Rachel had several promotional commitments organised by Magnavid — but she would juggle some free time, somehow. 'Of course. How about The Park Hyatt at the Quay? At 1 p.m.? We'll meet in the foyer.'

'Terrific. It'll be great to catch up.' He smiled again, a slow, lingering smile that said as clearly as words how much he was looking forward to being with her.

'See you then.'

Kerri and the journalist pack closed in. Vanessa, trying to concentrate on the questions being asked by two journos, watched an adept Kerri, after a conspiratorial wink, link arms with Curtis and move him off towards a long table near the back wall of the room. It was covered with tempting smorgasbord dishes.

Later, as the crowd thinned — only the die-hards staying on for the booze — Kerri, with two champagne flutes in her hands, passed one to Vanessa who, for the moment, stood peacefully alone at the window, looking at the harbour view.

'Well?'

Vanessa straightened as she sipped the champagne. 'It's going very well, I think. Good feedback so far.' Her tone was distracted because, having turned towards Kerri, she saw Curtis involved with a group of people on the other side of the room. She wondered what they were talking about. 'The media seemed on side, but I'm not sure about the movie critic from the *Sun-Herald*, he's a dour kind of chap.'

Kerri let Vanny's remarks about the journalists and the critic go over her head. 'And ...?' She stared expectantly at her friend.

Vanessa blinked and stared back. 'And what?'

Kerri pursed her lips and waggled a finger at Vanessa. 'You can't fool me, Vanessa Forsythe, I've known you for too long. *Curtis.*' She gave her friend her cat-that's-swallowed-the-canary smile. 'I saw your face when he came in. In fact, both your faces lit up like Christmas tree lights. I can tell when something's going on. Curtis has the hots for you. I thought he might when I was at Amaroo with Heather. That's why Nova got so upset — she realised Curtis couldn't fall in love with her because he was in love with you.'

Vanessa shook her head, but also had the grace to blush at Kerri's amazingly accurate revelation. 'My God, you should be writing fiction. Where did you get such an idea?'

But ... Kerri's words set her thoughts off on a tantalising tangent. Could it be true? Was Curtis in love with her and might he have been for years? Kerri Spanos was an insightful woman and she didn't make personal comments unless she was sure she was right. Vanessa's heart began to thud, increasing its beat dramatically as a shiver of expectation wafted through her body. What if Kerri's assertion about Curtis was true ...?

'Just think about it.' Kerri was warming up to the subject. 'He's changed towards you over the years, hasn't he? He couldn't stand you when you first met, you told me that at the reception in Darwin. Then he saw you change, adjust to outback life and watched

463

your commitment and love for Amaroo grow. And, another thing, how many men, related or otherwise, would donate part of their liver to save a child. It takes a special man, one with deep feelings, to do that. Curtis is that type of man, the quiet, patient kind who doesn't push himself forward.' She gave a nod of approval. 'He's a lot like my Yannis.'

Kerri stopped to give Vanessa time to absorb what she had said. 'As well, luv, he's been divorced for years but hasn't found anyone else. Never even looked at another woman, most likely.'

'Finding eligible women in the middle of nowhere isn't easy; women of any kind are pretty hard to come by,' Vanessa explained as she pondered Kerri's words.

'You're right about that.' Kerri subjected her to a searching look then, forthright as usual, asked, 'Okay, Vanny, my girl. What about you, what do you feel?'

Vanessa shook her head as if she wasn't going to reply but then the expression in her eyes changed, at first confused then it became positive. 'I'm in love with him,' she said simply, the truth of it evident in her features and her accompanying glorious smile. 'I don't know how or when it happened but ... that's how I feel.'

'I knew it! Of course you are. And what are you going to do about it?'

'I don't know. I don't know if he ...' she broke off, gathered her thoughts. 'We're going to have lunch tomorrow, and later, Kyle and I will fly to Amaroo for Regan's fifteenth birthday, in four weeks time.'

'I see,' suddenly Kerri sighed with exasperation. 'I know your temperament, waiting isn't your strong suit. I can't believe you're prepared to wait an hour, a day or a month to find out how he feels. If you are it *can't* be love.'

Vanessa should have been irked that Kerri knew her so well but, curiously, she wasn't. Kerri was right. She didn't want to wait another day ... another hour.

'Are you worried about Bren, what other family members might think if you and Curtis get together?'

'No.' She wasn't. With everything that had happened she didn't think there would be any problems in that regard. She was being given the opportunity to find happiness again and she would not let it slip away from her. Her real concern was Curtis's feelings for her!

Kerri looked towards Curtis then back at her, and jerked her head in the obvious direction. 'Then why are you standing here talking to me when ...?'

Vanessa smiled her thanks and began to work her way through the thinning crowd towards Curtis. Reaching him, and trying to ignore the fact that her heart was racing and her knees trembling, she took his hand and whispered, 'We have to talk — now!'

The evening breeze made it cool on the club's deserted patio but Vanessa was unaware of the air chilling her bare shoulders because she had other things on her mind.

'What's up?' Concern was evident in his eyes. He saw her shiver and took off his coat, placing its warmth around her shoulders.

For a moment or two she savoured the heat from his body transmitted through the coat's material, then, with considerable difficulty she attempted to organise her thoughts. 'I want to ask you a question.' She took a deep breath. 'Just one question, and I want a yes or no answer. Nothing more, nothing less. Okay?'

Bemused but with his curiosity roused, he shrugged casually, 'I guess so.'

Vanessa licked her lips. She swallowed the lump in her throat and pulled his coat more tightly around her, and hoped he wouldn't notice that her hands were trembling. 'Are you ...' her throat muscles began to tighten. 'Curtis, are you in love with me?'

'What?' He half-turned away to cover his shock.

'A *yes* or *no* answer, remember.'

She waited ... and waited — it seemed an eternity, but was in fact only a few seconds during which her hopes see-sawed between need and despair. Why was he taking so long to reply? Finally she had to prompt him. 'Well?'

Curtis turned to face her again. His normally inscrutable gaze, for once reflected what he felt, what he had hidden from her, and everyone, for so long. 'I don't know how you found out but,' he chuckled deep in his throat, 'you wanted a short answer, it's ... *yes*.'

Vanessa's smile widened to its absolute limits. Radiance and delight lit her features and, the light from a lowering half moon made her look stunningly lovely. Deep inside her being she began to give way to feelings she no longer had to keep under control — they were raging through her body and spreading to her heart and her soul.

'Oh, Curtis, that's wonderful. Fantastic.' She could drop the barriers now, the self-control. 'It's the answer I wanted to hear because ... *I love you too.*'

She watched him blink in amazement but he recovered fast and stretched out his arms invitingly. There was no hesitation on her part as she glided into his embrace and, the way he held her tight — as if he never intended to let her go — confirmed his love for her.

As their lips met, Vanessa's last conscious thought for several minutes was, that later there would be time for questions and answers, and they would talk about their future with Kyle and Regan, and a new beginning at her beloved Amaroo, for all of them.

THE END

## ACKNOWLEDGMENTS

To my literary agent, Selwa Anthony. To my editors: Nicola O'Shea, Vanessa Radnidge, Linda Funnell and Pauline O'Carolan. Michael McFadden, Taronga Park Zoo. Alan Ross, Dreamworld Helicopters. Rachel Oates-King. Dr Kenneth Oey. *In the Middle of Nowhere* and *Riveren, My Home, Our Country*, by Terry Underwood. *Outback* Magazine. Joanne Brookes.

And a special thanks to Terry and John Underwood of Riveren Station, Northern Territory.

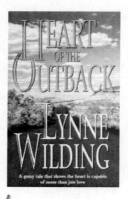

## HEART OF THE OUTBACK

Fiery and ambitious architect Francey Spinetti is a young woman on her way to the top.

When wealthy magnate CJ Ambrose introduces her to his business empire – and a career-scarred local cop, Steve Parrish – everything seems to be falling into place, including her love life.

But the harsh outback landscape holds more secrets than Francey could possible have imagined, and more enemies too.

As CJ's empire becomes embroiled in murder, Francey will need to call on all her strength and determination to survive.

0 7322 6744 7

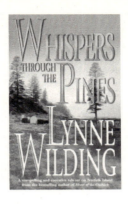

# WHISPERS THROUGH THE PINES

Barrister Jessica Pearce is brilliant in the courtroom until a personal tragedy tears her life apart.

To help her recover from her trauma, husband Dr Simon Pearce decides they will move to Norfolk Island. Here amidst the idyllically serene landscape, Simon hopes Jessica will rebuild her life.

But strange, inexplicable things have Jessica questioning her own sanity on an island scarred by dark secrets from its convict past.

Is the beautiful Jessica fighting a losing battle and drifting deeper into emotional instability, or are the strangely sinister forces on the island responsible for her problems?

ISBN: 07322 6476 6

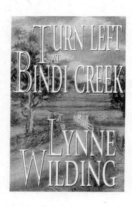

# TURN LEFT AT BINDI CREEK

When Jason and Brooke d'Winters move from the city to the small town of Bindi Creek in western New South Wales, it seems the couple's dreams have come true. The townsfolk welcome them with open arms, Jason's practice flourishes, and Brooke is the perfect country doctor's wife and mother to their three children.

But a devastating accident shatters Brooke's home and happiness, forcing her to confront events from her past as shock waves race through the tight-knit community.

Wes Sinclair, Jason's best friend, is a staunch ally. Others, such as Sharon Dimarco, are waiting to see Brooke fall. And even Wes has an agenda of his own.

What could be so terrible to make Brooke change her whole life? And how can she and Jason go forward when their world has been turned upside down?

0 7322 6795 1